BRITTNEY HART

Cinnamon Muffins

First published by Brittney Hart Writing LLC 2024

This novel is entirely a work of fiction. The names, characters and incidents portrayed in it are the work of the author's imagination. Any resemblance to actual persons, living or dead, events or localities is entirely coincidental.

First edition

ISBN: 979-8-9896358-4-9

This book was professionally typeset on Reedsy.
Find out more at reedsy.com

A note
to the world-weary:
Keep to your stargazing.
If your eyes become dull,
the stars always have
some sparkle
to spare.

Contents

Acknowledgments

My beta-reader, Susana Puche Saud, was the most instrumental help I could have had. Dear one, you are incredible.

Triggers for this novel include: panic attacks, self-harm, suicidal ideations and attempts, physical abuse, severe neglect, bullying, homophobia, near-death experiences, and graphic violence.

1

Cold, Cold Ears for a Cold, Cold Boy

I t's cold. Taylor can't even find his hat. Maybe it's lost somewhere in the sleeping bag with his other clothes, maybe it fell off when he dragged himself out from under the bridge to look at the stars. His ears are freezing, and the sweat matting his hair to his forehead isn't helping. Despite the sweat, he's still shivering- it's dark and probably below freezing, if the clouds of fog that puff away to count his breaths are any judge. He just wants his hat. He just wants to be warm.

Taylor should have accepted Dalton's goddamn jacket at lunch. Dalton wouldn't have asked for it back. Even if he'd wanted it back, Dalton would have just laughed and bothered Todd for his coat and joked that Todd's rich enough to buy another coat *unlike us poor, poor peasant folk.*

The joke is much funnier at ass o'clock at night (Taylor's dead phone can't tell him whether it's nine at night or two in the morning) curled up in a sleeping bag filled with all of Taylor's gross-smelling clothes, trying to keep warm under the igniting winter wind promising to turn the wisps of clouds, which had only dusted the moon before, into a real star-darkening storm. Taylor laughs, and it echoes around the underbelly of the bridge before being carried away on that pre-storm wind.

Another shiver lights up every nerve on Taylor's skin, and all the ones under the skin too— if there are any there. He's not sure that there are. Todd would know. Taylor could text him and ask if his phone wasn't dead, or if there was an electrical outlet under the bridge on Clearwater Street, or if he had money to replace the charging cord that broke when some Junior in his history class stepped on it this morning. If Taylor could text him, Todd would be able to explain the whole thing about nerves and where they are and aren't very clearly, very concisely, and then he would tell Taylor and Dalton to go to bed if they don't want to get sick.

That's what he said to Taylor, last time Taylor slept at his house. It was snowing, so Taylor said they should all hang out at Todd's, and Dalton had been more excited than anyone else so he didn't have to sell it too much. Todd had told Taylor then that Taylor didn't look so good- "your face is kinda red, dude. Do you want my mom to check on it? Give you something OTC?" Taylor can't remember what OTC means right now, but he had known at the time and he had said no, don't worry about it, I'll be fine. Because Taylor Macready only had $32 to his name when he set up his sleeping bag under the bridge four weeks ago and that ran out quick because he's a fucking idiot. He couldn't afford medicine for a cold, OTC or otherwise.

It's been a week or so now, though, and the cold has only gotten worse. Yesterday, even Jaxson Dixon had said he looked like shit when Taylor was vomiting his guts out in the bathroom where he and Jaxson usually spent the entirety of third-period English. He'd told Jaxson to shut his fucking trap

2

if he didn't want to get hit. He hadn't really meant it. Taylor's kinda grateful to Jaxson in more ways than he'd like to admit because Jaxson takes care of his little sister Juniper-Maisie and Juniper-Maisie takes care of Taylor's little sister Hellen and if Taylor dies from this stupid cold then Jaxson might end up taking care of both of them. Or maybe the girls would take care of Jaxson- they're getting awfully tough now that they're in high school.

Taylor is wondering if there's a god out there that has it out for him specifically and this cold is a punishment. It feels like punishment. And maybe he deserves it. Dad was always reminding Taylor that he deserved it- whatever 'it' happened to be. And Mom kept telling Taylor to get out of the house more. This is it. His parents were right and Taylor was wrong and this cold is the whole universe telling him to go fuck himself.

And he wants to.

Taylor Fucking Macready. Taylor bum-ass, piece of shit, selfish, worthless, infectious Macready.

If he had a rope, he'd string himself up from the rebar poking out from the bridge. If he had a gun, he'd only pay for one bullet. If he had a knife, he'd get his blood flowing one way or another. If he could afford the OTC medicine from Todd's mom, he'd chug the whole bottle like a cup of fucking water and hope it was the kind you can die from.

But he has none of these things. Just a cinder block from the nearby parking lot as a combination table-and-chair, a sleeping bag filled with his own clothes, his backpack, and bone-chilled shivers that wrack his frame.

Oh, and his hat is probably somewhere around here. He really loves that hat.

3

The stars that had been valiantly battling the clouds for primetime viewership in the sky have grown too tired to try. They all sink behind a thickening veil of darkness that doesn't waste time with promises before dropping the first stiff snowflakes onto Swisher, Iowa. It's time, then, to drag his stinky, sticky sleeping bag of clothes back under the bridge. No more stars to watch, and the snow will make everything wet and colder than it is. But Taylor is so tired now, from the shivering and from the cruel beckon of what comes when he's stopped shivering, that he just watches the snowflakes instead. If he ignores how fast the snow is picking up the pace, he can pretend the snowflakes are stars rushing out to meet him. Accepting him. It would feel nice to have someone rush out to meet him.

Taylor loves the stars. He'll join them someday soon. He'll blow his brains out or take too much of something or wrap a rope around his neck or maybe even spice it up and slit his veins open, and then he'll be a star and he'll float in the sky, millions of millions of miles from the next star over, way too far for anyone from Earth to reach, and nobody will be contaminated by whatever it is in his fucking brain that makes him so awful. He can just be a star and watch Hellen graduate and watch Dalton and Todd get amazing careers and watch Jaxson get out of this town that treats him like shit and watch Wes Post meet someone who doesn't mind how much he twitches and they'll all grow old far, far away from Taylor. And Taylor will finally be fucking happy.

The day before yesterday, Taylor stole someone's cinnamon muffin off of the counter at Post Family Coffee. He doesn't even like cinnamon. But he was hungry. Nobody in Swisher is hiring, and Taylor ran out of money over a week ago. So he had to steal the muffin. Either the cinnamon or the stealing from Wes genuinely-fucking-good-kid Post made Taylor so nauseous that he threw up the muffin an hour later, and he hasn't eaten anything since. But it's okay- Taylor's not even hungry. He promised Dalton earlier that he wasn't hungry. Hasn't been hungry since he threw up the cinnamon muffin. But he still feels bad because Wes probably had to set out another cinnamon muffin and call the order out again. Wes is too nice for Taylor to infect, so Taylor didn't go back to Post Family Coffee after that, even though he likes to sit in the heated coffee shop and watch Wes move like a bee in a hive behind the counter, even if he's never actually talked to him much. Wes is still nice to look at, long brown hair he never brushes and big, big brown eyes like oversteeped tea.

Taylor's train of thought spins and spins with the snowflakes that are getting lighter and fluffier as the storm picks up. He can't pretend they're stars anymore, they're too big for that, too close when they settle and melt into his burning, shivering skin. If he tries hard enough, the snowflakes can be cold fingertips brushing his face, or wisps of soft brown hair. The fiction is unsustainable because Taylor has four classes with Wes Post and his soft brown hair, and Wes jumps out of his skin every time Taylor glances at him. Nobody wants to be friends with the guy who picks fights like flowers.

His eyes flutter shut as the weight of the snow presses him still. Behind his eyelids, he can see the stars again, in every brilliant color that Taylor doesn't know how to name.

Maybe this is a punishment. Maybe this is a homecoming. Maybe the snowflake-stars rushing out and landing with quiet kisses on Taylor's sweat-damp face is what it means to go home. He'll just wake up as a star.

Great. Now he doesn't have to find a rope.

He cackles until it shatters into a cough.

* * *

Wes Post is taking a walk. His anxiety is pulsing in every heartbeat and keeping him awake, but if he walks far enough and fast enough, he'll be so exhausted that he can fall asleep by 11:00 and stay asleep until 6:30 and have enough energy tomorrow for his precalc test. Nobody else will be stupid enough to be out and about at 9:36 at night either. Especially not in this cold weather. Great for Wes's piece of mind, but not for Mom's.

Mom had actually advised against Wes going, but Dad reminded her, in his roundabout way, about how poorly Wes slept if he didn't have his pre-bedtime walk. Wes's mother relented on the conditions that she would wait up for him and that Wes would bring his parka, even though Wes rarely felt cold enough to need a parka while he was walking- snow or no snow. But he took the parka with him anyway to make Mom happy.

Wes actually puts the parka on about six minutes into the walk when the snow picks up and up and up until the pretty flutter of fragile flakes becomes the harsh screech of poofy blizzard-spawns. Wes considers turning around. It's snowing pretty hard now. And it's windy. But Wes will never get to sleep if he turns around now, and he's got that test tomorrow— he hopes he's prepared enough. He needs to sleep tonight. So he'll muddle through. He pulls a fidget toy from his pocket and clicks it a few times as he walks, trying to calm down. It's just a walk. He won't die just from a walk. Even if it's freezing cold and snowing in piles.

A rough cackle echoes from somewhere below the bridge, and then crumbles into a grating bout of coughs.

His heart skips a frozen beat. Maybe he will die just from a walk.

What the fuck was that? Aliens? Zombies? Nazis? Some sentient chicken nuggets that all morphed together into one giant McMonster and now have the intent to destroy anyone who doesn't pledge their life to veganism?

No. No. Think about this logically, Wes. There were no flying saucers, or general town-wide hysteria, or Third Reich flags plastered to the town hall, or chicken-nugget goo dripping into the water supply. None of that at all. No warning signs of any kind to indicate that something like that is going on. So nothing to panic about.

Unless it's a homeless person with a knife trying to sneak up on Wes and kill him and rob him and leave his body in a ditch in Ecuador where nobody will ever find it. Never mind how his body would get from Iowa to Ecuador. There is potential for dying just from a walk. Wes stretches his fingers to avoid yanking on his shirt. He likes this shirt, and it's not deformed from his anxious tics yet.

Think it through. How can Wes maintain a sense of control in a situation like this? He can't think clearly if he doesn't stay calm.

Alright. There's a big stick. He can defend himself with that. He can sneak up on the homeless person with the knife before they sneak up on him. Then he'll be okay. He can stay calm here. He can.

So Wes picks up the big stick and he creeps around the corner, quieter than the snow on the wind. But there's nobody there. *Hallucinations!?* is Wes's knee-jerk, nervous thought, but he can be calm. He knows he can. He's been practicing being calm and meditating and taking his medication and everything. No. He's not hallucinating.

The snow lies peaceful and undisturbed, even as it continues to pile up in drifts. Nobody has even walked in the area since the snow started falling. Under the bridge, when Wes ventures farther down, is a hat. A yellow hat. Wait, Wes knows this hat. He stares at it every day in Physics. And English. And Precalc. And History. It's the same yellow beanie Taylor has had since eighth grade when Todd and Dalton got him a new one because the one he wore in elementary school was too small (from four seats back in their eighth-grade homeroom, Wes had overheard them telling Taylor that Todd bought the yarn from a really high-end shop so it would last forever and Dalton knitted it together with help from his grandma. It was too big for Taylor then and it always fell in his face, but it fits pretty well now). Why is it half-covered in snow under a bridge? If there is one immutable fact about Taylor Macready, it is his yellow beanie framing the organic ebb and flow of bruising on his face. He wouldn't leave this hat anywhere.

Did Taylor get hit by a bicyclist who thought he was a penguin? Did he get dragged away by a bear? No! No. Stay calm, Wes. He can stay calm. He's nervous, sure, but Wes will just grab the beanie and give it to Taylor tomorrow. Taylor's probably looking all over for it. It'll give Wes a reason to talk to Taylor anyway.

But then there's another cough. It's right behind Wes— *oh fucking Christ he's gonna die*. He flinches, but nothing ever

8

makes contact. When he tentatively turns around, nobody is there. But there's a new patch of color in the snow. The color of Wes's wooden dining room table when he spilled cherry-flavored medicine on it that one time. Wait. That's human skin. There's a person buried in the snow.

Okay, this is getting pretty out-of-control, but Wes can handle it. He's not a kid anymore. He's a grown-ass adult now, almost, and he can—he can—Jesus Fucking Christ that's Taylor Macready buried in the snow next to a bridge at 9:47 pm.

Fuck meditation and fuck control and fuck keeping calm Wes scrambles to unearth Taylor like some fucked up hybrid of a dog in a backyard and an archaeologist in a tomb. Taylor doesn't look right. His face is too red. He's shaking so hard that if he and Wes put wigs on, people would probably get their identities backward. And why is he sweating? Taylor never sweats- he's always complaining about how it's too cold, even in the summer. Wait, wait, wait. Let's back up even further: why is Taylor in a sleeping bag in the snow with no yellow hat on at 9:49 pm next to a bridge?

Wes has no answers for this.

But Taylor is clearly freezing cold. Maybe it's a dare. Who knows. But Wes knows he doesn't look comfortable, so he goes to shake him awake. And then physically recoils because fucking hell, this boy is throwing off heat like he's got a job as a furnace and four starving children to feed. That's not healthy. Shit. Shit that's a fever. And he's not waking up. Isn't that really bad? Is Taylor already dead? Wes stops panicking, momentarily, when Taylor begins trying to cough out words.

Of course, he's just reciting the words to "New York, New York," by Frank Sinatra with the tone-deaf quality of a hungry

9

cat waking you up three hours before your alarm, and after the chorus he can't be encouraged to respond to Wes for anything.

Wes is beyond panicking now, he's halfway into an anxiety attack and he decides that Taylor needs to get warm enough to stop shivering—isn't that how you stop a fever?—and he hoists him up with as much of his body strength as he can muster this late at night and begins the dead sprint home to find Mom still waiting by the door with the porch light on. She's usually asleep by now so she can wake up early to open the shop with Dad, but Wes has never been happier to have her hovering.

There is a careful progression of phases that Mom goes through between the time that she can make him out in the thick snow and the time that Wes reaches the porch, and he can read them all.

1. Oh, thank goodness, Wes is home. I was worried.

2. He's still not wearing his parka. That boy needs to take better care of himself.

3. Why does his parka look so much bigger than before?

4. Wes is carrying someone who is wearing his parka. I am worried again.

5. What kind of circumstance requires Wes to be carrying a person home at ten pm!?

6. I trust my son. There must be a good reason for this. I will help him and ask questions later.

Wes is extremely grateful that Mom makes this final decision, and that she opens the door for him and pushes him inside and tells Dad to take Taylor and walks Wes through his breathing and settles him down and has given him some hot tea just as Wes is lucid enough to drink it.

2

This Weird Guy Lives on a Suburban Pullout Couch Now

Wes takes a long sip from the steaming mug, not reacting to the temperature even though it must be scalding. The tea is decaf- Martha Post hates it when her son drinks caffeine before bed.

"Th-thanks, Mom," he says softly.

Martha nods. "Want to tell me why you're bringing home unconscious boys in the middle of the night?" She's biting back a frustrated, worried scream because she knows it won't help.

Wes nods back. "He wa-was sleep-eeping under the b-bridge by C-C-Clearwater Str-St-Street."

Martha is not pleased with how much Wes is stuttering. Nowadays, he only stutters that bad when he's panicking. She leans back in her chair and gives Wes a sympathetic smile and she gives herself a sigh. "Alright, kiddo," she says, "I'm going to leave the rest of this conversation for tomorrow when you're more relaxed, but I do want to know what happened." It won't help anything to get Wes all wound-up and scared right before bed.

"Honey?" Richard Post calls from the living room, "This kid's running a fever. We still have that acetaminophen in the cabinet?" Well, that explains why her son, bleeding heart that he is, sprinted home with him. Now the only question is literally everything else.

"It's the blue bottle next to the decongestant medicine, dear. Look in the medicine cabinet."

"Found it. Thanks, honey."

Wes has downed half of that decaf tea, and Martha decides it's bedtime now. Her son looks as wired as an electric panel during business hours, but she knows he'll turn off like a circuit breaker the moment his head hits the pillow.

"Alright, Wes," she says, patting his elbow to prompt him to stand, "let's get you to bed." He's taller than she is now, but there's still the stubborn part of her muscle memory determined to scoop her son into her arms and rock him like he's a toddler.

"B-bu-b-but Mom, T-Tay-aylor's-" This is that Taylor? The one her son can't shut up about? The one he gave a free cinnamon muffin to the other day? That Taylor? Martha swallows a smirk.

"Taylor will be fine, kiddo," she reassures him. "Your dad and I will take care of it. You go to sleep so you can be ready for that test tomorrow." That reminder works to get him to acquiesce to bedtime.

It's rare she's up for his bedtime, and she savors the walk to Wes's room and the way he kicks his shoes off and falls into bed. His feet almost hang off the edge. Martha had been right about him being like a circuit breaker; he's already asleep. Maybe he's mostly grown up now, outgrowing a lot of their help, but she tucks his comforter around his shoulders and turns off his lights before going into the hallway to meet Richard.

"How's Wes?" he asks

"Wore himself out panicking. He's asleep now."

Richard sighs heavily. He hates when Wes gets that anxious. It makes him anxious, Martha knows.

"How's Taylor?" Martha asks.

"Is *that* Taylor?" Richard huffs an incredulous laugh. "How did Wes manage to find him?"

Martha shakes her head, telling her husband, "He was too freaked out to say."

With a lopsided grimace, Richard says, "Yeah. The kid's got that fever I told you about— hotter than a windshield in an Arizona summer— and he's coughing like he's trying to give his lungs up for adoption."

Martha winces a little in sympathy. "You think he needs a doctor?"

"No, I don't think so, but we can take him to see one to-morrow if that medicine doesn't kick in." He looks at Martha dreamily. "You remember when you caught pneumonia, and we had to intubate you for a whole three days?"

"I remember," Martha replies with a smile, "you brought a stack of books with you and didn't leave the room once."

Wes wakes up at 5:58 am the next morning, having slept so hard and so soundly that his face is creased with the wrinkles in his pillowcase and he's still in last night's jeans. Sprinting home and having a panic attack while lugging around 175 pounds of human boy will do that to you.

He does his typical morning routine, brushes his teeth, scrolls mindlessly through apps, takes his medication with a glass of water, does his morning stress-release meditation, throws some clothes on, and it is only when he heads downstairs to get coffee and breakfast that he passes the living room, glances at the pull-out couch, and almost screeches.

Of course, his medication and meditation are worth their salt, so he does not panic like he did last night. He just stammers his way through half of an explanation before realizing that Taylor is still sleeping, and therefore neither hearing Wes's explanation nor caring where he is in the first place.

He looks better than he did last night though, Wes remembers that much. He's not breathing so hard, his face is less red, and he's not coughing every other breath, for starters. Wes sees a cold pack that's fallen off of Taylor's face, and one of those medicated patches that Mom used to put on Wes's chest when he got sick and couldn't stop coughing. He goes to fix the cold pack— that's probably part of the reason Taylor isn't so red today— but it's lukewarm and floppy now. The sheets are soggy where the condensation soaked into them. Wes heads to the kitchen, swaps out the used cold pack for one fresh from the freezer, and heads back to the living room to set it on Taylor's forehead.

Wes can't control Taylor's physical condition, but he can help improve it. He has steps he can take, things that are in his control.

Now, breakfast. There's a note, as there is every morning, on the counter.

Wes,

Dad is already out at the shop, but Mom is staying home to take care of Taylor. Don't worry, he's in good hands. When you get home, we want to talk to you about last night. We just want to know what happened, nobody is in trouble. Good luck on your test. We know you're going to do great.

Love,

Mom and Dad <3

Alright. See. Nobody is in trouble. Wes feels a knot of anxiety he hadn't been fully conscious of evaporating, now that he knows his parents definitely aren't mad at him. If they were mad, they wouldn't have put a heart at the end of the note. That's just science.

He leaves without really feeling too anxious about Taylor— Mom can take care of sick people way better than Wes can, so he wouldn't have been much help. It's only once he's on the bus that he thinks: Oh, shit, Taylor is going to miss the test, and Oh, shit, Taylor's clothes are still in the snow by the bridge, and Oh, shit, Taylor is going to be so confused when he wakes up. But he stops the train of thought there. He can't control those things. He can't change them, so he can't fill up his brain with worry about them. Wes takes several clarifying breaths and fidgets with the sensory cube in his pocket.

What can he do about the situation? He can tell their precalc teacher that Taylor is sick, and ask her if Taylor can take it another day. He can grab Taylor's clothes on the way home after school today. He can trust that Mom won't leave Taylor hanging. These are the things Wes can do personally, things he has the agency and capability to do. There's no need to panic. Nobody is mad at him and there are things he can do to remedy his concerns.

By the time he's adequately calmed himself down enough to sit through class, the bus is pulling up to Swisher High School, and Wes gets out of his seat and turns Ella Fitzgerald's voice down just a bit on his headphones to squeak out a 'thanks' to the bus driver and head into class.

Now time for the real challenge of the day: he's got five classes to sit through, and no yellow-hatted head to stare at.

* * *

Todd is not a stupid kid, and neither is Dalton, for the record, but Dalton definitely isn't sure what the hell Todd is talking about at lunch when he says, "Taylor isn't here today."

Sure. Yeah. Statement of fact. But he said it in that tone of voice that means that he means something else by it. Dalton blinks at him from across the table to ask him to clarify.

"Taylor never misses school," Todd explains, itching a spot between his braids. "I mean, he ditches English, but he's always *at* school. I don't know," he shrugs, "it just doesn't sit right with me."

Now Dalton can see the issue. And he agrees with Todd's feeling. "He's been acting weird for a few weeks. I saw him taking a shower in the locker room after school last week."

"Did you ask him why?" Todd asks.

Frowning, Dalton shakes his head. "You know how he gets when you ask him stuff like that-"

"You mean when you ask him anything."

"He gets all squirrely. Like defensive, but it's us so he's trying not to be mad? Ya know?"

"Yeah, Dalton, I know," Todd sighs, "I don't want to jump

16

to conclusions, but shit's weird. He got really nervous when I pointed out his cold the other day. Practically sprinted out of the house."

"And yesterday it seemed like he couldn't even remember where he was." Dalton's frown deepens, "he said he wasn't hungry, but he *looked* hungry."

"Everyone looks hungry to you, Dalton," Todd says.

Oh, suddenly this isn't a safe space for a man with a maternal heart? Dalton throws his hands up in a small, exasperated gesture. "I had banana bread," he cries, "and he said he wasn't hungry. To banana bread. That doesn't strike you as near-death behavior?"

"As someone who doesn't like bananas, no it does not."

Leaving his impossible bestie to his banana-hatred, Dalton rolls his eyes and notices, "Hey, isn't that Wes Post?" Todd peeks behind him and, yep, there he is, with that brown hair that's only gotten longer since elementary school. How that twitchy mess of a guy manages to handle that much hair in a food service position is beyond Dalton's comprehension.

Wes is staring right at them, occasionally shuffling his feet like he might step towards or away from them, but can't decide which. He's muttering to himself, but he always does that. Nobody minds it anymore— even the teachers hardly bring it up unless he's muttering the answers to a test while they're taking it (the other kids sitting in the back never tell the teacher if they hear it though, because Wes's answers are always right and sometimes a kid needs that A). It's even weirder to see Wes at lunch. Everyone knows Wes disappears at lunch— who knows where to.

Still, as ignored and flighty as the phenomenon named Wes is, he's hard to ignore when he's staring right at you with the possible intent to socialize. Very awkwardly.

"Oh, so it is," Todd acknowledges, "should we invite him to sit with us?" There are four chairs at every table in the cafeteria. Usually, it's Taylor, Todd, and Dalton, with one empty chair that is occasionally pulled away to supplement somebody joining another group, but today they have all four, and two are empty.

They watch him for a minute without making it too obvious they're watching. Will he come or will he go? He's an entertaining kid, even if you don't know him. Always doing something. That's what Taylor always says, anyway. Taylor only ever really puts a sentence together once in a while, but half the time he does it's about Wes. Dalton is just thinking that he'll take the jump, make eye contact, and wave Wes over to sit down with him—for Taylor's sake, if not Wes's—but Wes decides just a half-second before that he's got somewhere else to be and he takes his lunch and flees from Todd and Dalton's view.

"Weird," Todd mutters.

"Totally weird," Dalton agrees.

* * *

Taylor feels too hot, and too cold. He does have his hat now, so he's got that going for him. Bone deep shivers are twisting his spine and his blood feels like it's simmering, letting his muscles cook dry. His chest doesn't feel like it'll stab him for not coughing though— nice and cool and empty in there. How pleasantly comfortable, even if the rest of his body isn't. Is he dead? Is this what happens when you die? Is that why his chest feels so cold and empty? Has his cursed soul left him? Can he begin anew?

Oh. Wait. No. He's on a bumpy pullout-couch with springs poking through the mattress. That's one point for alive.

But where? Taylor's first thought is that someone called the cops, and now he's back home, but that can't be it because they don't have a pullout couch. It had been a thing. Dad wanted one when Taylor was twelve and their old couch broke after Taylor ("son of a bitch") jumped on it and Mom had been dead-set against it. "Why," she had argued, "so we can have bums couch-surfing in our living room all the time? Not in this house."

Well then, Taylor is currently, apparently, a bum, couch-surfing in someone's living room. But whose?

Green wallpaper. But that's not narrowing it down. It means he's not in Dalton's house, because his house is cream paint, and it's not Todd's house because Todd has a guest bedroom and no pullout couch. The couch is clearly unused to use, but that's not the kind of thing anyone knows about anyone else's couch. Taylor can barely turn his head without feeling like he might break out into coughing, but he turns it anyways to see what he can see, lives with the scraping bout of coughs, and sees nothing that narrows it down any further. A bookshelf, an end table with a glass of water and a crossword puzzle book, an armchair with a blanket thrown over the back. Taylor hasn't been to nearly enough houses to know if anyone does crossword puzzles or keeps hand-knit blankets on their armchairs. Taylor Macready knows he's not the kind of kid who gets invited to other kids' houses. Parents take one look at him and quietly tell their kids he's not a nice boy, if the kids themselves didn't already know that in the first place.

19

Dalton and Todd are exceptions. They practically picked him up by the scruff in kindergarten—before *anyone* can have a reputation—and now they're stuck with him, even if they wish they weren't.

Footsteps pat-pat-pat down the hallway until Taylor sees a tall, broad-shouldered woman with dark brown hair in the archway to the living room. She looks familiar, but Taylor can't parse where he's seen her in the jelly-thickness of his stream of consciousness.

"Oh, you're awake then, Taylor?" she says sweetly. It's not an actual question, and doesn't require an answer. Taylor gives a tiny nod anyways. Something defensive curls in his gut, and it rises to guilty nausea. What kind of disrespectful, couch-surfing bum doesn't even thank the woman letting him use her couch? Her pillows? What must be at least four comforters?

He opens his mouth, despite the way his throat feels like it's filled with sand. "Th-"

"Don't you even worry about it, Taylor," she cuts him off, voice still far-off and a little vague as she settles into the armchair. He nods again. No wonder his parents don't love him, he thinks— although he's not exactly certain why he thinks it. Maybe because he didn't say thank you right.

"You look confused," the woman says softly. Taylor blinks. He is, but it's a very general kind of confusion, and between the illness and the medicine, he could hardly put together a novel sentence if he tried. He's got no clue what *she* thinks he's confused about, but he is very confused. The woman pulls the knit blanket into her lap and flips open the crossword puzzle book. "Don't worry, Taylor," she says airily, "I'll still be here when you wake up."

Taylor croaks, "No." No way she's doing that. This lady's definitely got better things to do than babysit Taylor's stupid, sick, contagious, disrespectful, bum, couch-surfing ass while he sleeps. His voice strains at even the barest use. Saying "Go" is almost too much for his throat to take. She doesn't move, so he repeats, "go." She doesn't seem to hear him, but she does leave the room. Taylor doesn't have time to be relieved that he's not going to be a burden before she comes back with a new ice pack and places it, gently, on his forehead, and readjusts the four layers of blankets. A shiver spasms through Taylor's spine, his shoulders, his chest. He coughs.

Fighting every step, Taylor falls back asleep.

3

Tic-Tac-Toe

Wes walks home, even though it's below thirty degrees. Because if he walks home he can pick up Taylor's clothes. Taylor is less likely to be mad if Wes picks up his clothes for him— even if he'll probably fit in Wes's old clothes, more or less. Wes decides, after a few seconds, that he's not going to think about Taylor, groggy in the mid to late morning, cradling a mug of coffee that Wes made him between his hands and occasionally taking a sleepy sip, wearing one of Wes's old t-shirts and some pajama pants, smiling at something funny Wes said and just looking beautiful in the golden light coming through the kitchen window. No. No more of that. Wes will get nothing done if he thinks about things like that.

Maybe he'll save that thought for later. As a treat.

Taylor's clothes, conveniently, are all stuffed inside his sleeping bag. Inconveniently, his sleeping bag is almost completely soaked with partially-melted snow. Ew. And heavy, fuck. But he's already determined that he's doing this, and Wes does not give up on the things he's determined to do. So he hefts up the sleeping bag like any other 50-pound coffee bean bag and treks the last few blocks home and flops it in the laundry room by the side-door and then finds his mom sleeping on the armchair and Taylor sitting straight up and staring at her with an intense enough glare to level maybe one and a half small city blocks. He's got weird-looking— familiar-looking—red marks on his wrists and hands. No skin broken, but like he's been scratching at them.

Wes forgets how to speak for a second. Because Taylor Macready is in his living room, conscious and lucid, wearing *Wes's* pajamas, which is a new record for their level of interaction. The previous record-holding interaction had been Wes accidentally smacking Taylor's forehead with his chin that one time in the hallway when neither of them was looking where they were walking in sophomore year. They sit near each other in Physics and English and Precalc and History, but Wes is way too scared to talk to Taylor Macready, no matter how much he likes him. That said, maybe Taylor does or maybe he doesn't remember that as vividly as Wes does, because Taylor, after noticing Wes, crosses his arms defensively. Like maybe Wes might be ready for a fight or something.

"I-I-I-I-I um," Wes takes in a centering gulp of air and releases it slowly, "Glad to see you're up, T-Taylor."

Taylor lets his scratched-up arms fall to rest on his lap. He opens his mouth. Closes it. Swallows thickly, like it's painful. Then gestures around with both arms in a motion that succeeds in looking exasperated, with both the exhausted and confused connotations.

"Oh! You're in-n my house," Wes explains, "Tha-that's my mom."

Taylor nods slowly, digesting his thoughts. After a few

seconds of this, Wes remembers to unglue his shoes from the floor of the hallway and he retrieves a pad of paper and a pen and hands them to Taylor. Taylor stares at them for another good minute, as if he's forgotten how his hands work, or maybe he doesn't trust them. But he must decide his question is worth asking because eventually, slowly, uncertainly, the pen in his hands traces out:

why?

'Why' what? Why is he here? Why did Wes bring him here? Why is that his mom? Why is Mom here? Why is Wes here? What does that mean! Wes doesn't realize he's getting anxious until he feels his hands stretching themselves apart in that habit he grew to uproot the habit of yanking on his clothes and scratching at his skin. Another centering breath. He can be calm. He knows he can. He is a capable person. He can stay calm.

Taylor doesn't seem to have noticed the brief freakout—and who's to say that moment lasted anything longer than half a second? Wes steps through the archway and fully into the living room.

"I f-found-ound you in the snow last night when I was ou-o-out for a walk. You were s-sick so I carried you here. Dad g-gave you some medi-dicine." Wes figures he'll answer all of it in one fell swoop if he just explains the whole smorgasbord of events. "Mom s-stayed-d home to take c-care of you."

If his expression is anything to go by, this did not answer Taylor's question, but he starts scribbling again so Wes figures he'll wait—not anxiously, not anxiously at all—until Taylor shows him whatever clarification he's thinking of. Unfortunately, Taylor doesn't give Wes any clarification, just a random fact.

you dont stutter that much at school.

Wes blinks a few times. He's not even anxious now. That pulled the metaphorical rug from beneath him so fast that he's just kind of not even feeling the floor. He's wondering why Taylor would notice something like that. They don't talk much. Taylor's right, Wes hardly ever stutters like that anymore, just once in a while or when he's anxious, but it's jarring to hear it from someone else—especially when that someone is sick on the pullout couch in your living room and you've almost never spoken to each other. He says, "I g guess I'm just nervous because you're here."

Apparently, this was the wrong thing to say. Taylor nods thoughtfully, stands up, and starts walking towards the door. What!? Why!? Why is he leaving!? He can't leave—and that isn't Wes's stupid little crush talking! Eyes watery with congestion and forehead flushed, Taylor has an off-kilter lilt to his step as he makes a slow-gaited break for the front door. Wes meanders him back to the couch with an easy tug on one elbow. Taylor sits. Wes winces. They stare at each other for a minute like something might come of it. Nothing does.

Wes takes the silence as an opportunity to count things in the room. His therapist says that can sometimes work better than breathing, and breath seems to be in short supply at the moment. Sixteen scratch marks on the green wallpaper. Seven wrinkles in the curtains on the window. Three people in the room. There. Calm. See? Wes is fine. Taylor is fine—although he should probably still be laying down.

"Are you hungry?" Wes asks, doing his best to make it seem like he's as calm as he wants to be. If he acts calm, he can make himself calm.

Taylor takes too long to respond, so the slight negative

shake of the head goes ignored because it is clearly a lie. Wes wonders what kind of food Taylor likes, then weighs the likelihood of Taylor telling him (which is not likely at all, because Taylor is being both testy and vague—the former because of who he is as a person and the latter because he's sick), and decides he'll just make soup. Everyone likes soup. Sick people love soup. It's like food, but it's a liquid so you don't have to put all that effort into chewing.

He heats up a can of soup in a pot while he sips a cup of water to the bottom, and then pours half the pot in a bowl with a spoon and hands it to Taylor, who looks inexplicably frustrated and angry. It becomes rapidly clear that Taylor either doesn't like soup or doesn't like Wes, but he's not saying which it is.

The spoon doesn't leave the bowl. The soup begins to cool. Taylor is literally just staring at Wes, expectantly. Eventually, with a frustrated grimace, Taylor scribbles on the notepad.

is there more soup

"Yeah?" Wes keeps his voice down. He doesn't want to wake up Mom. Arm movements are doing their best to replace words for Taylor, but they're so abstract that Wes understands literally nothing of what he's trying to communicate. "W-what are those motions supposed to mean?" Wes is trying not to laugh, and mostly failing. Taylor flips him off briefly before writing on the notepad again.

YOU

dumbass eat some food

Is this? Is this what it looks like when Taylor cares? What the hell? Why didn't he just say it like a normal person? Although, Wes supposes as he wanders into the kitchen to get himself some soup, it's not like Wes Post is really a paragon of normal either.

"Look, soup," Wes says with only a little bit of teasing, "now we're both eating."

Taylor narrows his eyes, but sips the soup slowly with the spoon. Then the spoon is quickly abandoned and Taylor drinks the whole bowl—noodles and little vegetable bits and all—in a few seconds.

"So you were hungry," Wes comments. Holding out his bowl, he offers, "Want mine? I don't usually eat much."

Taylor shakes his head hard enough that he starts coughing again, despite the cooling chest patch still attached to the front of his shirt. Wes is surprised that the coughing doesn't wake Mom up, but she's always been a heavy sleeper. She slept through that thunderstorm in middle school that brought half a tree down on their roof.

"Are you sure?" Wes insists, "I can make some more soup in a jiffy too."

Taylor shakes his head again. He's got his nails from his right hand buried in his left arm. It's not drawing blood, but it looks painful. "H-h-hey, hey d-don't do th-t-tha-that!" He grabs Taylor's hand and pulls it away from his arm and just holds it, trying to keep his breathing in control. He didn't cause this. He probably didn't cause this. Taylor is in control of his own actions, not Wes. Wes can be calm. He can be calm.

When Wes unscrews his eyelids, Taylor is staring at the mess of their combined hands on the thick old comforters that Dad had piled onto the pullout couch last night. Taylor's hands are rough, and there's little tiny scars on the knuckles of his fingers, probably from splitting them open so often—Taylor's always hitting something. Wes's hands have all sorts of little scars too, mostly burns from the machines at the shop.

27

Wes retracts his hands and passes Taylor the other bowl of soup. He'll make more if he feels hungry. "Here. I'm done. If you don't eat it, I'm going to throw it out." Taylor grumbles quietly—Wes thinks it sounds like an expletive—flips Wes off for just a second, and then takes the bowl and finishes it just as fast as the other one. "Cool," Wes says. He feels a little better. "Be right back."

The medicine cabinet in the hall bathroom is always a mess because nobody in the Post household gets sick often enough to use it anymore. Wes got sick a lot when he was little, the way kids do, but not so much now that he's a little older. So it's a pain in the ass to find the cough drops, and they end up being in the second drawer in the vanity anyway, but Wes does find them and go back to the couch. Of course, it's empty.

Taylor is in the kitchen. Doing the dishes from the soup lunch—linner? It's something like four now.

"Oh, thanks for that," Wes says. He wishes Taylor would sit down, but he's already done the dishes, so there's no helping that. And he does appreciate it.

When Taylor turns, Wes expects another middle finger, but what he gets is a very small, very real smile. Not to be dramatic, but Wes literally almost has to sit down. He hasn't seen Taylor smile maybe ever. Wes wishes he had a photographic memory, or even better an actual camera. He wants to play those two seconds on loop every day for the rest of his life. What the fuck.

Then, of course, Taylor is the one who literally has to sit down, because being sick kicks your ass, and Taylor stumbles on nothing and ends up crouching on the floor and Wes has to help him to his feet and shuffle him back to the living room couch. Mom rouses herself with the commotion (maybe Wes screeched a little, but that's fine), and demands to know why Wes had let Taylor out of bed, look at him, he's gone pale! But she's not actually mad, and she makes Taylor take more medicine before Wes gives him a cough drop.

"Alright, I'm going to go make myself a snack," Mom says, "and we'll have dinner with Richard when he's home from the shop." She disappears into the kitchen.

Wes has no clue what to say, so he doesn't say anything. Taylor sucks on his cough drop for a while, and then he clears his throat with enough success not to cough at anything and says, "Sorry."

Which is absolutely out of left field, as far as Wes is concerned. The only thing Taylor has done is the dishes! Why is he sorry?

Reading his expression, Taylor adds, "For causing trouble." He does a half-cough that seems to mitigate the necessity to cough aloud. "I didn't mean to get your family caught up in my bullshit. Or you." He's frowning, angry almost, at some indecipherable speck on the comforter.

Wes doesn't quite get it, so he doesn't respond. Instead, he asks the question that's been on his mind since 9:47 last night: "Why were you sleeping in a sleeping bag in the snow?"

Once again, Taylor doesn't respond for several minutes. A few times, he opens his mouth to say something, a lie most likely, and then closes it again. He peeks at Wes's face. Grumbles. Sighs. "I live there."

"In the snow? In a s-sleeping b-bag!? U-un-under a bridge!?"

"Dude, calm down, it's not a big deal."

"It's a huge fu-f-f-fucking deal! Why are you l-living under a br-bri-idge, dude!?"

29

"Because I won the lottery—why do you fucking think!?"

"J-jes-je-j-jesus-us ch-c-chri-c-"

"Wes—I'm sorry I yelled. Calm down, dude."

"Ack! I-I-I-I a-am-m-am-m ca-ca-lm-alm."

"How the fuck do you do this?" Taylor mutters under his breath. In a normal volume, he says, "Wes, look." And Wes looks. And Taylor has his tongue stuck out, a pen balanced on his nose, and his eyes crossed. Wes huffs out two strangled chuckles. Now that he has successfully obtained Wes's attention, Taylor draws a little crisscross on the notepad. In the center of the grid, he marks an 'x' and hands the pen to Wes. "Your turn."

With shaking fingers, Wes grabs the pen and marks an 'o' in one of the corners. It's a shitty 'o,' all wobbly and uneven, but Taylor doesn't seem to notice. Just marks an 'x' in the adjacent corner. He can see what Taylor is doing now, but it doesn't mean it's not working. Wes puts his next 'o' in the corner opposite. Taylor's next 'x' sits beneath his last one, and Wes cuts him off at the bottom. Then Taylor is trapped between two options for loss, so he draws his next 'x' in a random spot, with a frowny face on top of it. Whether placebo or some actual psychiatric bullshit, Wes's hands are steady when he puts his last 'o' in one of the two winning spots and draws a little smiley face inside it.

Words leave Wes's mouth with the even keel of any other day. "Was t-this your strategy? Distract me by making a weird face and challenge me to tic-tac-toe?"

"It worked, didn't it?" Taylor says—kind of smug and kind of indifferent. Then, in that half-angry way again, Taylor says, "Sorry."

"No, I'm s-sorry," Wes insists, "I'm t-trying to panic less.

I shouldn't have let my worry g-get me so worked up."

This sentence clearly doesn't sit right with Taylor, because he's still frowning. But then again, maybe Wes is just reading too far into things. Taylor visibly emotes only once in a while, the rest of it is just what Wes sees because he's spent so long staring at him that by now he's almost got a sixth sense for it.

No. No. Wes knows what he sees. He won't second guess himself. He can stay calm. Taylor looks a little consternated, a little confused.

"Wes, your dad's on the way home," Mom calls from the kitchen. Wes thanks his lucky stars that the walls are thick enough that she didn't hear him freak out. She would have helped, of course, but it would have been embarrassing. "Are you and Taylor both okay with chicken?"

Wes looks to Taylor for confirmation, and gets nothing— Taylor is still half-angrily glaring at the comforter—so Wes calls back, "Sounds great, thanks Mom!"

Mom will be on the phone with Dad while she makes dinner and he drives home, Wes knows. So now he's got to talk to Taylor... about something. Anything. Taylor coughs once or twice, so Wes hands him another cough drop, and then puts the whole bag on the end table next to the couch.

With sudden interest, Taylor starts trying to fumble around to look for something. When he resigns himself to not being able to find it and being too dizzy to get out of bed, he asks "Is my backpack still under the bridge?"

Oh. Wes hadn't thought to check under the actual bridge when he went back for the sleeping bag and clothes. The snow had drifted with the wind and piled up in little dunes underneath the bridge, so he hadn't seen anything by chance either.

"My phone's in there," Taylor mutters.

"Sorry."

"'S not a big deal. I was just gonna text Todd and Dalton. Tell them I'm sick so they don't flip out over me missing school yesterday."

"I can text them?" Wes offers.

Taylor shrugs, "If you've got their numbers. I don't remember them."

That's kind of an issue. "I'll go grab your backpack," Wes says, and he stands up, and then Taylor literally yanks him down with much more force than necessary, leaving Wes to yelp in surprise and sink into an ungraceful heap on the edge of the pullout couch.

"Don't." Taylor coughs. "It's not a big deal." He looks a little... embarrassed?

Wes can understand not wanting people to go out of their way, so he nods. "I'll grab it when I go for my walk tonight," he proposes instead. "If I walk the same direction I did last night, I'll pass right by it." With another half-angry frown, Taylor nods before going back to staring at the comforter.

4

Who's Got Taylor Macready's Number?

Richard Post picks up a loaf of his wife's favorite french bread from that expensive artisan bakery he's not fond of on the way home—she was up every few hours last night checking on Taylor, even though Richard had insisted both that Taylor would be fine *and* that if she really wanted to check he could help. She had insisted in return that she couldn't help but worry *and* that he needed to sleep since he'd be running the shop alone while she stayed home.

Now, tonight, over dinner, they'll be discovering how exactly their son left the house without so much as a hat and came home with a sick teenage boy. Kidnapping isn't likely, but it isn't entirely out of the question—after all, this is Swisher, Iowa, and kidnappings have their (very justified) reasons more often than not. Maybe their son has been meeting up with Taylor in secret for the past several months, and Taylor collapsed while they were making faces at each other in the park. Richard remembers when he was younger, making faces with Martha at the park...

But anyways, he walks through the front door and passes

the living room, where Wes and his friend are sitting in the most petrifyingly awkward silence Richard has seen since he himself was a sophomore in college. He'll let that simmer until dinner—it will enrich the conversation, he's sure.

Only when he is fully in the kitchen does Richard sing, "Hello, dear."

And Martha sings back, "Oh, hello, honey. Dinner is just about ready."

After a quick kiss on the cheek, and after setting her bread down on the counter, he sways from the kitchen to his bedroom to change out of his coffee-stained clothes and wash his face.

"Dinner," Martha calls, and he can hear Wes helping her set the table, and bickering with his friend about not letting him help set the table.

"Taylor, you can barely walk without wobbling, you're not about to carry a stack of ceramic plates around."

Taylor mumbles something that doesn't carry through the walls as well as Wes's voice does.

"Will you just si-sit down? Fine, you can help with the silverware."

Yes, this will certainly enrich the dinner conversation.

He comes downstairs and the table is set, the boys and Martha are all sat down in front of their plates, and Richard takes his spot next to Martha. Wes looks jumpier than normal, but not anxious—just, nervous. Like any seventeen-year-old boy sitting next to his crush at dinner would be. Richard smiles. Taylor is staring with borderline-murderous intent at the tablecloth, like he expects it to rise up and try to strangle him. Richard's smile wanes.

"So," Richard begins, "how is everyone today? Taylor,

feeling any better?"

Taylor's eyes don't leave the tablecloth, but his back straightens just marginally, just for a second, like a reflex. What a strange reflex to have. "Yessir," he mumbles, "sorry about the trouble."

"No trouble at all," Richard assures him. "I remember when I was your age, I had mono for six weeks."

"You did!?" Wes cries. Oh, maybe Richard hadn't mentioned that before. "What happened!?"

After considering for a moment, Richard decides this is not a great dinner table topic. "Oh, you know. It was all fine after that."

"After what!?" Wes shouts.

"I mean, there was all that mess with the store running out of crackers, but basically it all turned out okay."

"What does that mean, Dad!?" Wes demands, arms waving. A soft chortle erupts from behind a muffling hand, and everyone is a little surprised to see it come from Taylor, whose eyes are warm and kind for just a moment before he sees the table staring and he returns to glaring semi-murderously at the tablecloth.

"So, Wes," Martha begins the conversation that they all know will have to happen, "Taylor," she ropes him in too, and he does that tiny little back-straightening thing he did before as she talks, "as parents, we just want to know what happened last night." She's using that one tone of voice she has specifically curated (and Richard has one too, for the record) for when she's discussing something Touchy. Very even, very kind, very open.

Wes looks at Taylor, as if for permission, but Taylor is still studying the tablecloth. "I, u-um, I went on my wa-walk last

35

night."

"No need to be anxious, son. We're not going to be mad," Richard reassures Wes.

Taylor's black eyes dart from the tablecloth to Wes's pinching expression and back again. His brow furrows ferociously, and then calms a little into something more manageable, less aggressive, but still fierce. "I was sleeping somewhere I shouldn't have been," Taylor says, "He didn't do anything wrong."

"'Sleeping somewhere you shouldn't have'... Taylor, sweetie, what does that mean?" Martha asks. Taylor recoils from the question.

Wes's hands are fidgeting up a storm in his lap. Taylor's face is getting stonier and angrier by the second. Richard is afraid dinner may not go as swimmingly as he'd hoped.

Taylor shoots Wes one more glance that Richard is starting to think is an attempt to look nervous and then says, "You can tell them."

"Wh-what!?" Wes stammers.

Martha almost rises from her chair to start helping him through some breathing, or another calming technique, but Taylor intervenes first: "Drink this," and he hands Wes a glass of ice water, "catch an ice cube on your tongue."

Wes doesn't think, just immediately does it, and the concentration required to catch an ice cube with his tongue distracts him from his panic long enough to diffuse it.

Martha almost gapes, Richard blinks owlishly. That's... new.

They've been to online seminars and they've read the books but to see someone just *help* their son without thinking anything of it or hesitating or panicking themselves—Richard feels a little emotional, actually. A switch flips in his head and he no longer cares where Wes found this kid, he just wants to know if Taylor is willing to stick around.

While Wes chews on his ice cube, Taylor explains, "I was sleeping under a bridge."

"In all that snow!?" Richard exclaims. He hadn't meant to shout, but he checked Taylor's temperature last night, and he had avoided saying how bad it really was because he knew Wes was in earshot. Taylor had been halfway delirious with a fever of 103, and still shivering. Richard had given him as much of that medicine as was safe to do, and hoped he wouldn't need to take him to the hospital by morning. If he was asleep under a bridge when it was cold enough to be snowing, it's a wonder he survived until Wes found him.

"I t-tripped on him, actually," Wes says, looking a little calmer now that the ice cube has been chewed and swallowed, "he was kind of buried in there." That's Iowa snowfall for you—Richard remembers when he and his friends buried their buddy. Poor Frank. He had volunteered though. It's a good thing he ended up being mostly fine. They were all kids anyway, then.

"Why were you sleeping in the snow under a bridge?" Martha's got that fire in her eyes that Richard knows very well. She won't set this one down. She has made this Her Problem. "Do I need to call your parents?"

With a shrug, Taylor replies, "I mean you could call them, but they won't really care."

"What..." Richard wants to sigh, or groan. What exactly does that mean, 'they won't care'? Well, he knows what it means, but is Taylor being serious? Is there actually a parent out there who would just kick their child out? In the middle of an Iowa winter? "Why do you say that, Taylor?"

Taylor's eyes snap up from the tablecloth, his shoulders square, and he glares at Richard. Viciously. Like Richard is a threat. Like Richard might be an idiot. There's so much vitriol in that expression that Richard actually doesn't know how to respond.

Anyway. The point has been communicated. Taylor's parents kicked him out. Taylor is homeless.

Taylor gets up and leaves the dinner table without another word. He's trying to look intimidating. Richard thinks he looks hurt.

* * *

Monique Feldman does not expect a text from Wes Post at nearly eleven pm on a Friday. She doesn't actually remember who he is at first. Wes Post? Isn't that the same last name as the coffee shop? But then she remembers. Oh! That one kinda nervous kid from school. She was assigned to work with him as a partner in English one time. He didn't make her do all the work, which was a welcome change, but he talked way too quietly when they were presenting it to the class, so that was kinda awkward. But she does remember him. What she doesn't know is why he's texting her at eleven pm on Friday. They haven't spoken since the project. The last text in the chain is

Wes: We got a 97 overall
Monique: Cool thnx
Nice working w you
But tonight there is a new text. And a weird one.
Wes: hey do you hav Todd's number?

38

Or dalton?

No. No, Monique does not have either of those numbers. Why would she? She never talks to those guys. She doesn't have any classes with Todd, and she only has Physics with Dalton, and they've never partnered together for anything. She never hangs out with them. Why would Wes ask her—at eleven pm no less—for their numbers? Why not ask someone who actually knows them? She's sure even her boyfriend, Harley, and his friends would know better than her—or, more likely, Taylor Macready, that asshole's always with them—

Oh.

Oh, Monique understands now.

See, Monique has English with Wes. She also has History with him. Which means she has them with Taylor too (even if Taylor never shows up to English). And Monique is not blind. And it would take someone blind, deaf, and possibly mentally impaired to miss the way those two moon at each other throughout class. Wes is tall, so he sits in the back and just stares. Taylor sits in the middle of the room and puts his head on his desk so nobody notices him peeking at the back row under his arms. But Monique still notices because she could pass these backwater fucking classes any day of the week and twice on Wednesdays when the cafeteria serves pizza that's actually edible, and she's always bored out of her mind.

But Taylor Macready is not exactly an approachable guy, even though he's about her height, and someone who gets nervous enough that his voice sounds like it's going through a cheese grater for a presentation to a class of twenty-six kids is not exactly going to start a conversation with someone like him without precedent. Everyone knows—just like they know Monique Feldman can pass Precalc, English, Physics, AP

39

Government, and History in her sleep, backwards, at a death metal concert—that Taylor Macready will rock your fucking shit if you so much as look at someone *else* sideways. He's just an angry kid. In a town like Swisher, Monique can respect that. Hate the sinner, love the sin.

But that leaves Wes Post's problem: How to approach this bastard. He's much more likely to take a sideways approach and try and talk to Taylor Macready's two friends first: Dalton Aarons or Todd Richards. Everyone knows that those are the only people Taylor Macready tolerates, god knows why, and they are much friendlier.

There we go. Now Monique remembers Wes Post and knows why he's texting her at eleven pm on a Friday night.

One more question: do we want to make him squirm?

Hmmm.

Were this a question of do we want to make Bart Chomski squirm, or Monica Briers, or even that fucking piece of shit Freddy Peters, Monique would say yes. Wholeheartedly. Without reservation. She's taken a lot of shit from a lot of people, and she'll dish that right back out if she thinks they deserve it, but she's not sure Wes Post does. I mean, he sucks at presentations, but he's one of the only people she's ever worked with who hasn't made her do all the work in a project. That, if nothing else, puts him in her good books.

She'll give him his information. He's a good kid.

Oh, shit, she forgot she doesn't have the numbers.

Monique: *gimme a min*

So Monique switches text conversations and texts Celsee. She knows Celsee likes Dalton, and Celsee doesn't sit around and wait for shit to fall out of the sky, so Monique knows Celsee will have Dalton's number, whether she's put that to use yet or not.

   Monique: hey celbel

   u still got daltons number?

   Celsee: wtf why???

   Girl i s2g if u want to make this a two player game i will fuck w u /hj

   Monique: Ew

   Gross

   No.

   Some guy is asking for it

   Celsee: ???

   Asking for dalton's number???

   Don't all the boys know each other??

   It's super sus if this guy doesn't ALREADY have daltons number

   I do not want u talkin to creepy guys bb

   Monique: its wes post

   Celsee: oh

   Oh that makes sense then

   Omg is he finally gonna like???

   TALK

   to macready???

   I will give u this number if u promise to keep me updated

   [contact shared: My Mans Who Aint My Mans Yet But He My Mans]

   obvs change the contact name <3

   Monique: 1 why r you so invested in someone else's relationship?

   2 thanx

   Celsee: bc i am a bored woman in a very small school

   Monique: 3 ur contact name oml XD

   Celsee: what can i say i am a pinnacle of comdy

*comedy

Monique: alright since u care so much i'll keep u updated if i find anything out

But i am not putting effort into this, celbel

Celsee: <3<3<3<3<3<3

And Monique changes Dalton's contact name and shares it with Wes.

[contact shared: Dalton]

Wes: dfhj

Sorry, I droppd my phone

Thank you, Monique! I appreciatte this! I'll give you a free coffee sometime at th shop

Monique: no prob

see you monday

Wes: See youu then! :D

With the little :D emoji and everything. Why is Wes Post such a good kid?

Unknown: Hi Dalton, I'mm sorry for texting so late. This is Wes Post.

I got your number from Monique.

Dalton: oh heyyy wes

Dalton is not very surprised by this text. Not even at 11:36 pm. He saw Wes in the cafeteria earlier. Wes is thinking about something—and that something probably has to do with one of Dalton's two best friends, specifically the pissy one with the yellow hat and the secret stargazing hobby.

"Hey, Todd," Dalton says into his headset, "Wes just texted me."

"Real shit?"

"Yeah. Said he got my number from Monique."

"Rushing B," Todd says about the video game they're playing, but he seems more focused on the drama than the game, "Dude, he actually got your number instead of Taylor's? I guess he's a little more scared of Taylor than we thought."

"I mean, I guess—" Dalton gets shot in-game and curses, "fucking camping bastard. But I mean, if *you* didn't know Taylor would you try to start a conversation with him?"

"You know what? That's fair. He's been beating the shit out of people since elementary school. I wouldn't mess with that guy if I didn't, like, personally know him."

Dalton: wuts up bud

[contact added: Wes]

Wes: hey um

Are you in a headspacce to receive information that could be strssful?

Well, that's one way to start a conversation.

Well, he's out for the round anyway. "Hey, Toddster, I'll be right back."

"Why? What did Wes say?" Todd sounds distracted, and from the spectator's view of his game, Dalton can see he's occupied by two people on the other team trying to box him in.

"He asked me if I was, and I'm quoting here, 'in a headspace to receive stressful information'."

Todd scoffs, still distracted. "Dude, Dalton, that's weird. What does that even mean?"

"I've got no fucking clue."

"I mean, I guess he's trying to be considerate."

"Yeah, I guess. I'm going afk."

"Go for it."

Dalton: ummm ya sure?

43

Go w ur traffic

Wes: so I've got Taylor at my house right now

"TODD!"

Dalton watches Todd get shot in the head with the sudden distraction, and doesn't feel remorse even when Todd snaps, "Dude, don't scream in my ear! What? Did a South American country's government collapse?"

"NO, DUDE, WEIRDER."

"Well don't make me guess just tell me!"

"YA KNOW HOW TAYLOR HASN'T LOGGED ON TODAY, LIKE, AT ALL?"

"Yea, he's not answering his phone either. Weird, but not weird enough to justify your screaming."

"HE'S AT WES'S HOUSE"

"He's *where*!?" Todd screeches.

Dalton is now standing up from his chair. "YOU HEARD ME."

"CLEARLY I DID NOT BECAUSE I JUST HEARD YOU SAY HE IS AT WES POST'S HOUSE," Todd says, and damn, this would be more fun if they were in the same room and could record, together, a voicenote so embarrassing that Taylor might actually sock them in the jaw if he were to open it around Wes.

"THAT IS WHAT I SAID," Dalton yells back. His dad yells up asking if everything's okay, and Dalton shouts down that everything's fine. He doesn't mention what, exactly, is going on, because his dad doesn't exactly love Taylor.

"NO FUCKING WAY," Todd is still shouting, in his massive upper-middle-class mini-mansion where even that volume doesn't make it to every corner, "WHAT THE FUCK."

"Alright, alright, Todd. We gotta calm down. Wes's still

typing and I need to respond."

"You tell me EXACTLY what that kid says— and whether he kidnapped Taylor or slept with him."

Wes: he got really sick.

Dalton dutifully conveys the words, "Wes says Taylor got sick," even though his smile is starting to falter.

"Yeah, we knew that," Todd says, excited, unable to see that faltering smile. "Why does that mean he's at Wes's house."

"I don't know, man, the guy's still typing." Dalton's stomach is twisting.

Wes: and I don't know if you guys know where he's been living, but that made his condition a lot worse too.

"'Where he's been living'? What the fuck does that mean?" Dalton mumbles. He's starting to get nauseous.

"What's he saying, Dalton?" Todd demands, but Dalton is too busy putting locker-room-shower-shaped pieces together.

Wes: H'es okay now though!!

Wes: but I've got hiss stuff at my house right now. My parents said he can stay here for a while, so that's finee, but since you'r his friends, I thought you shoul know.

"Holy shit," Dalton breathes. The floor is gone. The game is gone.

"What?" Todd laughs, "Did they really do it?"

"Dude," Dalton says softly, "Todd, I think we fucked up."

Silence infects the mic. Eventually, Todd says, "What do you mean?"

"When's the last time we went to Taylor's house?" Dalton asks.

A beat of silence. It isn't a good sign. Todd has the best memory out of the three of them. "Get to the point," Todd says, nervous.

"No, seriously," Dalton says, "when was the last time we went to Taylor's house? I can't remember and you're smarter than I am. Todd, when's the last time we actually saw Taylor go home!?" The world has whited out and every nerve in Dalton's body is singed with this awful wrenching.

Neither of them says anything for long enough that their respective headphones stop trying to pick up noise.

"Fucking hell, dude," Todd whispers, his voice sounds a little hoarse, "you're not actually saying-..."

A blip of the outside world creeps in when Dalton dies again in-game. He hadn't realized the next round had started. "I don't know if I'm reading this right," he says. "There's no way I'm reading this right."

"Dalton, don't freak out," Todd interrupts. Taylor is better at calming Dalton down, but Taylor is, apparently, at Wes's house. And has been. For who knows how long. Todd can't remember the last time he went to Taylor's house either, which means it's been a while. "What did Wes actually say?"

Dalton reads the texts off quickly, voice beginning to clench. Todd listens and feels his toes go a little numb.

Shit.

They knew something was wrong. They knew. They were talking about it at lunch. They knew and they should have done something. Taylor never would have let them, but they should have done something anyway.

Dalton suddenly realizes it's been several minutes and he hasn't responded. "Shit, what do I say back?"

"I don't know, man," Todd replies hollowly.

Dalton: is Taylor ok
Wes: he's okay

46

His phone is deaad though

And he didn't remembr anyone's number. That's whyy I had to get it from Monique.

Dalton: ok

ok Todd and I are going to meet up w u guys

Whats ur address

Wes: ljksa

Sorry I dropped my phone

You guys can come over, but Taylor already fell asleep.

[location shared: IIome]

Dalton says, "I'm going to drop an address in the chat. Meet me there ASAP."

"Is it Wes's house?" Todd asks. It probably is. He can't think of anything else that would be address-shaped and relevant at the moment.

"Yeah," Dalton replies. There's the sound of shuffling, of socks and shoes being pulled on. "He says Taylor is asleep."

"I'll pick you up on the way," Todd tells him.

5

Fingers In Their Bloody Little Graves

Wes is fidgeting. Taylor is trying to get Wes not to fidget so much. There's nothing to be stressed about. Why does *Wes* feel so much pressure? Taylor is the one who has to tell his friends that he's been homeless for four weeks. There's no pressure for Wes. Wes just has to send the physical text. Taylor should be freaking out.

Is he though?

No.

Just kicking himself.

Who the fuck did he think he was? Just gonna strike out on his own? Taylor Macready, look at him go—he's really got something going for himself. I mean, if he saves up, he could get a nice area rug to go with the cinder block he dragged from a parking lot to use as an easy chair, or he could get a cool desk lamp—if he had a desk. Or electricity. Jesus Fucking Christ, what did he think was going to happen? He would miraculously survive an Iowa winter living under a fucking bridge, turn eighteen, and just fucking graduate with no goddamned incident like his parents didn't kick him out because at least they understood that he was wasting space under their roof—fuck Taylor Macready.

"T-Taylor, stop that."

"What," Taylor snaps. He didn't mean to snap. He really didn't mean to. You know what, it's better this way. If Taylor snaps at Wes then Wes and his parents will see what Taylor is really like and they'll hate him and then they'll kick him out too and then he won't infect them with whatever the fuck is wrong with him. It's better this way.

But here is Wes. Unfolding his hands so gently, prying them from the skin of his arm—when did they get there? When did they start drawing blood? Taylor's ears are ringing... why? Why can't he feel anything except Wes's fingers on his, and why are Wes's fingers so cold?

"Taylor," Wes is almost whining, it's almost funny, "you're bleeding."

Good. That's probably good. Taylor deserves to bleed. He's got mistakes he needs to pay for. He's done too much bad. "Fuck off," Taylor mutters, but his teeth click with their chattering when he does.

"Alright, we're waiting for Dalton to respond," Wes explains, as if Taylor hadn't spoken, "I'm going to get medicine. The nighttime one. You're shivering again."

"No," Taylor insists, firmly, angrily, defensively. "That shit makes me tired." He doesn't want to fall asleep before he knows how Dalton and Todd react. He needs to hear whatever they have to say before he goes down. If they say they don't want to fucking see his face again, maybe he'll just not wake up from that nap. He needs to know beforehand so he can plan if he should wake up.

Unfortunately, Taylor's fever really is starting to spike, and he couldn't get up to stop Wes from getting the stronger nighttime medicine if he tried. He stares at his fingers instead of moving. There's a little bit of blood- not enough to even coagulate, or build up into drops, just enough to color his nails a little red-orange. He hates it. Ugly fucking color. Ugly, jagged fucking nails. He rakes them up and down his arms until they find the uneven little spots they'd been sitting in before and Taylor digs them in there again. The pain keeps him tethered. He'll stay right here with the pain. The rest of him stays collected in a tight, tense, pissed-off little puddle at the top of his head, but his nails and his arm are there. Everything else spins and spins and spins around that point of contact. That pain is his control center.

"Here, swallow this," Wes sounds a little calmer now. He probably just needed a moment away from Taylor—Taylor knows he's scary, he knows that he probably freaks Wes out just by being around. Wes probably wants him to leave.

And Taylor will. The second he can stand up and stop being such a pathetic sack of shit, he'll go. That would be best. Taylor takes the fucking medicine. Wes brought him water to take it with—why is he so nice? Why can't Wes understand that Taylor won't say no to these things? That he'll just accept them and take advantage of Wes? "Good," Wes says softly, calmly. He sends another text on his phone. He puts the phone down and sets the hand on Taylor's shoulder.

Taylor recoils immediately, the echo of pain not inflicted ringing in every nerve like a burn. "Don't fucking touch me," he hisses.

No—shit. Why can't he just interact like a normal fucking human being? No wonder Wes hates him!

Wes doesn't seem to notice the vitriol, just says, "Alright, I'm going to take your hand now." It isn't a question, but Wes gives Taylor plenty of time to say no. Then there's his cold, gentle fingers again. Both hands take their time to lift Taylor's nails out of their bloody graves. This time, one hand stays with Taylor's, fingers locked together, Wes's thumb rubbing fidgety circles in the hollow between the metacarpals on Taylor's thumb and first finger. His other hand types out some messages to what must be Dalton, but Taylor's focus is on the hand holding his.

He wants to cry. Nobody has touched him this delicately since... since sixth grade when Todd and Dalton threw him a birthday party because Taylor's family didn't want to for the first time and the hug Dalton gave him was just a little different than his normal hugs. Taylor doesn't deserve it. He doesn't deserve this. Can a person die from being too cared for? From being handled too kindly?

"Gonna kill me," Taylor mumbles, and he can feel himself half-gone in sleep, even though the medicine should take another thirty minutes to kick in.

Putting down the phone, Wes uses his other hand to pull the covers up around Taylor's neck, pull Taylor's beanie further over his ears, and wipe a drop of water off of Taylor's face. Who knows if he's been crying or if that was something irritating his eye.

"They're not mad at you," Wes says sweetly, oblivious to the fact that they're having two totally different conversations, "if anything, I'm the one they're gonna be m-mad at."

With his free hand, the one attached to the arm covered in raised, red flesh and the tiniest little baby scabs, Taylor grabs what he can reach— in this case, Wes's oversized pajama shirt— and hoarsely whispers, "Go away," before falling totally asleep.

Dalton's waiting on his driveway at precisely 11:56, about two minutes before Todd's car growls onto the pavement—his dad was headed to bed as Dalton was headed out, but he just said have fun and come home safe. It's absolutely bonkers that Wes is even awake to text them, much less let them come over to talk about this whole mess.

And fucking hell, what a mess it is.

Todd's a broken record of "how could we not have known" and "I was so stupid," and Dalton's a broken record of "I'm just so glad he's okay, dude." Not that Taylor is actually okay. But it could have been so, so much worse.

It's all they can talk about on the way there. Nothing else seems to matter, really. It takes less than six minutes to get to Wes's house, and Dalton vaguely wonders why he didn't just walk.

Dalton gets a text as Todd switches the engine off. And then five more in rapid succession.

Wes: don't knock on the door
Taylor is sleping
And my parentss
Jst comm ein
It's not locjed or anything
Sorry

"He says just to go in," Dalton informs Todd, showing him the texts when Todd gives him a look.

The door opens easily. It feels wrong that way, as if Dalton and Todd expected it to stay shut, or at least make an effort to do so. It's Taylor they're looking for, after all. But the door opens like it's used to opening easily and often. The house is dark, but not quite in an eerie way, just unfamiliar. Less like a deserted alleyway and more like a crossroads. Whatever moonlight can be spared to reflect off the snow and shine through the big window next to the kitchen table puddles in the home's main hallway.

"D-Dalton? Todd? Is th-that y-you?" a voice rings through the walls, and Dalton and Todd follow it to the living room. At the source of the voice they find a picture that is about as far from any reasonable idea of what they might have to confront that night as can be expected at just past midnight at a barely-not-a-stranger's house. Wes looks no less awake than he was when they saw him in the cafeteria earlier today, and is twisted a little uncomfortably sideways, the one free hand he can use waves awkwardly to greet them. Attached to Wes's non-waving hand, and to the corner of his shirt, is Taylor, curled up like a baby, tucked under four layers of blankets, and mumbling a little in his sleep. Dalton wonders if he is hallucinating this. He looks at Todd to check, and Todd looks like he is also wondering if he is hallucinating this. Which means, in all likelihood, they are hallucinating nothing, and Taylor is actually willingly physically touching someone, and sleeping, and looking so much softer than they have ever seen him—conscious or not.

"That's, uh" Dalton says after a brief wave to respond, "that must have been some cold medicine."

"Uh, um, it h-hasn't... it shouldn't have taken effect yet," Wes mutters. "I think he's just tired."

Well, there really is absolutely nothing Dalton can say to that.

Todd sure can though, because he asks, "Is this why you

told us to just come in?" in a tone like he can't really believe what he's looking right at.

Wes nods, a jerking motion that rattles his shoulders. "He's like a cat."

"What do you mean?" Dalton asks. He's resisting the urge to coo like a grandmother, or maybe cry.

Both Dalton and Todd are immensely glad that he asked when Wes says, "Watch," and lifts up the hand that Taylor's sleeping body has apparently taken a shine to, only for Taylor to unconsciously pull the hand back closer to him, mumbling something unintelligible without waking. The same reaction occurs when Wes tries to pry Taylor's fingers off his shirt. "He won't let go. I have to pee so bad."

"Okay, first, I'm taking a picture," Dalton says, whipping out his camera.

Todd nods wisely, "We'll need concrete evidence to prove to Taylor that this happened."

Wes twitches a little, but doesn't object. Dalton takes three pictures, the last one with flash because the first two didn't turn out very good— the flash makes Taylor's face wrinkle and open up slowly into wakefulness.

"The fuck're—" Taylor mutters, blinking and trying to move (and then realizing the weird angle he put his shoulders into in order to hold both Wes's hand and his shirt), letting go too abruptly, saying "fuck" at a normal volume, re-remembering Dalton and Todd's presence, thinking very hard, and announcing a third time, "oh, fuck."

"Thank god," Wes whispers, "I'm gonna go pee," and he scampers off down the hall.

Taylor pulls himself to a sit, muttering all the while, "Shit, fuck, fuck, goddammit, fuck," so quietly that Todd and Dalton would not be able to hear it were they not granted a special sense of hearing by the silence of partially-asleep houses past midnight.

It becomes apparent to Dalton before Todd that the emotion Taylor is trying to express is anxiety. Unfortunately for all, Dalton is a seventeen-year-old boy, and does not know how to respond to this knowledge.

"How you feeling, dude?" Dalton asks instead.

Taylor's face goes harsh and stony too fast. His friends almost feel the whiplash in their own brain stems. "Fuck," Taylor mutters, and his voice sounds shredded—Todd hands him a cough drop from the open bag on the end table. When he's got that in his mouth, he says, "Sorry. Didn't mean to cause trouble."

Cause trouble? Cause trouble!? Dalton sits down in the open armchair with a huff of ironic laughter, mostly because he is a dramatic bitch, but he genuinely feels that way too. "Taylor Macready, I will fucking kill you, the fuck you mean 'cause trouble'?"

"Dude," Todd chides. Not disagreeing, just cautioning. Todd's always been better at keeping his shit composed under pressure.

"I know," Taylor whispers, too softly—softer than they knew that he could speak. "Sorry."

"No!" Dalton cries, then lowers his voice when he hears it ricochet back at him from the unused corners of the living room, "Taylor, no! I am not actually going to kill you."

"Jesus fuck dude," Todd adds, "I can feel your fever from here. You need to rest."

"But I lied—god, you guys must hate me," Taylor sighs. He looks exhausted. Like. Bone-deep, heart-droopingly, soulcrushingly exhausted. And the worst part is—the part that's really making Dalton sweat—is that he can't remember Taylor looking any better.

"No!" Dalton insists.

"Sh, Dalton, Wes's parents are still asleep—Taylor, we don't hate you. Come on, man."

Taylor's face crumbles a little further. "Why?" he hisses. He sounds angry.

But Dalton knows better and he wraps Taylor in a hug that Taylor tries to run from for a second, and then he just settles into it like his bones liquefied and he can't hold himself up anymore. Todd knows better too, but he's not as good a hugger as Dalton—what he can see from his vantage point, however, is Taylor's face. And Taylor's going through seventy-three emotions in half as many seconds.

Then Taylor sniffles and calls into the dark (without looking, no less), "Wes, stop hiding."

"I thought he was still peeing," Dalton says, letting go of Taylor.

But Wes tiptoes anxiously from the hallway and peers into the room with a guilty look and a self-conscious wave, "S-sorry. Didn't want t-t-to interrupt."

Todd shrugs with a small half-grin, "That's Taylor, I guess." The best hearing of anyone they know, and the worst sense of smell.

Wes is blushing, which you can barely see in this light, but it's still a little visible. So something magical happens.

Between Dalton and Todd, they have seen Taylor's face go red exactly one time: it was when Taylor overheard Stephen Barbary talking shit about Dalton's mom less than a month after the funeral, and Taylor went visibly red with anger about nine seconds before he beat the everloving shit out of Stephen.

What they are currently seeing is approximately the opposite of that: Taylor is blushing because Wes is blushing and that, for homosexual reasons, has had an effect on him. But Taylor's face is red in a similar way. Dalton resists the urge to laugh, because Taylor's face is as red as Wes's and they're just staring at each other for about ten seconds before Taylor stands up and says, "Bye," and begins to walk to the front door. Wes or Todd could have easily dragged him back, but Dalton is a football player, and just picks him up and carries him back. Taylor is too exhausted to protest, so he grumbles.

"No, you're laying down and sleeping now," is the general gist of what three people are trying to say at once.

"I thought you guys were here to grill me about all that shit," Taylor says, looking too genuinely confused to laugh at.

"No, dude," Dalton insists, "we just wanted to check on you."

Todd nods, "We were seriously worried." By his expression, 'worried' is an understatement. He looks haunted. There's something in the set of his narrow shoulders that wonders about the spare rooms in his house that Taylor could have easily fit in. Something in the flatline of his mouth that can see, probably better than Dalton ever could, the outline of how bad this could have been, if not for Wes.

"But if we get to ask questions," Dalton seizes his chance, "how the fuck did Wes find you? No offense Wes."

Wes nods, hands up in a little shrug. "None taken."

Without moving off of Dalton, Taylor shrugs weakly. "I dunno man, he tripped on me or somethin'. Ask him."

Eyes turn to Wes, who squeaks, takes a breath or five, and explains in super-fast words, "Okay, so I was out on a walk, and I heard a noise, and I followed it and it sounded like it was coming from under a bridge, but I didn't see anyone there? So I was about to head back home, but I did actually tr-trip on T-T-Tay— on him."

"How did you not see him?" Todd interrupts. Taylor might not be as big as Wes or Dalton, but it's hard to miss a whole-ass person.

"H-he was, um, b-buried in th-the snow."

"He was *what*!?" Dalton cries, earning a reprimand from Todd and a grumble from Taylor.

"S-s-so I br-b-brought-"

"Wes," Taylor leans off of Dalton to look Wes in the face. He doesn't say anything else, just suspends the room in flabbergasted silence and waits for Wes to re-orient himself. Then he turns to Dalton and says, "Fuckin' chill out, dude. I'm too tired for this bullshit." And he promptly re-collapses onto Dalton, who has not one singular goddamn clue who Taylor Macready has been recently replaced with—or, if this really is his best friend, what the fuck this cold medicine is doing to him (it really is the latter at this point. Now that the medicine has infiltrated his system, Taylor could barely tell a tree from a soda can if you asked him. He'll barely remember any of this by morning).

So Wes finishes telling Todd and Dalton what happened, and they listen, and by the whole three sentences later, Taylor is already sound asleep with a broken fever and not a dream behind his eyelids. Todd and Dalton promise that they're coming back tomorrow to figure this out when everyone is conscious.

6

A Quiet Saturday on December 12

Wes doesn't remember walking to his bed upstairs, but he certainly wakes up there at 7:03 in the morning— an hour and a half later than normal, even on a Saturday. Usually he falls asleep by midnight at the latest, after a walk if he needs one, and wakes up by 5:45 or 6:00, but last night he was up until at least 1:26, so it follows that he'd wake up later too, especially since yesterday had been not just long, but really fucking stressful.

Today, Wes decides during his morning meditation, his goal is to calm himself down before he gets to the panicking stage. He wants to have zero anxiety attacks today. That, he thinks, is reasonable, attainable, and tangible—the three things that his therapist said to look for in a daily goal when he saw her last Monday before she left for a vacation to Tahiti with her kids. No panic attacks is a goal she would approve of, Wes thinks. He can logically keep track of it, it's not insurmountable, and there is a definitive line between reaching it and not. Nice.

He almost breaks that goal fourteen minutes later when he gets to the kitchen to make some breakfast to find Taylor already meandering around in the kitchen. Wes catches him just as he's cracking an egg into a bowl.

"What are you doing!?" he shrieks, because Taylor should *not* be up and about yet, probably, and even if he should be it's jarring to walk downstairs and see your crush making you breakfast. Wes will probably die of a heart attack before Taylor manages to get settled anywhere else.

"Fuckin' chill," Taylor says, with no real anger. "I'm making breakfast. Your parents left a note, by the way."

Wes fidgets with the sleeves of his pajama shirt in the archway to the kitchen. "They always leave a note."

"Aight. I'm making scrambled eggs. Can't cook for shit other than that." Taylor's body language is as loose as it ever gets, which isn't very loose at all, but it makes Wes bite his cheek around a smile.

Inching into the kitchen, he offers, "I can help?"

"No," Taylor snaps. There's the slightest twitch in his frown that Wes understands to mean that Taylor's still got half of that sentence stuck in his trachea. He does that a lot, Wes has noticed, says something but means something else— not something different, just more than what came through (or maybe Wes has been staring too much, who's to say).

But Wes can't sit still while Taylor—whose pallor has improved immensely overnight, if nothing else—makes breakfast, so Wes pulls out a bigger bowl and insists, "then I'll make pancakes." He gets a dirty look, which he pointedly ignores. Taylor shouldn't even be awake right now, probably, he doesn't get to be bossy.

"You won't even have time to make the fucking pancakes before I'm finished with the eggs," Taylor grumbles. It's a weird, non-angry kind of grumble. Wes might chalk it up to

Taylor's throat still bothering him, except for the slight frown.

Without taking any time to try and untangle whatever has Taylor grumbling and frowning without actually being angry, Wes pulls out a whisk and replies, "We'll see, I guess."

Mixing with one hand, Wes's eyes drift to read the note his parents always leave him in the mornings where they open the shop.

Good morning Wes (and Taylor),

We've gone to open up the shop. Make sure Taylor takes some more medicine when he wakes up, we don't want that fever spiking again! Wes, you don't have to come in for the afternoon shift, we've got it for today (but tomorrow we'll need your help with the church rush). Taylor, make yourself at home. When we get home, we want to talk about options for where Taylor is going to live. Nobody's upset

See you both at seven (we're going to eat lunch at that cute cafe down the street),

Mom and Dad

Wes has pancakes on the griddle by the time Taylor is starting to get to the scrambling part of the eggs—the speed makes Taylor's expression pinch into what could be surprise, if it was kind of annoyed. They finish their respective dishes at the same time, and Taylor is fuming, just a little. With no eye contact, for fear that Taylor would snap or Wes would laugh, they make their plates and sit down at the kitchen table with some glasses of water.

The silence is awkward for a minute. What the fuck are they supposed to talk about? The weather? It's been normal as any other Iowan city. How they've been? Well, Wes already took his meds and Taylor will be taking fever medicine after they finish eating, so that's already kind of a known variable. They haven't ever really technically spoken to each other like normal human beings.

"Were you looking at the stars or the snow?" Wes blurts. He hadn't meant to. Shit. That's like, the worst thing he could have brought up. Wes is certain that the last thing Taylor wants to talk about is why, exactly, he was sleeping next to the bridge instead of under it when he almost died of exposure.

But, without any emotion—no animosity or nonplussed-ness or even any special amount of apathy—Taylor replies, "Kinda both." He takes Wes's silence as an incentive to venture another two sentences. "Mostly the stars, but then it started snowing. Got too tired to move."

"Oh," Wes nods. Pauses to take another few bites of eggs. They're pretty good eggs, despite what Taylor had said about not being able to cook. "Do you like stargazing?"

For just half a second, Taylor's eyes light up, like Wes had guessed the right answer and now Taylor feels free to gush, but the lights go out just as fast as they came and instead, Taylor shrugs and eats more pancakes. "I mean, I fucking guess. I'm shit at it though."

"How can you be shit at looking at the stars?" Wes blurts again. Shit. Dammit. He needs to learn how to shut his mouth. Clearly Taylor didn't want to talk about it. Why did he bring it back up?

One of Taylor's hands abandons mealtime to scratch at his other wrist. Wes wonders if Taylor will need, like, some band-aids or something to keep Taylor from fucking his arm up too much. Or long sleeves that are harder to roll up.

"I only know a couple constellations," Taylor admits, like it's a mistake that he needs to correct. An egregious sin, or something.

Finishing his eggs, Wes replies, "I mean, that's a couple more than I know." He stacks his fork and knife on his plate in an I'm-done kind of way. "And who said you need to be good at something to enjoy it?" That's what Wes's therapist has always told him.

It gives Taylor something to chew on, that's for sure, while Wes rinses both of their dishes and puts them in the dishwasher. When he's done, Taylor is staring at him, expression half-angry again, and he bites his cheek before turning away from him and facing the window. For absolutely no reason. But whatever. So Taylor isn't super fond of him. Ouch, but Taylor isn't super fond of anyone whose name isn't Todd or Dalton.

"Did you take your cold medicine?" he asks anyway, because if there's one thing Wes Post can handle, it's peer rejection.

"Fuck off," Taylor mutters, which feels like unnecessary salt on a fresh wound.

"Dude, what the fuck?" Wes snaps, and regrets it even without looking fully at Taylor. Less fast and less hard, he says, "Wh-Why— Why are you being so rude?"

And Taylor whirls back around. "Why are you being so fucking nice!?"

"What are you talking about!?" Wes has no recollection of being nice in any capacity that would be considered weird, or even mentionable. If anything, he's been overly-anxious (having your crush dumped on you with a cold like a stray cat will do that) and a little bit more sassy than he'd usually venture to be. He's got no clue what Taylor Macready is even

63

referring to.

But Taylor is adamant and frustrated.

And Wes doesn't know what to do about that.

So he stomps to the bathroom, grabs the daytime, non-drowsy cold medicine from the cabinet, and stomps back to hand it to Taylor, who grabs it with a huff, shoves a tablet out of the blister-pack, and swallows it dry. In retaliation, Wes refills Taylor's water glass from breakfast and shoves it at him, and Taylor yanks it into his grasp and swallows the whole thing in three gulps before practically slamming the cup on the counter.

For some reason, they both crack up laughing.

The rest of their conversations that morning go about as well.

Dalton created the groupchat: Concerned Parents™

Todd: oh no, Dalton's making more groupchats

Dalton: u know it bb ;)

Wes: Oh

Uh

Hi guys!

Dalton: im sure u r all wondering y i have gathered u here today

Todd: we're really not

Wes: I would actually like to know

Hey fuckwad why is wes in this chat and not me

Asldkfjj

Sorry

That was Taylor

Todd: Taylor be nice to Wes

jfc I'm really fitting the """"Concerned Parent"""" sterotypes here

My instructions still stand

Dalton: Taylor, if u were in this chat it would not be called concerned parents, it would be called concerned parents and their wayward delinquent child

Besides isn't ur phone like dead

Todd: dalton will u get to the point so I can keep researching??

Wes: Taylor is still peevedd. He went to the livng room to sulk

Todd: ...

Hey Wes

How did you become proficient in Taylor's coding language in less than 2 days?

*Dalton: ^^^*

BIG MOOD

HOW DID U DO THAT

IT TOOK ME YEARS BEFORE I COULD TELL IF HE WAS HAPPY OR SAD

Y E A R S

Wes: ??? I ddon't know??

What doo you mean?

He's just got a normal face?

I don't think he likes me, butt I can tell when I'm pissng him of more than normmal?

Todd: hmmm

Dalton: hmmmmmm

ANYWAY

I made this chat because my son is apparently homeless and, as his father, i cannot let this stand

Todd: I thought we talked about this this morning Dalton??

Dalton: yea but Wes should know too

I mean Taylor is kinda crashing there rn

Wes: what did youu gys come up wthh?

I'm sure my pareents willl et him stay here, but he'd either be sharing my room or leeping on the couch

Imma go live under the fukin bridge again if u guys try to make decisions without me

Fukin watch

Im not 2 ffs i can take care of myself

That wwas tYlor again. He's back from the living roomm.

Todd: 1.) Taylor did you forget that you got sick and were LIVING UNDER A BRIDGE??

2.) we aren't trying to make decision without you, your phone is just dead

3.) I told you already, be nice to Wes.

Wes: fuck u todd

Im fine

Todd: clearly, you're not

Dalton: is wes letting u type or r u stealing his phone?

Wes: im stealin it

hes pissed abt it .

But fuck it he was gonna be pissed abt somn i do anyway

Todd: Alright, I'll get right to it so Wes can have his phone back sooner.

Taylor, my parents said they'd be fine with you crashing at my house for a while.

Wes: tf

No

Why would they say that

You don't need to do that.

I don't want to make trouble for anyone.

Todd: you wouldn't be making trouble for anyone.

Dalton: fr dude have u seen Todd's house? Yall could go 3

weeks and not even pass each other in one of the two kitchens

Todd: the basement bar doesn't count as a kitchen

Dalton: IT HAS A FRIDGE AND A STOVE IT COUNTS

Wes: Taylor ggave me back my phone.

He says "I'm done talking to idiots""

Oh sory he said i wasn'tt supposed to tell you that

Lasdkjkaio;;;

wes is a liar i didnt say shit

Taylor is angry withh me now

Todd: alright but i am taking this as consent that he's going to come to my house tomorrow at noon

Wes: he says "whatever, fucker"

Todd: Wes you are invited tomorrow too, of course

Dalton: ofc we cannot forget the newest member of the Squad

Wes: askdjf;a

sorrry i dropped my phone

I'm part of your squad?

Todd: yes

Was us ambushing you in your house at midnight an unclear orientation??

Dalton: XD

No but fr fr wes u r a verified squad member

Wes: Taylor is evenn mor maad at me noww i thnk hee objects

Todd: please hand taylor the phone..........

Wes: its not my fault

I s2g

Todd: Taylor I told you to be nice wtf

Wes: dude i fukin was

But he's cryin now

I dont know what i did wrong.

Dalton: why tf did wes say u were mad then?

Wes: idfk

genuinely no fukin clue what i did

Todd: then ask him????

You emotional banana???

Wes: brb

Dalton: why is this 30 mins more eventful than the previous three years of my life combined

Todd: same

Dalton: toddster imma play some siege, you finna join?

Todd: sounds good. who tf needs premed research anyway fuck that shit

wes/taylor, text us when you get this figured out.

I'm going to see all three of you at my house tomorrow at noon

With taylor's stuff

Because i will be booking a weekend trip to hell before i let my best bud go homeless while my house has two spare bedrooms????

"Why are you crying?" Taylor asks in the stilted way that someone who has never been on a farm or seen a horse girl movie might approach a bucking horse.

Wes sniffles, "I'm not. I'm not crying."

After a minute of waiting to see if they're going to address this blatant lie and getting nothing, Taylor insists, "You were."

And Wes insists, "N-not anymore."

And Taylor decides to move on entirely. "Why?"

"I do-do-d—" Wes gives up on that sentence and starts another, "I would prefer not to say."

"Why not?"

"It–t's kind of embarrassing."

"Do I look like I give enough of a shit to judge?" Taylor asks, giving his best impression of someone approachable (he's a bad actor).

"I'm still not gonna say."

"Fine, fuck it. At least I can tell Todd I tried."

"Okay."

They're sitting next to each other on the pullout couch. There had been a rerun of a movie that, to their distracted attention spans, wasn't horrible, but out of all the times where they wrestled over Wes's phone, they must have pressed too hard on the remote, because now they're watching Jeopardy on mute. Both boys are too stubborn to change the channel, because they'd have to find the remote first, which would require communication. They suffer in silence for, if you're counting like Wes is, 82 seconds.

Then, apparently, Taylor can't take it anymore.

"Are you gonna tell me why you were crying now?"

Wes flinches—bad habit—but snips back, "Are you going to be a dick about it if I do?"

After mulling it over for another ten seconds, Taylor shrugs. "No more of a dick than normal."

But what can Wes tell him? That he got a little too emotional because nobody his age has called him a friend, said they wanted to be his friend, or even really spoken especially kindly to him in years? That he was so happy that Todd invited him over that he broke down in tears? That makes him sound like a freak. No, Wes can't say any of those things. "It was nice of Todd to invite me over too," Wes comments instead, hoping it sounds casual and not the damning, mountainous confession it felt like.

Brown eyes, the color of a sunset in the woods, slide over to stare at Wes. One calloused, scarred hand wraps itself around Wes's before Taylor can even remember what he's doing enough to stop himself. Wes won't complain about the support.

And once the hand is there, it would draw way more attention if Taylor were to snatch it back, so entwined with Wes's it stays. Most of the night before is fuzzy, but Taylor remembers Wes *unfolding his hands so gently, prying them from the skin of his arm*, and Taylor thinks 'hell, I can do that shit.'

"Are you sitting on the remote?" Wes whispers.

"No. Are you?"

"No... I think it might have fallen behind the couch."

Neither of them moves. If they want to grab the remote, they'd have to stand up, which would require letting go of each other's hands, which would require bringing attention to the fact that they're holding hands at all.

"Who even hosts Jeopardy now?" Taylor asks blandly.

Wes shrugs, still a little shaky. It's about lunchtime now, and his meds kick his *ass* if he's not regular about mealtimes. Wes thinks his mom might chide him for missing lunch later, but he doesn't want to get up to make anything. "I don't think I've ever actually watched an episode all the way through. I dunno."

Each in their own heads, Wes and Taylor zone out on the couch, occasionally making a stupid joke about Jeopardy, and what it looks like these people are saying. The TV is still muted.

Wes hadn't even noticed that Taylor was commenting less and less as he sank deeper and deeper into the back of the couch, but he certainly notices when Taylor finally tips over, asleep, and lands smashed against Wes's side. It doesn't look

70

comfortable, but Taylor must be exhausted to fall asleep that way—and without the help of the sleepy side-effect of the nighttime cold medicine either! This event (and make no mistake, this is an event. In fact, if Todd or Dalton were here, they would tout this as the weirdest thing to happen in Swisher since Elvis's tour bus broke down as he passed through in 1972. It. Is. An. Event) does, of course, turn Wes's face bright red.

Is this? *This* guy? This person leaning against Wes's shoulder, drooling a little on his flannel? Is *this* guy the same person that Wes stares at for five out of his six instructional school hours? The same Taylor Macready that Wes has seen deck someone across the jaw for saying something rude to Todd? Is that the same person who has, yet again, claimed possession of Wes's hand while unconscious? The cognitive dissonance between seeing Taylor at school and seeing him asleep, muttering wordlessly into Wes's shoulder, is astounding. Briefly, Wes wonders if he'll die from this much excitement—because 'joy' isn't quite the right word, even if he is happy, that won't be what's killing him here, it will be the heart-stopping excitement of trying to use his one free hand to take a picture—because he didn't get a picture of Taylor's smile yesterday, and he'll be damned if he misses another opportunity to document Taylor Macready being human.

The picture turns out blurry and awkward, but he sends it to Todd and Dalton anyway. He hopes he's not overstepping, but Dalton seemed so interested in getting a picture last night that Wes thinks he'll appreciate it.

Groupchat: Concerned Parents™
Wes sent an image: img_026.jpg
Wes: is this normal for himm!?
Is this just what he's lik when no one iss around?

Todd: ummmm

I don't know how to say this

But literally NOT AT ALL???

Dalton: alsdjjas r u telling me taytay is WILLINGLY PHYSI-CALLY TOUCHING U!?

HE BARELY LETS ME HUG HIM

I KNOWN THIS MAN FOR LIKE 20 YRS

Todd: we're not even eighteen???

Dalton: T W E N T Y YEARS

AND NOW HERE HE IS!

PRACTICALLY LAYING IN WES LAP!

WTF BRO

I WANT A HUG FROM SLEEPY TAYTAY

Todd: seriously wes how did you manage to make him do that?????

We need to know,,,,,, for science

Wes: um

Crazy story guyes

He just... did that on his ownn

He's kind of drooling on me

Does he normally talk in his sleep?

Todd: I wouldn't know he practically never sleeps

Wes: !?

Dalton: fr fr dude even when we have sleepovers he's awake when we fall asleep ad awake when we wake up

We've genuinely had conversations abt whether or not hes secretly like some kinda cryptid

Todd: can I take this to mean you two figured stuff out?

He said you started crying earlier?

Dalton: Q~Q

Wes: oh

Yeah

Uhmm, yes?

We'ree okay i mean

I just don't knw if he likess me very much?

He just seems angry all the time. Even when he's happy he's angry.

I think he's trying. I think I'm the problem.

Todd: Wes,,, buddy,,,,,,, no

That's just Taylor

He's just like that

*Dalton: ^^^*

He's just an angry person

Wes: why?

Dalton: uhhhhh

I'll be real honest w u bud

Idfk

I've just known him forever and he's always been that way

Idk if there's a reason or if that's just how he's wired

Todd: yeah, same. It was never a question I thought about???

Taylor is just how he is

I guess.....??

The rest of Saturday passes the same way. On Sunday morning, Todd sends them a panicked text about helping his grandma, who is having an episode and has wandered away from her retirement home, so they don't meet up Sunday at noon. Wes goes to the coffee shop to help his parents with the post-church rush (which has gotten so much easier since the pastors of the rival churches in neighboring towns stopped claiming Swisher, Iowa was either in the spot where the biblical figure Rebekah was born or that it is the spot where the Antichrist will be born). Taylor is persuaded to stay home under threat of every member of the Post household raising the alarm and calling a city-wide search if he isn't at home when they get back. By Monday, Taylor's clothes have all been washed and shoved back into the sleeping bag, which has also been washed, and is serving as an oversized backpack for Taylor. His phone is still dead, but a new charger will be five bucks at the gas station on the way to school.

7

An Interesting Day on Monday, December 14

School on Monday is... interesting. Nothing is innately different than normal, but for Wes and Taylor it feels abnormal. They walk to school together, and Taylor buys his charger from the gas station while Wes fidgets and tries not to make eye contact with the meth addict staring at him outside the window. They go to their lockers separately, but then they have Physics. Together. Mr. Fieberg is an open-seating kind of guy, so they naturally sit together because Wes is yammering Taylor's ear off about how he researched the different production methods and ingredients of methamphetamine drugs once (he's still nervous about the gas station guy).

Mr. Fieberg certainly notices. Both because he's too smart to be teaching high school Physics and because he's just That Kind of Guy. The two weird-ass kids who intentionally sit alone and avoid everyone else in class, and everyone everywhere else on campus (with the exception of Wes's two friends)? Suddenly sitting next to each other? Yeah, he notices.

Doesn't say anything though, for the same aforementioned reasons. Just keeps an eye on them while Taylor, miraculously, doesn't look at his phone during class, even though it's plugged in and charging under his desk, and Wes makes it through the lesson without muttering to himself too much.

Mrs. Merino-Ott notices too, for the sole reason that Taylor Fucking Macready—her number 1 problem student, who skips class with number 2 problem student Jaxson Dixon (who is apparently out sick today, for real, his parents called it in), but who manages to get exactly 69% on every godforsaken text, quiz, and homework assignment she assigns—is present and a-fucking-parrently ready to learn about the English language. For once in his life. She's glad to see it, even if he's only showing up to stare at Wes (who would be a pleasure to have in class if he could make, like one friend so she doesn't have to pair him up with Monique every project). Today was supposed to be a dissection of "The Yellow Wallpaper," but now it's devolved into a group vent about how little society has progressed with mental illness. Wes almost has a meltdown when they talk about how it used to be viable to think a person was living in your walls (because some houses have enough space in there to fit full people), but Taylor whispers something to him that makes him laugh so hard for a minute that Wes forgets to have the rest of his breakdown—but then Taylor refuses to share the joke with the rest of the class, so nobody else laughs and Wes quiets down quick too.

Precalc is the same soup, reheated. Mrs. Woolley does her best to make it fun, but there just is no way to make logarithms entertaining unless your name is Harley Daniels and you "just think they're neat." Everyone else takes notes in silence and tries not to make this any harder than it needs to be and, on good days, flings sticky hands at each other from across the room. Taylor flings one at Wes, and it sticks to the center of his forehead—which Mrs. Woolley chastises with a soft clearing of her throat that turns Wes's whole face bright red, shoulders to ears. Taylor rolls his eyes at her, but she pointedly misses it in favor of asking him to try the problem on the board. Which he does, failing horribly and potentially purposefully at it and sitting down with a heavy *fwump*.

And then, finally, lunch. After a morning filled with more math and English than anybody realistically wants to deal with, Wes and Taylor are relieved to hear the bell that releases them to the cafeteria. Wes packed them both lunches ("I w-was up-p late last n-n-night and we had a lot of l-left-tovers," he had explained nervously while Taylor shoved the paper-bag into his backpack this morning), and they're both going to sit with Dalton and Todd at their usual table.

Of course, a day can only go so well for so long, and so Alex Morenson accosts Wes while Taylor is dropping off his books at his locker down the hall.

"Wha-wha-wha-what's wrong, dipshit?" Alex sneers. His gaze rakes over Wes derisively, although he has to look distinctly up to make eye contact and taunt, "Did you get l-l-lost, like a wittwe babwee?"

And Wes has been alone at school long enough to keep a straight face. Actually, dissociating a bit, Wes mulls over how Alex could really be more effective at making fun of Wes in the future. These insults are low-tier at best, and none of them really hit home. Wes got lost on campus during a panic attack once, and, sure, it's a dick move to bring it up again, but he could be saying much more hurtful things. The only thing that vaguely registers as emotionally damaging is the fact that Alex went out of his way to try and hurt Wes's feelings. But none of the rest of it really registers as significant enough to cause harm. He's heard it all before. He's the Weird Kid. He's been twitchy since elementary school, and in a high school class of something like 300 people who have all known each other since kindergarten, even if you work your ass off and get rid of most of the twitching, the stammering, the anxiety, everyone still sees you as the Weird Kid who twitches and stammers and has anxiety. Wes has had bullies, the same general set of them, all his life. They get tired of it quicker if he doesn't react.

Only, Wes is hoping Alex gets tired of it really fast today, because if Taylor comes back from dropping his books and Alex is still around, Taylor might just decide to go to lunch without him. Bullies aren't always hurtful, but they're usually a pain in the ass. Nobody wants to be friends with a kid who has bullies, just like nobody wants to be friends with a kid who has lice. It's understandable, if scary. Wes still isn't sure if Taylor really enjoys his company, or if he's just too apathetic to tell Wes to shut the fuck up and go away. If Alex Morenson is to be believed, Wes is worth less than the shitty, discolored, 2-cent-per-square-foot linoleum lining the school's hallways.

Then, out of absolutely fucking nowhere, Alex is knocked to the ground. Like, flat on his ass type of knocked to the ground. Nose-bleeding, jaw swelling, kind-of-crying type of knocked to the ground. When Wes snaps to look, it's genuinely Taylor fucking Macready huffing, "Shut the fuck up," and then turning to visibly exclude Alex from any further conversation.

Nobody else in the hallway pays Alex, or Taylor, or even

Wes, any mind. Making a fuss out of whoever Taylor decides to whack is a good way to be the next person Taylor whacks (Taylor got to meet the superintendent once by doing that in Freshman year). Honestly, Wes doesn't even have time to panic before Taylor is wandering aimlessly into the cafeteria. Not a care in the world.

"Don't get left behind, Wes," he calls behind him, and Wes takes a few big steps to catch up.

In the wake of his most recent fight (if you can call it that), everyone clears out of the way in the cafeteria. As if Taylor might punch them across the face next. Like Taylor might be in a bad mood. As if they can't see that barely, just the tiniest bit, Taylor is *grinning*. Wes is flabbergasted.

It wasn't like Wes hadn't been able to defend himself. He has a solid four inches on Taylor, and he does all the heavy lifting at the coffee shop since Dad threw out his back a few years ago, so he has muscle to back himself up. Being able to knock a kid flat onto the shitty, discolored linoleum was never the issue. Wes could have done that any time (and if the look on Alex Morenson's face is to be believed, maybe he should have done that at some point). The only thing had been that Wes never thought it would be *worthwhile* to beat the shit out of his bullies. He knew that if he punched Alex Morenson, he'd have to punch Scotty Mallinson next, and then Darius Adrian, and then on and on until eventually half the school would be tangled up—and fuck, it just seemed like more trouble than it was worth. Might as well just sit there and dissociate until they're done, right? Better that than to fight and fight until he has no clue how to put down his fists.

But Taylor has already fought half the school at some point or another, a lot of people twice, and he just added Alex

Morenson to that list. For Wes. Who definitely shouldn't feel flattered and a little flustered. Definitely shouldn't be going just a little pink in the cheeks about that.

But Todd and Dalton absolutely notice this, and haven't yet heard what happened fifteen seconds ago, and they watch Taylor drag Wes to sit in the empty chair and then sit down himself. Clearly, something happened with Taylor and Wes, but damn if Todd and Dalton know what that something is.

"So, uh," Dalton begins awkwardly, "how was... Precalc?"

"Y-y-you punched that guy in the face!" Wes shouts, voice cracking.

Todd immediately looks to Taylor. "You punched someone in the face, Taylor?" He doesn't sound mad. Just disappointed.

"Maybe," Taylor answers coolly.

"At least tell me you had a good reason?" Todd sighs. He's the only one who cares enough (which Taylor doesn't) and is level-headed enough (which Dalton isn't) to try to explain Taylor out of trouble. It works sometimes, Todd's explaining, but usually on the basis of Todd's reputation and intentions, not Taylor's.

Taylor shrugs. "He was pissing me off," he claims, which is clearly a lie because Wes whips his head around to gape openly.

Todd decides not to push it. If Taylor doesn't want to say anything, fuck it, it's probably fine.

Ever the mediator, Dalton asks, "Hey, Taylor, I brought too much banana bread again. Want some?"

And then the second-most unlikely thing to happen in Swisher High School happens. And Taylor pulls a homemade lunch out of his beat-up, seven-year-old backpack. And he says, "Nah, I got lunch." And anyone who doesn't know

Taylor misses it, but Taylor's eyes are shining like he's holding out the pedigree certificate of a goddamned prize-winning racehorse. He's just barely not smiling.

Friends of Taylor Macready know that he hasn't brought a homemade lunch to school since first grade.

Wes doesn't know this, but he still blushes more and stares at his lap self-consciously. Like they won't see his sympathetic nervous system light up the flare signal of incoming oxytocin if he changes the angle of his face. "All right," Wes relents (although nobody is sure what, exactly, he's responding to), "but you can't just punch people because they say shit to me."

Neither Dalton nor Todd realize what Wes means until Taylor asks, "Why not?" and takes a bite of what appears to be a peanut butter and honey sandwich.

"We'd be here all day," Wes insists. He's kind of laughing. Neither Todd nor Dalton has seen Wes laugh before, not like that. Not ever.

Taylor swallows, nods, and says, "It'd be a great fucking day." He's also kind of laughing. Neither Dalton nor Todd can remember seeing Taylor laughing. On the outside, they laugh too, but on the inside they're thinking *oh shit*.

At the end of lunch, Todd and Dalton stay behind when Taylor and Wes go to their respective fourth period classes.

"You ever seen him laugh like that?" Dalton asks quietly, watching them walk away.

Todd gathers up all his AP textbooks and holds them defensively over his chest. "Fuck, dude, I can't even remember seeing him *smile* like that."

"We fucked up, Toddster."

"I think we did."

81

Because they've known Taylor for almost their whole lives and they saw how he acted and they never bothered to ask *why*.

Wes has art after lunch, and Taylor has drama. Neither of them chose their electives, they have it in common that they filled their class schedules with the required courses (math and English and history and science) and then got to the elective section that was every kid's favorite and went *oh shit I have no hobbies* and left it blank. Therefore, random assignment, and different classes.

Wes walks Taylor to drama, which is on the far side of campus in a weirdly-shaped building, before walking himself back to art. Both Taylor's teacher, Ms. Porter, and Wes's teacher, Mrs. Herrick, notice when they walk in looking noticeably different than last class.

Mrs. Herrick sees Wes walk in about four seconds before the bell, four and a half minutes later than usual. She sees him sigh a little, smiling at himself, and sway into his seat, and she sees him pull out his sketchbook and start doodling before she's even finished writing the day's prompt on the board. It's 'Capturing Motion,' but that doesn't seem to matter to Wes, even though he usually agonizes over *what is that even supposed to **mean*** for at least ten minutes before he'll touch his pencil to the paper. She's so curious that she makes sure to walk past his seat, which she usually avoids so he doesn't panic and think she's scrutinizing his work. He is not 'capturing motion,' he's drawing a beanie covered in—what? Is that dirt? Snow? Well, it's certainly a hat laying on the ground that he's drawing. But she'll let it slide. He's certainly capturing something in motion, it's just not on the page. And she's a fucking *art* teacher in *high school,* if they don't want to draw what she wants to draw what is she gonna do? Sue them?

Ms. Porter sees Taylor meander into the room—on time, for once!—and drop his backpack against the back wall with the others and wander to sit on the floor in front of the risers that make up their faux-stage at the front of the room. His hat's about to fall off, instead of being pulled so low over his face that it's almost covering his eyes, and he's just kind of... staring into space. Ms. Porter wants to ask if something is wrong, but she also doesn't want to risk the three months she's spent building up Taylor's trust in her not to intrude on his personal life. He's like a stray cat: you can't just pick him up and start coddling him unless you were thinking stitches are a nice aesthetic choice. Instead of texting—and Ms. Porter heard from Mrs. Merino-Ott today (not in conversation, they're in different departments and don't have much in common, but in passing, while Ms. Merino-Ott was talking to Mrs. Hunter as Ms. Porter walked by) that Taylor showed up to her class today without a phone too—Taylor just stares at the wall of inspirational quotes opposite the window until Ms. Porter is ready to start class. She doesn't want to admit how much of the time that she should have spent pulling up the slides were instead scrutinizing which quote had caught Taylor's eye so much. A sophomore, Brenna Uribe, pulls Ms. Porter's attention to class again, and she smiles and turns on the projector and they all choose a favorite animal to briefly research and then act out. Taylor picks a possum, lays in the middle of the room, and stares out the window at the muddy piles of snow while he plays dead.

Then class is over and she sends everyone out, except Taylor.

She doesn't have a great reason, and it's against her better judgment to meddle, but just this once— "Taylor," she smiles.

"What." And he doesn't bother pretending that it's a question, which is honestly a little refreshing.

But she sees her mistake instantly. Gray-sweatered shoulders stiffen and straighten, offensive and defensive, and just a minute ago he'd been relaxed, laying in the middle of the room pretending to be a possum. "Hm... nevermind. Go ahead to your next class."

He shrugs, and she sees his hand move to flip her off (he's done it before, to her and to every other teacher, but nobody has ever effectively stopped him from doing it, so even surprise seems a moot point), but he restrains it by grabbing his backpack instead and walking to whatever class he has next. Ms. Porter thinks he looks excited, and she frowns thoughtfully.

Wes is one of the first kids inside Mr. Bloomquist's classroom because he's a fast walker and Mrs. Herrick's room isn't far, but he isn't the first. Of course, the teacher is there, scrolling on his phone like he couldn't give less of a shit about whatever goes on outside of the times he is being paid to watch, but so is Monique Feldman, who is also a fast walker but doesn't need to be to beat everyone else to last period history because her AP Government class is also taught by Mr. Bloomquist, so she doesn't even have to get out of her seat between fourth and fifth period. To Wes, it's a little intimidating.

Monique is an intimidating person, and no amount of English projects together softens that. She won't hit you (she's grown out of the physical violence of youth), but Wes has seen her decimate people with her words. She made Freddy

Peters cry once—which is a feat, sure, but the scariest was when Sean Temmerman tried to argue pro-life in English and by the time she was done with him he had to go to the counselor's office because he'd had a nervous breakdown and he was at home "sick" for two days. She was much easier to text than to see in person, where you couldn't turn your phone off if she decided to eviscerate you on the politics of using the intersectionality in the 1920's jazz scene as a scapegoat for the subsequent Great Depression.

And today, her eyes are set on Wes the moment he steps in the room.

"Wes," she sings, and he nods, and she continues, "how was your weekend?"

Which, for context, is such a weird question for Monique Feldman to ask Wes Post that Mr. Bloomquist looks up from his phone to observe the conversation vacantly.

"U-uh, fi- I guess i-it was, uh- oka- alright-t?"

Other students filter in around him, but he stays cemented to his spot in front of Monique's desk, feeling increasingly stuck there.

She smirks, and if Wes isn't imagining it, there are some teeth in there. "Do anything fun?" Mr. Bloomquist makes a little face at this, like they're speaking in code and he only has one soggy half of the cipher.

"J-Jesus- er, I-I uh, I me-mean- all I- I j-just-"

"Wes, look, I found a leaf," Taylor mutters flatly, and drops it into Wes's hand while Mr. Bloomquist drops his pretense of occupation and Monique drops her whole face. Truly, Monique hadn't meant to tease Wes too badly, but she did want to know what use was made of the information she gave him. "Hey, Monique," Taylor's greeting is a little flat, almost annoyed?

It's out of place, and Mr. Bloomquist almost laughs. This is unexpected. Well, nothing like the least likely friendship in the whole of Swisher High to spice up classes otherwise occupied by the idiot high school boys who think they're experts on history because they know a handful of WWII facts.

The bell rings, and Wes realizes what has happened. "Wait, Taylor, why did you hand me a leaf?"

Taylor drags him by the shoulder to a seat towards the back of the room, away from Monique, who seems confused and a little disappointed to see them go. "Dunno. Cool leaf," he replies, and for Mr. Bloomquist, Monique, and all the idiot high school boys who think themselves historians, it means nothing, but to Wes and Taylor it means exactly what it was supposed to mean.

8

Who's Going To Be Home For Christmas?

By the time class is over and everyone is done dissecting the Federalist Papers (if one more kid mentions Alexander Fucking Hamilton, Taylor is going to lose his shit), Taylor, Wes, Monique, Mr. Bloomquist, and every other godforsaken student and teacher in Swisher High School is ready to go home and potentially never come back. They will come back tomorrow, because it's Tuesday and they are all legally obligated to attend school in America (except Damien Cosuleanu, who technically has dual citizenship, so who knows if he's legally obligated—but he'll show up too). But they don't want to. All they want to do is go home, eat something, sleep, and, in a few students' cases, die.

Taylor is among those unhappy few. He can't get Ms. Porter's face, almost saying something after class, out of his head. Her eyes had been on him during class too. The expression is stuck under the bed of his nails, and he itches his wrist, absently. The little band-aids over the bruised scrapes

87

from the weekend push his fingertips closer to the heel of his palm than usual. It's still comforting. One little spot of control in a world built to confuse him.

What the fuck had Ms. Porter actually wanted to say? The twist of her mouth detailed not just concern but pity, worry, maybe even a little condescension. It makes Taylor's intestines twist over and over themselves. She doesn't know shit. She shouldn't know shit. She couldn't—she's not that intelligent—is she?

Taylor's phone is capable of turning on now, but he doesn't want to turn it on. God knows Hellen has tried texting him. There's no way she hasn't, unless their parents took away her phone too. For texting when they don't want her to be. That's how it starts. First it's her phone and then she's a useless piece of shit because she didn't take out the trash and then she doesn't deserve to live in this fucking house because she dropped a plate and then she's homeless living in a sleeping bag under a bridge—

"Taylor? You're scratching off your bandaids," Wes squeaks, and the anxiety makes his footsteps bounce off of the shiny, refrozen surface of the snow. It crunches underfoot, and Taylor tries to retrain his point of control to making the loudest crunch he can when he breaks the crisp snow-shell.

His fingers attempt to press the bandaid back against his skin, but it doesn't stay. After a few pounding, crunchy steps, it unsticks and flaps uselessly. So he rips off the other half. People always compare doing painful things quickly to ripping off a bandaid, but Taylor doesn't feel it lift away. He feels the cold, empty space on his skin where the bandaid had been before though. The sharp wind stings, but ripping off the bandaid hadn't.

"What's up?" Wes presses.

They're still walking, but Taylor's world stands still for a long minute while he tries to come up with an answer. These thoughts aren't rational—are they? And either way, it isn't like Wes would get it. They've known each other for what? Three days? How could he condense his life into few enough syllables to say anything before his throat closes around the words and chokes him back into numbness?

He shrugs.

Wes shrugs too, expression exasperated and stressed about the lack of response, but they keep walking and he doesn't press anymore.

They're almost home when Todd texts.

Groupchat: Concerned Parents™

Todd: are you guys still coming over or???

Dalton: wut

???

Wes: were we meeeting up today?

Todd: oh,, whoops

We were gonna yesterday

But then my grandma

So I thought we rescheduled for today??

Dalton: oh shit how is grammy toddster btw

Wes: me and taylor ar free

If we end up meeting up

Sorry

He ain't sorry don't let him apologize for shit he didn't do

This is taylor btw

And my phone is charged now

add me assholes

Todd: ahaha whoops sory for the confusion guys!!

Grams is fine, She's back in the nursing home
Dalton: im free today too
Lets link bitchesss
Make this a thing <3
Wes: don't make it weird dalton
And can u fuckin add me already
I'm giving wes his phone back bc he looks like hes gonna cry but i stg if nobody has added me in the next thirty seconds im gonna kick ur ass

Within half an hour, Wes and Taylor are at Todd's front gate.

They almost debate climbing it— Taylor says it's fun and Wes says he can't possibly climb someone else's gate— but Dalton shows up on their heels too fast to get headway on the argument, so they walk in like normal people.

They sit in Todd's basement on the big gray couch, each of them are offered a soda from the stocked minifridge underneath the basement's bar, and each of them takes one.

"So my parents say it's fine if you stay here," Todd shrugs. That wasn't what they had been talking about, but Todd is smart enough not to start too abruptly with the meat and potatoes of it. He's known Taylor for too long to try it. "There's two spare bedrooms. Go ahead and pick one. God knows we don't use them." He's trying to be as nonchalant about this as he can, because he's seen Taylor turn down Dalton's banana bread while his stomach growled, and he doesn't want Taylor to turn this down. "Just one issue, they're going out of town for that medical conference starting next week—"

"Next week!?" Wes screeches, "but— that's—! That's

90

Christmas break! At least tell me they're going to be back before the 24th!"

Todd rolls his eyes. "Nah. They go every year. I mean, it's fine. They still leave presents and we have a family dinner together before they leave and when they get back, but it's the only one of these conferences all year." Todd shrugs, like he isn't hurt by it, "What am I gonna do? Throw a fit?"

"I mean, you could," Taylor snickers. Taylor and Dalton have been taking turns for years, trying to convince Todd to make trouble for his parents at least once in his young life. Todd never does.

Todd laughs, something like relief heady in his veins. It's still just Taylor, who he's known since kindergarten. And the tension of the room is broken a little. Todd seems a little less pressed about his parents being gone for Christmas (again) anyways. "But as long as you're okay with it just being me and you on Christmas, bring your stuff over whenever," Todd says. His tone is final—as if this has already been decided. Less of an offer of housing and more of a signing of a contract. And, though Taylor bristles a little, he doesn't actively protest. This is a win, Todd thinks.

Dalton *does* actively protest. "No, no. I am not okay with my two best buds spending Christmas alone in an empty house!" he says. "That sounds, like, super fucking depressing! Not okay. Not happening. I am inviting myself over for Christmas. Wes, you're coming too."

"*Ah!*" Wes startles. "I am!?"

"Do you not want to?" Dalton asks—and he suddenly realizes he hadn't considered that Wes's family might actually like spending Christmas together.

"N-no!" Wes screeches, "Yes!" he flexes his hands flat like

91

a twitch, "Fuck, uh—I want to..." he falters and restarts more slowly before the stammering can set in, "spend... Christmas... with you guys..." and then he tacks onto the end, "if that's okay?"

Dalton wants to squeeze the daylights out of him (and he's probably the only one present who *can*, size-wise). Todd grins a little, trying to be casual about it, saying, "If you can come, it'd be cool to have you." Taylor fixes Wes with an inscrutable glare before redirecting it to the pile of the carpet.

Elaborate pillow fort plans are made (mostly by Dalton, with notes on structural integrity by Todd and Wes). Video games are selected for the occasion (only Todd has played the Bioshock series before, but he swears on anything anyone cares to name that it is "both metaphorically poignant and a really fucking cool fps"). Wes promises to bake some cookies, and Dalton makes him promise not to start without him. Taylor, by the end of it, has said maybe five words total in the past hour, but he's smiling. Soft and small and real.

"At a friend's house?" Martha Post echoes dreamily. Hm. Not what she expected her son to ask. But he seems excited. She exchanges a look with Richard, and he has a knowing smile. They had been talking just the other day while they closed the shop about how much they were dreading another Christmas of shoveling driveways and slipping on road salt. Richard had emailed her ("email, Rich? Really, now. You could at least have texted it to me like you've been alive past 1995") an ad for plane tickets to Rosarito. She had smiled and marked the email 'read,' because as nice as the thought was, she didn't want to drag Wes across the continent for Christmas; he already gets so nervous on planes.

But if he was already asking to spend Christmas with friends...

"Well, sure, Wes," Richard replied with less preamble than he might have used if he weren't thinking the same thing as Martha.

That, and, would it really be so bad to let Wes spend his eighteenth Christmas with a boy who looks at him like he personally paints the sunrises every morning?

They say yes maybe a little too easily, because they're remembering those plane tickets and they're remembering when Wes panicked and Taylor calmed him down right there, just like that.

And, later, after really making sure that it's okay with Wes and with Taylor, they book those plane tickets to Rosarito. Richard tells Martha, when she asks if it's a good idea to leave them alone, that 'some quality time will be enriching for everyone.' And then she slaps his arm and tells him to stop referencing Wes's third birthday like that.

* * *

On the way to school the next morning, Wes offers Taylor a cinnamon muffin from the shop— "leftovers. We don't sell them if they weren't made that day"— for breakfast. Taylor smiles one of those tiny, real smiles. The ones that are just for Wes, who does nice shit like bring an extra muffin for Taylor.

"Nah. I hate cinnamon," Taylor replies. Ever since he stole (and then immediately puked up) that muffin from Post Family Coffee, cinnamon has tasted even worse than usual.

Inexplicably, Wes loses his shit. "You hate cinnamon!?" he

shrieks, "How long have you hated cinnamon!?"

Taylor tries not to be too thrown off, but that was a *hell* of a reaction about cinnamon muffins. "Uh, forever," he answers nonchalantly and, out of a passing curiosity, he asks, "Why?"

Wes mumbles something to himself and Taylor only catches 'dumbass.' When Wes feels like he can speak without stuttering, which takes a minute more of walking past the bus stop that sometimes takes them to school, Wes starts way back before the beginning: "That one time. Before you—er, uh, before you lived with us. I left a muffin on the counter for you," and Taylor absolutely wants to react to that— although *how* he's going to react will be as much a surprise to him as it is to Wes— but Wes's still going. "You'd been hanging out in the shop for hours but you never ordered anything—" *because he didn't have any money* "—so I left a cinnamon muffin on the counter for you—" *and it was the only thing he'd eaten since the day before* "—but I didn't know you hated cinnamon! I would have put something else on the counter!"

"What!?" Taylor barks sharply, and, out of necessity to conceal less desirable emotions, his word is half of a laugh. He tries to act normal, despite the fact that his worldview is crumbling and he has no idea why anyone, Wes Genuinely-Good-Kid Post included, would do anything so batshit insane as leaving a muffin out, for free, for *Taylor Fucking Macready* of all people! How can Wes be so naive as to think Taylor wouldn't have taken advantage of that? How can he think Taylor wouldn't have eaten as many muffins as he put out? What does the world look like through eyes so kind? It takes a lot of effort to hike his jacket higher on his shoulders in a way that doesn't seem terrified and grumble, "Dude it doesn't matter, that was so long ago." His face feels hot and his stomach feels slippery. He wants to change the subject, and fails horribly— "Why did you even leave anything on the counter if you didn't know I needed food?"

And Wes is fidgeting like crazy with a little swirly fidget toy, looking terrified, and he rambles, "Because I've had a crush on you for, like, two years and I was figuring I should at least try to talk—"

He stops mid-sentence as the part of his brain that controls and records current events, like telling Taylor Fucking Macready that he's had a crush on him for, like, two years in a conversation about cinnamon muffins, catches up with the part of his brain that tells people things, like telling Taylor Fucking Macready that he's had a crush on him for, like, two years in a conversation about cinnamon muffins.

If it wasn't for the rush of road traffic and the Christmas carolers on Faraday Lane and the non-migratory birds and the gradeschoolers who cross the street perpendicular to theirs, you could hear a pin drop.

When Taylor feels circulation leave his fingers and pool in his overflowing heart, he says, "What?" as flatly as anyone can say that in the current circumstances.

Wes's face isn't all red, but it's red in his cheeks and ears and collarbone, plus the tip of his nose but that's probably because it's 37 degrees outside and not because he's embarrassed. "So, clearly this was not how I wanted to say this—"

"Clearly—dude, what the fuck?" Taylor is panicking maybe more than Wes. Wes likes *him*? Why!?

"—and, honestly, I wasn't gonna say anything at all!" Wes continues to ramble, "I totally get it if you don't return my feelings or whatever, honestly it's not a huge deal—"

"It's fine."

"—If you just want to pretend you never heard that, go ahead- fuck, it's probably kinda hard to unhear th-th-thin-thi- stuff. B-but, uh, j-just don't worry about it—"

It's a great distraction from his own emotions, trying to calm Wes down, and Taylor tries to interrupt, "I said it's fine don't flip out about it."

But Wes doesn't seem to hear him, stammer sticking to more words. "—s-s-so yeah. If you're uncomfortable, that's understandable, I get-t that. You can just go ahead and move in with Todd, and you don't have to talk to me anymore—"

It slips out: "Feeling's mutual, dumbass," Taylor growls. And he has to growl it, and he has to call Wes a dumbass, even though he normally wouldn't. Otherwise... otherwise he might get so soft that the cold wind would blow him away, up into the sky. Something in Taylor, just for a second, doesn't want to join the stars yet.

For about three seconds, Wes stares at him like he expects him to elaborate, or maybe his brain is rebooting. He's got to look down a little to make eye contact, but Taylor won't let him because he doesn't want anybody to see what's in his eyes, least of all Wes.

They continue to walk to school.

"So," Wes begins again, nervous but less panicked, "does this mean—"

"No," Taylor says flatly.

Wes's steps stutter, and he takes two long strides to catch back up and mutter, "Oh. Sorry for assuming, I just thought that..." he trails off, and then back in "ya know, since we both... " and when Taylor still doesn't offer anything, he gives up pretense and just asks, "Why not?"

And Taylor stops at the crosswalk of Green Street and Alentis

Road and says with the gravity and forethought of a much older man, "You deserve better."

No matter what Wes thinks to say to that, it dies in his chest, withering in frosts of confusion and heartache, and then the crosswalk illuminates to tell them to step into the street.

9

Tension on Tuesday, December 15

Mr. Fieberg notices the tension right off the bat. Yesterday they were two peas in a very weirdly shaped pod and today they won't look each other in the eyes. They still take a seat right next to each other, but they are doing their best to look as occupied with absolutely nothing as possible.

And then Jaxson Dixon, whose parents called him out sick yesterday despite being the type of people that sometimes remind Mr. Fieberg that he's a mandatory reporter, enters the room and he sits on the desk and asks Mr. Fieberg if his girlfriend still has that annoying-ass cat.

Personally, Jaxson likes cats about as much as anything else that breathes, but he knows two things about Mr. Fieberg:

1.) Mr. Fieberg was about to go bother Taylor and Wes, and Jaxson thinks it'd be better if he and every other nosy fucking teacher at Swisher High School would lay off, and

2.) Mr. Fieberg hates cats.

And the distraction serves until the bell rings for class to start and Jaxson slides into one of the chairs across from the lab table claimed by Taylor and Wes—whom he has known in different capacities for a while, and never together. Taylor sometimes joins Jaxson in the bathroom during second period English to talk shit about their parents, and they've known each other more or less forever because their sisters are inseparable. Wes is sometimes eating lunch in the bathroom when Jaxson goes to take a piss or have a quiet moment or cut his hips open, and when Wes looks like less of a basket case, Jaxson invites him to sit with him and Collin behind the gymnasium. Doesn't look like he'll need help sitting with anybody anymore—but isn't this interesting.

Jaxson's gone for *one* day and, apparently, the school goes to hell!

Ms. Merino-Ott takes one look at Taylor and Wes— followed closely by Jaxson Dixon, who is also, miraculously, attending her class—and sighs. Whatever's going on, it's developed in an unhappy direction.

They couldn't have fought, or Taylor would be doing whatever he usually does to pass her class downstairs in the boys' bathroom, probably with Jaxson, but Wes looks like a lovelorn schoolgirl who's going to die of consumption in two days and Taylor looks like he shit his pants. And they're sitting right next to each other in the back row. And Jaxson Dixon is talking enough, in the seat across from them at a table in the back, for all three of them.

Honestly? Ms. Merino-Ott is just glad that Wes Post somehow managed to convince her two ritual truants to grace English class with their presence.

Jaxson manages to get Wes to open his mouth twice, Taylor once, before the bell rings and class starts and Ms. Merino-

Ott has to find some way to make a class full of high school seniors in a rural Iowa town understand that Shakespeare is neither high-brow nor heterosexual. Jaxson Dixon, despite never having seemed interested in anything even remotely related to English, is strangely helpful in that—and it makes Ms. Merino-Ott wonder why he spends her class doing fuckall in the bathroom if he's really that interested in Sonnet 20.

Mrs. Woolley notices nothing unusual, because she's already got her hands full trying to get Harley Daniels to be quiet for just a few seconds about the Pythagorean theorem to Sarah Stanley— the class isn't even talking about the Pythagorean theorem, they're talking about logarithms! She's toeing a fine line between endeared by his enthusiasm and frustrated by his distraction, and before she knows it the bell has rung and she has taught these poor kids almost nothing about the logarithms that will be showing up on their test this Friday before school lets out for Winter Break.

Each department at Swisher High School is located in one building, with classrooms located on the outer doorways of the building and one room in the middle. The middle room has doorways connecting it to each of the classrooms in the building, and one hatch leading to the roof, but no exterior exits. When the school was built, like ninety-six years ago or something, this room was intended for private teacher's meetings. When there was an attempted school shooting six years ago, these rooms were rebranded by the faculty as "safe" rooms. Nobody really gives a shit though, and mostly, they're used for the teachers to eat lunch in without having to interact with highschoolers for one brief, wonderful, thirty-six minute period.

The Math teachers get along fine. The science department would get along better if Mr. Keyes would shut up about his failing marriage and four dogs. The Social Sciences department gets along horribly because Mr. Co is a dick, Mr. Bloomquist an apathist, and Mrs. Williams sits with the English teachers. The Arts teachers tolerate each other. The English teachers get along like leaves in a tinderbox.

"Jaxson Dixon finally showed up for class today."

"You're shitting me— Carolyn, that's great!"

"Boy was talking about Shakespeare like he knew the guy personally—"

"Carolyn, if you say another word about Shakespeare I'm gonna lose it."

"Calm down, Maria!"

"She knows Shakespeare is off limits in the lunchroom! I can't rehash this debate! It was the 6th Earl of Oxford or I'm a zombified cow!"

"For Christ's sake, you're rehashing it right now! Shut up!"

"Oh, Erin, how's the GSA coming along?"

"Ugh, don't remind me— front office is trying to throw more shit in my face. It's like they know I don't have the time to fight them on it."

"I forgot, you just got back the Freshmen papers on Lord of the Flies, right? For English 1?"

"Yeah. I wish they'd let me teach honors again this semester. I can see the promise in some of these kids, but you tell them to write a three-page essay and I'm convinced they intentionally make their writing worse."

"Actually, I've been reading a study—"

"You're always reading a study, Tamiyoo."

101

"Shut it, Petra! I was reading a study, and— oh, shit, I forgot what I was saying. Well, anyways. It had something to do with confidence. I'm sure it did."

"Speaking of, guess who else actually made it to class today?"

"Carolyn Merino-Ott, I swear to god, if you're shipping students again I'm calling CPS. Leave them alone!"

"You mean leave *us* alone."

"Okay, but this one will actually make you guys jump a little. Then I'll drop it, I swear."

"Fuck, fine. Who're the lovebirds?"

"Wes Post—"

"Oh, really, don't tease him. I feel bad enough for that kid already."

"Poor guy... I always had to pair him up with someone when I had him last year."

"Okay, but I'm actually interested. Who's the girl?"

"Taylor Macready."

"You've got to be shitting me."

"Carolyn, you can't be mean about it! Wes is so... well, he's so... shy."

"Yeah, there's no way he would even talk to a kid like Taylor Macready! That boy..."

"He's rude, for one thing."

"I've never even had him in my class and I know he gets into fights."

"One of the girls in my fourth period this semester—you know Sandy Liu?— told me he punched a kid twice in the face yesterday. No reason. Just walked up to him while he was talking to some other kid and knocked him on his ass."

"That boy's going to be arrested one of these days and I

won't be surprised when it happens."

"Can I finish? I have my reasons, you know."

"Oh, get on with it, Carolyn. Lunch is almost over anyways."

"Before last weekend, I'd never seen either of those boys with another student even once—"

"Well, sometimes I see Taylor Macready walking with two other boys. Todd Richards and Dalton something-or-other."

"Yeah, Todd Richards and Dalton Aarons. They're both sweet kids. No idea why those two hang out with a boy like *Taylor*."

"Sorry, go on, Carolyn?"

"Right, so, Taylor Macready never even shows up to my class. But yesterday they walked in together— I shit you not they were practically holding hands, and today, same story. They've been sitting right next to each other."

"God, Carolyn, I wouldn't hold out hope for this one."

"I dunno, she's winning me over. I had Taylor Macready last year. Anyone who can get that boy to come to a class discussion of metaphors has probably got him wrapped around their finger. I had Dalton Aarons *and* Todd Richards, and neither of them could get him to come."

"Ah, shit, that's the bell—I've got prep period after this, anyone wanna send a TA to help me grade quizzes?"

"I've got Frankie Rubio making me some copies, but I can send them your way when they've finished with that."

"You're a doll, Erin."

Fourth period, Mrs. Herrick recognizes nothing amiss with Wes, but Ms. Porter stifles a groan when Taylor refuses to participate in any of the class activities. Again.

Mr. Bloomquist watches Wes Post scamper into the room and sit in his spot in the back row while avoiding Monique Feldman as obviously as possible. She rolls her eyes, but takes the hint. Pity. Mr. Bloomquist would have loved to see something interesting in class for once.

Taylor Macready strolls in and plops himself right next to Wes Post, and they say absolutely nothing to each other, and Robert Bloomquist has never seen two kids happier to sit next to each other and say absolutely nothing. The rest of the class files in shortly after, and then the bell rings, and not four minutes into class an office aid enters the classroom door and stands politely, waiting for Mr. Bloomquist to have a moment for their errand.

Frankie Rubio is a quiet, heavyset senior who tested out of half the classes they were supposed to take in high school, but opted not to graduate early. They seem to know the secrets of this school before the walls have heard them. Their fifth period is office aide, and they always know a lot more about the errands they run for the front office staff than the front office staff does. Mr. Bloomquist has some respect for a kid who's here just to learn the things school isn't intentionally teaching them.

After setting the class to some busywork, Mr. Bloomquist meets Frankie at the door.

"Taylor Macready to see the principal," Frankie says, even-keeled and smiling.

Taylor, who isn't far away, hears his name and flips Frankie off. Frankie ignores him and says, at the same volume, in the same tone of voice, while looking directly at Taylor, "it's about an incident of violence yesterday before lunch."

Mr. Bloomquist shrugs, beckons Taylor over, and for some

reason, Wes Post feels the need to join.

"No, just Taylor," Mr. Bloomquist tries to say.

Frankie smiles again and says, "No, Wes can probably come too. He was involved, after all."

How interesting. Wes is built like a freight train, now that he's almost an adult, but being as shy and nervous as he is Mr. Bloomquist never thought he'd get violent with anyone.

How very, very interesting.

"Alright, go then," Mr. Bloomquist says, and Frankie leads Taylor Macready and Wes Post out the classroom door and to the front office.

"Oh, Frankie," says the woman with the thick Midwestern accent working the administration desk, "where'd you just come from? I didn't realize you'd left, I just got back from lunch!"

"Hi, Ms. Connie," Frankie answers warmly, "Just picking up a couple of kids."

"Oh?" Ms. Connie drops her glasses off her face, and they hang by a beaded strap around her neck, "And what are these two doin' in the office?"

Taylor shrugs. Wes twitches. Frankie smiles and replies, "Kid named Alex Morenson said that Taylor punched him yesterday before lunch. Wes was there too, apparently."

Ms. Connie's bright face darkens, but Wes pulls on his hair with one hand and blurts, "H-he only hit-it him because he was t-tr-t-try— picking on me!"

Frankie's smile widens.

Ms. Connie's expression shifts from darkness to shadows and she almost succeeds in restraining a smile. "Well, good-ness, you two! Sit down— Frankie, will you be a dear and tell the principal I'll handle these two?" When Frankie stops smiling so wide, she waves her hand and adds, "and if that man has a problem with it, you tell him he's got a direct phone line to my desk and he knows how to use it. Don't let him give you any trouble." And Frankie nods and steps into Mr. Morales's office, grin re-affixed to their face.

"Now, why don't you boys tell me what actually happened yesterday?" she prompts, "Because I have met Alex Morenson and I have heard the things he says to people when he thinks nobody can hear him when I'm getting in my car after work."

Taylor offers her nothing. He crosses his arms and looks out the window. He'll take his L. He doesn't need this olive branch or whatever the fuck. He knows, deep in his soul, that Ms. Connie will only be acting nice until he's fucked up enough times, and he'd prefer to save himself the disappointment of it all.

Wes, however, is only getting more worked up. He's never been to the office for anything outside of that one time he got lost during a panic attack. "A-Alex M-Mor-Morenson just-t lik-ikes to fu-f-fuc- mess w-with me. Y-yesterday, T-Taylor-"

"Ms. Connie," Taylor interrupts, "can you give me some paperclips?" Ms. Connie looks shocked, and doesn't move. "Please," Taylor adds flatly. After a hot second of searching, she sets a little clear, plastic container labeled "100 Paper-clips" on the desk. Taylor hands it to Wes and tells him, "Make the longest paperclip chain you can." Wes, whose breathing is starting to go shaky, nods and begins to string them together.

Ms. Connie is still staring, blankly, like she's not sure what the hell to do about this.

"Alex Morenson is an asshole," Taylor explains simply. "I

saw him being an asshole, and I stopped him from being an asshole. If you're gonna give me detention or suspend me, just do it. I don't give a shit."

Ms. Connie is still staring, blankly, like she's still not sure what the hell to do about this, when the desk phone rings. She answers it mechanically, though her voice is anything but. "Mr. Morales, I thought I'd be hearing from you," she says saccharinely into the receiver, "yes, they're right here. No, actually, I don't think I will. No—… Well—… Are you going to let me talk or is the staff going to have another discrimination meeting on Friday instead of leaving on time? Thank you. I've resolved the matter… I don't care 'who it is,' Cesar, they're kids. I don't care that he's done it before. Well, for god's sake, Cesar, you can't be goin' around judging teenagers based off of a few incidents, they'll get a complex— you know, Tamiyoo was telling me about a study she read the other day— oh, alright, fine, but these kids are going back to class. Yep. All written up. I'll hand-deliver it to your office in about five minutes but they've missed enough class as it is for something like this. Alright. Alright. Yep, thank you. Buh-bye."

Ms. Connie sets the phone carefully into the cradle, sighs knowingly, replaces her glasses on the edge of her nose, types loudly on her keyboard, and peers at them above the rim of her glasses. "Wes, sweetie, you feelin' alright now?" Wes nods mutely, paperclip chain dangling from his fingers. Neither he nor Taylor know what they're supposed to say after that phone call. "Alright," Ms. Connie smiles, "now you two get back to class, and Taylor?" for the first time in his life, Taylor feels inclined to listen to an adult, and pauses to look back at Ms. Connie. "Try not to get into too many fights, alright?"

He nods.

Jaxson invites himself to walk home with them, which means, of course, that Collin is coming too. Jaxson also invited himself to sit with them at lunch.

"I just feel like we haven't hung out in so long, Taybee Baby," Jaxson sings while they walk. Wes thinks this nickname is hilarious, but Taylor threatened Jaxson with serious, hospital-level assault before the backstory could be revealed.

Taylor grumbles back, "That's because we were never close."

"Don't be mean, we're friends," Jaxson insists.

Collin smiles a little awkwardly and says, "W-well, sorry for bargin' in on you fellas like this, Jax was just wantin' to know how you two got so close so quick!"

"Babe!" Jaxson groans, "You're not supposed to tell them that!"

"Gosh, sorry, Jax."

"S-Sorry," Wes interrupts, "are you two...?"

Jaxson bats his eyelashes dramatically at Collin, who averts his eyes bashfully. "You didn't know?" Jaxson says. Internally, he's wondering how anyone at Swisher High could have missed that he and Collin were dating. It's been an open secret to everyone but the adults since Freshman year. Eventually though, he does ask what he meant to, "But, actually, Wes, buddy, what happened this weekend? You two are awfully close all of a sudden—"

"Shut your trap, Dixon," Taylor says. He only calls Jaxson that when he's upset with him.

But the anger of Taylor Macready, who solves everything in the ways that Jaxson is too familiar with to be scared of, has never meant much to Jaxson Dixon, and he presses on, "And I'm not getting anything from that brick wall, so tell me.

What happened this weekend?"

"It's really not my place to say," Wes mumbles, fidget toy clicking in his pocket where his hands are shoved.

"Whose place is it then?" Collin asks, not really meaning much by it.

But Taylor snaps, "Mine. Shut the fuck up about it." When Jaxson glares at him, he flips him off. The anger of Jaxson Dixon has never meant much to Taylor Macready either. Knowing how somebody's little sister treats them does that to you.

Wes's parents almost rush home from the shop when they hear Wes has friends over. They've barely heard of Wes *having* friends, a development from less than two days ago, much less *inviting them over.* But Wes convinces them it's fine, as long as they're okay with it, and they are, so Taylor, Jaxson, Collin, and Wes sit on Wes's pullout couch watching cartoon reruns because it's the only thing they could agree on for the better part of three hours.

It's unexpectedly comfortable.

Jaxson has shed his 4-year-old parka (or, *he's* had it for 4 years- it looks like it could very well be older than any of the boys in this room). He's just wearing one of his crop tops, one of the ones the school couldn't find enough of a problem with to stop him from wearing it on campus. Before 7th grade, nobody had ever really seen Jaxson out of his ugly-ass parka, but something shifted in eighth grade, probably around the time when Jaxson cut ties with Freddy and Harley and Bart. All of a sudden Jaxson wore nothing but crop tops. Maybe he'd finally grown out of the ugly parka, maybe he was just feeling a new look, but after some point nobody could remember the last time they'd seen him in the parka. That was all well and fine until freshman year, when Jaxson threw some lingerie layers into the mix, and some girls joined him with those, and the school got a sexual harassment lawsuit that got plastered on page two of search engines all across the country.

Of course, page two of a search engine is still page two, so nobody ever actually heard about it— but in Swisher, Iowa? Jaxson Dixon was forgotten once the principal bullied him into wearing crop tops with no bras underneath and no profanity on them, but the girl whose parents started the lawsuit moved out of Swisher fast, and everyone has heard, by now, of how well she's doing in San Diego. It's a small town. Once you get a label, it stays stuck to you like a bright red A, even if you do your damnedest to tear it off.

In the winters, Jaxson wears a parka that's clearly third-hand and he claims is a gift. Good money goes for the gift being from Juniper-Maisie, and that's even without Hellen having to tell Taylor anything. Everyone knows Jaxson's willing to work an odd job or two when he needs something, and every May he almost fails his finals because he works himself silly at some part-time or another so he can buy his little sister a birthday present.

Taylor usually makes Hellen something out of what he finds around the house for her birthday. Not that he's likely to be at home for her birthday this year.

"What're ya thinkin' about?" Collin asks Taylor. It's commercials, and Taylor is still staring directly at the center of the screen, so it's safe to say he's thinking. Lost in thought, even. He certainly didn't notice Jaxson drag Wes out of the room to help him make popcorn.

"Nothing," Taylor says. He doesn't know Collin Donahue at

all, really. Nobody does. His parents are in the PTA, which is embarrassing for a highschooler, and he's generally a nervous guy— but in the polite, unobtrusive way that gets you branded 'a pleasure to have in class,' and passed along without anyone looking any deeper. He and Taylor have, by some stroke of dumb luck, not had a class together since middle school, and even then they kept distance because Collin's PTA parents would string him up in the yard for being *seen* with Taylor Macready. They don't even know he hangs out with *Jaxson*, whose reputation skates by on being pretty and charismatic and pitiably poor.

"Oh," Collin wrings his hands, "'cause you sure look like yer thinkin' about somethin'."

Taylor shrugs, "Where'd Jaxson get his parka?"

At that, Jaxson swings into the room and throws himself onto Collin's lap. "You like it, Taylor? It was actually a gift from my precious younger sister."

"Real shit?" Taylor answers. It's not a question. He's not super surprised, if anyone was going to be giving Jaxson Dixon a gift, it would be his kid sister. Still, it makes him miss Hellen. A little. Not a lot. Just the way she would sometimes come sit in his room for no reason. Or how she tried to make him a pet cat out of a sock when dad chewed him out for asking. Just little shit like that.

Wes, who knows about the Dixon family the same way everyone in town other than Taylor and Hellen Macready know about the Dixon family, says, "That's nice," with a smile. Most people in town don't smile when they say that though. That's just Wes Too-Fucking-Good Post. And then he says, "Taylor, you asshat, you're sitting on the remote," and Taylor realizes he'd been staring at Wes for so long he didn't realize

111

he accidentally butt-muted the TV.

10

Voice Like a Beehive, Punch Like a Sting

When Wednesday starts, Taylor feels like the color the sky chose to dress in that day: a dingy blue-gray that promises precipitation of some sort, but storms almost always miss Swisher by half a mile, and Taylor knows that this time, just like every other time, they'll be denied the catharsis earned by the lack of sunlight.

Wes and Taylor get up and get ready for school. For breakfast, Wes hands Taylor a leftover blueberry muffin from the shop, and they make their lunches together ("Dude, I'm almost an adult, I can make my own lunch"). They don't get five minutes into their walk, however, before they find Collin and Jaxson waiting for them at the bus stop.

"The fuck're you two doing here?" Taylor asks. They don't live on the other side of the school like Dalton and Todd, but they don't live, like, right next door or anything. Besides, everyone knows they just walk to school together. Since Freshman year that's been how it is. It's out of character for them to suddenly include other people in their plans.

But Collin waves enthusiastically enough to convince you he's still who he was in elementary school, and Jaxson swings himself off his boyfriend's shoulder and grins wide. "We wanted to walk with our new friends," Jaxson sings.

Taylor doesn't like this. Suspicious. The two gay kids who talk to each other almost exclusively (other than second period English in the bathroom sometimes) all of a sudden want to hang out with Wes, Taylor, Todd, and Dalton? It's kinda weird.

Wes doesn't seem to see a problem with it. Which is both sweet and probably because he's been living under a social rock since fucking infancy.

Fuck it. Beats walking to school alone while Wes stares at him with something adjacent to anger but too close to confusion to be called either. At least Collin and Jaxson make for a good buffer after yesterday morning— whatever Taylor is supposed to call that.

He had thought his answer to Wes's confession was very straightforward, but now anytime it's just them, Wes looks at him so intently. He'll open his mouth like he wants to say something eighteen times in a row, but nothing ever comes out. If he's pissed, Taylor wishes he would just say it. That way he could at least face it head-on.

Despite Ms. Connie's words yesterday, and the amicable chatter of his friends, Taylor wishes he could find something, or someone, to hit. Or maybe just to hit him. Maybe getting some sense knocked into him would do him good. Maybe Dad was right about that one thing.

Wes doesn't get it. He literally cannot wrap his fucking head around any of it. He doesn't have time to worry that Jaxson and Collin— who everyone knows never talk to anyone but each other, and the kids in the GSA on Fridays after school— might suddenly be interested in him because they want to harvest his organs or something. He's got more pressing matters. Like the fact that Taylor Macready— the very same Taylor Macready that handed Wes a cool leaf for no reason other than to calm him down and who punched Alex Morenson in the face because he was bothering Wes and who treats Wes like a real, human person worthy of kindness instead of a zoo exhibit— has not only reciprocated Wes's romantic feelings, but also turned down dating him for not one single goddamned reason.

What is he supposed to do about that?

Is there anything he *can* do about that?

Mr. Fieberg calls him to the board twice in class (apparently, Wes is the only person in class who understands the equation and isn't actively hiding it today) and he doesn't so much as flinch because he's lost enough in his head that he doesn't even really register getting up from his seat, much less the eyes (eyeseyeseyes) that are watching him complete the problem with perfunctory accuracy.

Taylor doesn't act any different than normal. If Wes didn't know better, he'd say Taylor had forgotten that conversation entirely. He does his work normally, talks normally, makes a normal amount of eye contact— Jesus Christ, he's not even sitting closer than normal!

After a whole class period of careful observation, Taylor is acting entirely normally. For Taylor. Wes has decided, by the time the bell that sends them to second period English screams, that normal for Taylor is very different from normal for everyone else. Wes doesn't have a large sample size for this data, but nobody else has ever sat that close to Wes. Nobody else has ever put their arm around his shoulders for just one single, casual second. Taylor only does it once in a while, when Wes is walking slow and he wants him to speed up, but that's more than anyone else. Nobody else taps out the same rhythm of the song Wes had been humming while he got dressed this morning with the tip of their pencil. Nobody else gives him tiny, real smiles that disappear when observed like whatever particle Mr. Fieberg had been talking about.

Maybe Wes is reading too much into all of it.

He is thrown back into awareness of his surroundings when Taylor speaks for what might be the first time since school started this morning. "No," he says flatly, just a bit less nonchalant than usual.

Wes has missed whatever conversation or request incited the refusal, but Ms. Merino-Ott is happy to recap. "It's not a lot Taylor, you just have to read your assignment to your table group. If you want, I'll walk away so I don't hear anything, but you have to participate in class."

"I don't want to."

"Taylor, this kind of belligerence isn't going to get you anywhere. You're almost eighteen— I don't want to call your parents."

And Jaxson Dixon and Rose Uribe, the other two members of the table group, miss it, but Taylor flinches. Not so much in his body as in his face. Same way he did when he was sick and Wes tried to set a hand on his shoulder. Ms. Merino-Ott sees it too, on account of having worked with highschoolers for about seventeen years now and observing Taylor since she had him for Freshman English.

She almost takes it back. Almost comes up with a witty retort and says "alright, who cares, you're outta here in another semester." It's such a small thing. Who really cares if he reads his short story assignment out loud? If it makes him uncomfortable, she shouldn't push it. She feels her feet dangling over the precipitous drop at the line she just crossed.

Taylor just says, "Fine. I'll go last." He's hoping the bell will ring and he'll end up not having to read his assignment with the group after all. Ms. Merino-Ott nods placatingly and leaves them alone, feeling like a guest who has overstayed their welcome in a strange place. She wanders off, trying to look nonchalant and collected, to Monique Feldman's table group to see what they have to say about the assignment.

The assignment was flippant. Prompt: whatever gets your creative juices flowing. Ms. Merino-Ott had planned on accidents happening and not being able to finish her unit on sonnets until Friday, but the only accident to happen was her over-cautious planning, and instead she found herself with three empty days before Winter Break. Out of her ass, she'd made up a creative writing assignment. Write one Tuesday night, workshop it Wednesday. Thursday she'll review plot structures with them, and Friday will be a movie day. Even for something supposedly easy, it's *hard* to get highschoolers to willingly share a creative piece of any kind.

Wes stares around his table group with eyes blinking hard to stay focused on his immediate surroundings. Nobody has really moved. They're all looking at Ms. Merino-Ott, and at each other, and at Taylor, who is glaring at a little pile of eraser shavings like he hates it personally.

Rose goes first by her own hesitant, shaky volition. She read an incredibly well-written story with no real plot. Just a description of a place filled with people who each lead their own interesting, boring lives. Everyone says it's good. Nobody brings up the part where it has no plot because they don't know Rose well enough to give her criticism. And her words are pretty so who cares about plot.

Wes doesn't want to, but he says he'll go next. He gave his story a title, because he thought it had to have a title, but now his title feels stupid because Rose didn't have a title and—fuck. Taylor nudges his shoulder. And it shouldn't feel so stupidly, cozily intimate, or soft, because for all outward appearances it wasn't, like, a soft nudge. It had *looked* like the kind of nudge that you give to some guy you barely know and don't especially like all that much, but it had *felt* like the lightning between clouds; soft and electric. But Wes's neck still spins ninety degrees to blink owlishly at Taylor.

Wes doesn't want to, but he says he'll go next. He gave his story a title, because he thought it had to have a title, but now his title feels stupid because Rose didn't have a title and—fuck. Taylor nudges his shoulder. Wes spins to blink, owlish and bewildered, at Taylor. It wasn't a panic attack, it was barely even *panic*, but he still noticed. He noticed and he even gave Wes a nudge, not a particularly special-looking nudge, but it was enough to ground Wes and reintroduce him to the present moment. Who the hell notices such a small thing? There is a sudden onslaught of conflicting desires to either curl into himself and cry or grab Taylor by the shoulders and kiss him.

But he manages to do neither of those things and instead get himself back in order. He coughs awkwardly and skips his title altogether to read the rest of his story. It's kinda shitty, and Wes knows it. He's not great with storytelling, written or verbal. He's at least that self-aware. It's about a child running from what, at first glance, is a monster, but ends up being a figment of the kid's imagination. Everyone tells him it's good. Rose is polite about it, in a very distant kinda way. Jaxson might mean it, but who knows with Jaxson. Taylor doesn't look at him when he says it, so Wes can't tell if he means it.

It's alright, even if nobody meant it. Wes might be more anxious than a meth head in a police station most days, but reading the thing out loud was scarier than the thought of someone not liking it. Who cares if they didn't like it. Wes's never written anything before except that brief stint in 5th grade where he was certain that if he didn't write things down then the past might rewrite itself constantly. As long as he doesn't have to share anymore, he can stay pretty calm.

Jaxson's story is, of course, because it's Jaxson Dixon and he's actively trying to prove everyone wrong, about everything, every day, impeccably written. It's something with complicated, almost-run-on sentences with flawless grammar that you can lose yourself in, and it's about a prostitute killing herself. Taylor says, "That's kinda fuckin' dark for a class assignment."

Jaxson grins, Cheshire, and says, "I wanna see if I can make Ms. Merino-Ott shit her pants a little."

Rose, distantly polite, says it's very... interesting. Wes asks what made him think of something like that. Jaxson shrugs and says his mom gave him the idea. Nobody asks about that.

There's eight minutes left in class. Taylor groans, and almost leans in to ask if they don't want to talk about Jaxson's some more, so he can get out of this, but Ms. Merino-Ott is glancing their way every few seconds. Taylor flips her off. Ms. Merino-Ott, already feeling a little guilty about her earlier intrusion, but also a woman with a spine built out of cement and rear, raises an eyebrow and turns back to Monique Feldman's table to ask about something in Celsee Steven's story.

Seven minutes left in class.

"Fuck it, whatever," Taylor mutters, and then yanks his notebook out of his backpack and begins to read out of it.

There's nothing very special about the writing style. If something were to be said about it, it's conversational. Matter-of-fact, no-bullshit narration. But it's captivating. To Wes, anyway. He'd say he's biased, but even the uncomfortable stilt of Rose's shoulders relaxes into something like attentive interest as Taylor unfolds a story of a girl passing out fliers for an event she knows nobody will attend. It should, for all intents and purposes, be boring as fuck. But there's something suspenseful and captivating in it. The girl is thirteen and afraid of something that the story doesn't address outright. She's clutching the fliers for the neighborhood picnic with trembling, sweaty, clenched fingers. People keep passing her and she keeps getting more desperate— she doesn't just advocate for this event because she thinks it's neat— she needs this event, for some reason. Nobody is taking her wind-wrinkled, handmade fliers though— they're all just passing her, not even glancing her way, and she feels like she's choking on their hatred—

That's the end of the story.

"And that's it?" Jaxson balks, "It just ends there?"

Rose nods tentatively, asking the same question.

With a shrug, Taylor replies, "I dunno. Didn't finish it."

"Why not?" Wes asks. There had been plenty of time to finish it last night, or this morning before school. Just one sentence. Something for catharsis. For closure.

Taylor shoves his notebook back into his backpack. "Didn't know how."

As always, Mrs. Woolley is behind schedule, and the last class before break will be their logarithms test. So, they manage another class where she tries to convince them that they've learned this material, and maybe four students believe her. Wes isn't paying attention. He's thinking about a girl passing out fliers with the desperation of the dying. Taylor isn't paying attention either. He's staring at Wes.

Harley Daniels is paying attention, but who gives a fuck about Harley Daniels.

* * *

Ms. Connie sits with the English teachers for lunch today. Usually, fourth period is her lunch break, but she's got Rayshawn covering her desk right now because she asked nicely and he's a sweetheart. She tells them the latest gossip from the office: today Frankie Rubio brought the office staff cookies that they made in home ec, and she finally finished that stack of incorrectly-filed registration forms for the Spring sports this year, and yesterday Principal Morales tried to give a kid a suspension for punching another kid in the nose.

"If we were suspending kids every time they got into a fight on campus," Ms. Connie tells the teachers, "we should be starting with that snot-nosed little asshole who keeps leaving those notes in the African Heritage Club's self-care note box—because I know it's Henry Milton, and that boy has gotten in just as many fights."

The English department laughs. Tamiyoo asks who, if not Henry Milton, Ms. Henrietta "Connie" Constance saved from suspension.

Connie giggles, and it's the special magic of her friendship with the English department that the sound is full and a little nasally instead of tinkling and hollow like a bell, the way it is when she's in the office. "The funniest thing, ladies, so Frankie Rubio is supposed to be bringing Taylor Macready to Principal Morales, but he's got this six-foot-something monstrosity of a kid trailing behind him—"

"You're kidding me, Connie—" Petra Liu gasps, glancing at Carolyn Merino-Ott.

"Did the monstrosity have hair like an unstyled L'Oreal model? Past his ears, brown, unbrushed?" Carolyn asks Connie.

"Well, I mean, yeah," Connie says, taking a bite of her salad, "Why d'ya ask?"

Carolyn smirks at the other assembled ladies of the English department— plus Tamiyoo Williams, the psychology teacher, and Henrietta Constance, the administrative desk attendant.

Connie rolls her eyes, "Don't you smirk at me, Carolyn, I want to know. What's the scoop? This Taylor Macready was an interesting boy."

"You tell us what happened in your office and I'll tell you what happened in mine," Carolyn offers.

Connie swallows another bite of salad before assenting. "So, Frankie Rubio walks these two right by my desk— like they wanted me to see them, I swear— and, we all know Frankie, so I say hi, and they say hi, and I ask what brings them through my way. Georgia had taken me to lunch—"

"Aw," Sarah Hunter coos, "such a sweetheart."

"Yeah," Connie's smile flashes brilliant and soft for a moment before she continues, "yeah, so I was just settling back into my desk and Frankie says Taylor Macready punched

Alex Morenson yesterday at lunch—"

Tamiyoo Williams interrupts to say, "What were we just saying yesterday? That boy's trouble."

"Well hold your goshdarn horses, Tamiyoo!" Connie says, gesturing widely with her arms, Tamiyoo holds up her hands and resettles in her seat. "So, you ladies know how I am, and you know how I feel about Alex Morenson, and Wes was halfway to having a meltdown in the middle of the office, so I told Frankie I'd take it from there and I told Taylor and Wes to sit down at my desk and I asked why Taylor punched Alex Morenson." She pauses for dramatic effect. "Wouldn't say a word. Sat there with his arms crossed for a good five minutes. His big friend, Wes, started trying to explain for him, and the poor kid's voice sounded like he was talking into a fan."

"Oh, poor thing."

"When I had him last year, he would get like that anytime he got too nervous."

"Well, he was certainly nervous— pulling on his hair, the whole nine yards." Ms. Connie pauses to take another bite of salad. Lunch is halfway through and she's only had three bites of her chicken cobb. "And Taylor was staring at him— I thought he might be gettin' angry at him about it— and he turns to me and asks me for paperclips!"

"Paperclips?"

"Oh yeah. Paperclips. Even said 'please.' I was so surprised I just handed him the little box I keep in my desk. And he hands the whole box to Wes and told him to make a chain of 'em. Long as he could."

A chortle of confused humor works its way out of Maria Albert's nose.

Connie nods eagerly and continues, "Then he tells me he

punched Alex Morenson 'cause the kid was— I'm quoting here, ladies— 'being an asshole,' and told me to do whatever I want for punishment, said he didn't care." She takes another bite of her salad.

Carolyn gives an impatient shake of her head. "What did you do?"

"You ladies know what I heard that Alex Morenson say when I was getting in my car last Tuesday— I didn't do a thing. That kid needs to get what's comin' to him." Between another bite of salad, Connie continues, "And of course Principal Morales felt the need to stick his nosy beak into it—"

"Oh, of course he did—"

* * *

In the student cafeteria, more than halfway through lunch, Dalton is staring at Wes, who is staring at Taylor in agonized confusion. They've exhausted everything Dalton and Todd can think of to say. Dalton's got nothing to report other than horrible, awful fucking boredom from history, trigonometry, and physics. Collin's only contribution is that he's excited for the school play that they'll be starting once everyone is back from Winter Break. Jaxson talks for as long as he can about how insufferable his third-period engineering class is, but he exhausts that after a while too. Todd has only one anecdote of Freddy Peters (with whom he has second-period AP government) going on a thinly-veiled rant about how gay people are diseased and need to be eradicated... totally unprompted. The class had been discussing Thomas Payne.

Freddy Peters being an ignorant asshole is nothing new. The

weather is more interesting, because at least that changes. So now, more than halfway through lunch, the stagnation between Wes and Taylor is palpable, and uncomfortable. Dalton is staring in the hopes that Taylor will read his mind, as he does on occasion, and tell them what's up.

It's Todd who says, "Alright, what gives. What happened with you two?"

Jaxson's eyes go flinty, and Dalton can tell he knows what went on, while Collin remains outwardly oblivious, which means it was either physics or English, but nobody says anything.

Taylor just shrugs, eyes casting out the window as casually as possible.

That leaves Wes, who wrinkles his whole face into one big question mark. Eventually, when Taylor makes it clear that he's not opening up, even under duress, Wes asks Dalton and Todd, "Did you guys know that Taylor is that good at writing?" The way Taylor's eyes snapped to look at him, almost betrayed, would make anyone think Wes had meant something malicious by saying it so plainly. The way Wes's eyes are glowing with more than wonder, almost adoration, would let anyone know that he didn't think the question could have hurt.

But it clearly did, and nobody at the lunch table— with its six chairs now, and doesn't that feel strange after years of it being just three— knows how to calm those waters or unrock that boat. So nobody says anything. Jaxson looks like he might, but the words die in his cheekbones and never make it past his lips.

The bell rings for class, and Wes is only just beginning to realize that nobody answered his question. Dalton has never felt further from Taylor. Last week he would have said he knew both of his best friends like the back of his hand.

After school, Taylor tells Wes to walk home without him. "I got somewhere to be and your parents want help with the incoming deliveries."

"Somewhere to be?" Wes echoes blankly. Nothing had been said before about Taylor having somewhere to be this Wednesday after school. But Wes isn't his keeper and he hardly knows everything about him, so he says sure, alright. See you later. His parents did want help with unloading this week's deliveries of coffee beans, and organizing the storeroom. Ever since his dad hurt his back, Wes is the only one who can lift the giant bags of beans with anything like ease. So Wes goes home and Taylor begins to walk downtown.

Taylor doesn't actually have somewhere to be. He just has a hitch in his bones and he needs someone to set it right again. His insides feel mushy and confused and he doesn't want Wes to be part of the fallout of what happens when he gets what he needs. First time in fifteen years that Taylor has wanted someone other than Todd and Dalton to not be around when he gets his bones unsettled like they are now.

He hangs out just next to the back door of a few different bars, hoping to catch some drunk and disorderly who's already looking for the same thing Taylor is. It's a little early to be drunk and disorderly though. He waits a while. When his stomach starts growling he considers going into someplace to eat, but he doesn't have any money. Maybe he could steal someone's food— that'd be two birds and one stone, after all— but nah, he doesn't want to show his face inside these places. Then they might start to know him. Look at him the ways teachers have looked at him since elementary school. The way his mom looked at him, sometimes. Why does he still miss his mom?

See, this is why he needs someone to set him right again. He can't go home.

And here comes a lady and her boyfriend. They're both obnoxious types. She's screaming at him that *that was so embarrassing* and he's screaming back *he was looking for that fight, Jess*, and she's saying *no, you were looking for that fight*, and Taylor is thinking *perfect*.

"Is this guy bothering you?" Taylor asks, too-loud and six kinds of stupid.

They respond at the same time with "Yeah, he is," and "No, this is my wife."

With bared teeth and a set jaw, Taylor smirks, and it feels less feral than it looks, and he says, "Lovers quarrel? Marriage falling into a train wreck?" He looks directly at the man, who was already looking for a fight, according to the woman, and spits his words between his teeth. "Let me guess, her ex-boyfriend thinks he can take you?"

It's a perfected skill, getting someone else to throw the first punch every time, and that shit sends Taylor stumbling a little.

The wife sees Taylor spit out some blood. He bit his cheek, but she can barely see that in the shadows where the streetlights don't reach. She realizes Taylor wanted this too and gives up on convincing her husband and starts a brisk walk toward what must be her car in her cheap wedges.

The husband whacks Taylor on the side of the head, and Taylor punches his chest where it meets his shoulder, but he left his torso wide open so the husband knees him in the stomach because Taylor isn't as tall as this asshole so it's not a

127

hard reach. Taylor pushes him to the ground and starts wailing on him, but the husband gets wise and turns his head to the side after two good hits to the cheek, so Taylor's knuckles hit old concrete and bust open bleeding. The husband shoves Taylor off him and kicks him, flatfooted, in the chest, tries to kick him again but Taylor blocks it with his forearm. Then the guy kicks him with the toe of his boots, right in the back, three times, and Taylor realizes those are steeltoes and he does not want to be on his ass next to the drunk asshole in steeltoes, and he rolls to his stomach and bounces into a crouch and stands up and runs off and it lasted something like thirty seconds but it felt infinite and it felt fucking pure.

When the guy is out of sight and he's halfway back to Wes's, he slows to a walk. Breathing that hard makes the bruises on his back itch and throb. He can't tell if his heart is pounding because he was running or because of the fight, still hot enough in his mind to cauterize the uneasy web of emotion that's been wrenching him apart all day.

Everything hurts, and it's finally, finally comfortable. His mind is a carefully balanced blank. He smiles to himself and discovers a bruise is making itself at home at the intersection of his nose and cheek. Doesn't feel broken though, even though it's bleeding.

It's getting kinda late. It might have been something like 8 or 8:30 when that couple finally walked out of the bar, so maybe it's 8:40 now? Taylor pulls out his phone to check the time. 8:49. Wes and his parents have probably already eaten. That's good. Taylor can eat later, or get something from a fast food place. Shit, right, no money. One of these days he's gonna have to get a job so he can stop mooching off the Posts. He already feels shitty enough— but if he focuses on the buzz of pain scorching his chest and the bootprint on his arm, the shame is less intense.

On purpose, Taylor takes the long way to Wes's house, so he doesn't get there until 9:15. Maybe Wes's parents will already be in bed. They wake up real fucking early to man the shop for the breakfast rush, so they go to bed real early too. Taylor doesn't want them to see him. To look at him the way everyone looks at him. He doesn't want Wes to look at him either— Wes who jumped when Taylor tried putting his arm around his shoulders that morning— Wes who hummed some song Taylor had never heard and tried to make Taylor a peanut-butter and honey sandwich for lunch, with baby carrots in a tupperware container— Wes who wanted to know more about the stupid short story he wrote for English class— Wes who has a voice like a beehive, low and bumbling and anxious and filled with honey— Wes who is sitting on the front porch with the porchlight on trying to figure out logarithms and failing miserably because he's too distracted waiting to see Taylor when he gets home— Wes whose whole face falls and makes the incredible adrenaline-buzz Taylor had just seconds before evaporate, and suddenly Taylor feels the cold and realizes he's just wearing a flannel and jeans and his hat is almost falling off and he shivers.

When you're about to get your shit kicked in by a guy in steeltoe boots, you don't have time to think about what you're feeling for a boy with a voice like a beehive.

He is dragged inside, and the heat feels oppressive, even though Taylor knows it's cold because this house is always cold in the ways that make you not want to get out of bed in the morning. He is sat inside the bathroom. Wes actually makes him sit on the counter so he doesn't have to lean down to see him, and it feels intimate even though Taylor knows it shouldn't. Or maybe it should, given yesterday morning's confessions.

No. It shouldn't. Wes deserves better and Taylor won't take advantage of him any more than he already has.

But he can have this one night of Wes poking at the scabs wherever they have sprouted on his body— can't he?

11

Salt in the Wound

W es feels the compulsive need to vomit when Taylor steps into the porchlight. He'd been doing his homework on the porch because Mom and Dad were getting ready for bed and the shower always sounds like the fucking end times from downstairs because the drain isn't great, and he'd wanted some quiet to figure out what exactly logarithms are for, or at least how to do them. Even after they went to bed, Wes was too lazy to go back inside.

And then Taylor starts walking up, Wes can make him out in his flannel and yellow hat, even in the shadows of the unlit part of his street, and then he's climbing the porch steps, grinning a little to himself, kind of sharkishly, and Wes wants to vomit because *who did that to him.*

Taylor doesn't protest when Wes drags him into the house, although his sharkish little smile is replaced with something guilty and depressed, and he doesn't protest when Wes practically sets him on the bathroom counter to get a better look at him— a blazon of violence.

His face is more purple than peroba-wood tan, and he's

bleeding honey-like rivulets from his nose and his teeth and the side of his forehead, just next to his temple. His flannel's dead-hydrangea brown is deranged with sleet-dissolved grime and cuttingly-clear bootprints, from his front to his back to his arms, like a pattern imposed on top of the chunky plaid. One of his fists is an incohesive bouquet of blood at the knuckles. The knee of one side of his jeans has been torn open like skin to reveal red-dyed road rash freckled with grains of concrete.

Wes stumbles through the obligatory *what happened, who did this, are you okay*— but neither he nor Taylor even really register the words. For a moment, staring at Taylor sitting on his bathroom counter covered in blood, Wes is both glad his parents are in bed and convinced he should go get them.

But what are parents gonna do? Wes's been better than either of them at first aid for years. Par for the course when you're clumsy with anxious tics and a tremor and spend a lot of your day surrounded by hot or sharp objects in a coffee shop. His parents are more likely to make Taylor clam up inexplicably. The urge to wake them passes.

So Wes moves to grab the first aid kit from the cabinet next to the showertub with shaking hands, and Taylor leans against the mirror behind him.

"D-don't m-m-move," Wes tells him.

Taylor crosses his arms a little more gingerly than normal and grumbles, "I'm fine. Don't freak out."

With practiced efficiency, Wes counts his steps and his breaths on his way to the laundry room to grab a clean rag and on the way back too. He makes Taylor scoot over and runs the rag under hot water, and when Taylor tries to be a stubborn asshole about how he's not a baby and doesn't need anyone fawning over him, or something, Wes slaps the side of his face that isn't bruised with the dry half of the rag. Taylor still winces.

First, the blood. Can't see anything about the injury with all the blood in the way. And if Wes narrows his focus to that, considers it clinical as opposed to personal, he can manage this more easily. He's not squeamish, but Taylor's staring directly at him with an emotion Wes can't place. That makes it hard to stop his hands from shaking enough to be careful. He starts with the knee, because that's farthest from Taylor's face, so he doesn't have to look at him while he rinses it with the rag, eases the debris out of the grooves of injury, disinfects it with rubbing alcohol, and dabs some bacitracin cream on it with the biggest bandaid in the first aid kit.

When it comes to the torso, Taylor both refuses to remove his flannel and insists that nothing is bleeding under there, so he's fine. Wes can't easily argue with that (and he doesn't want to seem like he just wants to see Taylor shirtless— because he doesn't; this is strictly clinical, professional, medical). But now all that's left is his hands and his face, and either one feels too intimate to touch.

Goddammit, he shouldn't have even started this because now he has to finish it and everything still feels like a tidal wave of emotion that Wes can't begin to process because *fuck!* Taylor Macready likes him back and he *still said no* for a reason that Wes can't even *begin* to wrap his head around!

"Wes, it's not as bad as it looks—shit do you not like blood?" Taylor's got his hands on either side of Wes's face, saying, "Shit, ok, you get out, I'll clean this up—"

"No!" Wes's voice cracks on the word, and he clears his throat. "I-I, uh- I d-don't f-freak out at blood."

133

"Then why are you still stuttering?"

"Because I've got a stutter."

"Yeah, one that only comes up when you're stressed."

"Will you shut up and let me do this for you?"

And whatever dickweed retort Taylor was cooking up is lost in his lungs when Wes pulls one of his hands off of his cheeks— the one covered in blood— and starts rinsing it with the warm, damp rag. The source of injury seems to be his knuckles, which are scraped raw and torn up. Wes tries to be gentle, but Taylor's other hand is gripping the bathroom counter tight, so he hurries.

"We don't really have any bandages this shape," Wes murmurs, digging through the first aid kit.

Taylor's voice is choked and awkward, "I'm not gonna die."

"If you don't cover it until the scab forms then it'll get infected!" Wes cries, "What if the infection t-turns into sepsis and you d-d-die!?" It's only when he looks Taylor straight in the face that he sees his face is red like cherry cough syrup on the dining table, and the blush is infectious. "I-I've done this a hundred times— lemme just find the tape." He actually hasn't bandaged split knuckles before, only imagined it. He'd never considered that the other hand might be gripping the bathroom counter or that the jaw would be set hard with pain. He keeps his eyes on the web of medical tape and gauze until the tissue-paper ridges of flesh unearthed on Taylor's fingers are safely wrapped.

But now comes the face. Shit. Wes can't look him in the eyes but there's no way not to when he's gently— gentler than that, he's doing his best not to hurt him— wiping the blood off of his eyebrow, and his chin, and his lips.

"Your nose isn't broken," Wes says.

Taylor says, "I know."

"Why is your mouth bleeding? Did you b-bite your tongue?" Wes asks.

Taylor answers, "No, inside of my cheek."

"The cut on your forehead isn't bad. The bruising is gonna be worse," Wes says.

Taylor says, "I figured. The cut's just from the guy's wedding ring."

Wes puts a bright blue bandaid over the cut above his eyebrow, just next to his temple. Then he realizes Taylor is sitting on the bathroom counter and Wes has stepped close enough to be standing between his legs and *oh shit* and Wes hops back far enough to bonk his head on the wall and Taylor breathes like he hasn't breathed in days and Wes giggles with a lightheaded kind of giddiness and says "O-okay, let's ge-g-get- grab you an ice pack. Or seven."

Somehow, it's 10:26 already.

Taylor's face is still cherry-cough-syrup-on-the-dining-room-table red, but Wes has managed to distract *himself* out of self-consciousness by talking about how he's gotten pretty good at first aid with cuts and scrapes and burns because he's a clumsy idiot in a coffee shop— and he shows off his newest addition to his bandaid collection on the side of his palm where he let it rest against the roasting machine for a little too long this afternoon.

The sound of a stifled laugh erupts from behind Wes and he turns to see Taylor with a hysteric little smile accented by tears. He's crying. Taylor is crying.

Wes actually yelps— quietly, at least. He doesn't know where this is coming from— okay, probably it's from the fact that Taylor, for some reason, willingly went out and got his ass kicked— but why now? Why after the danger has passed and he's safe and taken care of? Why cry now, while Wes is pulling ice packs out of the freezer in the dark?

But, for whatever reason, he's crying, and Wes slowly, hurriedly, the way you might try to pick up a possum playing dead in the middle of the road, wraps Taylor in his arms. That makes it worse, and he starts crying harder, but both fists work their way into Wes's shirt so he can't back up.

More than not knowing what to say, Wes's whole brain fucking short circuits. What is he supposed to be doing here? What can he say to comfort someone when he knows not one single goddamned thing about what's wrong? He can't honestly say things are going to be okay, because maybe they aren't. He can't say he's safe, because what if he isn't. He can't say it's alright, because it probably isn't. Not if Taylor fucking Macready is crying.

But only one of them can be breaking down at a time, so Wes just holds him in the kitchen for a minute.

The next morning, the note Wes's parents leave him on the kitchen counter says they are leaving this afternoon, before the boys get home from school. They have left the shop all closed up, with a sign saying their hours won't be regular again until after Winter Break— they tell Wes any hours he wants to pick up during break are his own choice, but any money the store makes in those shifts is fully and completely Wes's to do with as he chooses.

(If this was last year, they would have just left the store open and told Wes to close up whenever he felt overwhelmed. Because last year he wouldn't have had anything else to do while they were gone. But it's not last year, and Wes has friends to hang out with now, which is what makes them feel comfortable going on this trip at all. The money arrangement is their way of an apology for leaving with such short notice, and without him— even if he does hate planes and warm weather.)

The note also tells Wes that they love him, and they'll call him at the layover at LAX and when they land in Rosarito, and to have fun with his friends. The note tells Taylor that he can stay as long as he likes, and that they expect to see lots of him regardless when they're home in January. The note tells both Taylor and Wes that they will call them on Christmas to reveal the location of their hidden Christmas presents.

Wes reads the last two parts aloud to Taylor, who is throwing peanut butter and honey and bread into two separate sand-wiches and shoving them aggressively into reusable plastic sandwich containers.

"Why'd they get me a present?" he grumbles, "I'm not their kid."

Wes doesn't have an answer because, technically, Taylor is right. Richard and Martha Post have never gotten their son's friends any Christmas presents before— although in the past that was always because Wes never had any friends with which to set that precedent.

In the end, while Taylor is stuffing baby carrots into reusable plastic pouches, Wes answers, "I dunno, 'cause they like you?" Of course, this makes Taylor's face go stonier than before, angry in a real way, almost vindictive.

With lunches made with hateful affection by Taylor, and breakfast muffins provided from the coffee shop leftovers in the cabinet, they begin the walk to school.

They're still surprised, although Collin argues they

shouldn't be, when Jaxson and Collin are waiting for them at that bus stop again. From what Wes has seen of them during the few, kind gestures of lunches he has shared with them behind the gym, it's probably more safety in numbers than anything. The GSA is held in a locked room on Fridays for a reason.

While they walk, and Jaxson laughingly tries to goad Taylor into telling him 'what the fuck happened to your face, dude,' it occurs to Wes that they could have taken the bus today. Him and Taylor could have taken the bus yesterday too. It's not a long walk, but it's cold as anything.

It's Thursday, December 17th, one week exactly before Christmas, in *Iowa*. The high today is 35 degrees. They could have taken the bus and been a heck of a lot warmer for it.

But if they'd taken the bus, Collin wouldn't have slipped on the road salt that's stuck onto the sidewalk and bonked his forehead on a lightpole and said "Fudgenuggets" like it's a curse word, and they wouldn't have all laughed. If they'd taken the bus, Taylor wouldn't have walked slow enough to let Collin and Jaxson get far ahead so he could ask Wes quietly, softly, if he wanted to borrow his jacket— "you're shivering, dipshit, why didn't you wear your parka?" If they had taken the bus they would have had to pass Freddy Peters, who sits at the front every day, and Taylor probably would have punched him and started another fight. Or maybe Jaxson would have beaten him to it— everyone knows that Jaxson Dixon will use any excuse to get at Freddy Peters. They've hated each other since seventh grade, even if nobody really knows why.

Maybe Harley Daniels or Bart Chomski know, but they still hang out with Freddy Peters, so they're not talking.

But Wes does know that the walk is worth it, because he

walks into Mr. Fieberg's first period physics class wearing Taylor's jacket, and Jaxson is laughing at them both for it.

Mr. Fieberg notices Taylor's face. It would be much harder not to notice when a student who had been perfectly healthy and unmarred yesterday walks in looking like a splatter-painted canvas. He doesn't comment on it. Mostly because if a teacher wanted to comment every time Taylor Macready walked in looking like he got into a fight, they would actually lose enough instructional minutes over it to be significant. Mr. Fieberg just glances at Wes, then at Jaxson, and then he wanders off to talk to Danny Chon before starting the class.

Ms. Merino-Ott doesn't mention it either. She's still a little self-conscious after yesterday. Threatening to call Taylor's parents had definitely been a Bad Thing, even if she doesn't know why, so in recompense she doesn't look twice when he comes in bruised to shit. She just delivers her power point about crafting plotlines and character arcs and tries to ignore Jaxson Dixon's side comments detailing the poignant examples of character arcs that he has gleaned from pornhub.

Mrs. Woolley scrunches up her face when they walk in. She asks if Taylor wants to go to the nurse. He says no. Then she asks if he wants to go to the counselor. And he says no again. And Mrs. Woolley wrings her thin little hands and says alright, but she's always there to talk, and Taylor resists the urge to roll his eyes until he's sitting in his seat and her back is turned.

And then lunchtime. Taylor drags his feet the whole way there. He makes every excuse— says he has to pee, spends forever putting his shit in his locker and getting his lunch out, walks at the pace of a fucking snail— and it's making Wes a little bit crazy. Not that lunch is some huge event or anything, but Wes hates being late. Makes him nervous.

"Everyone else is p-probably already there," he stammers, a little annoyed. They're right at the swinging doors to the cafeteria, but Taylor doesn't want to enter. Taylor shrugs. "Let's go already, T-T-Tay— ugh! Let's just go!"

"Trouble in gay paradise?" comes the mocking voice of Freddy Peters from behind. Harley Daniels opts to roll his eyes and scroll through his phone instead of getting involved, but he and Bart Chomski are there too.

As always, Bart Chomski tries to mediate, "Dude, leave it," he reasons, "the principal won't listen either way." This makes no sense to Wes or Taylor, but Freddy, Bart, and Harley all seem to be on the same page.

And there they are. The epicenter of Swisher High School. Always together, always starting shit. The staff mostly turns a blind eye because their moms are big in the PTA and the HOA and the town hall meetings, but the students collectively hate them for the same reason one hates a black mold infestation. Persistent. Annoying. Hazardous.

Taylor doesn't initially react, and Wes is doing his best to be somewhere else, mentally. They miss their millisecond of a chance to squeeze out of this by walking away just a fraction of a second too slow with Taylor's sticky snail-paced feet.

Freddy Peters doesn't like that they didn't react, and he doesn't like Bart trying to tell him what to do, so even as Taylor and Wes make their way in the other direction down the hall, he pushes. "Y'see, Harley," addressing the only person who isn't openly opposed to his shit-disturbing, and who doesn't look up from his phone, "this is what happens when a couple of gaywads get together: it doesn't end well for anyone. First Jaxson gets with *Collin Donahue*, of all the freaks. Now these two? It just doesn't end. It's a *disease*, and both of them have it. That's why we have to—"

"Fuck it," Taylor mutters, "let's go, dipshit."

"What was that?" Freddy taunts, "Fairy wants to fight?"

"Sure," Taylor says, and he comes with a left hook so fast that it genuinely unbalances Freddy, despite his size advantage.

Freddy grins, malicious and planning. Wes knows that Freddy Peters never starts a fight he doesn't want, or one that he can't finish. Freddy brings up one knee and slams it into Taylor's stomach.

And the strangest thing happens. Taylor just... falls over.

He doesn't get back up.

One part of Wes clams up and goes rigid, but the part of him that's in control of his arms and legs goes right for Freddy Peters' fucking throat. A Sophomore year summer in boxing classes two counties over comes back like riding a bike and, after a minute, Wes feels somebody dragging him off of Freddy Peters— it's Bart Chomski saying *dude, chill, you're gonna*—

And then Bart shuts up because Jaxson is wandering out of the cafeteria, and he surveys the scene and sends his foot into Bart's knees and grabs Freddy by the collar of his jacket and headbutts him and steps on his hand and punches him right in the nose.

"This is a hate crime," Freddy whines, stifling a small trickle of blood from his right nostril. "The gays are trying to kill me."

Harley Daniels rolls his eyes again and asks, "Are we fucking done here? Have you made your point, Fred?"

Freddy grumbles, "I'm telling Principal Morales that the gays are trying to kill me."

Jaxson cackles, high and manic. "Was this for attention!?"

141

he snaps, "Still, Freddy? What the fuck is wrong with you?"

Freddy snaps back, "No, this is about getting homosexuality banned in Swisher! Come on, Bart."

And then they skitter back the way they came, still too entrenched in their own little world to recognize anything outside of themselves.

"A-a-are they actually t-tr-t-trying to ba-b-ban being gay?" Wes asks, adrenaline buzzing in every nerve, while he and Jaxson catch their breath.

Jaxson waves a hand, "I mean, maybe, but they can't get far. I think it's illegal to try." He rubs at his nose. There's a bruise growing just between his eyebrows from the headbutt. "Anyway," he nods to Taylor, "what the fuck happened to you, bitch?"

Taylor replies inexpressively from the floor, "He got me good."

"C-c-can you st-st-stand u-"

"Breathe, Wes."

And Wes does. Then tries again. "Can you stand up?"

"Sure." And Taylor tries. He gets almost to his elbows before he falls back down.

"Jesus— Jesus Christ, are you d-d-dying!?"

"I'm fine, Wes. Don't freak out. Jaxson, can you, like, I dunno, do something?"

And Jaxson would love to, but he's also a little unnerved by the part of this where Taylor can't get up, so he hesitates. He hardly feels the panic rising in his gut, and he hardly feels himself murmuring, "I don't know why he isn't getting up. Why isn't he getting up?" In all the time Jaxson has known Taylor, Taylor *always* gets back up.

It only takes maybe a few seconds for Collin to exit the

cafeteria next. As he opens the door, he's mumbling, "Now just where did Jax run off to," and as the door closes behind him he's saying, "Well there you are, I was gettin' worried you'd be doin' somethin' stupid without me, and look, I sure was right. You three're all kinds of messed."

First, Collin tells Wes that everything is going to be fine, and to try to breathe, then he makes sure Taylor isn't dead, then he checks on Jaxson's forehead, and then he says, "Why ain't nobody helpin' Taylor off the floor?"

Taylor immediately says, "Because I don't need help," and proves himself wrong by not even justifying his body with an attempt.

Collin forcibly pulls Taylor to his feet, and then they all walk into the cafeteria together.

Nobody mentions the fact that it definitely looks like these three got into a fight— because it's Taylor Macready, and it's expected— but they stare a little because now there's also Jaxson Dixon with a bruise on his forehead and Wes Post with scratches on his neck and face.

Dalton and Todd, however, groan before Collin can even finish telling them that there was a fight in the hallway.

"Wes, what the fuck did that to your neck?" Todd asks, "It looks gnarly."

Wes hadn't realized that he had gotten scratched at all, and Jaxson answers for him, "Bart Chomski's disgusting fingernails. The guy never trims them, just bites them a lot."

Dalton feigns a gag, then moves on to ask, "And Jaxson, is that bruise from another of the Three Musketwats?"

With a grin, Jaxson nods, "Freddy Peters."

Taylor glares at Dalton and Todd, trying to cow them into silence. It doesn't work because they've known him for too long.

"Going by the band-aid," Todd deduces, "Freddy Peters didn't do that to your face."

"Fuck off, Todd."

"Dude," Dalton whines, "you can't keep doing that. Go to the gym or some shit, like a normal person!"

"Do what, fellas?" Collin interrupts. He has no clue what they're talking about, and neither, to an extent, do Wes or Jaxson.

Todd grumbles something about *delinquent son, bullshit*, and then says, "Stop me when I'm wrong, Taylor. You were... pissed about... something, I don't know; so you went out and found someone willing to kick your ass, but underestimated just how badly they would kick your ass; you dragged yourself home— er," Todd gets uncharacteristically self-conscious over that slip-up and quickly corrects, "to Wes, I guess, and he patched you up (thank you for that, Wes) but, and this is just a wild shot in the dark, you didn't tell anyone how badly that guy you picked a fight with kicked your ass, and that's having repercussions now."

"Congratu-fucking-lations, Todd," Jaxson giggles, "that's the most sarcasm I've ever heard from you."

"How many times do you think Taylor has done this over the years?" Todd deadpans.

Even Dalton is stone-faced for once. "How bad is it actually, Taylor?" he asks.

Taylor shrugs.

Dalton rolls his eyes, trying for playful if serious won't work, and says, "Don't think I won't pull your shirt off like a dirty toddler in the middle of the cafeteria," and he pushes out of his chair and starts yanking on the edge of Taylor's t-shirt collar. Everyone laughs, and Collin finally rediscovers his appetite and begins to dig into leftover chicken-fried-rice. Jaxson steals the carrots out of Collin' food. Wes nibbles his sandwich, made by Taylor this morning. Todd sips his juice pouch and tells Dalton and Taylor to knock it off, stop acting like hooligans. Dalton says *yes, dad*. Taylor flips Todd off, but he's smiling a bit more than he was before lunch.

Mrs. Herrick sees the scratches on Wes's face and neck and gasps aloud, asking him if he's alright, if he needs to see the nurse, does he need any help. Wes says he's fine, thanks, and goes back to his exploration of beginner's optical illusions.

Ms. Porter sees Taylor, bruised and walking funny, and sighs heavily, but doesn't press it, just delivers her lecture on Oscar Wilde's plays.

Wes arrives second, after Monique Feldman who stays in her seat between fourth and fifth period, to Mr. Bloomquist's class. Mr. Bloomquist is still on his phone, but he peeks over the edge of the wallet-case when Monique gasps and meets Wes where he's standing in the middle of the room.

"Wes, what happened to your face?" she demands.

"Um, it's kinda a long story-"

"No, I mean who did you fight."

"Oh, Bart Chomski and Freddy Peters."

Mr. Bloomquist chuckles to himself, and pretends that the humor was found in his phone screen.

Monique frowns. "Those fucking dickwads," she grumbles, "I'm gonna have to talk to Harley about those two. They're not redeemable people but he just goes on and on about how they're the only friends he's ever had, and change is hard. God, it's all so messed up—"

"Monique, since when was Wes your couples' counselor?" Taylor asks. He slipped into the room about ten seconds ago and has been listening to the tail end of her rant. Wes is too polite to tell Monique that he both doesn't know what to do about her boyfriend and actively dislikes him. Taylor seeks to be as impolite as possible on a daily basis, and therefore has no trouble telling Monique Feldman to leave Wes alone. Even if she does make Taylor nervous once in a while.

Monique gives him a dirty look and sits back down next to Allison, who is only marginally less of a loose cannon, and continues telling her about how much she hates all men. Mr. Bloomquist drops his phone into his desk drawer and rolls his wheely desk chair over to Wes and Taylor.

He does not stand up from the chair, but he does ask, "Alright, what happened to you two?"

"Huh!?" Wes twitches. Mr. Bloomquist is actively uninterested in anything he's not paid to pay attention to. Wes never thought he'd have to deal with Mr. Bloomquist interrogating him!

"Nothing," Taylor says flatly.

Mr. Bloomquist grumbles, and swivels in his chair, but presses the issue in an uncharacteristic show of concern. "Did you two fight? Come on, what happened?"

Taylor and Wes glance at each other. Wes chuckles at the thought of fighting Taylor. Taylor says, "We didn't fight. Freddy Peters and Bart Chomski picked a fight before lunch."

Mr. Bloomquist does a double-take at each of them. He doesn't laugh, but he grins. "You two?" he clarifies, sounding a little excited and a little flabbergasted, "Freddy Peters picked a fight with you two about that? I thought for sure he'd go after the Dixon kid, or his boyfriend, what's-his-name...

Donahue."

"Why do you a-ask?" Wes wants to know.

The bell rings. Class is supposed to start, but most of them are enthralled watching Monique and Allison discursively eviscerate one of the kids who never shuts up about Alexander Hamilton and WWII, Darius— Darius mentioned something about gay marriage being unnatural and both girls lost their minds.

Mr. Bloomquist, content with the class being occupied for a minute, leans closer, conspiratorial, and explains, "About seven minutes ago I get an email from Principal Morales. Freddy Peters and Bart Chomski and Harley Daniels come waddling in, covered in bruises, saying they're victims of a hate crime. They say a bunch of homosexual kids jumped them for being straight. Of course, Principal Morales isn't stupid, so he told them to go back to class or go home, and to stop picking fights, but it's also Freddy Peters, and we all know how that kid's mom is, so Morales sent out an email asking teachers to give their fifth-period classes a talk about acceptance."

Taylor can't help but mutter, "You're shitting me."

Mr. Bloomquist gives him a look about the language, but continues with a nod. "I won't be doing that, because I think it's stupid and nobody is checking— and I've got tenure, what are they gonna do about it?" He takes a breath, and another, and then looks at Taylor and Wes and laughs again. "But, man is it funny to know that Freddy Peters picked a fight with *Taylor Macready* to try and prove that he was a victim of a hate crime." Mr. Bloomquist doesn't bring up the other part, about them being gay, because it's so much funnier to him that those three hooligans went to the one kid who would fight a mayfly

147

and tried to say he 'targeted' them for anything.

Then he swivels his chair again and rolls away to break up the fight on the other side of the room. Allison has Darius by the throat and Monique is giving the synopsis of queer history in America to anyone who's listening to her over Darius's death throes. Mr. Bloomquist tells them to knock it off and they do, sort of. Allison stops trying to kill Darius anyway.

And the lesson continues as if Freddy Peters didn't intentionally get himself beat up to try and prove that homosexuals are a danger to society, and as if he didn't convince Darius of the same, and as if Mr. Bloomquist didn't willfully ignore Darius getting his ass beat for believing that. No, currently it is time to learn about the inception of the electoral college and how useless and stupid Mr. Bloomquist believes it to be.

12

Things Can Still Hurt Without Bleeding

After class, Jaxson and Dalton (no friendship has ever formed faster) accost Wes and Taylor outside Mr. Bloomquist's classroom, with Todd and Collin in tow.

"Wes. Wessy. My main man Wes," Jaxson says with a wicked smile, "your parents are out of town, right?"

Wes shrugs Dalton off where he's clinging and stammers, "U-uh, yeah?"

Dalton grabs both of Wes's hands and spins him in a wide enough circle to cut off the flow of foot traffic, and the group catches a few annoyed glares and a few surprised glances, but they don't move. "You should let us come over for a sleepover."

"It's a school night!" Wes cries.

"I don't have any homework," Todd counters. "Do you?"

Collin shakes his head. He looks nervous, inexplicably. Almost quiet enough to miss, he says, "You sure would be helpin' me out a ton." He's worrying his lip between his teeth, and there's scabbing evidence that he's been doing it all day. "My parents are headed to a PTA meeting, which means they'll want me to hang out with Freddy Peters and his bunch, and—" he glances at Taylor briefly, and then shrugs, "I— well, I don't do as well with fighting."

Mostly to Wes, but definitely including everyone in a tacit pact, Jaxson says "Come on, Wes, we won't trash your house— I promise!" He winks at Taylor, which is the only indication Taylor or anyone else gets that Collin is much more nervous than he lets on (which is a metric fuckton of nervous) and that Jaxson is operating as a distraction.

"*He* promises," Dalton laughs, "I never promised anything." When Taylor elbows Dalton's stomach, Dalton rolls his eyes and changes his tune. "Fine, fine, I won't be a pest."

Wes wrings his hands, but when he looks around, all the faces are friends. He grins. "Alright. You guys can come over." He's never had many people over before. Monique visited once for an English project, Taylor now temporarily lives with them, and there's been a few people who've been over for an hour or so at a time, but now— this will be *five* people! At once! In his house! Like he's got not just *one friend*, which would have been inconceivable a week ago, but a *group* of friends!

There's cheers all around, and everyone begins the forward march to the Post household. As they walk, they exchange the latest gossip— Mr. Co is still missing, Mr. Fieberg won't shut up about how much he hates his girlfriend's cat, Allison tried to kill Darius for saying gay marriage was unnatural— and complain about the weather ("too damn cold," "it's December in Iowa, Todd, what do you want?" "I dunno, less cold?") and debate on what they're having for dinner, pizza or Chinese.

"It's Wes's house," Dalton says, "he should pick!"

"You're just saying that because you both want pizza!" Jaxson insists.

"Wes, Taylor, and Collin haven't said anything," Todd points out, "so far it's just you two yelling at each other—let someone else give an opinion."

"And what do you think, Todd?" Jaxson asks, "you think Mr. Meng's is better, right?"

"I think both of them are gonna give us all indigestion."

"Pft. What do you know anyway? Okay, Collin? Babe? It's gotta be Mr. Meng's."

Collin frowns, blinks hard, and his eyes light up in a manic way, "Sure!" he forces. "Whatever's the least trouble."

Dalton and Todd and Wes and Taylor laugh at the joke. But Jaxson falls behind the group a little so he can come up behind Collin and wrap him in his arms and ask, "You alright, cute stuff? You're sounding a little, uh, nervous." He knows how Collin gets when his parents are too much. That's why he suggested a sleepover. Will Collin's parents kill Jaxson and punish Collin in ways that might violate the Geneva Convention? Likely, but Jaxson has until tomorrow to brainstorm another brilliant plan to keep his boyfriend as far from his parents as possible.

Collin sighs heavily and leans into Jaxson. "Sure thing, Jax." Jaxson wiggles him around, because that wasn't an answer, and Collin grumbles and giggles and says, "Alright, alright. I'm tryin' to be okay today, but it ain't workin out too great. I just wish—" he stops himself. "Nevermind. Sorry, Jax, I'll try to get it in check."

Jaxson wants to say no, don't be sorry, *he's* sorry, but Collin is already catching up to the group in a few running steps and asking them what they're laughing about.

Jaxson rakes a hand through his hair. To himself, or maybe the sky, he mutters, "Today just sucks."

Wes doesn't have any gaming consoles, since he's never had anyone to play them with, so they make do with his PC by taking turns absolutely fucking up a medieval action RPG character's life and getting him arrested for pickpocketing as many times as possible. They're trying to get an arrest in every inn, hamlet, and town in the game. Unless the guard says anything rude to them: if the guard is rude then they kill him and wait for another, nicer guard to bring them to justice. It's fucking hilarious.

Taylor doesn't even want to play because Dalton and Wes are significantly funnier at it. So he watches and laughs and eventually everyone starts dropping off and falling asleep. Todd— the lightweight— goes down first, almost mid-laugh, and they all make fun of him for it.

A while after that Collin crumbles. He's got Jaxson curled sideways on his lap, and somehow isn't super fucking uncomfortable with Jaxson's bony shoulder digging into his side.

When it's Wes's turn to fuck around with the character again, Dalton drops like a bag of sand on the bed.

When Wes yawns (he literally yawned, bleary-eyed and sleepy, and Taylor is not thinking about that at all), Taylor offers to take the controls. Wes says yeah, alright, sure, and then falls asleep immediately on the bed next to Dalton. Taylor would take a picture if Jaxson wasn't still awake and watching. He dicks around with the character, makes him join the thieves guild and get caught on every mission. Around one in the morning Jaxson says he wants to go explore a cave system, Taylor says fuck, man, go for it, and sits on the floor next to where Todd passed out. While Jaxson is distracted fighting some dwarves, Taylor puts a pillow on the ground and pushes Todd's head onto it so he won't wake up with a stiff neck, and covers him with a blanket so he won't get too cold.

It's only when Taylor's eyes shoot open from a dream he hadn't realized he'd been having that he recognizes that he'd fallen asleep at all. It's a comfortable way to wake up, once the nightmare wears off. This is how it always goes at sleepovers with Taylor, he can never sleep peacefully when there's so many people so nearby.

Wes and Dalton are still dead asleep on the bed, and Todd is still passed out on the floor, and Collin is scrunched in the office chair, but the dining chair that they had set in front of the computer is unoccupied and Jaxson isn't in the room. The energy of the house is tilted sideways and pressed flat. It doesn't feel like a late-night piss break. Taylor doesn't like the queasy feeling his stomach has about it. He scrubs his eyes out of dreamland and steps gingerly over Todd and around the office chair and out of Wes's bedroom.

The bathroom light is on, which means Jaxson is probably in there, but the door is open, meaning he's probably not peeing. When Taylor passes the door, Jaxson has a little, thumb-sized package of replacement blades to fit into a safety razor opened up on the counter.

Jaxson says, "Hey, dude, what's up?" As if that's a normal response to any of what Taylor is seeing.

Taylor just sees Jaxson with a fresh razor blade he dug out of the medicine cabinet. And he knows what people do with fresh razor blades that they've dug out of medicine cabinets. And he says, "Dude, what the fuck."

Jaxson knows he can't hide it, but he still tries to reason, "It's nothing. Go to bed." He's sitting very still, like Taylor might not see the blade pressed to the skin if he doesn't move. When Taylor also remains absolutely still, he adds, "Really, don't worry about it, you're dreaming. Just go back to sleep. You won't even remember this happening when you wake up." This lie has worked countless times on Juniper-Maisie, when she was little, and it worked once on Collin.

Taylor can't even think. Doesn't understand anything going on around him. Static is creeping into his ears, his feet, his chest. The world is made of TV static except that razor blade between Jaxson's fingers and the guilty look on Jaxson's face. He unglues his feet from the hallway carpet and steps into the bathroom and says, again, "Dude, what the fuck."

"Sh! Don't wake anyone up," Jaxson hisses. Taylor hadn't realized he'd shouted. "Why are you even awake?"

Taylor doesn't panic easily, but when there's a guy about to slit his wrists in your friend's bathroom at a sleepover, there's not a whole lot of other ways to react. He moves to pull on his hat, and realizes it fell off while he was asleep. "Jaxson—" he feels like he should say something, but he has no clue what to say. Should he go get Collin? Collin would know what to do. It's his boyfriend after all. If he didn't flip his lid— would Collin flip his lid? Jesus fucking Christ. What comes out of Taylor's mouth is a ragged "Why?"

Jaxson giggles the way people giggle when they're about to cry and are trying to hide it. Jaxson is hiding it better than most. "It's a bad day," he says. "Just go back to bed, Macready. I'll see you in the morning."

"No fucking way," Taylor snaps.

In the back of his mind, the part of him that he was last week is telling him that this isn't his problem, and that if Jaxson says he's fine, he's fine. That part of him was too terrified for himself to be worried about anyone else, and that part of him had no examples of care to draw from, but it's been an eventful week and Taylor will deal with the fact that he is now a person he hardly recognizes later, when Jaxson has put away the fresh razor blade he dug out of the medicine cabinet.

The part of Taylor that put a blanket on Todd a few hours ago and let Collin help him to his feet this afternoon and made Wes a sandwich this morning snatches another of the stack of fresh blades from the thumb-sized box and shows that he cares in the only way he knows how: by doing. He says, "Whatever you do, I do."

Jaxson blinks. Says, "No— dude, put the fucking razor down."

"Sure, when you do."

"Jesus— Taylor, no. I'm built different. I'll be fine." Jaxson runs his free hand through his hair, razor blade still gripped firmly between two fingers resting on the bathroom counter. Taylor doesn't relax, because Jaxson is still talking. He picks his way around his words as he tries to explain, "If I slit my wrist, we all wake up tomorrow and go to school; if you slit your wrist, we all drive you to the hospital."

Taylor has no clue what Jaxson's talking about. He's not sure Jaxson knows what Jaxson's talking about. He doesn't put down the razor blade.

Jaxson giggles again, but it's a little more hoarse, and his eyes are a little wetter. He's thinking about how, once, he wished someone would find out. Wished they would tell him to stop. Wished they would care. Collin cares, now, but now the razor blade is a habit and Jaxson just needs something to hurt and he wants Taylor to go away so he can hurt in the peace of this unfamiliar bathroom.

He starts to dig the edge of the blade in—determined to call Taylor's bluff— but Taylor *actually* copies him and Jaxson drops the razor when he sees the blood start to well up on Taylor's forearm.

"Dude what the fuck!?" he screeches, standing up, putting some distance between himself, the razor he stole, Taylor and the well of red beginning to drip down his forearm. To someone, maybe Taylor, or himself, or the shadows of their little sisters in the corners of the bathroom, he rushes to clarify, "I didn't think— Jesus, I didn't think he'd actually—" but, even to the shadows, he can't get the sentence out.

Within about fifteen seconds Wes slams open the door and skids into the room, followed by Todd, the lightest sleepers.

What Wes sees is both Jaxson and Taylor halfway through slitting their wrists, and Jaxson is laughing and crying and Taylor is looking at Jaxson in the same angry way that he stared at the comforter on the pullout couch that first day after Wes brought him home.

He doesn't want to panic, he tries to stay calm, but when two of your friends are slitting their wrists in your bathroom at a sleepover, there aren't a whole lot of other ways to react. He immediately bursts into hiccuping tears. He can't even think clearly enough to speak. He's stammering on the outset of a word but he can't get past the first syllable.

Todd is also panicking, but he crushes the feeling in favor of storming into both Taylor and Jaxson's personal space and carefully removing the razor blade from Taylor's fingers (he practically drops it into Todd's hand) and then he makes sure the cuts aren't going to kill anyone (they're not, neither of them is longer than an inch nor bleeding profusely) and then he moves to comfort the two who are crying. He snaps (he doesn't mean to snap), "Taylor, can you calm Wes down, you're better at that."

So while Todd asks Jaxson what's wrong, what happened, why, Taylor shuffles up to Wes, almost embarrassed. "Wes. I'm not dead. Jaxson's fine. Why're you crying?"

There's three different stutter-starts where Wes tries to answer and is cut off by a wave of his own tears. When he finally gets more than a word out, it's "y-y-y-you-ou we-ere g-g-gonn-nna-... why— *fuck*— w-w-wou-would y-you?"

And finally, seeing it on such an open, trusting face, Taylor can categorize the feeling he felt when he entered the bathroom: fear.

Not fear for himself, fear for someone else.

"Sorry," he mutters. "Sorry." For no discernible reason, he feels his eyes well with tears, and he pulls Wes into a hug so nobody else can see him crying. "Sorry," he repeats. "I didn't— I mean, I wouldn't—" he can't finish the sentence. Drawn by the noise of Wes's slowing tears and Todd's quiet nudges to get Jaxson to talk to him and Jaxson's giggling sobs, Dalton and Collin meander towards the bathroom.

Dalton says, "What's going on? Bathroom party?"

Todd doesn't want to answer that. Why should he? He barely knows what's going on! But everyone else is crying, so he answers, "I don't know but Jaxson and Taylor were playing with sharp objects."

Collin hears this and perks up, scans the bathroom, sees the razor, and lets out a barking laugh that doesn't sound happy. He laughs and laughs until everyone is a little freaked out, but he doesn't stop. Just keeps laughing.

"Can someone please explain at least one part of this bullshit to me!?" Todd demands. His voice stretches itself thin like a rubber band before it breaks.

Jaxson mutters, "Not if I can help it."

"Ha-ha, very funny, Dixon," Todd jabs, "What the fuck were you and Taylor doing!?"

"Nothing!" Jaxson cries, "Just leave me alone! I'm *fine!* I was almost done anyway." He feels like a cornered animal, caught rifling through the garbage.

"Almost done what!? Cutting yourself!?" Todd snaps, which is the first Dalton is hearing of this and it shows in the widening of his eyes, the sudden set of his jaw.

Collin's laugh gets a little higher in pitch.

"I'm not going to explain it to you," Jaxson starts to hiss, defensive, "I can't—"

Collin's laugh cuts off abruptly and stomps past everyone else into Jaxson's space. "Jax," he snaps, barely three inches from his face, "if you do this again I'm through. With everything."

Which leaves Jaxson with an ultimatum that he doesn't even have to think about. He lets a few more tears roll before scrubbing all evidence of them away with the heel of his palm and crossing the room and pulling Collin into a hug and planting a kiss on the top of his head and whispering, "Okay. Alright. Sorry, babe. I'll tell them. Don't you leave me."

"You bet yer sorry ass I won't," Collin sniffles back, eyes steely and dark and spilling over onto his cheeks.

Taylor has recovered enough from the shock of almost accidentally slitting his wrists to try and save a guy he's known for almost a decade but only been friends with for a little less than a week to peek over Wes's shoulder. Jaxson is holding Collin the same way that Wes is holding Taylor. Taylor doesn't know how uncomfortable that makes him, but he does know he's not ready to let go. Wes deserves better, but Taylor can have a few seconds, right? Just for now? He'll let go soon.

He blinks, and he has been shuffled into Wes's bedroom with everyone else. It's not even five am. It was barely three when he found Jaxson in the bathroom. What happened in the interim? People are talking, but Taylor can't decipher the words. Someone has their hands in his hair. He both feels entirely outside himself and like his blood is scraping his veins with a cheese grater.

"No we didn't *plan* it," Jaxson is saying heatedly, "Taylor just came into the bathroom and did that."

Dalton moans, "How come I've seen my best friend break down more this week than in the entire rest of our lives?"

"Can we focus?" Todd asks sharply, stressed, "Please? Jaxson, you wanna explain yourself?"

"Not really."

"Jax, please."

Jaxson sighs like he's breaking under too much weight. Taylor remembers hearing him sigh like that when they were sitting on Taylor's back porch maybe six years ago listening to their little sisters play dolls, and Juniper-Maisie's doll and Hellen's doll were arguing about where to bury the only boy doll they had, because Hellen's doll had killed him for being mean to Juniper-Maisie's doll. The girls had been laughing. Jaxson had sighed just like that.

"I like hurting sometimes," Jaxson says. Taylor feels the skin on his face crinkle more than he registers any emotion like concern. "It's just. It's just nice. Sometimes, ya know?"

"What!?" comes from three voices, and Taylor can't tell if one of them is his or not. Probably not, because he gets it. Hellen and Juniper-Maisie are friends partially because their brothers are cut from the same cloth.

Dalton asks, "Dude, why!?"

"I dunno. It just, ya know, like, sucks me in, I guess? Like, for a second there's just one little fucked up thing instead of all the bigger fucked up things. It's nice."

"Nice!?"

"Wait," Wes says, and that voice is so close that Taylor realizes he's still right next to Wes, still holding onto his t-shirt. "Wait, how long has th-this been going on?"

Jaxson replies sardonically, "I don't keep a diary log of it, Post." But he rolls his eyes back as he thinks and he eventually says, "I dunno. Maybe seventh grade?"

Because in seventh grade he lost all three of his friends in one day because they decided it wasn't worth it to be friends with a gay boy.

They spend several hours untangling What Happened To Jaxson Dixon. Taylor fades in and out of focus, but he gets the picture. Jaxson's parents suck ass, he knew that, and they always apologize with dollar-store snack cakes after they go too far with the corporal punishment. Before seventh grade, even when he would hang out with Harley and Freddy and Bart, they said the bruises looked badass. They never asked where he got them. Probably they knew, and just didn't care. After seventh grade, his parents started deciding he was too big to punish, but Jaxson still got low. He'd use whatever. He's got a few cigarette burns. Some cuts. Some little dots where he'd stick a safety pin in and wiggle it around. Collin caught him once, last year, and made him promise to cut it out, but Taylor knows better than anyone you can't just quit a habit like that.

"Jesus, dude," Dalton mutters.

They're trying not to freak out about it. Be cool, ya know? But when you find out a guy you barely know has been opening himself up with razor blades for six years there aren't a whole lot of other ways to react.

Taylor, for his part, says nothing, feels nothing, and is altogether exactly as ignored as he would like to be tonight. Just stews in the new information and tries to remember every time Jaxson Dixon has ever come to school with long sleeves for his crop tops and high-waisted jeans and holds tight onto Wes's t-shirt as a tether to reality.

13

Near Misses

Wes doesn't sleep at all for the rest of the night. Everyone else falls back asleep for those wee hours between five-thirty and seven-thirty, but Wes stays wide awake, resisting the urge to pull Taylor closer—which would be practically impossible, Taylor is already curled up halfway in his lap holding onto Wes's t-shirt. That's part of what's keeping Wes awake, actually. Taylor being this close makes his skin feel like a thousand static shocks and he feels as wired as ever.

Jaxson's issue is also a lot to take in, and Wes was not blessed with a natural affinity for sleep anyway, so he just stays awake and thinks about it all.

It makes sense— puts some puzzle pieces in place, answers some nagging mysteries— but fuck. Who leaves behind a friend when they're at their lowest and being treated like shit at home!? Even Freddy Peters and his lot aren't that cruel, right? No, apparently they *are* that cruel, and Wes laments several times in the few solitary hours of consciousness that he didn't get a few more hits in on Freddy's stupid face.

When Wes is very sure that everyone is asleep and definitely not looking at him, he carefully pries Taylor's arm from his t-shirt. The cut in the crook of his elbow isn't big, and the blood is all dried down where it smeared on his forearm, but there's a cut there, right above the fading marks where Taylor had dug his nails into his skin the first night he stayed on the pullout couch. He had clung to Wes that night too.

Neither Jaxson nor Taylor had been willing to talk about what went on in the bathroom; Jaxson because of the way Collin was looking at him and Taylor because Taylor hadn't responded to much of anything last night. The unresponsiveness worried Wes a little, but he didn't want to freak out more and make everything more complicated, so he focused a lot of energy on staying calm, allowing his mind to feel what it felt without allowing those feelings to overwhelm his body. It worked as best it could, in the circumstances.

God, what a week for his therapist to be out on vacation.

He grimaces at the new little cut. At the crescent nail bites from earlier in the week. At the bandages wrapped around Taylor's knuckles from Wednesday. Todd and Dalton hadn't seemed worried at all for Taylor, despite all the injury his body is accumulating, and Wes remembers seeing Taylor stumble into class looking worse than this— and before he'd always thought it had been cool in a tough-guy way, had thought Taylor must not even feel pain because he's already had so much of it. But here he is, clutching Wes's t-shirt and sleeping like a rock. Wes can still feel the phantom of the spot where Taylor's tears soaked through his sweater on Wednesday night when he cried for absolutely no reason in the kitchen. Just because Taylor has felt pain before doesn't mean he can no longer feel it.

And Wes finds the shattered image of this monolith so much lovelier.

He's been running his fingers through Taylor's hatless hair for hours.

When his phone goes off, Wes vaguely wonders who could be contacting him in such wee hours of the morning, but he opens his phone to a text from his parents in Rosarito, an hour behind them.

Mom: hey sweetie- just checking in

Everything still okay at home?

Your dad and I got caught in a layover at LAX for a few hours, so we just got to our hotel

Ready for your math test today? You said you had one for logarithms, right? I know you can do it! We believe in you!

I know this isn't the same as our morning notes, but we just wanted to say we're so happy that you have some friends to spend the holidays with! Text me when you're out of school

Wes checks the time on his phone. Then he screeches loud enough to wake up Todd, Taylor, and Collin, "It's s-s-seven-thir-thirty!"

Dalton drags his head up about an inch off the floor where he'd fallen asleep and slurs, "So? It's Saturday."

Todd has more of his wits about him, "No, it's Friday! Shit!"

Everyone is a flurry of activity, pulling sweaters over shirts, trading sweatpants for jeans, donning hats, taking meds, and Taylor and Dalton work together to make six lunches for everyone while Wes throws muffins at everyone as they exit the house. The whole way there, Todd is bemoaning his lack of preparedness for his Calculus test, and Jaxson is reminding him dude, it's fucking Calculus, that class isn't made to be passable and Mr. Simon is a well-established dick about it.

Collin says he still hasn't memorized his lines for the Hamlet reading they're supposed to be doing in his second period Advanced Drama class, and Jaxson pulls up the lines on his phone and helps Collin give them a live performance as they speedwalk to school.

They split up at the school's front gate and go their separate ways, each making it to class with about fifteen seconds to spare.

Mr. Fieberg gives them a surprise quiz instead of collecting the homework that neither Taylor, Wes, nor Jaxson did last night, which is a blessing and a curse because who the fuck actually knows how to solve these fucking equations?

After the quiz, potentially as an apology, Mr. Fieberg turns on the Bill Nye the Science Guy film of popular choice (the photosynthesis one, the farthest they could manage to get from physics) and lets that play until class is over.

Ms. Merino-Ott, as promised, turns on a movie as well. "How the Grinch Stole Christmas." She spends most of the class chatting with Monique Feldman and Celsee Stevens at their table near the front. Taylor and Wes and Jaxson, and even their tablemate, Rose, snicker at the Grinch's bitterness, and they all joke that guy needs to *get a life, take up knitting, I don't fuckin' know, something.*

Mrs. Woolley, having prepared herself for the beehive buzz of excited seniors ready for their last Winter Break of high school, is especially stern when she directs them to their seats, passes out the tests, and demands silence for the duration of the test. Wes has been on edge since almost being late this morning, and Mrs. Woolley has to come to the back row twice to ask him not to mutter the answers out loud.

Before lunch, there is an assembly.

Principal Morales gives a brief spiel on the importance of flu safety measures (washing your hands, not sharing drinks, etc) before handing the mic off to Danny Abelman for his yearly Hanukkah talk. Ever since his family got the school district to make all Winter Breaks inclusive of Hanukkah, he gives a big old speech about it on the last Friday before Winter Break. He calls it educational, but after three years of this shit, the power point is only new to the freshmen.

Then Freddy Peters comes up, allegedly to talk about acceptance, and delivers a thinly veiled speech about the threats to American values that is only barely not openly calling for a ban on homosexuality in schools across America, and when it doesn't catch, he ends it on a solemn note and sits down as if the silence is poignant and not crickets.

Awkwardly, Principal Morales releases them to lunch.

"Taylor, you did not pack us baby carrots," Todd says, in as shocked a tone as Todd ever sounds. If he weren't so surprised, you would be able to tell that he's flipping through a thesaurus in his head trying to find the right word to describe the emotion he's feeling about Taylor packing him baby carrots with a peanut butter and honey sandwich and one leftover sugar cookie from the coffee shop. He can't find the right word at all, but it makes him smile, and giggle. Friends of Todd Richards know that he hasn't brought a homemade lunch to school since sixth grade.

Taylor flips Todd off.

Dalton seizes the opportunity to be dramatic. "He insisted on baby carrots. I tried saying that a sandwich was enough, but he was all '*no*, we need to be healthy.' And then he called me mean names."

Collin, who had forgotten that Taylor made them all lunch this morning, says that sounds out of character for Taylor, and it is. But Taylor is going red in the ears about it now (not that you can see his ears from under his hat, but the color leaks into his cheeks eventually, and those are visible), so they change topics to making fun of him for his blushing, and then he tells Dalton that he will kick his ass for mentioning it one more time, and Collin distracts everyone with a hyperbolic retelling of how disastrously Polonius' speech went in his second period Advanced Drama class, as delivered by Tina, the senior, who really should be better at this by now.

Jaxson, who everyone knows hasn't had a single lunch packed for him by anyone in his life, stares at the baby carrots for so long that Todd asks if he doesn't like carrots. Jaxson nudges him and says shut up, who doesn't like carrots? Then he stares at the little cut in the crook of his elbow. He's too tired to parse it all out, but he looks at Taylor and squints between him and Wes for a second when nobody is looking.

Collin has fourth-period trigonometry with Jaxson. After that it's fifth-period history, also together. Then Collin can choose to either go home to his parents, who spent most of Wednesday night and Thursday morning being downright mean, and will be meaner still since he stayed out without permission last night, or he can hang out with his boyfriend, who still hasn't explained himself after last night's hullabaloo.

Jaxson has never been able to handle Collin when he's

peeved. They're not even to Mx. Indi's door when Jaxson drags Collin to the side of the hallway and pins him there and says, "What."

Collin gives Jaxson an unimpressed face. If Jaxson weren't so clearly upset today, Collin would hold it against him more that he absolutely knows what Collin is upset about. But he is clearly upset today, and Collin isn't cruel, so he spells it out.

"Yer not bein' fair, Jax," he explains, "last night was scary, and you won't tell me what happened!"

"If I tell you what happened will you stop looking at me like that?"

"Like what?"

Jaxson's expression is dramatically aghast and he throws his arms out in a wild gesture of exasperation, but Collin just crosses his arms and waits for Jaxson to answer. He does, slowly, laughing, nervous, "Like you don't like me or something, I dunno."

The bell rings. They should be in trig now, but Collin knows Mx. Indi won't notice or care about their tardiness. Sighing, trying to let go of the frustration before it becomes something closer to anger, Collin smiles at Jaxson, "Alright, Jax. You tell me what happened last night and I won't be mad at ya."

"Thank you," Jaxson exclaims dramatically, "Fuck, you'd think I murdered your firstborn, the way you were staring at me."

And Collin rolls his eyes and drags Jaxson into Mx. Indi's classroom. The teacher doesn't acknowledge their entrance in the middle of an explanation of how, exactly, this class potluck will go down.

On a row of desks pushed to the front of the room, there's all kinds of sweets and some little goldfish crackers and some kind soul brought mini water bottles. Collin and Jaxson had forgotten that Mx. Indi had made today a class party— 'to celebrate the time of rest, if nothing else,' they had said when they announced it.

Well. On the not-so-bright side, they did not bring any treats, and therefore have to wait to be last to go up and get any of the donut holes Racquelle Turner brought. On the bright side, this gives them plenty of time to talk.

Those who brought the treats get in a neat little line at the front of the room.

Collin says, "Alright, start talkin' mister."

Jaxson has never had trouble telling Collin about anything. He'll get clammy around other people, but when it's just him and Collin, he's an open book, as long as Collin asks. Today is no different. "So, you know my folks have been getting shitty to me and Juniper-Maisie ever since Jeremy moved out." Collin nods, frowning. Jaxson has only really touched the tip of the iceberg with what his parents have been like since his older brother moved out a few months ago, but even that hasn't been pretty. "Yeah, so, this weekend," Jaxson presses on, "they're all on my ass about how I'm never gonna get anywhere and I'll still be living on their couch at thirty and they can't handle how selfish I am. The usual stuff—"

"Jax, you know it ain't true, right?" Collin interjects. He feels like Jaxson knows, but he's saying it so casually, and Collin understands better than anyone how deep words like those can cut. How deep they *have* cut.

"Sure, yeah," Jaxson waves him off, not because he doesn't appreciate it, Collin knows, but because it's hard to do anything other than brush those words off for a barely-18-year-old boy, "but it doesn't feel great when they say it, ya know?

And then on Tuesday they start laying into Juniper-Maisie too: telling her she looks like a whore and that she spends too much time with Hellen and no boys are gonna want her—"

Collin winces, exclaiming, "They don't know yet!?"

He and Jaxson stand up to get their snacks, now that the people who brought them have gotten their share and sat down. They pass through the line quickly, picking their favorites— goldfish and a few donut holes for Collin, those shitty pink sugar cookies and a brownie for Jaxson— before sitting back down at their seats. Mx. Indi glances at them, probably wondering why Jaxson, their favorite, didn't greet them as cheerfully as usual, but then getting distracted by a conversation with Racquelle Turner.

Once they're seated and Jaxson is confident nobody is looking at them or listening in, he replies, "Collin, my dad gave me a black eye and wouldn't let me come home for three days when I even hinted that I might be gay." His face darkens when he says, "I told Juniper-Maisie to keep that shit under wraps. Maybe bi is better to them, but I'm not risking it on my baby sister."

"Aw, man..." Collin murmurs. What else can he say? Jaxson takes a bite of the shitty pink sugar cookie and Collin squeezes him sideways in a little hug.

"Yeah, shit sucks," Jaxson jokes, "it be like that, but so anyway, I told my old man to shut his fuckin' trap about Juniper-Maisie, and I told my ma that she looks more like a whore when she puts on her goddamn pajamas than Juniper-Maisie ever has."

Collin laughs. Jaxson grins a little too. "Well, they didn't like that. Me and you hung out on Wednesday, you know how I was feeling—" which is to say, damn near suicidal, "and then Thursday Freddy just kinda," Jaxson's voice cracks a little, "kinda put the last nail in that fucking coffin, I guess." He laughs, but it's dry and empty, "He hit Taylor so hard he didn't get up— I've never seen Taylor not get up, Collin." This sits heavy between them. Not that Taylor and Jaxson were super close besties or anything, but Taylor is like a big old rock. You never expect it to change. It's scary when it does. Jaxson moves on, both of them trying hard not to think about what it's like to be the kind of person people compare to a big old rock, "Freddy just picked Wes and Taylor because he knows they're *just* starting to get comfortable with being gay. I just—" Jaxson shrugs, "I dunno, I just didn't wanna have to think about it anymore. I wanted to take the edge off."

The pun doesn't provide any of the humor Jaxson meant it with. Collin pulls a face, "You promised you'd stop."

"Sorry, babe."

"Don't sorry me!" Collin cries, just under the din of the class, "You *promised*." After he caught Jaxson in their tree-house putting out a blunt with his thigh, Collin's anxious brain echoes all the ways he knows a person can hurt themselves. Collin hates that, of all the people to fall in love with, he had to pick one who likes to bleed. Collin is not great with first aid. "I have half a mind to go back to bein' angry with you," he grumbles, but there's nothing angry about it, because there's no sense being angry anymore. It would only make things worse. He leans into his boyfriend's side and shoves a donut hole in his mouth.

That gets Jaxson's smile back, just a little. "Well, I'm still here now. Not like I killed myself."

"Not funny," Collin snips, mouth still full of donut hole.

"Yeah. I, uh, I pulled the blades out of Wes's razor—"

"Ewww."

"Oh shut up, his razor *kit*. Because he's one of you rich heathens who has a fucking safety razor. But, uh..." Jaxson's voice trembles again. Which is weird, because for Jaxson, all of this is par for the course, except apparently it isn't, because his voice is trembling. "Uh, Taylor must've woken up. He came into the bathroom and saw what I was doing, er, about to do. He just stared at me for, like, thirty seconds" he laughs, kinda, incredibly cognizant of the cacophony of the class party happening around them, "and then he grabbed one of the razor blades— I should have stopped him but I was kinda panicking. I kept trying to tell him he was dreaming, but he wouldn't listen. He told me that he was gonna do whatever I did."

"What!?" Collin hisses, thinking of how utterly empty Taylor's eyes had been last night, how he had just tucked himself into Wes and not moved until morning, "Why would he do that?"

Collin's shoulders stiffen, and a palpable wave of stress welds him to the shitty plastic chair he's in so strongly his knuckles go white. "What?" he whispers, like that's the only word he's got in him. He thinks of how utterly empty Taylor's eyes had been last night, how he had just tucked himself into Wes and not moved until morning. "Why would he do that?"

"He was trying to stop me," Jaxson says, eyes downcast and arms pulled in tightly.

"But..." Collin trails off, eyes darting to where Jaxson's jacket covers the inch-long cut in the crease of his elbow.

Jaxson explains, "But I thought I could call his bluff— because what kind of idiot would actually do that?— so I started, but then he *actually* copied me, and I freaked out, and then Wes and Todd were in the bathroom and it was a hot mess and then, I mean, shit it was just a *hot* mess."

Collin's jaw hangs open. "Jax!" he stammers, "Babe! You're telling me he—"

"He's fine!" Jaxson promises, "Tiny little cut. Matches mine."

A slow exhale, cortisol cut with norepinephrine. "Thank goodness."

"That's what I'm saying! I didn't think he'd— I didn't think..." Jaxson sighs and finishes his second cookie. "I mean, I dunno. I guess I didn't think he cared that much."

Collin nods. He's thinking about the baby carrots from lunch.

Fifth period passes in a blur of mind-numbing in-class essay-writing. Wes finished ten minutes early, then saw that nobody else was done and pretended to be writing for another five minutes, and then watched Allison turn in her essay, then Monique, and then he turned in his essay, sat down, and the bell eventually rang to dismiss class for Winter Break.

Wes doesn't scream for joy like the other kids when Winter Break begins, but he does try to be the first out the door so he can avoid all the crowds, a strategy that doesn't work at all because long legs have never been able to outrun the truly feral hordes of over-excited teenagers trying to escape school. In genuine Swisher fashion, the horde really is feral, and they trample a freshman a few feet behind Wes in the hallway. Wes is jostled by the crowd for one overwhelming second that he's sure will be the end of his young life before one bandaged fist closes around the hood of his jacket and Taylor yanks him out of the fray. Better to wait it out, even if that option includes being pressed right against Taylor in the corner behind a doorway.

It's not the first time they've been so close, but every time since the Cinnamon Muffin Discussion on Tuesday morning has been increasingly awkward. Wes still has no idea why Taylor would reciprocate his feelings and then say they couldn't date, but whatever emotion fuels that sentiment plays out on Taylor's face every time they're this close. It makes Wes's insides twist and scream and his fingers feel around in his pocket for something to fidget with while the tsunami of excited violence passes.

Once the horde thins, Wes mumbles a stuttering thanks, and Taylor gives him a sideways look that could almost be a smile, if it didn't look so tortured, and they walk to the front of the school.

They're almost to the big, metal front gates when they hear, "Taylor Thomas Macready, what kind of trouble have you gotten yourself into now?"

Taylor flinches, stops, turns. A moment of unadulterated panic flickers in his expression, but it's gone even faster than it came— either because the panic has passed or because Taylor has buried it. Wes shivers.

To their left, standing with Juniper-Maisie Dixon, is Hellen Macready. Hands on her hips. Chin held high. She stomps up to them with the indignation of a church mother on her way to berate a recent divorcee.

"What do you want, Hellen?" Taylor mumbles. It's not... nice, or even soft the way Wes has seen Taylor be with him, but it's unusually meek— for Taylor anyway.

Hellen folds her arms and growls, "I want to know why I haven't seen you in, like, a month." Juniper-Maisie, who had been texting, swinging her legs over the edge of the table she'd been sitting on, pockets her phone and stands next to Hellen with a polite wave. Everyone knows Juniper-Maisie Dixon doesn't get involved in anything. Hellen doesn't acknowledge Juniper-Maisie's stalwart presence next to her, just continues, "You never came home, fuckhead! You know Mom and Dad don't care, but I do! Why didn't you ever text me?"

Wes twitches and fixes Taylor with a look. A *how the fuck does she not know that you're homeless* kind of look. He would say it out loud if Taylor's expression wasn't so collapsed and desperate and *sensitive*.

For the first time, Wes wonders what, exactly, preceded Taylor living under the bridge on Clearwater Street.

"I figured Mom woulda told you," Taylor says.

Hellen shuts up real quick. The too-fast way. She takes Juniper-Maisie's hand and begins to storm off, "Let's go, Juniper-Maisie. We can pick on your brother next."

"Alright," Juniper-Maisie says with a giggle, like she didn't hear a word of that.

"Wait," Taylor calls, "Hellen!" Hellen stops. She turns. Taylor asks, "What did Mom do?"

Hellen loses the ability to hold eye contact. Juniper-Maisie asks her if she wants to go. Hellen shakes her head. "She didn't do anything yet," Hellen murmurs. "But every time I try to ask why you haven't come home yet..." her voice cracks, but she does an admirable job of finishing her sentence anyway, "Every time I ask, I feel like she might— the way she used to... to you..."

Juniper-Maisie squeezes her hand, "I know, Hells, I know. Com'ere." With her arms safely encompassing Hellen's waist, Juniper-Maisie shoots Taylor (and Wes! Who is doing his best to be a fly on the wall and not be too awkward and also maybe find a good time to leave this conversation, since it's clearly not meant for him!?) a vicious look.

The sun cowers behind a thickening coat of black clouds.

Stumbling back, Taylor starts to escape, but is called back by Hellen, who is recovering herself now. "No, Taylor, wait." Taylor stops. He turns. Hellen asks, "Text me, alright? Just so I know you're not, like, living under a bridge or some dumb shit like that." She laughs, and Juniper-Maisie smiles, and Taylor chuckles, and Wes laughs in a surprised, unhinged kind of way.

It's the first noise he's made since the start of the conversation, and Hellen finally notices him. "You're... Wes, right? Your parents own the coffee shop?"

"Huh!? O-oh, yeah," he waves the most awkward greeting he thinks he's ever waved, "Nice to mee-meet you, Hellen!"

Unlike her brother's first conversation with Wes, she has the tact not to mention how much Wes is stammering. Just smiles, says it's lovely to meet him, and tells him thanks for taking care of her idiot brother. Wes says it's really the other way around, and Taylor says it really isn't, which sends Wes bright red and has both Juniper-Maisie and Hellen howling with laughter.

After Hellen threatens Taylor with death if he doesn't text her "like, at least once a week," Juniper-Maisie reminds Hellen of the GSA meeting they don't want to be late to— giggles and jokes, "you said we could harass my brother next!" The girls leave, and Taylor and Wes exit the school gates just as the first few snowflakes begin to sink from the sky.

"Hey, go home ahead of me," Taylor says. There's a pit of anxiety in Wes's stomach, remembering how well that went on Wednesday, when Taylor came home covered in bruises and scrapes. It must show on his face, because Taylor rolls his eyes and explains, "Todd just texted. His parents left for their trip this morning and he wants to finish up a project."

"But school just got out for break."

"It's due the day we get back. He's just being hyper-prepared again and wants me to listen to him read it out loud to work out the grammar or some shit."

"Oh," Wes murmurs. "Have fun?"

"Sure, you too," Taylor says. "You could take your parents up on that offer to open up the shop for some extra cash. Maybe I'll come get a hot chocolate or something when I'm done helping Todd."

The thought of seeing Taylor at work, for the first time since The Cinnamon Muffin, makes Wes a little giddy. He nods. They go their separate ways.

14

Self Care Can Be a Nap in a Scenic Spot

The snow, while it hadn't really melted from the last storm, exactly one week ago, is refreshing itself after a week of tire tracks and bootprints and harsh winter sunlight. It was a slow night at Post Family Coffee, and customers were sparse. When the sky had darkened and people stopped showing up, Wes closed up and went home. Texted Taylor that he would make him some hot chocolate when he got back. And now he's waiting in the living room, with the TV playing old Christmas movie reruns, in a t-shirt and pajama pants and socks.

His phone rings. It's Todd. Wes wonders if the reason Taylor never responded to his text was because his phone had died, and he answers.

"Hello?"

"Wes? Hey, can you tell Taylor to answer his phone?"

"What?" In an instant, Wes's throat has constricted to the barest needle of air. "H-h-he-he's not w-with you!?"

"What? No, why would he—" Todd stops abruptly. "Taylor's not at your house?" he asks, his voice deathly still and too-knowing.

"I th-tho-thought he was wi-w— at your house!" Wes screeches back.

The sound of rustling items— keys, shoes, jackets— can be heard through the phone. "Jesus Christ," Todd groans, barely within earshot of the receiver, "it's December in Iowa and my stupid best friend has the self-preservation of a fucking possum!"

Wes doesn't respond. The space in his brain usually reserved for putting one word in front of the other is currently dammed up with images of skin as red as cherry cough syrup spilled on a wooden table, of little coughs perforating Wes's eardrums, of Taylor stepping into the porchlight covered in bruises. His eyes are dammed up with tears. His throat is dammed up with bile and— dammit, he's not waiting around to figure out what happened.

He's got something he can do, in this situation. He doesn't bother hanging up on Todd or bringing his phone with him. He sprints out of the house at nearly midnight on Friday, December 18. It's still snowing (and Wes had been so excited for a white Christmas, even if Christmas is a week away), and he wishes the snow would all spontaneously melt. He should have asked Todd when, exactly, he last saw Taylor— if Taylor ever even went to his house for that project.

The snow isn't falling fast, but time feels slippery and evanescent to Wes. He's running, and little flakes are catching on his eyelashes, his coffee-shop scars, the hem of his ugly, hand-me-down Christmas sweater, the edges of the band-aids he's tried to stick on the worst parts of Bart Chomski's fingernail scratches, anything textured enough to stick to. He starts to feel like a snowman. A chill rattles his spine, despite his exertion and his stupid, nonexistent temperature response. He's only been running for ten minutes. He runs faster, breath hiccuping through his trachea, trying to get oxygen to his extremities faster, faster— faster, Jesus, Taylor might—

A hand yanks his shoulder backwards. No, that's not right— the hand just stopped him from running.

"Wes."

Oh, that's Dalton. He's panting. Wearing his thick, leather varsity jacket and still shivering. It must be cold.

"Can. You. Hear. Me?"

Wes nods, still unable to catch his breath, even after he's stood still for something like thirty seconds now. The lost time stretches infinitely across the mangled footprints in the snow, already being dispersed to wind and fresh flakes.

"Fuck, dude, you need to go home."

From somewhere beyond the darkness and snow, Todd calls, "Dalton! Did you catch him!?"

"Yeah!" Dalton calls back. "No, Todd, over here! Under the tree!" The hand that isn't holding Wes in place waves wildly to flag Todd down.

Wes lets out a high, cackling laugh when Todd almost gets lost in the Rorschach of darkness and snowflakes. How long have the streetlights been out? Is the storm that bad? The snow is starting to peter out. It's just windy now.

"Todd, he needs to go home. He can't be out here like this—"

"I know, dude. Can he even hear us?"

"If you talk, like, right in his ear."

"Shit, I don't know how to do this— uh, Wes, buddy. We need you to go home," Todd says, right in Wes's ear. "You're not even wearing shoes." He says it like Wes might not know.

180

He knows he doesn't have shoes on. Who cares about shoes? Taylor is out here somewhere with the self-preservation of a possum.

"You're going to fucking die if you don't get out of the cold," Dalton says, maybe harsher than he meant to, maybe more terrified than he meant to.

"Dude, shut it," Todd snaps. "Wes, listen. We're gonna find Taylor. You go home. Get warm, get changed, and calm down before you come back to help us."

Dalton has reined in the terror enough to try at optimism. "If we haven't already found him by then."

It's a thin veil, even to Wes, but Todd seems put at ease by it. "Right. See, Wes? We'll find him. But you're no use to anyone freezing to death in your pajamas having a panic attack in the dark."

Wes takes one gasping breath (and vaguely remembers that all of his breaths have come in gasps since leaving the house) and forces clarity to his eyes, and says "No."

"Buddy," Dalton tries.

"I'm helping you search."

Todd fixes him with a piercing look that would, under any other circumstances, cow him, nearly a foot of height difference be damned. But not this time— as it is, he isn't sure if he can stack his panic attacks. Just one at a time, one after the other. Maybe he'll flip out about Todd being pissed at him when Taylor isn't freezing to death somewhere in Swisher.

"You kn-know," Wes has to take a breath, mid-sentence, when he feels his chest tighten around his conviction, "I won't be able to calm d-d-down until he's safe." His resolve is rapidly crumbling as awareness of his surroundings, the whistle-wind and the dark and the sogginess in his socks, slams into his brain. But they can't all stack, so it's just one after the other. He can panic about frostbite when Taylor is safe.

"Dude," Dalton speaks softly and wraps his arms around Wes's shoulders. The sudden warmth makes him realize how cold he had been. The disparity is painful. "Go home." There is no context for a hug like this, and Wes's brain might short-circuit if he tries to process the emotion this inspires. His face is wet from snow that's melted on the leather of Dalton's varsity jacket. "If it makes you feel better, double-check everywhere on the way back. We'll look everywhere else in town until we find him." The tears that had felt frozen to Wes's eyelids melt and fall down his face with Dalton's heat. He shakes his head. Dalton presses, "Taylor will just feel shitty if you lose toes trying to find him in the snow in your socks." The laugh is fake and weak, cracking under the weight of the sentiment it supports, but it finally convinces Wes.

"O-o-ok-kay."

Todd looks at him funny over Dalton's shoulder. "Should we walk him home?" he asks.

Wes snaps, "Don't." He wouldn't be able to live with himself if they wasted time walking him home that could have been spent searching for Taylor. Wes's stomach is already curdled with fear.

He pushes off of Dalton and turns back toward his house. He'll go home. Change. Then head back out. Maybe bring a blanket in case he finds Taylor first. But fuck if he doesn't check every nook and cranny while he goes.

And that is exactly how he finds him. No cough this time. But Wes remembers this bridge, on Clearwater Street, and he can't help but go check. So he slides down the embankment to the little dip in the ground where Taylor had lived for four weeks before Wes found him, and where he's been hiding for four hours when Wes finds him again.

"Taylor!"

Taylor is laying on his back, entirely under the bridge, in a flannel and jeans. He doesn't even react at first, just turns his head against the concrete, dusted with a crystalline layer of powder that is heard underfoot more than seen. The streetlights aren't back on yet. But the moon is starting to show its cowardly face as the snow dies out, and Wes has been looking for shadows in the dark all night. He knew Taylor's outline on the ground even without light to distinguish its features by.

"Taylor?"

Taylor's voice mouths Wes's name, but his lungs don't provide the force to speak it. He looks kind of blue in some parts of his face, even the parts that aren't bruised, and it's exaggerated by the deep shadows of the bridge.

"Taylor, you fucker, answer me, are you dead?"

"Clearly not," Taylor whispers, "but thank you for the vote of confidence." He's not even shivering, and his skin doesn't give off any heat when Wes pulls him into his lap. "Wes, what are you doing out here with no shoes?"

Wes finds his own voice collapsing as he bites back, "Looking- f-f-for you. St-tu-stupid."

"Wes, it's alright. You found me. Relax..." Taylor's voice filters into almost nothing by the time it reaches Wes's ears, the stern insistence to be heard lost in the cold.

Wes's whole body twitches in an anxious tic that twisted up with a shiver and seized his hands. "Y-y-you c-c-ca-can't say th-that! You-"

183

"Alright," Taylor whispers weakly. "Alright then." He doesn't press it. Just brushes his fingers against the back of Wes's palm. His fingers are frigid, and, of course, Wes gathers Taylor closer, as close as he can get him, and holds his hands between their chests. Taylor starts to shiver in spaced out little spasms. His fingers squeeze Wes's wrist in familiar time. He's mimicking a breathing exercise— the one Wes had used after the in-class essay earlier that day. Wes feels himself sob, but begins to put herculean effort into calming himself down. Follows the example set by Taylor's hands.

Wes remembers what Todd and Dalton were trying to get him to do. Finally.

When he feels like he can talk, he whispers, "Taylor, we need to go home."

Taylor's eyes are closed. He doesn't answer, just nods. His face is pinched together like he's hurting.

But when Wes tries to stand, he can't. Limbs won't cooperate. Like dandelion vines have crept through the cement and through the snow and into his veins. Holding him down. He doesn't have the strength to get up. It's terrifying.

And, with one panic attack over, he's free to start anew. So he panics again.

"Taylor, I-I- I can't st-tand up."

"It's alright, Wes."

"B-b-but, wh-what-"

"Hey," and Taylor's eyes open to slits, the lids look ashen and blue, but too sallow to be swollen, "I ever lie t'you?" And he has. He lied about going to Todd's today. But they're both doing their best. So Wes makes another insurmountable effort to calm down even as his body begins to fail him.

His legs won't stand,

and then his arms give way,
and his eyelids collapse,
and his spine wilts in the weight of the wind,
and he's just wrapped around Taylor as his body stops shivering.

* * *

Taylor hears them coming before he sees them. Four boys in the middle of a night so silent not even the streetlamps dare buzz their interference are hard to miss. But they'll walk right past, bumbling around like that in the dark. They have flashlights, but a flashlights' vision is so narrow...

He tries to rouse Wes. Wes is louder than him, he'll be able to get their attention, but he's folded on top of Taylor, sleeping deeper than Taylor has ever seen. And he won't wake up, even when prodded. His eyelids wrinkle, but don't open.

"Wes," he tries.

No response.

"Wes, look."

Nothing.

"Wes?" the whole world becomes TV static again. "Wes, can you at least get off me? They're not gonna see us from the main road—" It hits Taylor that he might have fucked up. He might have ruined one of the few truly good things in this world. He might have killed Wes. "Wes? Please, Wes, you're— fucking hell, Wes, wake up!" His throat is shredded from cold and the sudden transition from whisper to scream, but he doesn't notice. "Wes, wake up. Wes, please, wake up— please, please, wake up!"

He must have made enough noise to be heard on the main road, because Dalton sleds down the hill on his ass, followed by an unsteady Todd, a frantic Collin, and Jaxson with an empty smile that drops when he moves to help Dalton untangle Wes from Taylor.

"Why won't he wake up?" Taylor's voice breaks on frost, "He's sleeping and he won't wake up."

"Fucking hell, dude—"

"He needs a hospital—"

"They both need a hospital—"

"With what fucking insurance? Maybe Wes's parents can afford it but I know for damn sure Taylor's parents don't have any. The hospital's just gonna throw 'em in a blanket. We can do that at home."

"Jaxson—!"

"Dalton, they'll call Taylor's emergency contact. That means his parents. You think it's gonna be good for Taylor to talk to his parents right now?"

"Todd, can you—?"

"Yea, yea, I'm— fuck, Taylor? Look at me, bud. Alright. Shit, shit, shit, uh— okay. We goin' to Wes's house or mine?"

"Wes's is closer."

"But his parents—"

"Neither of our parents are home!"

"We can't take 'em to Jaxson's house, he don't even have insulation— and my parents would never allow anythin' like that— and—"

"He doesn't need parents, he needs a heater. Collin are you looking it up?"

"Y-you bet! It says slower's better, like lukewarm—"

"Slower!? Really—? Todd, we need to get going!"

"Shit, dude, I'm trying! Taylor? Alright we're going to Wes's house, okay? Can you— shut up, Jaxson, I'm trying— can you walk?"

Taylor nods. Stands. Legs like bags of beach sand. He can't walk, but he can shuffle. And this satisfies Todd, who isn't big enough to carry Taylor. Dalton is already carrying Wes, almost running. Taylor can't keep up with that. So Jaxson, hilariously, scoops him up off the ground with his bony arms and runs too.

The heat in Wes's house feels oppressive, even though Todd immediately voices skepticism about it not being warm enough. Taylor tries to tell him it's too warm, but he's dizzy with the overloading sensations of body heat and fear. Did he kill Wes? Did he finally manage to infect him with the awfulness at his core? He just wanted to be alone for a minute— he just wanted to see the snowflakes rush out to meet him.

Dalton drops Wes on the pullout couch, and Collin deposits a protesting Taylor next to him before both of them run off.

Wes is so still. His chest spasms with a shallow breath once in entirely too long, and his eyelids begin to scrunch with pain that he is too weak to truly fight, but he is otherwise totally motionless. No fidgeting hands or stumbling mouth or biting his cheek. His lips are purple in the sallow overflow of light from the hallway.

"Is he gonna die?" Taylor whispers, watching Wes's breath leave his lips in harsh little puffs.

Jaxson has been assigned to keep an eye on them while the other three make a ruckus elsewhere in the house, shouting things and displacing the items they are shouting about. "No," Jaxson replies, "trust me, buddy. I'd know." For the moment,

Taylor can't remember why Jaxson would know, but he does trust him.

On cue, like an engine suddenly called to life, Wes begins to shiver hard enough to rumble the springs in the mattress.

Taylor hardly knows that anything else exists until Dalton comes in, wipes the tears off of Taylor's face and says something about how everything is gonna be alright.

And then Jaxson begins his upbraiding.

"—And you just thought he would actually go home!? The dude is six-and-a-half feet of walking anxiety whose go-to coping mechanism is his depressed fucking boyfriend!"

Todd snaps something, probably something witty, in reply, but he's farther away and Taylor can't hear it.

"Yeah, because Taylor is a paragon of fucking mental health— Jesus Christ!"

Dalton growls, "Everyone here is doing their fucking best," and the scariest part of all of this might be that Dalton is angry and maybe Taylor ruined two of the few truly good things in this world.

"Don't take that tone with me like I'm not right!" Jaxson sounds terrified. All of this is wrong. "You've been friends with this kid for ten years! You should know him pretty fucking well by now."

Collin is trying to diffuse it all. "Guys, I really don't think—"

"And it's one thing to not know what his parents were doing," Taylor wants to sit up suddenly. Make Jaxson shut up in any way possible. Jaxson wouldn't. He wouldn't. "But, fuck, you never thought anything was wrong until he disappears off the face of the fucking planet!?"

"Jaxson Dixon, you shut yer mouth right now!" Collin cries, accent thickening with the emotions behind his incredibly well-timed interruption. "Now I know yer worried, but what yer sayin' is just mean and you know it."

There is frigid, isolating, suffocating silence for several seconds, and Taylor thinks maybe he ruined all of the few truly good things in this world, and maybe this time they'll really hate him forever and he'll be alone in the cold again.

"Now, the wikihow is sayin' to put 'em in a lukewarm bath," Collin says, quieter but still very firm. Taylor has never felt more reassured by a firm voice. "I dunno how the faucets work in here. Can some'un help me out?"

The fight drains from everyone.

Dalton nods and his footsteps follow Collin's into the guest bathroom. They figure out the faucet, then the temperature, then the drain plug. Then they go upstairs and do the same thing to Wes's bathtub while Jaxson and Todd maneuver Wes into the bathtub, which immediately wakes him up with a spluttering of curses.

"GAH!! Taylor d-d-died and you didn't t-t-te-tell me!

Like a slug trudging through salt, Taylor heaves himself off the pullout couch and shuffles to the entrance of the guest bathroom. "Not dead," he croaks. Doesn't know why his throat feels so raw.

"T-T-Taylor?"

Todd and Jaxson squeeze out of the bathroom so Taylor can kneel next to the showertub. "Yeah, Wes."

"It-t h-h-hurt-urts-s."

Taylor nods.

"Y-you we-were sc-screaming b-but-t I c-c-c-couldn't f-find y-you."

Taylor nods. He can tell the stammering is from shivering now, not panic, but he stays by the tub.

Footsteps descend the stairs.

"Taylor," Dalton murmurs, "we have, uh, we have another bath upstairs... You're still shivering." He says it like he's not sure if Taylor knows, and, to be fair, Taylor didn't.

"No," he mutters.

Jaxson blows an exasperated breath from his nose. Dalton skips the middle man and grabs Taylor around the waist and hoists him into the air. Taylor doesn't fight it. Too tired.

"'M comin' back, Wes," he promises. And Wes smiles a thin, shivering smile back at him. To Dalton he says, "And 'm not gettin' naked."

* * *

After several hours, at something like five in the morning, Wes and Taylor are warm, dry, lucid, and drinking hot tea while packed into one collective mound of blankets on the pullout couch watching the only thing that's on so late (early?): Jeopardy reruns.

Meanwhile, in the kitchen, Dalton, Jaxson, Todd, and Collin are trying to simultaneously discuss and avoid the events of the night before while they pretend to make breakfast.

"I don't even know how to make pancakes," Todd grumbles.

Collin takes over smoothly from there, with the almost-precision of any stress baker. "What can we even do for 'm though?" he wonders.

"Other than sign Taylor up with a therapist?" Todd laughs.

Jaxson interjects, "Again, no insurance," with a sardonic smile. The smile is under duress from Collin, who has made it clear that he doesn't think fighting will help anything.

"Well, shit, I'm not a therapist," Dalton moans.

"But he needs help," Collin says, "even if we ain't the ones givin' it."

"Jaxson," Todd begins thoughtfully, "how did you know Taylor's family doesn't have insurance?"

Jaxson's eyes slide out of eye contact smoothly. "Our sisters are friends," he says, dodging the question.

Dalton snaps, "Jaxson if you don't cut it out with the vague bullshit..." but he doesn't finish the thought, also under duress from Collin.

From the other room, they hear the torn-paper edges of the first words out of Wes and Taylor's mouth since they got dropped in their respective bathtubs. Everyone lets some tension leak out of their shoulders, each in their own ways. They give each other little looks— looks that say, thank fuck, I thought they would be mute for the rest of their lives and we'd have to explain to Wes's parents whatever the fuck happened last night.

Nobody is really sure what happened last night.

There's a text chain, created at 10:58 on Friday, December 18. That's technically yesterday, but nobody has slept yet so it feels like today.

Unnamed Groupchat: Todd Richards, Dalton Aarons, Collin Donahue, Jaxson Dixon

[10:58]

Groupchat created by Todd Richards

Todd: taylors missing

wes went after him idk where he is either

can you guys help us look for them?

Collin: ????

Whaddaya mean Missing

Im puttin on my shoes

Jaxson: omw

Juniper–Maisie says her and Hellen saw both of them after school

Says that were right to be worried

Wont tell me wat happened tho

Todd: dalton and i ar handling the west side of town, can u guys get east?

we'll meet in front of the school

Dalton: if we havent found them by then

Who knows maybe wes found taylor first and just forgot to text us back

Jaxson: im not betting on that

[11:22]

Dalton: todd

Found wes

By the park

Hes not wearing shOES?

Todd: omw

Collin: is taylor with him?

Dalton: No

Toddster

Hurry

Jaxson: should me and collin come too?

Dalton: No u two keep looking

I think someone is gonna need to walk wes home

Hes like a fuckin zombie

Todd: jfc

Im by the park

dalton ??

Where u at????

[11:49]
Jaxson: oh shit wait i see u guys
By the front gate?
[12:39]
Collin: nothin at the coffee shop
Dalton: theyre not around the mall
Jaxson: nothing at the tree house
Todd: same,,
Nobody has seen him near the bars either
Dalton: should we tell hellen?
That taylor is missing?
Jaxson: probably no
Collin: meet by wes house?
Maybe they went home
Todd: Omw!
Dalton: see u there
Jaxson: omw

They hadn't found them until something like 2 am, when they were finally turning in and thinking there's no way their friends were stupid enough to be outside in that cold at that hour. They were certain that if they hit up the Post household one more time, Wes and Taylor would be there, watching tv on the pullout couch or sleeping or something.

And then Taylor's voice had cracked the frigid night with desperate, choked sobs and they had all nearly drowned in the sound and they found them, of all places, under a fucking bridge, off of Clearwater Street. Taylor was screaming. Nobody present has ever heard Taylor scream before.

Once they'd gotten them warm enough to leave behind the incoherent oscillation between catatonic and mumbling sobs, they were silent. And everyone was too scared to ask, so nobody really knows what happened last night.

But the tissue-paper edges of voices heard from the other room reassures everyone that they won't actually have to go to the hospital. Probably.

15

Time Spent as a Human Burrito

Wes finally realizes where he is after an indeterminate amount of time spent as a human burrito, watching Jeopardy reruns, sharing body heat with Taylor. He's not really sure how he got here, but he's sure it was because of something scary, so he avoids thinking about it. He can feel the textured skin of Taylor's arm pressed against his. Everything else is swaddled in softness that he recognizes to be one of the comforters that had been on the pullout couch. He must be sitting on the pullout couch. That's probably why he can see the TV, playing a Jeopardy rerun.

In similar, eddying tides, Wes becomes conscious. When he is fully conscious and aware, and has therefore exhausted any other distraction, he finally tries to remember why he is here, sharing a human burrito with Taylor on the pullout couch watching Jeopardy reruns.

It hits him instantly, like the memories had rung the doorbell long ago and had since been waiting, ready to run inside the moment he opened the door.

Holy shit.

He could have—

Taylor almost—

They could have died.

Wes remembers the feeling of dandelion vines tangling his legs, binding him to the ground, wrapping himself around Taylor to try and keep him warm— he remembers a bathtub, and he remembers Taylor screaming—

"Taylor?" he whispers, hoarsely, panicked.

There's an acknowledging shift in the human burrito, but Taylor doesn't answer.

"Taylor, you weren't, I mean you w-weren't-t-t actually going t-t-to— ya know?"

"Wasn't gonna what?" Taylor mutters. He scoots infinitesimally away from Wes, and the difference is frigid.

"Die," Wes whispers. "I mean, you weren't t-tr-trying to, right?"

Taylor doesn't answer.

A little ball of resentment makes itself known in Wes's solar plexus, not new but enlivened. His mind replays Tuesday morning, where Wes had told Taylor that he liked him, and Taylor had said he liked him back, and then Taylor had told him they couldn't date because Wes deserves better.

The resentment grows. Who had told Taylor that you needed to be good enough to be in a relationship? Who told him Wes was worth more than him— worth more than even the 2-cent-per-square-foot linoleum tiles at school? Who told him he was worth less?

The resentment sears hissing, spitting pain into Wes's ribs. Maybe it's resentment at a world that would push Taylor this far. Maybe it's resentment at Taylor for letting himself be pushed.

"Taylor. What were you doing out there?"

"Hm?"

"What were you doing out there?" Wes demands, "In the snow. You were laying outside in a flannel and jeans in fucking zero-degree weather— you almost died- wh-what-t w-were you d-doing?" Taylor doesn't reply, and the resentment glows white-hot and Wes steels himself and snaps, "Tell me."

"No."

Wes twitches twice, and the second time Taylor leans into him— as if he could keep Wes still by just being there. Maybe he can. It's an experiment.

"Why not?"

"Because you won't like what I tell you."

In a way, Taylor did just tell him— because they both kind of know.

Wes stares at the Jeopardy rerun. Disco History for 800. This ex-deejay hosted a mass burning of disco records in 1979. Who is Robert Dahl. That is correct. The resentment crackles as it superheats his bones.

And then his bones disintegrate. They turn to ash that blows away with Wes's breath. Nothing stops the resentment from using Wes's mouth to ask, "Taylor, what did you mean, on Tuesday morning?"

"Huh?"

"You said you wouldn't date me. Why not?"

Taylor shifts away from him again, body petrified into a glass bottle holding every emotion he's ever felt.

Wes shifts too, moves some of the blankets so he can look Taylor straight in his face. He makes it very clear he won't drop this. It takes several minutes of direct eye contact to make this point.

"You deserve better—"

"Yeah, but what the fuck does that mean?"

There's a shift in their burrito as Taylor also moves to face Wes more directly. "What do you want me to say, dude? I'm a piece of shit!" His eyes cast about the room. "Jesus, Wes, look where we are right now."

The smoldering resentment is bile creeping up Wes's throat. "S-so, so what!?" he asks, desperately searching for some part of Taylor's expression that looks worse than yesterday, or last week, or a month ago, because that would mean Taylor hasn't always felt like this. "I'm not supposed t-t-to help!? Just let you f-fucking freeze to death!?"

"I dunno! Maybe!?" Taylor's frustrated glare melts into a still understanding. "Y'know what, if it means you don't get fucking hypothermia, then yea. Yes. Let me freeze to death."

Wes snaps, "No!" eyes hot and body beginning to tremble at the joints. Someone remembered to give him his meds about half an hour ago, and he's never been more grateful for their assistance than this moment, because without them he knows he wouldn't have the strength to look Taylor in the eyes and scream at him like this.

"What do you mean 'no'!?" Taylor hisses back, and now his expression is new. There's fear in his eyes. What could he possibly be afraid of? Wes would never hurt him. "This isn't a fucking debate! If saving me means hurting you then I don't wanna be saved!"

"And I'm telling you that I'm gonna do whatever I can to help you, even if it fucking kills me." The words don't even surprise Wes once they've escaped his lungs. They echo back from the screen of too-quiet Jeopardy reruns and settle into the comforter-burrito with damning finality and Wes knows he means them.

"What the fuck!?" Taylor sounds like he's choking. He looks terrified. "No!?" he snaps, "Why would you do that?"

And it finally clicks what Taylor is so scared of. And it clicks what the anger was hiding. And it clicks what Wes has to do about it. "Because that's what boyfriends do," he says.

"What!?" Taylor looks ready to bolt, but the burrito and the stiffness of defrosting prevents him from getting much headway on the idea.

"Cool. Now that that's settled, hold my hand," Wes says, one hand seeking Taylor's out in the blankets. "My fingers are freezing."

Everyone in the kitchen is doing their absolute best to communicate through eye contact, because they don't want Wes and Taylor to know that they heard every word of that, but it's hard because there's *so much* to unpack. Where to start? Taylor's staggering self-worth issues? Wes's morbid lack of self-preservation? The fact that they, apparently, confirmed their feelings for each other on Tuesday morning, and then told nobody about it? The part where they're dating now?

Collin, for his part, flips another pancake.

Collin is not especially concerned about much of this. As long as nobody's dying no more, he's got bigger fish to filet. He loves his friends, but he also knows that after not one, but two consecutive sleepovers, neither of which had clearance from his parents, he's close to joining Taylor in the homeless department— and they can't all sleep on their boyfriend's pullout couches. Jaxson's trailer doesn't have one, and even after Jeremy moved out there's not even room to breathe in there (it's why he and Jax spend all their time outside, even if it's colder than all heck).

They hadn't really had *anyone's* house to go to before this week. Jaxson's house is chaotic and screaming and fistfights and so much broken glass on the floor that you can't take off your shoes inside. Collin' house is tight-lipped silences and oppressive watching and if you step on the eggshells—

You just try not to step on the eggshells or it turns into one of those nights where his parents Do Things and later Collin sits in his room and doesn't move a muscle until his mother calls him for breakfast.

He's never stayed out for two sleepovers without permission. When he and Jax first started dating, they stayed too late at that treehouse Jaxson and Taylor built for their little sisters in middle school and ended up sleeping there. It had been Bad when Collin got home. He Never Wants That To Happen Again.

He's got bigger fish to filet than whether or not Taylor and Wes have become Swisher's newest gay couple.

Todd makes eye contact with Collin— one of the pancakes is ready to be flipped. It's a little crispier than the others now. Collin is tempted to throw out the whole pancake. Nobody wants a fucked up pancake. If Collin hadn't been distracted, he would have flipped it on time. This is why he can't afford to spend time doing anything with his new friends: he gets distracted, and when he gets distracted his schoolwork slips and his parents buckle down with the rules and the groundings and then Collin fucks up the pancakes—

Jaxson sweeps in behind him and swipes the pancake off the plate, nibbling at it like a chipmunk. "Thanks, babe," he whispers, mouth full and smiling just enough to take the stress out of the slope of Collin shoulders.

In the other room, Taylor says something, low and grumbling, and Wes bites back with clipped, stutter-less efficiency. Todd is right by the archway to the hall and heard it better, he's laughing into his hand.

Dalton is whispering demands, "What are they saying? Toddster. My guy. What. Are. They. Saying," and Todd is shushing him, pulling out his phone, texting, and then Dalton is holding back laughter with sheer force of will.

Collin checks his phone.

Unnamed Groupchat: Todd Richards, Dalton Aarons, Collin Donahue, Jaxson Dixon

Todd: taylor asked if he had any say in whether or not he and wes are dating

wes told him to 'shut the fuck up'

Dalton: alkdfjln

XD XD XD

Jaxson: its what he fuckin deserves

last night was a hot fuckin mess

Todd: i mean i guess ya,,,,, but like,,,,,

Can u IMAGINE last week wes telling taylotr to stfu???

bc i Cannot

Dalton: it seems like just yesterday i was changing his diapers

</3

Now there is such foul language coming from his mouth

Todd: dalton,,, buddy........ U have known wes for like 5 days

Collin: wait I thought yall knew wes for a while?

*Jaxson: ^^^*

Yea

I would also like an explanation

Bc i have THREE classes with both of them

One of classes we have been assigned to a table together for months

And they only started talking to each other TUESDAY
Dalton: ok so heres the thing
Todd: collin the pancake is gonna burn
Dalton: we would love to tell u
Collin: !! thank you!!
Jaxson: i call the burned ones
Collin: heathen
Jaxson: i like them Kwispy
Dalton: but i would feel weird talking abt it without wes and taylors input
Ya feel?
*Todd: ^^^^*
Jaxson: ok aight so whats the plan then
We could interrupt their ~bonding moment~
Collin: well i dont wanna be rude though
Dalton: Collin. U have pancakes. Nothing is rude when u have pancakes.
Oh shit this groupchat has no name!
A TRAVESSTY
[Dalton Aarons Named the Groupchat: Babie its cold ousside]

As they enter the living room, the whole group shoves Collin out in front of them first, holding a stack of pancakes on the largest ceramic dinnerware plate in the Post household.

"Hey, y'all," Collin says, trying not to be too awkward, when two sets of eyes turn to stare at him.

"I forgot there were people in the house," Wes says with a sideways laugh. His whole face goes a little red.

Jaxson scoots out from behind Collin, swipes a burnt pancake from the top of the pile, and says, "We have pancakes and we have questions. Seeing as you two decided to lay down in the snow for four fuckin' hours last night and we had to peel your asses off the pavement, we are requiring you to answer them." He shoves the whole pancake into his mouth at once, and the regret at biting off more than he can chew slowly dawns on him as he tries to swallow.

"Fuck it," Taylor mutters, "ask away, but I ain't answering shit that I don't want to."

Dalton moves to sit at the corner of the pullout couch, and Todd sits cross-legged next to him. Jaxson and Collin squish into the armchair, and they pass the plate of pancakes around. They're all kinda biding their time. Jaxson, for one, has no fucking clue what he's even supposed to be asking here.

When it becomes clear that nobody else is gonna say anything, Todd sighs and says, "Taylor, you gotta tell Jaxson and Collin about your house."

Oh. That.

Jaxson scans Taylor's bruised face carefully, through the blanket pile, for signs of the rippling emotions that he can hide so well. It briefly crosses Jaxson's mind that Freddy Peters didn't fuck up Taylor's face— and Jaxson doesn't know who did. Sure, he could have gone out and picked a fight, but he also might have just gone home when Mr. Macready was in a bad mood.

Jaxson remembers when they were little and the Macreadys would leave Taylor with Hellen at the Dixon trailer when they dropped her off for a playdate, and Taylor would be covered in bruises and Hellen would be trying not to cry and Jaxson had known from the start exactly what that meant. The first few times, Juniper-Maisie would ask Taylor what happened— because she was still so little, and she didn't think other people's parents were like that (because that's what Jaxson always told her)— and Taylor would say he tripped, and when Juniper-Maisie stopped believing that he would say he picked a fight with one of the bigger kids.

That became the famous Taylor Macready lie: he picked a fight.

Sometimes he picked a fight. Sometimes he picked a bad night to come home.

Jaxson knows probably more than even Todd or Dalton about the Macready family. Hellen has always told Juniper-Maisie everything, and when they were little Juniper-Maisie told Jaxson everything— Juniper-Maisie's a tight-lidded box now, won't spill a secret for anything in a way that Jaxson really admires, but he's gotten enough puzzle pieces over the years to know that Thomas Macready beats the shit out of his son because, in seven-year-old Hellen's words, "Daddy doesn't think Taylor is his kid because he's got black hair and I have red hair."

Jaxson has always hoped Todd or Dalton knew more than him. That they were helping him somehow, in ways that Jaxson, with the same bruises, couldn't.

But Todd Richards and Dalton Aarons have been friends with Taylor Macready since kindergarten and somehow don't know.

Taylor and Wes make some pointed eye contact— which is the first indication, to Jaxson, that his guess at what this conversation is about could be wrong. How would Wes be implicated in the Macready household? Those two hadn't said a word to each other before Monday.

"It's your house," Taylor grumbles, "you say it."

"F-f-fine. Taylor's parents kicked him out."

Oh. Oh shit. That makes horrifying sense.

Last week, Taylor had stumbled into first period physics with the gait of a man limping towards death. Jaxson tried to mention it when they were alone in the bathroom during what would have been third-period English if they'd bothered to show up. He'd said Taylor looked like shit. Taylor hadn't responded, just vomited into the toilet and told Jaxson not to tell a single fucking person or he'd kick his ass. There was no way Jaxson could have known he was homeless. Even if his clothes were kinda gross. Maybe he just hadn't done laundry in a while— how could Jaxson have known! "Does Hellen know?" Jaxson asks. "Juniper-Maisie would have told me if Hellen knew."

Wes gives Taylor a glance that means he doesn't know the answer to this one.

Collin interrupts, "Wait, hang on, y'all. Where were you livin', Taylor? How long were you roughin' it?" He backtracks, a little intimidated by the glare Taylor is leveling him with, "If ya don't mind my askin'."

Wes answers part of that, "Under the bridge off Clearwater Street— Taylor, how long did you live there?"

Shrinking into the blanket pile, Taylor mumbles, "I dunno. Maybe a few weeks?"

"Weeks!?" half the room cries at once.

Dalton shouts, "Last Thursday was *not* the first snow of the year— how did you not die!?"

"The first snow wasn't too bad," Taylor insists, "I was covered by the bridge, so I wasn't gonna die or nothin'." He shrugs, "I came over to your house once or twice when it snowed. It's just that when Wes found me I was sick and stupid and decided to sleep out from under the bridge."

Jaxson echoes himself, "My point stands. How did Hellen

not *know*? Juniper-Maisie woulda told me if you really needed help."

"I don't need your hero complex bullshit, Jaxson."

"I don't give a shit," Jaxson growls, "tell me how you got kicked out without your fourteen-year-old sister knowing!"

"Because I never told her!" Taylor shouts. It rattles the springs in the pullout couch mattress. "I told my dad to eat shit if he was gonna bitch at me again, and he said he was done taking care of my sorry ass and he told me to get my stuff and get outta the house or he'd call the cops. So I left," Taylor's face is contorted with pain in ways that most of the people in the living room have never seen before. His breathing comes in bellows.

Todd and Dalton are both so terrified they feel themselves cement to the shaking springs of the pullout mattress. Taylor has never yelled at them before, not like that. Slower, quieter, Taylor continues, "Hellen was with Juniper-Maisie somewhere, I don't know. I was gone before she got home. I tried to avoid her at school 'cause I knew she'd feel bad." For just a moment, there's a carcass of a smile. "I wanted her to think I just moved out. Found an apartment somewhere, I dunno." His shoulders are hunched, blankets a protective barrier between him and the rest of the world. "I don't know." Nobody can see his nails buried in his arm.

In the blanket pile next to Taylor, Wes twitches. Jaxson can't see Taylor's face anymore, the only part of him that had been visible, because he's sunk so far into the blankets.

Dalton's got tears already running down his face. Todd hadn't spoken, but now he opens his mouth and says, "Okay. So let me break this timeline down. You get kicked out sometime in the middle of last November. You're living under

206

a bridge for three weeks? Last Monday, you got sick. Last Thursday, there's a snowstorm and Wes— that's when you found him, right? Because you texted us on Friday night." Wes nods. Todd continues, "So Friday Wes texts us, Tuesday, somehow, you two confess your undying love or some shit like that—"

Taylor lets out a barking laugh, and there's a release of tension.

Wes goes bright red, stammering, "I-i-it w-was an accident!"

"How do you confess on accident?" Dalton wants to know, laughing and wiping his face dry with his sleeve.

From his cocoon inside the blankets, Taylor says, "He was trying to apologize for feeding me muffins."

"You said you didn't like cinnamon!"

"It was the only thing I'd eaten in two days, Wes," Taylor replies, voice warm and almost chuckling, "I wasn't gonna complain about cinnamon."

Jaxson nods. He doesn't think much of that comment. Sometimes Collin will sneak food out of his parents' house for Jaxson when shit gets rough— and he hardly ever gets caught, so it's usually alright. He gets it.

Todd doesn't get it. His whole face wrinkles with guilt. "Dude, you could have—" he stops. Everyone can hear that he's choked up and they don't mention it. "Anytime, Taylor— you could have come to my house *anytime*. I wouldn't have asked any questions, if you needed me not to."

"Sorry," Taylor mutters.

"Don't be sorry," Todd says, "Just— I don't know— Just rely on us a little more."

Taylor shifts under the weight of that request and tries not to respond with a lie.

16

Secret Looks and Secret Phone Conversations for Secret Reasons

A
t maybe ten AM, when everyone is dozing in the living room, Wes's phone screams to wake him up with a call from his Mom's phone. He scrambles to answer it before anyone else can wake up, but nerves are still a little strung-out for everyone present, so everyone wakes up.

Dalton, sleepy-eyed but still electrically awake, gestures clumsily for Wes to put the call on speakerphone, and Wes acquiesces nervously.

Mom's voice is chipper— it's nine am there, which isn't early at all for her, since she's always up at six (or earlier) to open the shop.

"Hey there, Wes!" she says brightly.

"Hi, Mom—"

"Hi, Mrs. Post!" Jaxson calls loudly. Everyone turns to shush him, but he giggles and shrugs and pulls the extra blanket he's got more fully over himself. Collin glowers and slaps his shoulder. Wes twitches hard enough that his head hits the back of the couch. Nobody outside of the human burrito sees it, but Taylor leans into Wes a little more, like a lightning rod keeping electricity on the ground.

"Who was that, kiddo?" Mom asks calmly, trying very hard not to be too dramatically excited about the chance that her wonderful, charismatic, anxiety-riddled son might have invited a friend over without even asking.

Wes answers, "Th-that was Jaxson. Dixon. Me and Taylor and Todd and Dalton and Collin and Jaxson all had a sleepover last night. Kinda." It would be a lot harder to stay still and stutterless if Taylor wasn't acting as that lightning rod.

At half-volume, like she's holding the phone away from her face, everyone hears Mom say to Dad, "—a sleepover, Richard! Oh goodness!" Dalton makes a little face at Wes, conspiratorial and giggling. Dad's voice hums something about an event on a Cuban beach in the nineties that may or may not be related to the conversation at all, and then Mom laughs and says into the receiver, "Well, that's just great, kiddo! What'd you boys get up to last night?"

Everyone looks directly at each other. Oh no. How the fuck do they answer this?

Surprisingly, Collin comes to the rescue. "Well, Mrs. Post, it sure did snow a whole heckuva lot last night, so we mostly just sat around outside."

Mom buys it too. "Doesn't that sound nice," she replies a little distantly, "I hope you didn't get too cold out there in the snow!"

Jaxson can't help it, he laughs out loud, and Todd does too. Todd answers seriously, through his manic laughter, "Oh, no, Mrs. Post, we were definitely wearing jackets and everything—" he looks directly at Taylor, who has to unstick his nails from his arm to flip Todd off appropriately.

"Everyone is safe and warm here!" Dalton adds. He sounds a little nervous. He hasn't had a mom to lie to in a while, and he hopes he still knows how.

Mom is clearly too excited about Wes having his first sleep-over with friends to read too much into any of what the boys are saying. "That's wonderful, boys," she says, and Wes can hear the smile in her voice, the proud one that she used when Wes was little and he'd come out of therapy using words like de-escalation and coping mechanisms. "By the way, Wes, did you end up opening the shop? For the reasons I texted you?"

"*GAH!*" Wes screeches, diving for the phone and taking it off speaker. He finishes the conversation quickly while the rest of the room gives each other nonplussed looks around him. "Alright, yeah, I'll open the shop for a few hours today," Wes says. Mom tells him that sounds great, and not to push it if he feels overwhelmed. Wes tells her he won't push it, and then Mom says they're about to leave for some sightseeing and they say goodbye and hang up.

"I've gotta open the shop today!" Wes screeches. The whole room becomes a gallery walk of furrowed brows.

Except Collin, who smiles reassuringly and says, "Don't you even worry about it, Wes. We'll get outta yer hair so you can go open the shop fer yer folks without no worries!"

Taylor's got a glare leveled at Wes that's more confused than his normal glaring, but Dalton drags him out from the human burrito (and away from Wes's side) and says, "Me and the Toke-meister can drag Taylor outside for some Real Human Interaction!"

Todd foregoes agreeing with Dalton verbally (because Dalton usually doesn't care who agrees with him anyway) to clandestinely snap a picture with his phone of Taylor pulled

211

over sideways, tangled in blankets, hat lost somewhere in the mess, begrudgingly allowing Dalton to pat his exposed hair and kicking Jaxson for trying to poke his feet.

"I don't need human interaction," Taylor grumbles, "that shit sounds exhausting."

Wes giggles at him, and twitches hard with a shiver that works its way up his spine. Taylor's expression goes stony for an instant, then half-murderous, the way it was last weekend when Wes first met him and all he did was glare at the comforter on the pullout couch. He pulls himself away from Dalton and scoots back up next to Wes. "Nope. I'm staying here. Wes is staying here. You fuckers can go— especially you, Jaxson, stop tryna tickle my fucking feet, motherfucker—"

Jaxson, of course, is poking at Taylor's feet and teasing, "Aw, Taylor's had a boyfriend for forty-five seconds and he's already so protective!"

Dalton joins in on the fun by poking at Taylor's feet too until Taylor switches from kicking their hands away to tucking his feet under himself. Todd, once again, is taking pictures with his phone of Dalton and Jaxson laughing at a livid Taylor, of Jaxson and Collin holding back giggles on the loveseat, Wes and Taylor snuggled up in their partially-reconstructed human burrito. Setting aside the events of the night before and the fact that Taylor is still visibly black and blue, this is the most fun any of them has had in a while. And they all know it.

Still though, Wes says he really does gotta open the shop today, and Taylor tells him he's not going anywhere in this weather, and Collin reminds everyone that it isn't even snowing anymore, and Dalton gives the room a gorgeous (not gorgeous, actually genuinely atrocious) rendition of "Baby

It's Cold Outside," and Todd tells them he will leave or stay or whatever as long as Dalton stops singing, and, of course, Jaxson then joins Dalton in song. Wes, laughing with everyone, repeats that he really does have to open the shop today.

Taylor returns to glaring semi-murderously at the comforter.

Dalton, Todd, and Jaxson exchange a look. They all know what that look means or, at least, after almost 15 years each of knowing Taylor they've got some good guesses that land in the general realm of Taylor is kinda angry about something. Collin is the first to realize that they are all wrong when Wes gives Taylor an entirely different look than the one the rest of the room is exchanging.

Wes says, "Don't worry so much, Taylor," and Dalton's head literally snaps around to stare. Jaxson and Collin have one of those silent, couples-only telepathy sessions in which Jaxson says did you see that, babe by widening his eyes pointedly and Collin replies yea, sure, what was so weird about it by furrowing his brow and Jaxson purses his lips at him as if Collin is being intentionally dense.

"I will ask this once again, Wes," Todd says very calmly, "how did you become proficient in Taylor's coding language so fast?"

"Todd, I'm gonna beat the shit outta you—" Taylor grumbles, "I'm not a fuckin' robot!"

Dalton cries, "You say that, but you slept more in the last four hours than I've ever seen you sleep before!"

"And you're literally inscrutable as fuck—"

"Nice vocabulary word, Jaxson."

"Don't interrupt me when I'm making fun of you!"

"Plus," Collin adds, "you talk like normal even when your

face is all bruised up! Even I can't do that!"

Dalton laughs and pokes at Taylor's purple cheek and asks, "Do you have a lot of experience trying to talk with a bruised face?"

Collin scratches the back of his head and answers, "I was a pretty clumsy kid." (Taylor and Jaxson know better, for different reasons.)

Wes takes his meds, shoves handfuls of gummy vitamins at everyone ("Meds can be a group activity, probably?"), and takes another of the few remaining pancakes from Collin's stack. He and Taylor throw on fresh clothes and try to offer fresh clothes to everyone else ("Todd, come on, it's not Gucci or whatever the fuck, but we're almost the same size," "No offense, Taylor, but it's less about the brand and more about the fact that most of your shirts have holes in them,"). Everyone insists on walking with Wes to work ("What the else are we gonna do at 11 am on a Saturday?"), and they all insist it's not because of Wes offering them free coffee while he warms up the machines for the inevitable rush that comes any time Post Family Coffee is open during the holiday season ("Come on, Westlé, can't be that bad," "Last year we had to stay two hours late because we had a line wrapping around the block").

"I hate coffee," Taylor says flatly, "Don't make me any."

Collin laughs, "You sure picked the wrong boyfriend then, buster!" Taylor glares, and Collin blushes, "Aw, goshdarnit, are we not s'posed to talk about how y'all're datin'?" This is not the issue, but Collin is still getting used to talking like a normal human with a guy whose primary method of communication is glaring in different, nearly indiscernible fonts.

"Do you actually hate coffee!?" Wes cries, "But you come in all the time!"

"He does!?" Dalton exclaims. "How long has he been coming in!? My baby bestie is such a sneaky snake!"

"Don't talk about me like I'm not here, dipshit."

"Sneaky, I tell you! How has he managed to hide a caffeine habit from me and Toddster?"

Jaxson interjects, "Didn't we establish last night that Taylor hid the fact that he was living under a bridge from you for, like, two months?"

"Hey!" Todd insists, "Hey, two weeks."

"Three weeks," Collin correctly recounts, and then Taylor tells him he's not helping and Collin mock-salutes and apologizes meekly.

Rolling his eyes, Jaxson continues, "I think the issue might be that you two are just too trusting."

"Jax, you didn't know he was homeless either," Collin points out.

"Can everyone shut up about that!?" Taylor snaps, but it's got less bite than it would have had a week ago, and he adds, "The point is, Wes, don't make me any coffee."

Wes has changed a lot this week too. He doesn't miss a beat, just asks, "How about hot cocoa?"

Taylor's expression alone is enough to have Wes promising to make him a large one— which might or might not be worth the teasing Taylor gets for wanting a hot chocolate instead of a coffee at eighteen years old.

Wes is not nearly as clumsy around the coffee machines as his numerous bandaids had promised. He makes six drinks (even Jaxson's hilariously pretentious frappé drink) in record time, before the big, industrial coffee grinder in the back room has even warmed up enough to use.

Dalton comments that Wes doesn't twitch as much when he's making coffee.

"Just muscle memory, I guess," Wes says, "I've been making coffee since I was a kid, so it's kinda a comfort thing."

Jaxson sips his glorified-milkshake of a coffee. "I dunno, those machines make me nervous as hell."

Everyone sips their drinks in comfortable, warm silence for several minutes.

Dalton starts them back up, "Alright, so, Taylor. Tokes. We're going to the mall today, yes?"

"Do we have to?" Taylor moans.

"Yes," Todd insists, "you need t-shirts that don't have holes in them and actually fit you."

"I have t-shirts," Taylor grumbles. But when he makes eye contact with Wes, cleaning the blender, and he sees the clearly dubious expression peeking from behind the machines, he throws his hands up, flips the whole room off, and exclaims, "Give Jaxson your fucking charity, I'm fine." (Jaxson says his EBT card is charity enough, thank you very much).

Todd groans, rubs a hand over his face, and rationalizes, "Okay, well, we can't just sit in Wes's place of business all day. Let's at least get out of his way."

Wes starts to protest that it's fine, they can stay, don't worry about it, he really doesn't mind, but after a second he realizes that Todd is just trying to get Taylor to accept help and nods several times. "Yes, actually, tha-th-that might be, um, best." It is abundantly clear that Taylor does not believe his performance. He adds, "The customers get, uh, kinda crazy?"

And the first customer (drawn in, probably, by clairvoyant knowledge of the open/closed status of the Post Family Coffee

Shop) bounces in excitedly at that moment. It's an exhausted-looking mother who has either forgotten to remove her baby-halter or forgotten her baby in the car. She barely waits for Wes to greet her, just shouts her order at him and hands him exact change. Calmly— more calmly than any of his new friends have ever seen him in all of their 12 years of schooling together— Wes's fingers fly over the register buttons, he hands the woman a receipt, puts her change away, and makes the coffee. By then someone else has come in, slightly less rabid, but Wes was clearly right and the customers do get, uh, kinda crazy.

Taylor watches Wes do all of this with an expression that Todd, Dalton, or Jaxson might call 'peeved.' He's thinking about how smoothly Wes moves behind the counter, like a fucking liquid. Like he's made of syrup and honey. He's thinking about last night, wondering why a guy like Wes would even want a guy like Taylor around. He can't get a single word Wes has ever said out of his head, and his consciousness is swimming with it all.

"Fine," Taylor grumbles, "let's go to... wherever, I don't give a fuck."

17

Wrong Number

After leaving the coffee shop, Jaxson says Juniper-Maisie texted, so he's going home for a while, "have fun with your shopping spree or whatever, dipshits" (Taylor says it's not going to be a shopping spree because he will take anyone out at the fucking knees if they try to buy him anything). Collin says he's going home too, but it looks a little like an excuse to Dalton.

Well, that's probably fine. Collin is probably just uncomfortable spending the day with some guys he met, like, less than a week ago. Dalton thinks Todd might be pretty approachable, but Dalton knows he's big and he knows Taylor is scary.

Truth be told, Dalton is so extremely fucking jazzed to have more friends.

He can't wait for their Christmas sleepover. He already asked his dad, who's gonna go stay with Dalton's aunt for Christmas and New Years so he doesn't get too lonely.

Dalton, Todd, and Taylor walk to the mall, even though Taylor is both broke and violently against anything being bought for him. Todd says "fine, fine, okay, we won't buy anything, just window shopping," but he smirks at Dalton and Taylor knows Todd too well to believe him anyways so really Todd just said that to get Taylor to shut up with the threats.

It's maybe six pm when Collin gets a text message.

Wes Post: gelp
[Wes Post has shared their location with you]
Wes Post: plead
Collin: On my way!
Are you oky, Wes?

Wes doesn't respond. Collin is a little worried. Why would Wes need Collin's help, of all people?

Not that Collin doesn't like Wes! He seems like an awfully nice guy! Collin is sure that they're gonna be great buddies! But they've only known each other a little less than a week. Wouldn't Taylor be the first person he texts? Unless—

Unless Taylor is the one who needs help? Maybe it's like last night— gosh, it really don't feel like that whole mess was last night. It was so scary, but it feels like it was weeks ago already. Collin's got his shoes on and he Maps Wes' location while he runs.

Jeez, he'd been telling Jax they should try to meet more people, but has meeting more people always been so stressful!? Jax's thing in the bathroom the other night isn't nobody else's fault, but then Freddy Peters getting everyone all riled in the cafeteria, and then last night with Taylor and Wes goin' missing, and then today Wes is in trouble again!

Something in Collin' chest pulses with a familiar, angry pain. They're all still kids, technically— why do they have to go through such terrible things? They're all still kids, even if just barely, there should still be someone who was supposed to protect them. Who the fuck is protecting them? They're still kids—

And then Collin cuts that train of thought short. Puts the anger into running. He's still got to help Wes.

The Maps app leads him right to the coffee shop, but Collin doesn't see Wes immediately. "Wes!?" he calls, hoping that Wes just knocked over a sack of coffee beans or something, but knowing that's probably not it, "You out here, buddy?"

A less familiar voice says something Collin can't quite make out (it sounds a lot like 'agate' though), and he follows the echoes to the side of the coffee shop where, of fucking course, three kids from school are kicking a heap of clothes that is probably actually Wes.

Collin never really took martial arts classes as a kid— his parents were very careful to keep him away from such violence— but he's got the element of surprise and a lifetime of rage without outlet.

He slams a foot into the spine of one of the kids, who turns around and reveals himself to be Alex Morenson, already pivoting to lunge at Collin. But Alex Morenson's fighting experience is limited to him cornering people with his friends like a pack of hyenas, and Collin has always had worse odds. So Collin imagines Alex Morenson is his dad with a belt and slams his face to the concrete so hard there's road salt stuck to his cheek when he raises his head.

The second guy, Mathew Megans, whips around to try and get back at Collin, but he doesn't get a chance because Collin has already jabbed him in the throat. The third friend, who Collin doesn't know, had the forethought to sneak up behind Collin, and he pulls a thick piece of plastic that he found on the ground around Collin' neck, choking him. All three of them are giggling slurs through the blood they're spitting from behind their teeth, but Collin can't hear them over the rush of his own blood in his ears, picking up the pace to try and circulate the thinning amounts of oxygen in his body. Sparks pop like burning film in Collin's peripheral, and he vaguely registers his feet kicking and his arms clutching at his own neck, scratching his own skin off to try and get away from the cutting suffocation of the plastic trash garrote.

And then the pressure is gone. Collin hardly has the capacity to defend himself. He sinks to the ground, gasping for breath, until his vision and mind clears enough to register that Wes had shoved the third kid off of Collin, and now they're back to kicking him. In the chest. Collin coughs, wobbles to a stand.

He's had quite enough, frankly.

Collin grabs a bottle from the dumpster that used to hold cheap wine from the gas station and smashes it against the wall of the coffee shop, he hooks a foot around one of the guy's legs, and when he's on the ground Collin holds the broken end of the bottle just above his cheekbone. He whimpers, as Collin guessed he would, and his friends stop hitting Wes, and they all stare at Collin, crouched over their friend, dripping blood from where the plastic trash garrote cut into his skin, with a broken bottle poised over his face.

"Go," Collin says with that thin kind of calm that covers up what a grounding looks like in the Donahue household, "before I do something we all regret." Alex Morenson and his friend put their hands up placatingly and begin to inch out of the alleyway. Collin drags the glass over the final guy's face until a thin, red line begins to erupt with blood.

"C-Collin?" Wes says hoarsely.

Collin stops. This kid, whose name he cannot remember even when his blood stains Collin's nails, is not Collin's father or mother. This nameless kid is also a kid. Someone should be teaching him better, but he is a kid just like the rest of them.

He scoots back and lets his hostage go. All three attackers run off into the rapidly darkening night. He drops the broken wine bottle. His fingertips feel tingly and he tries to ignore it. Tries to force down the urge to scream and cry and make something, anything bleed. More important things to do right now, he tries to tell himself. Screaming can come later.

Wes is too big for Collin to pick up, so Collin just helps scoot him through the back door of the coffee shop into the stockroom, locking it behind him, and settles Wes sitting on top of a stack of coffee bean sacks, and turns on the lights.

Oh. Oh goodness. Oh fuck.

Collin debates who he needs to call while Wes tries to stifle his bloody nose with a paper bag he found on the floor of the stockroom. Taylor should know what happened, but Collin is not prepared to deal with an angry Taylor— no sir, not today and maybe not ever. Taylor is downright terrifying. He could call Jax, but Jax would ask a lotta questions that Collin doesn't have an answer to. Collin does not have an extensive contact list. He's got Monique Feldman's number but what would she be doin' here? Well, it's either Todd or Dalton then, and Collin knows Todd has a car.

Collin Donahue: Hey Todd! :)
  Todd Richards: hey collin
  hows ur folks house??
  Collin Donahue: Oh, you know, same old
  Hey Todd, your not still at the mall with Dalton and Taylor,

are you?
you're
Todd Richards: uh,,,
Yeah??
Why do u ask??
Collin Donahue: oh! Sorry! I won't bother you then!
Todd Richards: nah bro it's fine- ur my friend too now :))))
What's up???
Collin Donahue: okay, so this might sound kinda dumb
But could you come and pick us up?
Me and Wes
We're at the coffee shop
We might be a little scared to walk home
Todd Richards: Sure bud,, be otw soon
Y r u scared to walk home????
Collin Donahue: some guys might have come by the coffee shop and beat us up pretty bad
But we're pretty much ok!!
Nobody is dyin or nothin!
Wes might need a few ice packs though, haha
Todd Richards: sdfkj
wtf happened
this is taylr btw
Collin Donahue: oh! Hey Taylor!
I'm not too sure what happened, to be honest
Hang on lemme make sure Wes isn't fallin' asleep
Todd Richards: does he have a concussion
collin
collin
does he have a concussion
Is his head bleedig

collin

We're otw!! Be there in a few!!

(This is todd again btw„„ please make wes text taylor before he has a meltdown or somn)

Collin doesn't see the last several texts because Wes, in fact, did pass out for a second— he wakes up before Collin even gets to start panicking, but then there's a whole new problem because Wes begins to cry. Like, ugly cry. Like, coughing for breath, face red, shivering kind of ugly cry.

Well. Collin has no idea what to do about that. But he can certainly try!

"Wes, you holdin' up alright?"

There is, technically, a reply from Wes, but between the stuttering and the hyperventilating, Collin can't make it out.

"Does it hurt? Want me to grab some ice-" Collin tries, and then adds, "well, shoot, does the coffee shop even have ice?"

Wes nods, but doesn't point out where the ice is, so Collin stays seated, shifting awkwardly where he sits on top of the coffee bean sacks next to Wes. When Mom does this, anything Collin does just hurts, so he does nothing, and he waits for it to pass.

It has not yet passed when Collin lets Taylor, Todd, and Dalton in at the front door of the shop. Todd is the only one who bothers asking what happened, while Dalton starts grabbing Todd's first aid kit from the trunk and Taylor stomps directly to the stockroom.

Taylor is relieved that Dalton, after spending the whole car ride to the coffee shop badgering Taylor about *don't look so tense dude he's alright Collin said so it wasn't your fault*, opts to take care of the nasty looking gash on Collin's neck before following Taylor to the stockroom. Wes is sitting, almost curled up, on a coffee bean sack, rocking back and forth and sobbing. It's hard to even tell how beat up he is through the flinching, fidgety movement.

"Wes." No response. "Wes." Taylor isn't even sure Wes is hearing him. His hands, torn to shreds with what looks like road rash, tangle themselves in his hair and he starts yanking on it— a habit Taylor hasn't seen since middle school. "Wes, dude, you're hurting yourself." Nothing. And Taylor's getting a little desperate— desperate enough that he can't think of a solution fast enough. Before, if Wes was freaking out, he could just distract him with something and the panic would dissipate, but right now Taylor can't even manage to distract himself from the guilt and fear. How could he be stupid enough to think Wes would really trust him? How can he possibly be making this about himself right now?

"Wes—" but Taylor can't think of the right words, he's never been able to think of the right words, so he just unfolds Wes's hands, so gently, prying them from the skin of his scalp. Taylor whispers, "Please, stop hurting yourself."

Wes's whole body shivers with the weight of his next sob, and Taylor resists the urge to shut down, to lash out, to drop Wes's hands and leave him alone in the stockroom of the coffee shop. He tries to think of something that's going to help, anything, and before he can think of anything, his brain spits out, "Goddamn, you're outdoing me in how beat up we can get before Christmas. I'll have to find someone else to kick my ass to keep my spot as the resident punching bag of the group."

"I-i-i-if you d-d-o tha-th-that," Wes stammers between hiccuping breaths, "I wi-i-ill kill you."

Great. Fuck, Taylor feels stupid for saying it, but it got Wes's rapidly spiraling attention, so he'll take it. "Nah," Taylor says, "I'm just gonna go hang out outside a bar again. Pick a fight with another dissatisfied married couple."

Wes screeches, "I-is th-that what-t you d-do!?" He yanks his hands out of Taylor's and pokes at the healing bruise on Taylor's forehead, saying, "You just p-pick fight wi-ith guys out-outside b-b-bars!?"

"He does what!?"

And there's Dalton, at the door of the stockroom with a first aid kit, looking all kinds of concerned.

"Dalton, you should not be surprised by this anymore," Todd sighs, following Dalton into the room. "He's always get-ting in fights- oh, Jesus Christ, Wes, dude, what happened?"

And that would be the question, wouldn't it?

Because every part of Wes that's visible around his jacket and jeans is angry red or crushed purple. He's got one black eye that's on its way to swelling shut, his nose is bleeding, half his face is scraped up from the road salt, shoes, and pavement, and everything he's wearing is disgusting and wet from the post-snow slush in the alleyway. Taylor's seen enough fights to know about how this one went down, but he carefully avoids the part of his brain that could map this shit out like a stopmotion video and lets Wes and Collin explain it instead. Maybe it's not as bad as Taylor thinks.

"Th-the-they, um- well, I-"

"Take a breath, Wes," Todd tries.

Wes nods, fingers spasming in his lap, and Taylor grabs his hand just to hold onto some part of him. Wes starts to fiddle with Taylor's fingers instead of his own. It helps. "I saw th-them outside the shop while I was c-closing up-p. Alex

Morenson, and Mathew Megans and Jasper Liu. I kn-knew why they were here—"

"Were they threatening you?" Todd asks.

"N-no- er, yes," Wes stammers, "They do the same sh-shit to me at sch-school. So I kn-knew."

Dalton cries, "They beat you up at school!?"

"N-not at school."

"So other places!?" Dalton interjects again.

"They've been pretty quiet since I st-started h-hanging out with you guys."

Collin frowns, "'Cept today, I guess." Wes doesn't know this, but Collin told Dalton, Taylor, and Todd what he heard in that alleyway as they came in the door, that word that rhymes with 'agate'. Today wasn't a random happenstance, today was a direct result of what happens when you let resident asshole Freddy Peters stir up mini hate groups all around school with no consequences just because his mom donates a bunch of money to the PTA.

Wes shrugs, and it makes him wince from some bruise nobody can see under the shirt. Taylor's fingernails itch to dig themselves into his skin, but Wes's still got his hand, rubbing fidgety little circles between his digits. "I t-texted Collin when I went to t-t-t-take the trash out-t, and th-they-they were waiting f-for me. I th-thought I was texting Taylor, but your names are next to each-ch other in my ph-phone—"

Taylor shouldn't be so happy about that, about being the person Wes wants to call when he needs something. The guilt is still a stench so overpowering that it makes Taylor's eyes water, but the fact that Wes wanted to text him alleviates some of the pressure. Somebody wanted his help. Somebody wanted him to come. Somebody wanted him.

227

Taylor can't believe he's making this about himself right now.

Dalton says, "Alright, let's get you cleaned up." Wes nods and sits stiller than Taylor ever has while Dalton starts cleaning the road salt and asphalt grit from Wes's face. Dalton isn't always great with being gentle, so Todd, pre-med gifted and talented kid that he is, takes over eventually.

Taylor sees Collin has a ring of bandaids around his neck. They tried to fucking kill him- both of them. "Your neck," he says to Collin.

"O-oh!" Collin squeaks, "One of 'em got me good with one of those plastic things that hold the cans together, like at the supermarket? Wes pushed 'im off me 'fore he did any real damage though!"

"Collin, w-where did you learn to fight like that?" Wes asks. "I took boxing cl-classes when I was little, but th-that was— you—" he glances at Taylor, which is a clear enough indicator of how dangerous Collin is. Now, Taylor knows how Taylor got so good at fighting, even if nobody else does, and it isn't because he took boxing classes. If there's other kids— aside from the kids who actually take martial arts classes of some kind— who are as good as Taylor is at fighting, that's fucking bad, as far as Taylor is concerned.

"Collin-" he starts, but then Collin gets spooked by something.

His eyes go big and wide and he shifts in his coat and says, "I-I uh, I better text Jax. He's already gonna be all kindsa cross with me for not texting him first."

He goes out to the front of the shop, out of earshot. A few minutes later, when Todd and Dalton have almost finished fussing over Wes, Taylor gets a text.

Jaxson Dixon: Macready

I stg

Tell me the truth.

What the FUCK happened to my bf.

Taylor Macready: homophobes

wes texted him nstead of me

idfk

Jaxson Dixon: U r, without a doubt, the LEAST descriptive person in the world and i am going to kill u for it

Taylor Macready: we're at the shop come get me

ill kick ur ass

Jaxson Dixon: tayby baby i was kidding

Im not actually gonna fight u???

Taylor Macready: somebody better

Jaxson Dixon: tf r u on my guy?

Taylor Macready: wait hang on todds says we're meeting at his house now

see u there dipshit

Jaxson Dixon: aight

If my bf comes to ANY further harm before i get there i will hurt u

Wait no u seem to enjoy that

I will hurt ur bf <3

Taylor Macready: id like to see u try

18

Endearments to Disable Your Boyfriend

The first coherent thought Wes has had in what feels like years (but is actually only about half an hour), is *oh thank god, Taylor is here,* when Taylor grabs his hand and Wes realizes that he's been fidgeting with his fingers while trying to answer people's questions.

"Are you coming?" Taylor asks. Everyone else is on their way out of the room, but Taylor hasn't moved yet. He's staring, in that half-angry way, at their entwined hands. Wes thinks Taylor might not like holding hands that much, so he tries to take his back, but Taylor holds onto his hand more fiercely than Wes knows what to do with. "You wanna—" Taylor interrupts himself, "Wes."

"Huh?" Wes is hardly aware that he's even being spoken to.

"Dude, you're not even on this fucking planet—" Taylor blows a breath out through his nose and pulls Wes to his feet. "Come on, we're going to Todd's house."

"Why?"

Taylor asks, "Is it gonna make you feel better to know why,

or are you just asking because you feel like you should?"

Wes isn't sure how to answer, he's just very tired. He shrugs and lets Taylor lead him to Todd's sleet-splattered Jeep Compass. All five of them just barely fit, which means it's a pretty big car. The leather seats hold Wes's attention. So smooth, and barely used. Todd doesn't drive his car too often, not unless he's going somewhere far or his friends ask for a ride. There aren't a lot of kids in Swisher who have their own car, even fewer who have a car this nice, and Todd doesn't like to stand out. The car was a gift from his parents for his sixteenth birthday (everyone always knows what Todd gets for his birthday because his parents always invite the whole town to his parties) and it was brand new then. It's still the newest car in the whole of Swisher.

Taylor says "Wes," like this is the fifth time he's said it. Maybe it is. Wes isn't exactly the master of his faculties at the moment. "Wes, you wanna breathe with me? Everyone else is gonna do it too— right, Dalton?"

"What?"

"Right, Dalton?"

"Oh, yeah, sure."

Tapping out the time on Wes's palm, Taylor breathes in for four, holds for seven, out for eight. Four. Seven. Eight. Four. Seven. Eight. The music is calm and quiet. Classical? As they breathe, Wes can pick out the instruments: piano, cello, violin. Then his vision clears (how long had it been fuzzy?) and he can see that Todd is driving. Dalton is in the passenger seat. Collin is on one side, still looking a little frazzled. Taylor is on the other side, pretending to stare out the window but really trying to catch Wes's eye in the reflection of the tinted glass. When their eyes do meet, Taylor blinks, swallows, looks anywhere else and stops counting out breaths.

Wes swears he's in love, even if he's barely lucid enough to string the thought together.

"Where—" he wheezes a little, and realizes he's out of breath, even though he's been sitting in the car and has no good reason to be out of breath, "Where are we g-going?"

"Toddster is taking care of us," Dalton explains with a forced grin that's more heard than seen, "we're going to his house."

"You sure were out of it," Collin says, giggling, "You were answerin' questions an' all, but I know that look when I see it, yessir!"

The rest of the car gives a polite chuckle to cover up the fact that nobody has the slightest fucking clue why Collin would 'know that look'.

Nobody says much else in the whole three-minute drive to Todd's. Taylor is a warm presence on one side, and Collin is on the other side, itching at the bandaids on his neck. Wes wonders what he looks like right now. It's gotta be at least pretty bad, because Dalton is staring through the rearview mirror and Taylor won't look at him at all. Maybe unconsciously, Taylor is still tapping out the time on Wes's palm. Wes smiles around the bruises dawning on his face.

But the moment he feels that bruise radiate its feathery tendrils of pain from his cheekbone, every other bruise, scrape, and cut comes to vivid technicolor in his interoception. Everything hurts. From toes to crown, Wes's whole body is comprised of a connect-the-dots of different pains, from the sharp one cutting into his forehead to the dull one around his ankle. The salt in the wound is that, even though he's started to dry off in Todd's car, Wes is still soggy and covered in grit and grime from being rolled all over the disgusting asphalt next to the dumpster behind the shop. He feels hurt, he feels gross, he feels fear he feels disgust he feels anger he feels too much too fast—

—and he tries to narrow his focus to Taylor's tapping fingers on his skin.

He keeps himself collected in a tight, tense, pissed off little puddle at the top of his head, but Taylor's fingers are there in his palm. Everything else spins and spins and spins around that point of contact. That touch is his control center.

Todd types a code into the keypad at the gate to his driveway, and then they slide into the garage, and then Wes is being coaxed out of his seat by Taylor, and Wes follows in a haze just in case there's a chance he could hold Taylor's hand again.

"I'm gonna stab Freddy Peters right in his disgusting face," Jaxson says, emerging from the side of Todd's house.

Todd and Dalton both screech in undignified ways (Wes would have screeched too, had he been cognizant enough to know why Jaxson coming out of nowhere on Todd's sup- posedly unoccupied property was spooky), and Jaxson waves them off in favor of wrapping his arms around Collin.

Over Collin's shoulder, Jaxson scoffs, "Your fence is way too easy to hop for you to be surprised that I'm here, Todd."

"Well next time don't fucking materialize out of the blue when we're already nervous!" Todd screams.

"Shut up," Jaxson says with a faux-seriousness, "my boyfriend is injured and I would like to coddle him now." To Collin, he says, "Fucking hell, Collin, they tried to chop your head off!"

Wes just kind of stares. They did try to chop Collin's head off. Taylor says something ribbing, and Jaxson responds with something snarky, and Todd makes some sarcastic comment and Dalton laughs, but Wes doesn't really hear them. He feels very tired all of a sudden.

"Todd, I'm taking Wes inside," Taylor says.

Todd says, "You're right, it's cold as fuck out here," but Taylor wasn't waiting for a response.

Inside of Todd's house is warmer than outside, but still chilly in the way that houses that are *lived at* instead of *lived in* feel. Todd runs up a grand staircase by the entrance and returns with a sweater and some joggers.

Dalton laughs, "No offense, Toddster, but I don't think Wes's gonna fit into your hand-me-downs." He's probably right. Todd has a build that could be called academic, and Wes looks enough like a tractor that he might be able to run on diesel. Plus the four-inch height gap.

Todd nudges Dalton in the shoulder, "Shut up, they're way too big for me. Last year my parents forgot what size I wore, so all my birthday clothes were, like, three sizes too big."

"Dude, your parents got you a fucking Bape sweater and didn't get the right size!?" Jaxson cries, "I'm gonna sue."

"I shouldn't tell you about the Saint Laurent then," Todd jokes, and Jaxson screams something that gets lost in the 12-foot ceilings.

Taylor shoves Wes into a bathroom that Wes wouldn't have even known to look for amongst all the doors in the hallway to the left of the foyer and passes him the clothes and says, "If you're not done in three minutes I'm breaking down the door."

Wes barely hears him, and he stares at the clothes and wonders why Todd would loan him clothes after he caused so much trouble. Before he knows it, someone is banging on the door and saying, "Coming in."

Taylor looks pissed. "Dude, you haven't fucking moved."

"Huh?"

"Jesus fucking, alright, com'ere." Taylor unbuttons Wes's long sleeve, face going very red, and pulls it off his arms. "Can you—" he clears his throat, "can you get the undershirt by yourself?"

There's a joke somewhere in there about boyfriends and intimacy, but Wes can't find it in the scrambled mess of his brain right now. He pulls off his shirt, trying not to twitch too hard and get it stuck around his ears.

Taylor breathes, "Fucking Christ," under his breath. "Wes, are you... okay? I mean, fuck, of course you're not okay, god," he forces a laugh, but Wes can see tears building in the shine of his eyes. "You just got the shit beat outta you by some homophobes because you're dating me! And I don't know how the fuck to even help! Jesus! Fuck me— this is all my fault! If you had left me under that bridge, we wouldn't be here! You would be fine, and Collin and everyone else would be fine— fuck me!"

Wes shimmies himself into Todd's sweater. He doesn't bother looking at himself, because he knows it'll just freak him out. He can feel most of the bruising anyway, at the gauzy edges of his epinephrine-soaked perception. Even though his ears still feel stuffed with cotton, and he can't really assign names to the different objects in the room yet, and he can tell from the tremors in his shoulders that he's starting to hyperventilate again, Wes knows Taylor needs help too.

"Babe," Wes says, and immediately regrets using the endearment when it comes off his tongue clumsy and awkward, "this isn't your fault."

Taylor pauses mid-rant. His mouth keeps moving, like it might still believe it is ranting, but there's no sound coming out. It keeps opening and closing while Taylor's face goes bright red, rose-red, fire-red, starting at his ears and blooming out towards his cheekbones and neck.

"I heard yelling," Dalton says from outside the door. "Taylor, are you being mean to your boyfriend?"

Taylor's expression changes slightly, now half angry and half panicking. He's still mouthing out words with no sound.

Dalton opens the bathroom door. He takes in the scene and guffaws, and then calls everyone else in, saying "Wes broke Taylor."

One by one, Todd, Jaxson, and Collin poke their heads into the bathroom to gape and giggle. Then Taylor gets pissed and kicks them out, still wordless. He locks the door and backs up into the corner and finally gets his voice back enough to whisper, "What did you call me?"

Wes yelps out a surprised little sound. He hadn't thought that was what Taylor was reacting to! "Uh, I take it back!" he cries quickly, "I won't call you that again!"

"No!" Taylor snaps, "Wait— I mean— uh, fuck. I didn't..." He mutters, "I didn't hate it."

"Y-you-..." Wes is so fucking surprised by the fact that, of all people to enjoy cutesy endearments, it's this motherfucker, he's almost laughing. Almost. His ribs still hurt too bad to really laugh hard, but it's close. "Dude, er, wait," Wes clears his throat and, very self-consciously, says, "dearest."

Instantly, Taylor goes right back to red from his collarbone to his forehead. Wes has one thought to kiss every red spot on his face, but that still seems so far away. Instead, Wes grins a shit-eating grin and ignores Taylor's too-late plea of "no, wait, don't" and he sprints from the room, ignoring the bruises and scrapes on his legs, and skids to a halt in front of Todd, Dalton, Jaxson, and Collin.

They all look at him like he might have hit his head pretty hard. Maybe he has, but that's not the point. The point is, "Watch." And Taylor stomps over next to Wes. And Wes says, innocently, "Hi, sweetheart." And Taylor's face goes bright, vivid red and his pride and embarrassment are at war over whether to cover his face or not, and everyone blows up laughing.

"Holy fuck," Dalton screams through his laughter, "you actually, seriously broke him!"

Taylor opens his mouth with a barbed reply, but all that comes out is a strangled, "fuck you."

Collin does his best not to laugh too much. "Aw, come on, guys, don't tease him," he says, "I was just like that at first when Jax and I got together."

This gets a vaguely thankful expression from Taylor, and more bellowing laughter from everyone else.

"Collin is my only friend," Taylor says through gritted teeth and flushed cheeks, "fuck the rest of you."

Tensions feel diffused after that. Taylor tries calling Wes "babe," but he can only get out the first phoneme before his whole vocal tract starts playing possum.

Wes tries to insist that he doesn't need help getting himself patched up, "just gimme a first aid kit and I'll throw on some band-aids," but literally everyone shot that down.

"At least let me clean up that cut on your forehead," Todd says, maneuvering Wes back into the hall bathroom.

"It's only fair; you patched Taylor up on Wednesday," Dalton calls after them. "We're just returning the favor."

Jaxson asks, "Did you dipshits even check for a concussion yet? I cannot tell you the kinda trouble me and Collin have gotten ourselves into for not checking for concussions—" He cuts himself off, seeming to only realize what he's said after it's come out of his mouth.

Taylor, thankfully, misses what he said (or pretends to) and grumbles, "We get it, you're in love, shut the fuck up about it," as if Jaxson said something else entirely.

Happy to redirect, Jaxson asks, "And did Wes make sure to check your, ya know, personal areas?"

"I will kill you where you stand, Dixon."

Collin smacks Jaxson playfully on the back of the head, and Jaxson's attention is diverted to sticking his tongue out at Collin instead of needling Taylor. "Did y'all ever check Taylor's ribs after Freddy Peters kicked him on Thursday?" Collin asks, "'Cause he sure did go down like a sack of bricks."

"I lied," Taylor says as Dalton and Jaxson's eyes slide to him, and Wes squeaks out a negative response from the bathroom, "Collin is not my friend either."

"Well, sure I am!" Collin replies optimistically, "Friends make sure to check in with each other!"

It takes heckling, convincing, and a well-timed cutesy nickname from Wes (who is still being taken care of by Todd in the bathroom down the hall), but Dalton manages to get Taylor to let him poke at his torso, just to make sure nothing is really wrong.

Dalton pokes, and Taylor is under duress from Jaxson (who has promised to be much more invasive than Dalton, if Taylor lies or is uncooperative) to tell him if it hurts.

"Ow."

"Yes, that hurts."

"Ow."

"Ow."

"Ow."

"If you touch that rib again, I'm gonna knock you on your fucking ass."

Dalton eventually says, "Jesus Fucking Christ, where doesn't it hurt."

"The bruises are, like, four days old, dude," Taylor grumbles, "They don't hurt at all if you don't fuckin' poke them with your giant fucking football-player fingers."

Dalton clutches his fingers to his chest as if burned. "Todd," he whines, "Taylor is making fun of my fingers again!"

"Taylor, don't make fun of Dalton's fingers," Todd calls from the bathroom, followed by a little echo of a giggle from Wes.

19

Red Behavior Card

Todd orders pizza for dinner and pays with his parent's Wells Fargo Business Elite Signature Card®. He tips 30% because he, unlike his parents, believes that trickle-down economics only work through direct actions, like tipping your delivery driver 30% when you can definitely afford it. He also might still be feeling a little sore about his parents leaving for their yearly Christmas Conference Trip.

He's always a little sore around Christmas.

Todd and his friends go down to the basement and play around with his VR headset. Jaxson makes too many jokes about how lucky a "poor commoner" like him is to "have but a moment of enjoyment with the toys of the wealthy." Taylor tells him to shut the fuck up. Collin asks if he can have a turn, and can he switch the game to something where PvP is disabled. Dalton says "smacking people with our rubbery, digital hands is the best part!" Wes says VR freaks him out, and he and Todd watch the other boys making weird faces under the headset and crying out at digital perils.

The bandaids Todd put on the worst of the scrapes on Wes's

cheek and forehead wrinkle when he laughs. Todd's just relieved Wes sat still enough to get the bandaids on there, and clean the asphalt and road salt out of the injury, and throw some hydrogen peroxide on to prevent infection–

Taylor never lets Todd clean the asphalt and road salt out of his face. Taylor says "I'm fine, Todd, lay off" for two weeks until the cut that hadn't been too bad is oozing puss and still bright red and Todd snaps "for fuck's sake!" and has Dalton threaten to hold him down if he doesn't cooperate. And Taylor flinches the whole time like Todd might hit him.

"Thanks for patching me up," Wes says.

Without really meaning to, Todd replies, "Why are you such a good kid?"

Wes looks at him like his hair's on fire (maybe it is) and says, "I'm not."

They don't talk for a minute. Todd is trying not to let reality set in yet.

When Todd was four-and-a-half, just about ready to start school in the early kindergarten program, his parents sat him down and explained to him that there would be bullies. Todd was just enamored by the rare moment of undivided attention from both parents, so he listened extra carefully as his mom and dad explained how bullies could be any size or shape, with any face. They might use physical violence, they might use emotional violence, but they would certainly pick on Todd.

Without voicing it, Todd had known that his parents said this because Todd was small, and people picked on small kids. The movies told him that.

Mom had said that these things would surely hurt Todd's feelings. This hurt, she said gently, would help him grow. She reassured Todd that, if they could, she and Dad would hide

Todd from this hurt, but if they did then he would grow up "too sheltered" and he would never know how to navigate the world as an adult.

Todd, at four-and-a-half, had no clue what any of that meant, but he had nodded along sagely as if he understood.

Dad had said that Todd should never respond to those words. Todd should, Dad said firmly, not even react, because he is better than any of the names the other kids would call him. He muttered under his breath that he wasn't sure if things would be better or worse in a backwater town like this, and Mom had said it couldn't be worse than the city they had just moved from.

Todd, at four-and-a-half, had no clue what "words" his parents were referring to, but it was clear they meant a specific one, and so he nodded along sagely as if he understood that his parents were trying to brace him against being the only Black kindergartner at Swisher Elementary School.

And the next day, Todd stomped confidently to school in his nicest outfit (he dressed himself, which his parents thought was a wonderful show of his independence and they took pictures of the outfit with pride— after a few "fixes") and hung his tiny, shiny backpack on the hook with his name on it, and sat in the tiny, tiny desk with his name on it, and he smiled.

He was in school now. No more playtime alone with the nanny! He would have friends. He would make sure of it.

To his left, there was a little boy who was very tall, for a kindergartner, and his name tag read "Taylor." Taylor didn't smile, or frown. He didn't make any faces at all. He looked like a statue, just like the ones in the museums Mom and Dad took Todd to.

Behind Taylor, there was another little boy who was very chubby, for a kindergartner, and his name tag read "Dalton." Dalton was tapping on Taylor's shoulder and saying "Hey, hey, what's your name? Hey. Turn around. Hey, what's your name? Hey, do you wanna be friends? We could play on the slide together at recess. What's your name? Are you ignoring me?"

Todd waved at the tall, quiet boy. Taylor didn't wave back. Todd wanted to tell the chubby boy what the quiet boy's name was, since he could mostly read, but he wasn't sure how the "lor" sound was pronounced: was it like the first half of 'lord' or the second half of 'tailor'? He didn't wanna be wrong and look stupid, so Todd said nothing.

Eventually, the chubby boy turned to the girl behind Todd, she had very long hair, for a kindergartner, and her name tag read "Celsee." Dalton didn't talk to Celsee, and as his eyes moved past her, they reached Todd, and Dalton said, "Hi, my name is Dalton, what's your name?"

"My name is Todd," Todd said, trying to sit up so straight that he wouldn't look so small, for a kindergartner.

"Do you wanna be friends, Todd?" Dalton asked, "We can play on the slide at recess together. This is my other friend, but he's ignoring me and he won't tell me his name, so we'll have to ask him later. My mom always says to ask people things when they're in a good mood, not a bad mood."

"Yeah," Todd had replied. His toddler-brain hadn't heard anything after that first question. "Yeah, let's be friends Dalton."

At snack time, Dalton dragged Taylor by the hand to sit on the same mat with him and Todd. Dalton had an orange and a snack pack of goldfish. Taylor had half a package of graham crackers. Todd had a whole bunch of fruit snack packets. He gave some to Dalton and Taylor, and Dalton said thank you very much and Taylor said thanks— the first thing he'd said all day.

They sat next to each other on the rug for story time, and Todd helped Dalton when they did spelling practice, and, at lunch, they sat next to each other in the cafeteria.

At recess, Todd went up to the slide first, followed quickly by Dalton (who was insistent that the swings were next) and Taylor (who might have been having fun with them and might have just been just sticking around so nobody else talked to him). At the top, there was a boy who was very big, for a kindergartner, and Todd recognized him as the boy who interrupted story time three times and already had his behavior card on yellow, Freddy Peters.

Freddy Peters was already infamous, but he still had four friends. Todd wasn't jealous of Freddy Peters having more friends than him because his mom told him already that, with friends, it's quality over quantity. Unlike fruit snacks, where the opposite principle is true.

Freddy Peters had sneered that it was *his* **slide.**

Todd had said it's not his, it's the school's, "but if it's your turn now, we can share."

Freddy Peters said it's not his *turn* it's his *slide*, and he said Todd can "go suck a dick." Todd didn't know what a "dick" was, but he had figured that must be the word his parents were warning him about. Freddy Peters' friend in the puffy blue coat with a hole in the arm knew what that word meant, and he laughed at Freddy Peters for saying it.

"Why are you being mean to me?" Todd asked plainly, almost plaintively— almost. He was determined not to have his feelings hurt by the only boy in class who already had a yellow behavior card.

Freddy Peters called him a word that starts with an "n" sound, but Todd didn't hear the rest of it because Taylor had already pushed Freddy Peters off the whole play structure.

Taylor became the first boy in class to have a red behavior card, and he was the first one to have to sit in the timeout chair for the whole of craft time.

Todd didn't figure out what word his parents had tried to protect him from until he was already a third-grader and he asked them what they had meant and they had seemed surprised that he didn't already know.

Todd didn't figure out that Jaxson Dixon had told Taylor Macready what that word was— the word that Jaxson had heard from his parents all the time at home— until fifth grade, when he asked him. By then, Taylor had already had a red behavior card enough times that everyone in their grade knew better than to say it when he was in earshot.

Now, Taylor laughs and pushes Dalton into the couch cushions, and Dalton bitches and moans and tells Todd that Taylor is being mean to him, and for once Todd can't look Taylor in his bruised face and tell him to knock it off.

Instead, Wes tells Taylor not to push his friends, and Taylor throws his arms up like it's some unreasonable request, and Jaxson shoves Taylor into the couch next to Dalton.

Todd smiles and tries not to let reality sink in.

After pizza, everyone kind of sits around talking and tacitly wondering whether they should go home for pajamas and shit or not. "I've slept in jeans before and I'll do it again," Taylor grumbles stubbornly. Wes has somehow gotten Taylor squished up next to him, wrapped comfortably in his arms. Taylor's expression is daring anyone to comment on it, and Wes looks fucking giddy.

Jaxson, of course, has outgrown such childish embarrassment, but not the delight of sitting in Collin's lap with his head on his shoulder, which Collin relishes in as well.

Todd is saying that, of course, anyone who wants can borrow pajamas, "and I'm sure there's some extra toothbrushes around here."

Dalton says "nobody here brushes their teeth and you know it."

But Todd, apparently, did not know that. Totally unaware that this is the least significant thing to occur today, Todd starts insisting to Dalton (and, after a minute, Taylor and Wes and Jaxson and Collin too) that brushing your teeth is paramount to your dental health and nobody here wants dentures, do they? No, they don't.

Jaxson is kinda basking in it all. The easy domesticity after such a genuinely fucking absurd day.

Juniper-Maisie texted him this morning, asked him to come home and talk. She brought Hellen along too, teary-eyed and stiff-spined. The girls sat him down very seriously— more serious than Jaxson knows how to be— and Hellen told Jaxson that Taylor won't respond to her texts. Jaxson had tried to reassure her that Taylor was alright, and he was probably just being stupid, but Hellen interrupted him and told him it wasn't about her brother texting her back, it was about him being safe. She'd told Jaxson that if Taylor won't text her back, fine, he's an idiot, whatever, "but, please, Jaxson, make sure he's taking care of himself." Juniper-Maisie had given Jaxson a look that balanced puppy-dog eyes and a death threat, and

Jaxson promised he would.

"What am I supposed to say?" he had joked, "No? To those cute little faces?"

In the summer before she started fifth grade, Juniper-Maisie Dixon had said she didn't want to go home anymore, and she had taken her best friend, Hellen Macready, by the hand and they had packed what they deemed essential and they ran away.

Taylor had found out first because Hellen left him a note because she didn't think her big brother, stoic and aloof as he was, would ever bother looking for her. She had been proven very wrong when Taylor stomped right up to the tree she and Juniper-Maisie had been hiding from the world in, out of breath, after searching the whole town for seven hours. It was dark by then, and Taylor had never been good at climbing trees because he was scared of heights, but he climbed this tree and sat on the limb just below Juniper-Maisie and Hellen's and he said, "What the fuck were you thinking, Hellen?" Juniper-Maisie and Hellen knew Taylor barely well enough by then to hear that he had been worried. Taylor said, "C'mon. Let's go home. Jaxson will actually kill me if I let you get hurt." But Juniper-Maisie leaned close to Hellen and Hellen screamed that she didn't wanna go home anymore because Mom and Dad are mean to Taylor and Mr. and Mrs. Dixon are mean to Juniper-Maisie and Hellen doesn't think she needs adults for anything because they're all mean so no she isn't going home not ever.

Taylor had no answer for that, but he wasn't going home without them either. He'd get his ass kicked for that. So he waited.

Eventually, Juniper-Maisie said *besides, this is a nice tree.*

And Hellen nodded and said it was the best tree ever and no adults would ever find them this high because adults never look up. Taylor said, "How about a treehouse?" and, after some careful negotiation, the girls finally agreed to return home under the condition that Taylor build them a treehouse in this exact tree.

Taylor walked Hellen home first because Mom and Dad knew those two didn't ever go anywhere together and they didn't want a bunch of questions thrown their (Taylor's) way. Hellen waltzed in as if she had just been playing with Juniper-Maisie as usual, and Taylor walked Juniper-Maisie home, and the first thing Juniper-Maisie said to Jaxson was "I'm so sorry, Jaxson! I promise I won't ever run away again! I would miss you too much."

And Jaxson, who had thought Juniper-Maisie was at Hellen's house, said, "What the fuck are you talking about, Jamwich?"

And Taylor tried to walk away, but Juniper-Maisie grabbed him by the hem of his shirt and said, "Taylor promised to build us a treehouse, can you help him?"

And by then, Juniper-Maisie had started crying, so Jaxson just said, "Sure thing," to get her to calm down and then, "Why don't you go to bed? I'll come tuck you in in a minute." And when she was gone and as out-of-earshot as one can be in the Dixon trailer, Jaxson asked Taylor what the fuck happened— was Hellen okay— did anyone die or anything.

And Taylor had shrugged and walked away.

Jaxson and Taylor spent the rest of the summer building that treehouse. Neither of them talked at all because their entire relationship to that point had been built on their sisters speaking for them, and neither Taylor nor Jaxson knew what to say to each other.

Lumber was unwillingly and unwittingly donated by the logging yard on the other side of the woods. They only got caught once, and they ran so fast that the guy didn't get a chance to really see who they were. Jaxson, going into his freshman year of high school after an eighth grade spent bitterly alone, was growing into his charisma, and got the plans for how to build the treehouse from the Home Depot manager, operating as a distraction while Taylor stole the nails and hammer behind their back.

It was shitty and small and barely held the weight of the girls when they finished it in late June, but Juniper-Maisie and Hellen screamed for joy when they saw it for the first time and decorated it with pink sewing fabric that they found at a garage sale for fifty cents. Over the years, Jaxson has updated the treehouse with a better, wider, less flimsy foundation so he could spend the night here with Collin when their parents are both too much. He gave it walls the first winter after he and Taylor finished it, and he put a tin roof on last year. After asking anxiously for permission, Collin hollowed out a bit of the tree trunk and started stashing non-perishable snacks for when his parents decide food is a luxury.

It's as much a home for Jaxson as anywhere else, at this point. And the girls haven't used it in years, although Jaxson never took their pink garage-sale fabric out of the tree-branches.

Jaxson chews on the fact that the Macreadys really do pick favorites. He's not sure whether it's better or worse that the Dixons hit all their kids equally. Whatever. At least Juniper-Maisie and Hellen don't need a treehouse to feel safe anymore.

Now, Jaxson is leaning into the relative safety of Collin's

arms and smiling to himself that he doesn't really need that treehouse either. Not now.

Good. Let it rot, even if he loved it.

Out of a languid, passing curiosity, Jaxson lowers his voice below the conversation that Todd, Dalton, Taylor, and Wes are still having. "Hey, Collin, when was the last time you went to the treehouse?"

Jaxson feels it when Collin' smile drops, feels the rumble of breath in his lungs where they're pressed into Jaxson's back when he replies, "Can we talk about this later, Jax?"

The texture of the couch turns into linoleum underneath him, and Todd's basement is suddenly frigid. Jaxson says, maybe louder than he meant, "Collin, the fuck're you talking about?"

20

Understanding is the Only Way Some People Know How to Show Love

Collin squirms in Jax's glare.

Everyone is looking right at them, and Collin is a good liar, but he's also exhausted. And Jax looks real sorry about talkin' so loud now that everyone's eyes are on them. Collin is so tired of lying.

"Look here now," he says with a skittering smile to the group of boys, as if this were some gradeschool confidence, "if I tell you this, you can't tell nobody. Not a soul!"

Everyone nods. Jaxson's eyes are endless, oilslick pools of worry, right down deep as the ocean.

Collin face tries on several expressions before he finds one that fits what he feels. "So ya know I've been spendin' an awful lotta time with you fellas these past few days—and it's been fun! Problem is, I didn't get a chance to..." Collin trails off.

He had meant to say that he didn't get a chance to ask his parents for permission before running off on Friday night to look for Taylor and Wes.

But Wes's fingers are doing a funny, anxious little rubbing motion, and Taylor offers a hand, and Wes takes it and starts fidgeting with Taylor's hand instead. It seems to calm them both down. If Collin says that he left that night to go find them, they'll go crazy thinkin' it was their fault or something. It wasn't. Collin don't know much, but he knows this ain't nobody's fault but his parents'.

So Collin rephrases, "My parents don't want me comin' back home no more."

"They said that!?" Jaxson cries, oilslick eyes lighting on fire with the kind of rage people only feel for the assholes who hurt their friends.

"Uh, not in so many words!" Collin answers quickly, "But you know how they are, and I ain't been home in a few days, and I don't— I can't—" His voice fails him, sinking to a whisper. "I don't wanna go back."

The room is a mosaic for several seconds. Everyone is trying to wrap their heads around Collin's situation.

"They'll hurt you," Taylor understands instantly.

Collin nods.

Nobody moves, except for Wes's hands desperately trying to expend his nervous energy in fiddling with Taylor's fingers, trying to minimize the tics that are growing progressively more visible as the tension in the air escalates.

Taylor, maybe trying for a joke (Collin can still barely tell with Taylor), says flatly, "Homeless buddies."

And then Dalton snaps. In half. Like a rubber band. Collin sees the change in his eyes. In the tilt of his mouth before it opens. Dalton says, "No. No, you are not. Neither of you. Nobody is homeless." Collin is kinda too stunned to reply to Dalton's absolute nonsense.

"Uh, Dalton," Todd starts, but Dalton cuts him off.

"No, Todd! I can't fucking handle it anymore!" He shouts, throwing himself to his feet. "Nobody! Is! Homeless! And do you want me to tell you why?"

"Please do before Taylor's boyfriend has an aneurysm," Jaxson says, eyeing the way Wes's tics are entirely out of his control now that Dalton is yelling.

Dalton takes the hint, takes a breath, and says, "Nobody here is homeless because we're all together." Taylor and Todd scoff affectionately, and Dalton laughs too. "Laugh at me all you want but the power of fucking friendship is gonna be how we fix this. I will share a six-by-ten studio apartment in fucking Kalona before I let anyone here sleep outside of a warm bed. I have a fucking line, guys, and I'm drawing it. You guys are not allowed to be homeless. Not on my fucking watch."

Taylor replies, "That's the most I've ever heard you curse in a thirty-second span. I'm proud of you." Dalton makes a face at him that Collin thinks might be exasperated, but it's hard to tell because he's almost laughing.

Todd says, "Dalton, your sentiment is super admirable and the power of friendship is great and everything, but I have two extra bedrooms."

"You do not," Dalton insists, "you have, like, six."

"No, it's just two. The other rooms you're thinking of are my study, my parents' offices, the studio, the reading room, and the sensory room."

Jaxson barks out a laugh. "Rich people are fucking ridiculous."

Collin is still stuck on the part where he told these people he had a problem, and their first reaction was to defend him.

To protect him. To help him.

They're all still kids, technically, and they're all going through such terrible things. They're all still kids, even if just barely, and there should still be someone who was supposed to protect them. But that's okay. Apparently, kids can protect each other.

But Collin has missed a bridge in the conversation and now Dalton and Todd are initiating a game that they're calling "Overnight Hide and Seek."

"W-w-what's that?" Wes asks. The stammering clearly worries Taylor, who goes against all of the rumors Collin has spent his life hearing at school and wiggles closer to Wes like an attention-starved rodent.

"It's like hide and seek," Taylor explains, "but you sleep in your hiding spot."

"That sounds like the worst idea ever," Jaxson says, but he's laughing. Collin smiles too. He loves it when Jax laughs, sounds like warm water over cold gravel.

Todd launches into a more official-sounding version of the rules, and then they all scatter off to play.

Collin knows they're stalling. Sometime, they're going to have to confront all the bad shit that's happened to them. But instead, Dalton and Todd bring up a silly game to fall asleep, and Collin starts to love his new friends.

Wes and Taylor immediately break the rules of Overnight Hide and Seek by hiding together. You are supposed to hide separately. That's part of the fun. But Wes is still a little jumpy about Todd's house, since he's only ever been there once, and Taylor is still a little jumpy about being away from Wes for an extended period of time, since Wes was recently jumped by homophobes.

Besides, Taylor says he knows the best hiding spot in the house. Wes tries to argue there's no way Taylor knows a better hiding spot than Todd, because Todd lives here, but Taylor says "trust me, I've never been found once" and Wes is forced to think about how Dalton and Todd claimed to have never seen Taylor sleep around them.

Seeing the spot, Wes still insists there's no way they could both fit in there. Maybe Taylor on his own, but Wes is kinda big. Taylor tells him it'll be fine, they can both fit— he'll make them both fit, for fuck's sake.

And Wes couldn't think of any other worries to pitch out there so now they're both shoved into an empty cabinet below the counter in the basement kitchen (which is definitely a kitchen, not a bar as Todd had tried to claim). There was already a pillow and blanket there before they climbed in.

"I sleep here every time," Taylor explains, "sometimes I just crawl in here to see how long it'll take them to notice that I'm gone. They still don't know about it."

"They've never checked here once!?" Wes exclaims.

"I mean, would you? It doesn't look big enough to fit a person on the outside."

It doesn't. Wes had been extremely dubious that even Taylor would fit, and he had almost refused to climb in at all. He's not exactly claustrophobic, but he *is* afraid of crushing Taylor. But there's enough room, barely, for both of them to lay pressed right up against each other. Wes can feel Taylor's breath on the side of his neck, and he's doing his absolute best to be cool about that.

It doesn't help that his brain keeps reminding him that he and Taylor are technically dating, and that he should get used to this.

How the fuck is Wes supposed to get used to this? He feels like he's floating, and like every nerve in his body is on fire, and like he could die right now and walk confidently into hell knowing he lived the best life ever if he just got to sit here in this cramped cabinet in Todd's basement with Taylor. The only thing tethering him to earth is the sallow throb of the scrapes on his cheek from the road salt, and the ache of his bruised ribs.

It's pitch black in the cabinet, so Wes can't see around him. If this were ten years ago, he'd be terrified, but even if the edges of paranoid anxiety are creeping into the peripheral of his thoughts, he'll stay here forever if it means he gets to have Taylor this close.

Taylor's arm reaches above their heads and his hand squeezes sideways to pull something out from the drawer a foot above them. A button clicks- a flashlight. Now illuminated by the dim yellow light of a dollar-store flashlight, Taylor's glaring at the door of the cabinet like it has personally wronged him.

Wes surprises himself by knowing what the expression means.

Smiling, because he feels like he's been let in on the big secret of Taylor's weaknesses, Wes whispers, "Thanks. I don't like the dark either."

Then Taylor glares at Wes like he has personally wronged him. If this were a week ago, Wes would be terrified, but even if the nail-bites of uncertainty dig at the peripheral of his thoughts, he knows Taylor wouldn't be this close to him if he was actually mad.

Taylor grumbles, "One of these days, you're going to realize that I'm a fuckup."

Wes rolls his eyes. "Feeling's mutual, dumbass."

"The fuck is that supposed to mean?"

"It means one of these days you're going to have to realize you're not the only fuckup in this relationship."

"I'm sorry I wasn't there," Taylor blurts. It catches Wes so off guard that he momentarily forgets what Taylor could be talking about. Taylor pushes on, voice catching and tearing like a poorly-knit sweater, "At the coffee shop. Today. I'm so— I'm so sorry."

"Taylor..." Wes doesn't even know how to respond. Even thinking about what happened today feels so overwhelming. He doesn't know how to process it himself, much less help Taylor process it. It hurts physically, but emotionally it's such a nebulous, strange concept that someone would want to hurt you for what you are, not just something you'd done. It's sad. And there's the guilt of knowing that if he'd reacted faster, been more alert, more paranoid, he might've been able to fight them off. And there's the fear of what if it happens again. And there's just too much for Wes to even think about without his consciousness escaping his body.

But he wants to be in his body right now, curled up next to his boyfriend, even if that boyfriend is about to cry. "Can I take off your hat?" is what comes out of Wes's mouth. He barely knows he's saying it. Taylor nods, face turned down and away from Wes in the only way it's possible to break eye contact in such close quarters. It means that Taylor's forehead is pressed to Wes's collarbone when Wes moves to take off the hat.

Then Taylor flinches, and Wes stops.

For one stomach-dropping second, Wes realizes that he knows so little about Taylor Macready. Then Taylor wiggles one hand out from under Wes and pulls off his own hat and shoves it under the pillow beneath both of their heads. He does it so angrily, but he doesn't pull his face away from Wes's collarbone. It makes Wes giggle. But this close, Wes can feel through some intangible sensory data that Taylor is fragile, so he gently, slowly (slow enough that Taylor has plenty of time to say no, or move) settles his fingers in Taylor's hair. Taylor doesn't move except to grab two fistfuls of the sweater Wes is borrowing from Todd, so Wes presses his fingertips farther into Taylor's scalp, brushing the hair up and down with fidgety rhythm.

Neither one of them is sure who falls asleep first, but by the time they drift off their aches are foreign and their cares untethered.

* * *

If you wake up first the morning after a game of Overnight Hide and Seek, as Todd does, you know that your chances of being the winner are pretty good. Overnight Hide and Seek has never been about winning though, it's just been about Todd trying to get Taylor and Dalton to go to bed at a reasonable hour when they have sleepovers on school nights, because even at ten Todd had been responsible enough to know that you need eight hours of sleep to be productive in school (or, at least, that's what his parents told him when he asked if he could stay up a few more minutes to finish a TV show episode he was watching). It had been much easier to get his friends to bed if they were separate, so Todd proposed Overnight Hide and Seek one Wednesday night when he was ten and they played every weekday-night sleepover until they were Freshmen and felt stupid playing any game that involved 'Hide and Seek' in the title.

Had Dalton or Taylor been the first to wake up, they would have immediately sought the other players out to proclaim their victory or to stubbornly poke them awake just to bother them, respectively. Neither Taylor nor Dalton knows the true purpose of Overnight Hide and Seek, so they just think it's some weird game that they play to win. Dalton hardly ever wins because he sleeps like a bear and hides poorly, prioritizing comfort. Taylor wins sometimes, when Todd is particularly exhausted. Todd wins when he feels like it. But the game has never been about winning, for Todd. It's been about getting everyone to sleep.

And everyone had needed to sleep last night.

It's one thing for Taylor to go pick a fight with some drunk idiot, like he did Wednesday (god, doesn't that feel like a fucking eon ago); it's another thing entirely for Wes to get the shit kicked out of him by homophobes at his own place of business. Similar level of injury (assumedly; Taylor has and will always refuse to take off his shirt to show anyone how bad it really is). Different emotional impact.

So Todd has a few options this morning: wake everyone up and play up the 'fun game' aspect of Overnight Hide and Seek, or make breakfast for when everyone else naturally comes to the kitchen (it would probably just be an ungodly amount of toaster waffles, because the chef doesn't come in unless Todd calls her when his parents go out of town).

He goes for breakfast, and peels himself out from where he's tucked himself into the curtained-off bay window in his room to throw on some socks and slip downstairs.

Everyone could probably use as much sleep as they can get, and even if Todd woke them up he wouldn't know what to say to them. 'Good morning, the world is still as cruel as it was when you fell asleep'? 'I hope you slept well despite your numerous accumulating injuries'? Breakfast is an easier greeting to give.

It's only when Todd closes the door to his room silently behind him that he sees Collin wringing his hands in the hallway.

"Oh," Todd says, a little surprised to see Collin separate from Jaxson. They had said everyone has to sleep separately, but Todd had kind of assumed Jaxson and Collin would break that rule. Collin turns and Todd greets him with, "You won."

"I did?" Collin whispers.

"Yeah, seems like it."

"Do we go find everyone else now, then?"

"Let's let them sleep," Todd suggests, "Wanna help me make breakfast? You were pretty good at pancakes last time, and we have more ingredients here than boxed pancake mix."

Infinitesimally, the slope of Collin' shoulders relaxes. He nods and follows Todd down to the kitchen.

The pantry is a separate room from the rest of the kitchen, and Collin hesitates at the custom-made, balsa-wood lattice of the door. "You can come in," Todd presses when Collin starts to wring his hands again.

Collin flinches at the invitation and lowers his eyes. "Does this door have a lock in it?" he asks. Which is an absolutely bizarre question to ask about a pantry.

But Todd recognizes the look in Collin eyes as the same one he hadn't known how to interpret ten years ago when Taylor came over for the first time and stared at Todd's parents like they wronged him personally until they left the room.

Instead of answering, Todd says, "What do you wanna make? I'll grab the ingredients while you cook."

Collin decides on scones ("Jax loves it when I make scones, but my folks don't always let me and his oven don't usually work") and Todd locates and retrieves the flour, sugar, milk, butter, baking soda and baking powder ("Aren't they the same thing?" Todd asks as he hands them to Collin. Collin replies, "Not quite, but I sure as heck don't know the difference"), sour cream, and lemon juice.

"Shouldn't we wake everyone up?" Collin asks while he shapes the dough into little shapes (the recipe said triangles but neither Collin nor Todd care very much about that instruction).

"They'll come to the kitchen when they're ready," Todd replies with a yawn, "Want some orange juice?"

"But what if they're stuck. Or lost," Collin presses, "Yer house is pretty big."

Todd shrugs and pours his orange juice. "Dalton is going to be under the bed in the guest room next to my mom's office, because it's got the thickest carpet and the largest under-the-bed space. Taylor is in the cabinet in the basement kitchen, and Wes is probably with him. I thought Jaxson would be with you."

"I didn't wanna break the rules of the game," Collin mutters, moving the dough to a baking sheet lined with parchment paper.

"It's more of a suggestion really."

Collin puts the baking sheet laden with scones into the oven and washes his hands in the shiny, stainless steel basin of the sink. After bouncing on the balls of his feet for a minute, he takes a seat next to Todd at the island.

"How'd you know where Dalton and Taylor and Wes are?" he asks.

Todd smiles a tiny smile that he isn't fully aware that he's wearing. "Dalton always sleeps wherever's comfy. Since I hid in my room's bay window this time, that leaves his other favorite spot under that guest bed. Taylor always sleeps in that cabinet, has since we were kids. He's even got a pillow and some blankets in there. I make sure to take the out and wash them once in a while. Figured he'd bring Wes with him, but..."

"But what?"

"Don't tell them I know where they hide," Todd asks, "especially not Taylor. I get the feeling he wouldn't sleep at all if he knew that I knew about his hiding spot."

"Well why wouldn't he?" Collin wonders, "Wouldn't he feel better knowin' he's got you lookin' out for'im?"

Todd shrugs, "I dunno. He never sleeps around anyone. He doesn't like to."

"That's pretty strange," Collin murmurs, not because he means it but because he feels he has to respond with something normative.

Todd watches Collin face crease for a moment with performative confusion before falling carelessly slack to stare at the granite countertops with wide, wide eyes. He gets the feeling that maybe Collin has trouble sleeping too.

21

Haunted by the Scones of Our Past

Wes wakes up early, too early to know what time it is. When his consciousness comes around he registers two things: he hurts all over, and he is completely pinned to the floor of the cupboard by Taylor, who is still asleep.

Somehow, for the first time in his life, Wes blinks blearily, happily back to sleep.

When Wes wakes up again, it's because Taylor is moving around in his sleep, muttering a little. But before he can start romanticizing how comfortably Taylor fits between his arms, or how soft his hair is against Wes's neck, or how nice it is to wake up next to your boyfriend, Taylor makes a soft sound that is much scarier to hear than his usual sleep-mumbles.

It's a terrified, whispering whine. Like Taylor is in pain. Wes's heart skips a beat or three.

Maybe Taylor is in pain, since he's still bruised to shit. But he's never made a noise like that before? And there's the same noise again: unmistakably afraid.

"Taylor?"

Taylor doesn't wake up, but he kicks one leg into the back of the cabinet, and his hands grab fistfuls of Wes's sweater, and he lets out a choked, dry sob.

"T-Taylor!?"

Taylor snaps awake, his head ricocheting back to bonk against the drawer above them, and then he tries to squirm back and away from Wes, he's scraping in ragged breaths and bouncing off of all the interiors of the cabinet and then Wes opens the cabinet door by his head and squeezes out and then Taylor gets a door open, but he doesn't crawl out he just sits there, wheezing.

"T-Taylor, w-w-what's going on?" Wes asks. He hasn't had his meds yet today and he feels it acutely now. Taylor flinches, like he did last night, and he looks at Wes with bleary, unfocused eyes. Wes knows what this is. He's seen this a hundred-thousand times in the mirror.

Wes takes a steadying breath, focusing on the feeling of his bare feet on the cool tiles of Todd's basement kitchen. "Taylor," he calls, "you're alright." Taylor shakes his head, but the movement isn't decidedly negative. It's almost like Taylor is trying to physically shake off his panic. "You're okay, Taylor, look—" and Wes kneels down on the floor next to where Taylor is tucked into the cabinet, shivering and gasping, "Look, I'm gonna h-hold your hand, okay?" Wes knows that touching someone freaking out like this isn't always great, but he wants to get Taylor out of the cabinet— he bonked his head pretty hard, and Wes would hate to see him do it again. Wes's fingertips meet Taylor's arm at the elbow, and Taylor barely notices the contact, so Wes moves down the arm to grab Taylor's hand, and he slowly, gently coaxes him out of the cabinet. "Good, great. Thanks, Taylor," he murmurs, and pulls his hand back.

Taylor blinks a few times, hard, and rubs at his face. He holds his breath— and Wes wants to tell him to stop, don't hold it in, let it out, lean on me too. But Taylor holds it until he stops shaking and his eyes stop watering and then he lets it all out in a shuddering sigh.

Taylor opens his mouth to say sorry.

Wes talks over him, "Do you want a hug?"

Taylor doesn't answer, just leans into Wes and lets Wes wrap him in his arms.

"Bad dream?" Wes asks cautiously.

Taylor nods into Wes's shoulder. "Hit my head," he mutters, voice choked still.

"You sat up so fast you hit it on the bottom of the drawer," Wes explains. Taylor nods again.

"You—" Taylor bites his own tongue, and then tries again, "You still hurt? From yesterday?"

"Yeah," Wes says.

Taylor tells him, "It's always worse two days later." The words are muffled by the sweater Wes is borrowing from Todd.

Wes giggles, "Thanks for worrying. You wanna go see what's going on in the kitchen?"

"What're you talking about?" Taylor asks.

"Smells like someone's cooking," Wes says. "Can you not smell it?"

"Nah, I can't smell much of anything since I broke my nose," Taylor says, his voice sounds more even now. He still doesn't let go of Wes.

When Taylor and Wes slip into the kitchen, they're there just in time for Dalton to scream at the top of his lungs "OLY-OLY-OXENFREE!" Wes feels Taylor jump beside him uncharacter istically. Taylor hasn't let go of Wes's arm since he hugged him. He's just waddling beside Wes, holding his arm with both hands, like a toddler. Todd certainly stares, and so does Dalton, once he's done yelling. "Oh," Dalton says, "There you are." He's talking to them, but he's staring at the arm Taylor won't let go of.

"Got a fucking problem?" Taylor growls.

Dalton's eyes snap up to meet Taylor's now, a little confused by the ferocity, but he shakes his head no. "Collin made us scones," he says instead, trying to keep his voice bright. "We thought you guys might want some."

"Thanks, Collin!" Wes says.

Collin grins nervously, shoving his hands in the pockets of his borrowed pajama pants. "No problem, y'all. You sure did hide good though— we couldn't find you for nothin'!"

"Where's Jaxson?" Wes asks, he can feel his voice picking up in panic. He's still not sure how much he trusts Jaxson unsupervised after Wednesday night. Jaxson wouldn't do that again, would he? Even Taylor doesn't have any reassurance for Wes, besides his presence pressed into Wes's side. Maybe Taylor is scared too. Wes realizes he hardly knew Taylor understood how to be scared, and he shivers.

Todd seems to understand Wes's fear the quickest, and he answers, "Just peeing. He was sleeping under the couch in the sitting room when Dalton found him."

"I've asked you this three times, Todd, but what the fuck is a sitting room?" Jaxson says, swaying into the kitchen. He's left his jacket somewhere, so he's just in the croptop he was wearing yesterday, and Wes can follow the line of

Collin's stare to Jaxson's exposed waistline. Wes isn't sure what Collin sees there. To Wes, all he sees is too thin and tanner than expected, but Collin is preoccupied with it enough that Jaxson notices and smirks at him. Wes looks away, feeling accidentally voyeuristic, but his interest is piqued and his eyes dart to the hem of Taylor's sweater. He vaguely remembers how close they were last night, and registers that his hands must have brushed Taylor's waist, but he had been so focused on how warm and solid Taylor was that he hadn't had the extra space in his brain to take in shapes and curves. He wonders if Taylor would flinch at the chill of Wes's fingertips if they got greedy— but, no. Taylor had flinched last night when Wes tried taking off his hat.

"I've told *you* three times," Todd says, sipping orange juice from a glass so clear you can see the pulp through it, "it's, like, a living room— and stop looking at each other like that in the kitchen!"

Wes's spine snaps to attention, thinking he's been caught staring at Taylor, but Todd is glaring at Jaxson and Collin, not him. He's relieved, but still nervous, and his eyes dart around the kitchen until they land on the scones and his mouth waters for a moment before his stomach lets out a low, whining grumble.

Finally, after all this unbearable stillness, Taylor shifts against Wes, looking up at him. "You're hungry," he says flatly, voice low with exhaustion. Wes meets his gaze, twitching anxiously, and sees the sallow look of Taylor's face, the dark hollow of bags under his eyes. A tic wracks half his body and he wonders how much Taylor actually slept last night and, of those precious few hours, how much was nightmares?

"Yeah, sorta," Wes admits.

Collin grins at them from across the kitchen. "Well, don't just stand there, y'all! Grab a scone!" he says brightly, and Jaxson sweeps in behind him and wordlessly grabs a scone off the plate in front of him, and drags Collin, screaming laughing, by the waist to sit on his lap at the table in the breakfast nook. Todd scowls at the PDA, but a bite of his scone makes him willfully forget to be upset.

Dalton pulls the plate of scones closer to his spot at the island, and he throws one first to Taylor, who drops Wes's hand to catch it, and then one to Wes, who fumbles and drops it, and Taylor catches that one too before it can hit the polished tile floors.

"Good catch!" Dalton says.

"Eat," Taylor says, to both Wes and Dalton. He shoves Wes's scone into his hands and flops into a chair at the island.

As fast as he read Wes before, Todd reads Taylor, and he asks, "What's wrong, Taylor?"

Even Jaxson and Collin stop teasing each other over their eating habits to glance Taylor's way.

"Nothing."

Dalton leans over, pokes Taylor's ribs. "Taylor. Buddy. My guy. Main man Macready—"

"Nightmare," Taylor says, voice tight and terse. Wes finally takes a seat next to him at the island. He hadn't asked about the dream that had woken up Taylor in such a panic, he didn't think Taylor would want to say. It looks like he was right not to ask: Taylor's whole posture reads *closed*. Even as he nibbles on his scone in the light perfectly angled by the automated blinds over Todd's kitchen window, his shoulders are hiked in tense plateaus and his jaw clenches around the scone, and the set of his eyes are dark and forbidding.

"What was the dream?" Collin asks. In the too-bright desperation of his eyes, Taylor's tense shoulders could simply be reassured away, the way the tide washes stones smooth. "I always talk my dreams out after I wake up. Sure does make me feel better!"

"No." Taylor finishes his scone but doesn't look up.

Dalton leans in again, trying to get Taylor to open up a little. Taylor has been so open since Wes came into the picture, and this morning feels like a step backward, and Dalton just wants to nudge him forward so he says, "C'mon, Taylor, my good pal! Tell us your dream!"

Taylor snaps, "My dad killed Wes."

Dalton makes a face like this is pretty bad, but not anything some good conversation with friends can't fix.

Todd, trying to be reasonable and rational and kind, says, "But that would never happen, Taylor."

Wes's therapy-trained brain is already talking him out of being paranoid of Taylor's dad lunging from around the corner with a gun/baseball bat/brass knuckles/bare knuckles, already trying to follow Todd's rationalized logic. But then he happens to glance at Collin, who is staring at Jaxson, who is staring at Todd with a look that says Taylor might be right to be afraid.

Wes shivers. A tic seizes his arm and he yanks at his borrowed shirt for a second before he can help it, and it pulls against a bruise at his nape and he winces all over again. Taylor's head sinks to rest on the cool granite countertop of the island and his arms curl around him defensively.

God, what Wes wouldn't give to have his meds on him right now. It's usually not the end of the world if he misses a day, but the week has been maybe one of the most stressful of his life, and he could use the help. But he's got things he can do here, things he can help.

"I'm not dead," Wes echoes from the other day under the bridge, "b-but thanks for the vote of confidence." Taylor's eyes peek up from under his arms. Nobody else in the kitchen has any clue what Wes is referencing, and they don't ask. Wes says, "I'd like to see your dad try and kill me, Taylor."

Nevermind that Wes has no clue, at the moment, what Mr. Macready actually looks like, if he's bigger or smaller or more muscular or more intimidating than Wes. Maybe Wes would see Mr. Macready and be terrified, and maybe Mr. Macready would actually try and kill him, but this isn't about that. Isn't about reality. It's about making Taylor less scared of a dream about his dad. It's about making Taylor less scared of his dad.

22

Decorate Yourself in Violence, It Might Help

"I'm gonna go open the shop soon," Wes says when he's finishing his second scone, sipping some of Todd's ridiculously rich, organic, ethically-sourced tea made with care by a Keurig machine.

Todd, Dalton, Collin, and Jaxson all look at each other like *who's gonna say it*, but, of course, Taylor beats them all to it with a sharp, "No."

"Wha— why!?"

Collin, looking at the floor, says, "Well, yesterday it didn't go so well."

"So?" Wes crosses his arms, which undermines his point because they're decorated in bandaids that cover the roadrash from being shoved to the ground yesterday.

"No, Wes." Taylor's head is still resting on the granite countertop. He hasn't lifted it since he set it there earlier, when he admitted his nightmare.

Wes twitches and grumbles but can't come up with an answer before Dalton says, "Can we talk about how it's literally been one thing after another every day for, like, the past week!?" He laughs, but it's thin and his hands are shaking. "I'm a little nervous letting anyone go anywhere by themselves."

Surprisingly, it's Jaxson who agrees first. "Not gonna lie, same. It feels like every time someone goes off by themselves it goes fucking sideways." Collin pushes into Jaxson's shoulder, a comfort for both of them.

"I can't say I disagree," Todd says, "and I've got enough room for everyone to stay here until..." he pauses, looking around the room as if his friends might have answers. "Until we stop being fucking disasters, I guess," is what he ends up saying.

"I'd need to go home and grab some clothes," Dalton says, "but the neverending sleepover sounds absolutely fucking ideal, Toddster. You're a smart guy."

"Someone has to keep you from running headfirst into walls," Todd replies.

Jaxson says, "I gotta go check on Juniper-Maisie. And Collin—" he looks at Collin. He really looks. He looks for so long that everyone else looks too, and wonders. "Collin, how're you gonna—?"

"Jax, please, don't," Collin whispers. "I can't..." he doesn't seem to realize everyone can hear him when he says, "I can't go home, Jax. I can't— they'll—"

Jaxson is quick to say, "Okay." He busies his fingers petting Collin' hair, even if his eyes are wide and panicked as he looks around the room, begging for help. Even Taylor has lifted his head off the granite to make eye contact.

"Collin," Taylor says, "it's okay." The way he looks at Collin is a look that only they can understand. His dazed, groggy expression goes flinty and he says, "We're not gonna let anything happen to you." Which is absolutely the furthest thing from what anybody expected to come out of Taylor's mouth.

Taylor is thinking about how Collin helped him up off the floor last week when Freddy Peters knocked him flat. It's so rare that anyone helps him up after anything.

Collin, in his trusting way, takes in Taylor's face: the bruises that are yellowing at the edges and the knuckles still wrapped in bandages, the hardened break in his nose that's been crooked as long as anybody can remember (even though Dalton and Todd *know* his nose was straight when they met in kindergarten). Collin, in his trusting way, believes Taylor.

Jaxson, with a slight nod, thanks Taylor for taking the words out of his mouth. He smiles, fakely, for Collin and says, "Taylor's right, Collin. We've got you. Anybody trying to hurt you would have to get through me and him and they would have to try to get through Wes and Dalton's dumb, burly asses— and Todd would probably have had them thrown in prison for some law they broke when they were six by the time they got through there."

Everyone laughs a little, for each other's benefit, because maybe it will become funny if they pretend it is, even if Todd and Dalton and Wes don't understand what's going on at all.

They still don't know exactly what happens in the Macready household, or the Dixon and Donahue household for that matter.

"Okay," Todd says, scrabbling for control in a world where he knows he has very little, if any. "Okay, here's what the new plan is." Everyone turns imploring, thankful eyes to Todd, and he continues a little faster. "Nobody goes anywhere alone.

Taylor don't even start looking at me like—"

"No, I think that's a good idea," Taylor replies before Todd can get started preemptively defending himself. "Between Collin's parents and whatever the fuck went on yesterday at the shop, I think it's a good idea not to be alone."

Todd does not correct Taylor to say that he had also meant this to be a preventative measure for anyone deciding they want to, say, go pick a fight with a grown man outside a bar, or lay down in the snow for six hours. He just makes eye contact with Dalton, who blinks his understanding, and continues. "We can stay at my house, if that's okay with everyone?"

Nods all around. "Your house is kinda fucking sick, dude," Jaxson says with a grin. "You sure you're okay with a sleaze-ball like me getting your sheets dirty?"

Todd gives Jaxson a funny look, rolls his eyes. "You're not a wild animal, Jaxson. You don't have rabies. Just remember to take your shoes off at the door."

Jaxson laughs a little sideways.

"You're so anal about the shoes at the door," Dalton laughs.

"Not me," Todd insists, "my parents. But that's besides the point. Everyone takes their shoes off at the door. Everyone stays here. Everyone will go together to pick up people's stuff."

"But I still want to open the shop today," Wes says. His eyes bore right into Todd's, the organizer of this new plan.

Taylor grumbles and sets his head back down on the granite countertop.

"Why are you so dead-set on opening the shop?" Dalton asks, instead of negating him like Todd can tell he wants to. They all want to. They all want to wrap Wes in blankets again, like they did on Saturday and protect him by keeping him with

274

them, surrounded by them. It would be easier.

Wes immediately breaks eye contact and studies his fidget-ing fingers. "I—" He struggles for an answer. "I want the extra money," he eventually settles on.

It's a weird answer, but Wes refuses to go any further. He's set on it, and that's that.

Taylor grumbles a few times into his arm, and that's the only noise in the room. Todd feels a little well of panic behind his throat. Jaxson is still running his hands through Collin' hair, trying to keep him calm; Wes is biting his lip and making fleeting, nervous eye contact with Todd and Dalton in turn trying to defend his choice; Todd and Dalton are looking at each other for answers, for reassurance. They're already in such precarious stasis, such careful safety.

"Fuck it," Taylor grumbles, just a bit louder than his other grumbling. "Wes, what's your parents' phone number?"

"What?" Wes looks sharply at Taylor, who has not lifted his head yet, "Why?"

"I'm gonna beg 'em to give me a job, I guess."

"Wha—!?" Wes squeaks. "A-at the shop!?"

"Yeah." Taylor pushes his face so far into his arms that his hat starts to slide off. "If you're going to open the shop, I'm coming with you. I'd feel dumb as shit just sitting around though. And you need help there anyway."

"I d-do not need help."

Taylor finally peeks up at Wes, ignoring everyone else in the room, to say, "Wes, you can do it alone, but that doesn't mean you should or that you have to." It's kind and true and hilariously, obliviously ironic.

"Taylor's right, Wes," Dalton says, trying for one problem at a time.

Jaxson interrupts, "Can we all acknowledge, for posterity, that Taylor Macready, the pot, has just looked Wes Post, the kettle, in the eyes? Taylor, you heard yourself say that, right?"

"Shut the fuck up, Dixon."

"No judgment, Tayby Baby, just checking your self-awareness." Jaxson laughs in the space where the shadows of their little sisters sit, still burying their one Ken doll in the dirt. "I think we can call this character development."

Todd goes with Dalton to pick some stuff up from Dalton's house. Collin goes with Jaxson to pick some stuff up from Jaxson's house. Taylor goes with Wes to open the shop.

"You really don't have to do this, Taylor."

"I'm already here," Taylor says, "And I'm not leaving without you unless I'm chasing the assholes that did this with a fucking bat."

Wes gives Taylor a glare, like no you will not be getting into any more fights I don't care what the reason. Taylor shrugs, flips Wes off venomlessly. "What am I doing first?" he asks.

"First, you're changing," Wes says. "Todd was right, you really do need new clothes—"

"Shut the fuck up about my clothes."

"But we have a uniform anyway. Come're, we keep extras in the back." Taylor pauses in the doorway of the stockroom, glaring. "Don't be like that, it's just a t-shirt," Wes says, rolling his eyes. "I've gotta change into one too. The one from yesterday is..." Wes trails off, biting his lip and twitching. "It's dirty."

"Wes, you—"

"Here's a t-shirt, tell me if it's the wrong size," Wes interrupts, shoving a random t-shirt at Taylor and turning to let him change.

It's the right size, and Taylor, anxiously starts to shimmy out of his flannel and into the green Post Family Coffee t-shirt.

"Hey, Taylor—" Wes starts, turning to face Taylor maybe half-second before it would have been safe to do so. As it stands, Wes pauses mid-sentence because he has seen Taylor's torso for the instant it took for Taylor to yank the shirt down.

Ordinarily, this would be exciting, maybe even a little thrilling. Seeing your boyfriend's abs or waistline, or even just more exposed skin than normal, would send chills up anyone's spine! But not today, because Wes had been too distracted by the patchwork mess of bruising all over Taylor's stomach to think about muscles or curves or skin or anything like that.

It actually takes Wes a second to remember that yesterday evening, with the homophobes, had happened to Wes himself, and not Taylor. He panics and questions his own memory, his own bruises, for a few seconds before remembering that Taylor had gone and picked a fight Wednesday night for no reason. When, in the absence of meds, that seems too flimsy of an excuse, Wes acknowledges the stretch of the bandaids on his forearms, the ache of the bruises on his ribs, the yellow he had seen edging around Taylor's bruises.

"T-T-Taylor w-wha-w-why—"

"Wes, it's fine. Don't freak out."

"How a-am I s-s-supposed t-to—"

"Hey, don't— I'm sorry." Taylor seems panicked too. He straightens the stiff edges of the shirt over his shoulders and opens his arms. "C'mere, um, babe."

Wes accepts the hug, wrapping his arms all the way around Taylor to remind himself that Taylor is still here, still okay. It takes him a second to realize that Taylor had called him "babe." Another second to realize that Taylor's neck is red-hot with embarrassment from it. Wes giggles.

"You called me 'babe.'"

Taylor grumbles inaudibly in response. When Wes is a little calmer, Taylor says, "See, I'm fine."

"You're not fine," Wes replies.

"Yes, I am. I can barely feel it."

"Do you think I'm stupid?"

"What?"

"Taylor, I'll bet if we pulled up my shirt it w-would look exactly the same. And it does hurt. A lot. It's fucking s-scary when someone has you on the ground." He puts a large, forceful effort into not dwelling on that, on how he had wondered if he should pretend to be dead or if the things they would have done to a corpse would be worse. But he won't think about that now, while he's safe. "D-don't try to tell me you're fine when you're not. I care about you too much for you t-to lie to me about that."

Taylor doesn't answer for a long time, but his fists tighten around handfuls of the sweater Wes is still borrowing from Todd. "I care about you too," he finally whispers.

Wes smiles into Taylor's hair.

"You want me to show you how to make a hot chocolate before we open?"

As before, the moment Wes flipped the sign to 'Open,' customers started in. Wes and Taylor agreed that Taylor would mostly work the register and Wes would mostly handle food and drinks. They threw some muffins that Wes whipped together insanely quickly and a few batches of cookies from dough stored in the storeroom fridge into the oven before opening, after Wes had made them both hot chocolate under the pretense of showing Taylor how to make it.

The first customer is a man in a suit (nevermind that no business in Swisher requires such strict dress code), and he orders a caramel macchiato with a shot of espresso and he pays with a metal credit card and he doesn't put down his cell phone once the whole time he's in the shop. After that, of course, is a disgruntled group of kids Taylor vaguely recognizes as Juniors from school, and they look hungover as fuck, and they order a complicated mess of drinks and food that Taylor has a hard time getting into the cash register correctly. Then there's a dad ordering for his family for breakfast. Then a mom on a roadtrip with her kid. Then there's fucking Frankie, from school, who looks at both Taylor and Wes with smiling eyes before ordering their coffee like they've never drank coffee before in their life and sitting down at a little cafe table to type at a computer like they're here every day. A few hours later, after Frankie has left, the entire English department (plus Ms. Williams, the psychology teacher, and Ms. Connie, who works in the office) comes through, tipsy at three pm.

"I told you— I told you!" Ms. Merino-Ott whispers to Taylor, "I told her."

Ms. Alberts slaps her shoulder, "Carolyn, you're drunk."

"You're drunk."

Ms. Connie shoulders to the front. "I'll have an iced vanilla mocha please," she says, breathless and almost desperate.

"Ooh, that sounds good," Mrs. Liu, who Taylor has never had personally but he's heard from Todd she never assigns homework, croons, and asks for the same thing.

Mrs. Hunter blinks at Taylor several times, like she's not sure where she is. "Taylor? Taylor Macready? Since when do you work here?"

"Since today."

Ms. Williams spies Wes over Taylor's shoulder and immediately exclaims. "Wes! What happened to you!?" She turns suspicious eyes at Taylor, and he tries not to take that too personally. It's difficult when she's tacitly accusing him of beating the shit out of his boyfriend.

Wes jumps, a little panicked at seeing his teachers daydrunk in his coffee shop and yelling at him, but he gives a wobbly Customer Service Smile and explains that some thugs came around the coffee shop yesterday evening.

Mrs. Liu giggles and slurs, "Why worry about thugs outside the shop when you've got one working the register with you!" Mrs. Williams laughs a little, but even Ms. Merino-Ott, possibly the drunkest one here, doesn't look at Taylor but at Mrs. Liu.

Wes actually puts down the frappe drink he was making, and he storms up to the counter, and he tells Mrs. Liu, "If you're going to talk that way about Taylor, I'll ask you to leave."

The teachers stare, Mrs. Merino-Ott gaping a little. Ms. Connie raises a pointed eyebrow at Mrs. Liu and Ms. Alberts says, in a very particular tone of voice, "Tamiyoo, why don't you take Petra out to the patio."

For some reason, a lump rises in Taylor's throat while he watches Mrs. Williams lead Mrs. Liu out, laughing to her, "Petra, you can't say that to kids! Especially not ones we teach! You know, I was reading this study the other day..." Wes watches them go with narrowed eyes, spares a glance for the remaining teachers, and gives Taylor a small, encouraging nudge before going back to finish making his drinks.

Mrs. Hunter pinches the bridge of her nose, blinking soberly, and says, "Taylor, honey, I am so sorry about that. She doesn't mean it. She's been drinking mimosas since ten am."

"But that's still no excuse for saying it," Ms. Connie snips.

Taylor says, "It's fine."

"It's not fine," Ms. Merino-Ott insists, pushing herself right up to the counter. She's still drunk, and her words slur a little, but she leans over the counter to look Taylor dead in the eyes. "It was mean," she tells him. "You're not a thug. You're a kid, a good kid."

The lump in Taylor's throat grows to a stinging behind his eyes. He can feel the whole coffee shop staring at him. They've gotta be staring. But Taylor has one thing in spades and that's stubbornness, so he clenches his teeth and swallows the lump in his throat. "What can I get for you guys? I have two iced vanilla mochas so far."

This might have been the wrong thing to say, the teachers give him peculiar looks. They order their coffees, some cookies, and a muffin, and pay with a card. Once they have their drinks, they leave with exasperated, embarrassed expressions. Ms. Alberts quickly shoves a twenty-dollar bill into the tip jar before following them out.

Taylor hears Mrs. Hunter groan, "God, that was embarrassing! Petra, what is wrong with you?" before the door of the shop closes.

Wes returns to his side to ask in a whisper, "Do you want to go sit down?"

"I'm fine."

"That was fucked up. You can go sit in the storeroom for a bit—"

"And leave you up here without help?"

Wes giggles, "You forget I worked the shop without help yesterday, and I do it pretty often on weekends too."

"I'm fine, Wes."

Wes sighs. He bites his lip and fidgets nervously for the first time since they started at the shop. "Alright," he says, "we're closing in, like, an hour anyways."

Then another customer comes in and it's back to work. Taylor is glad he's not great at the register yet, because that means it hoards his focus and there's no room left in his brain for words like thug.

23

A Karen a Day Keeps the Self-Respect Away

Towards the end of the shift, when the customers are less numerous and less demanding, Wes lets Taylor try to make a coffee. A simple one, just a mocha latte. Wes's hands guide Taylor's over the syrup pumps and the espresso machine and the fridge handle to get the almond milk and the steamer to heat it up. He leaves Taylor to cap the cup and put it on the counter while he takes an order at the register. Taylor thinks he did alright, but the second the order hits the pickup counter, he hears "This isn't my coffee" from a 56-year-old woman with a baseball cap reading "Road Trip Fam!" and a toddler on a leash attached to her belt loop.

"Mocha latte, right?" Taylor checks.

The woman rolls her eyes, sucks her teeth, and yanks on the toddler-leash when the kid starts poking at the coffee grinds on display below the register. "Iced," she hisses. "Iced mocha latte."

"Oh- uh, I can add some ice?"

"No, that won't work. It's not the same. You already

steamed the milk."

"What-..." Taylor feels his face heating up, embarrassment breeding shame and shame inciting rage. He tries to calm it down because this is Wes's shop and he can't be fighting random women because he fucked up their order (even if she definitely did not say "iced" anywhere in her order). He chokes out, "What would you like me to do about it, ma'am?"

"I want a new coffee, obviously!" she snaps, "And I'd say I want a refund, but I don't think your ancient cash registers even know how to tender returns on a debit card. Lord above, this is why all these mom and pop stores are closing down!" She yanks her leash-child closer when the kid starts tinkering with the display near the window. "I don't know why I let my husband talk me into coming here. Willy!"

A man with a matching baseball cap sidles up next to his wife. "This punk giving you trouble?" he asks, leveling Taylor with a suspicious glare.

But by now, Wes has finished the order at the register and he materializes next to Taylor. Taylor hadn't heard him coming and that's his first indication that the blood rushing in his ears is loud. "Everything alright, ma'am?" he asks politely. Below the counter, his hand taps against Taylor's.

The man mutters, "Great, another punk."

"Yes, I'd like to speak to the manager," the woman says, yanking her leash-toddler back from the display again. "Or at least someone over the age of thirty?"

"I'm the manager of this establishment," Wes answers saccharinely, "I can assist you with whatever trouble you're having."

"Your employee messed up my order. I want a new one."

"We can do that for you, ma'am. What was your order?"

284

The woman rolls her eyes again, exasperated at having to repeat herself a second time. "Iced. Mocha. Latte."

"Absolutely, I'll have that right out for you, ma'am."

"Thank you," she snaps, shooting Taylor a livid look, before dragging her toddler and husband to a cafe table to wait.

"Can you man the counter while I deal with this?" Wes asks. His shoulders are a little stooped and his eyes look tired. Taylor grumbles an affirmative and steps to the register, taking the next order from a girl who looks too young to even be drinking coffee.

A few minutes later, when Wes is done making the drink, Taylor watches listlessly as he walks it out to the woman and accepts her diatribe with more composure than Taylor could have ever managed. When he returns and there's no orders for a minute, he gives Taylor a sympathetic half-smile and a shrug. "K-Karens," he says, "we get at least one every day."

Towards five pm, the place empties out. Nobody wants coffee for dinner, apparently. They're stacking chairs, sweeping the floor, turning off and cleaning the machines, and that's when they see them.

Alex Morenson, with road rash and bruising obscuring half his face. Mathew Megans with a nasty bruise just below his adam's apple. Nathan Hepburn with a heavy limp. They're staring in the front windows. Wes is still in the stockroom filling up some new bags off coffee grounds to replace the ones they sold today in the display below the register so that he can show Taylor how to clean it and turn it off in a minute. Alex, Mathew, and Nathan see Taylor, and their resolve fractures, but it doesn't crumble. After an intimidated moment, they resume their boldfaced, mocking stare. Alex smirks.

Taylor drops the chair in his hands onto the table and goes for the front door of the shop. The bell twinkles as he slams it open and the sound punctuates Nathan Hepburn's feet hitting the pavement as he makes a break for it. Mathew seems torn between following Nathan and standing his ground. When Alex takes a step toward Taylor, Mathew decides to stay and pivots back toward them.

"Where's your boyfriend?" Alex sneers, as if that was a good way to get Taylor's goat or something. As if Taylor is upset at the implication of dating Wes and not, ya know, the fact that these three assholes tried to kill Wes and Collin yesterday.

"Who cares," Taylor answers. "Get the fuck out of here." He wants them to leave. Part of him wants them to leave. Part of him wants them to walk away, kicking their heels up, no fight in their shoulders the way it is now. The other part of him is itching for a fight, begging someone to set his bones right again, dying to feel his own blood trickle from his nose and his knuckles swell with exertion. He's letting Alex make the choice for him. Down the street, on the other side of the ABC Supply Warehouse, Nathan Hepburn's face peeks out, assessing the situation.

"We're not doing anything wrong," Mathew says. His eyes dart between Taylor and the shop. Taylor doesn't take the bait to look, because when he's distracted is when Alex will strike.

"Get out of here," Taylor repeats.

"Or what?" Alex is begging for it; feet set wide, shoulders square, hands flexing in and out of fists. He's smiling around the road rash.

The door bell twinkles again. Alex visibly falters, toes pointing sideways to flee instead of forward to fight. Of course, it's Wes's voice that says, "Get off my family's property or I will act in self-defense."

"What're you gonna do?" Alex sneers, as if Wes doesn't have several inches and more than twenty pounds on him. As if he thinks being gay somehow makes Wes less dangerous.

Taylor hasn't turned to see Wes's expression, but it sounds pretty close to bared teeth and murder when he says, "I'm gonna beat the shit out of you if you don't get out of here."

Something in that makes Alex and Mathew wiggle un-comfortably in their shoes, and they scoff and wander off, meeting up with Nathan at the other side of the warehouse and grumbling on home.

When they're far gone and not coming back, Taylor finally turns to see what in Wes made them change their mind today, he gets his answer in the hardened shine of Wes's obsidian-set eyes and the knife that they keep underneath the display of baked goods to cut slices out of the bread loaves. Taylor can also see the tremor working its way through Wes's shoulders, his wrists, his spine. He nudges Wes back inside the shop and locks the door behind him.

What Taylor wants to say is that what Wes just did was stupid, and he could have taken both those guys, and Wes is still hurt, and knives usually escalate fights rather than calm them down, but he turns around and sees Wes, one fist gripping that bread knife and his whole body shaking. Wes doesn't need to be reminded about how poorly that could have gone. He knows. "Hey, Wes, it's alright," Taylor tries, "it's fine. We're both safe. They left—" Wes isn't listening, fingernails starting to scrape through skin to draw blood. "Wes, your hand—" Wes's thumb has carelessly pressed into the blade of the bread knife, and the cut is dripping onto the floor.

"Who gives a fuck!" Wes snaps. His head spins to glare at Taylor and there's the bee-sting of an emotion beyond anger, beyond fear, beyond exasperation in Wes's eyes. "Have you even once considered that the feeling you have when you see me h-h-hurt is the exact same feeling I have when you're h-h-h-hurt? Why is it so h-hard for you to understand that I care about you!?"

Taylor stares. His brain feels fuzzy and full of buzzing, angry bees. He can barely understand the words Wes is saying, with the knife waving around in his other hand and blood dripping to the floor. Slowly, feeling nauseous panic creep up his throat, Taylor reaches for the knife. Wes lets it go easily once Taylor has a grip on the handle, and Taylor wants to sob with a kind of relief he doesn't understand while he sets it in between the upturned chairs balanced on the table behind him.

Free of the burden of the knife, Wes's hands go twitchy and then his whole body shudders and then his hands grab at his hair and he screams, "Do you not understand that it hurts me to see you hurting!? My worst nightmare is you being in pain, Taylor! And here you are! Picking fights with the express purpose of getting hurt!"

"I did it to get them to back off—"

"Bullshit!" Wes shouts. The fuzzy feeling in Taylor's head magnifies until his whole body feels ensconced in an angry beehive. Wes is still shouting, but Taylor can't understand the words anymore. Just angry bees and the pervasive fear of the guys who tried to hurt him and the woman who shouted at him earlier and the bruises under Wes's work shirt and the knife on the table and how loud everything is. Angry bees and fear.

It's a surprise when Wes's hand touches Taylor's cheek,

because Taylor hadn't seen Wes move towards him. Panic laces his veins, constricting them until Taylor is sure there's not a drop of blood in his body. Wes's other hand moves to settle between Taylor's shoulder blades and by then they've moved to the storeroom, and Taylor is sitting on the same bags of coffee beans that Wes sat on yesterday.

"Taylor, you're panicking," Wes says. But Taylor isn't. His chest is rising and falling in even breaths, his expression is as impassive as ever, there's barely any tears dripping from his chin. Taylor isn't panicking. This isn't what panic looks like.

But Wes still wraps Taylor up in his arms, holding him so tight he can feel the nerves he'd thought bloodless and inactive light up in recognition of the cool, soft pressure of Wes's body around his. Still wipes the tears from Taylor's face before tucking his head into Wes's shoulder. Still whispers, so much more audible than his shouting, that Taylor is okay, and that Wes is going to take care of him, and that they're both safe.

Time passes, but there's no way to tell how long. The first thing Taylor can feel is Wes buzzing with tremors around him, and he tries to push away— Wes is probably nervous, Taylor needs to help him, he needs to reassure him, Wes is shaking, Taylor needs to do something about it— but Wes's arms hold him tighter. "It's alright," Wes says, "take a minute. We're okay. You take a minute." Taylor doesn't feel himself cry harder, but he feels the shoulder of Wes's t-shirt when it's damp against his cheek. He can hear Wes shushing him, stammering, reassuring him. Only when his vision begins to zoom into focus- when he can read the clock on the wall as a quarter to seven, when he can see the shipping labels still stapled to the pallet leaning against the wall across the room, when the grinder machine becomes a squat cylinder instead of a shapeless color-smudge, does Taylor realize he hadn't been able to see any of those things before.

"Wes?" he whispers. He has to crane his head and look up to see Wes's face. Taylor is sitting in Wes's lap, with Wes's arms wrapped around him, holding fistfuls of Wes's shirt. He releases the shirt and stretches his fingers; they're sore from gripping so tight for so long.

"I'm sorry, Taylor," Wes whispers.

"For what? You didn't do anything."

"I yelled, and I h-had that knife in my hand. I shouldn't've—" Wes stops in time to spasm out a nervous tic in his neck. He needs to take his meds, Taylor realizes. "I'm sorry, Taylor."

"But I'm fine," Taylor says, but even his pride can't convince them both that Taylor isn't sitting, curled in on himself like a child, in Wes's lap with tears still staining Wes's shirt.

"You had a panic attack," Wes says, "That's not fine." Taylor can hear the edges of stammers at the onset of every syllable, can hear how carefully Wes is reining them in.

"That wasn't a panic attack." Taylor tries to explain that panic attacks look like what happens to Wes— with the screaming and the breathing and the crying— not what happened to Taylor. "That was... I dunno. It just happens sometimes when I get freaked out. But it's not a panic attack."

Wes searches Taylor's eyes for a moment. It feels like eternity to Taylor, who can feel that gaze looking right through his eye sockets and into his skull, scrying for truth that Taylor is desperately trying to obscure. "Alright," Wes says, "it's okay. We can bicker about it when you're feeling better."

"I feel fine."

Wes says, "You don't have to be fine, Taylor."

"But I am," Taylor insists, even though he can feel tears

choking out his voice.

"Okay," Wes whispers. His arms readjust around Taylor, and his fingers find the back of his neck and rub circles around the vertebrae there.

Taylor is asleep in minutes.

24

The Ignorance/Cruelty Differential

When Wes comes home from work carrying Taylor like a toddler on his back, everyone kinda assumes the worst. Honestly though, given Taylor's track record, it's totally fair that Todd's hand goes to pinch the bridge of his nose and Dalton feels like he's gonna be sick and Collin gets all squirrely and Jaxson reaches out a hand and asks what happened.

"Will you put me down?" Taylor grumbles, pleasantly surprising everyone with his consciousness and lucidity. "I told you they'd do this."

"To be fair," Todd says, "we have good reason to be worried."

"I'm fine." Taylor clarifies. "Wes, will you put me down?"

"But you're so cute when you're sleepy."

"Sleepy!?" Dalton shouts. "Okay, that's it. This is where I draw the line. My son is *sleepy* and I have not seen it! Not once! In my life!" He stomps his foot petulantly and says, "Taylor, we are duct-taping you to the bed in the spare room and you're gonna fall asleep! I gotta see it!" He's trying to get everyone to laugh, because the air is still so heavy from when they thought something bad had happened.

"Please be quiet, Dalton," Wes says.

Dalton immediately shuts up, even if only because Wes said it so seriously. It's actually such an uncharacteristic thing for Wes to say that everyone (sans Taylor, who really does look, for lack of a better word, sleepy) gives Wes a collective funny look.

But before anyone can ask Wes what's wrong that they need to be quiet about, Wes says, "Okay, Taylor. Bedtime."

And for once in their whole fucking lives, Taylor doesn't fight it. He doesn't insist that he's not tired or grumble uncomfortably like he has at every sleepover Dalton can remember. He just nods tiredly, pushes off and away from Wes, and says to everyone, "I'll be back in, like, an hour."

"Sleep well?" Jaxson says, looking out of his depth.

Collin, cheery and oblivious as ever, says, "Have a good nap!"

"You okay, Taylor?" Todd asks slowly. Because he thinks Taylor looks a little off and he thinks Wes is being weird. Weirder than normal.

Dalton knows Todd is smart, the smartest one here, most likely, and definitely smarter than Dalton, but he also knows that Todd isn't always right. He says, right after Todd, too fast for Taylor to have room to respond in an overdramatic voice, "Look at my son: all grown up! Taking naptime by himself!"

Taylor tells Dalton to fuck off, and Dalton laughs to make everyone else laugh, and they do, and Taylor wanders upstairs to take a nap at Todd's house for the first time in something like a decade.

As he's going up the stairs, still in earshot, Dalton says, "I'm making cookies."

"I'll help!" Collin cries, winces, amends, "If ya want me to, Dalton! Sorry for yellin' so loud, Wes."

The moment they hear a door close upstairs, Jaxson demands, "Yeah, no, what was that about?"

"Taylor just had the worst first day at work one can reasonably have," Wes says, very calmly.

"What happened?" Todd asks.

"I'm not sure it's something y-you would w-w-want to know."

"We're his friends, Wes," Dalton snaps, "We want to be there for Taylor even if shit sucks."

Maybe sensing the tension Dalton is trying not to let leak into those words, Collin says, "We can make cookies while we talk?"

"Good idea, babe." Jaxson kisses Collin' shoulder and takes the lead into the kitchen.

Dalton starts grabbing bowls and ingredients, and Collin starts putting everything together. Dalton would have no clue the kid was so nervous if his hands weren't shaking.

"So," Todd prompts, hands gesturing for Wes to continue as if this is some kind of business meeting.

Wes collapses into a chair. "There was so many little things, ya know? The w-whole English department came into the shop. Mrs. Liu—"

"From school?"

"Yeah. And Mrs. Liu called Taylor a thug! A thug! And then this stupid f-fucking Karen came in and h-h-harassed him f-for n-n-no r-re-reason!"

"Breathe, Wes."

Wes does, very intentionally, and clears his throat. "And

those guys from yesterday came by again. Taylor and I s-scared them off, but it freaked me out, ya know? And I was h-h-holding the bread knife, because they looked like they m-m-m-might h-hurt him, a-a-a-a-and—"

"Wes, it's okay—"

"But it's not!" Wes cries, and then takes a breath and lowers his voice, eyes glancing up toward the ceiling. "It's not okay," he says. "Have you guys seen what Taylor's torso looks like? From that fight he picked Wednesday night?" The only noise in the room is Collin frantically mixing the cookie dough together. "Taylor says it doesn't hurt anymore, but it looks bad. I was scared if Alex and Mathew hit him—"

"Like with Freddy on Thursday," Jaxson infers. Todd is horrified to know that he doesn't know exactly what Freddy Peters did to Taylor on Thursday, and from the look in his eyes, neither does Dalton. He remembers when Wes and Taylor and Collin and Jaxson came into lunch on Wednesday, and he and Dalton had been so preoccupied with letting Taylor know they didn't like him fighting people that they hadn't bothered to ask what had actually happened. He hadn't even asked. His lungs vacuum out and he tries not to cry.

But Wes just nods. "Yeah. So, I had this bread knife in my hand, and I was yelling at Taylor because I was scared that he w-was going to get, y-ya kn-know, h-h-h-hurt, and he started freaking out and he h-h-had a p-panic attack."

"What!?" several voices shout, out of sync.

"I felt h-horrible about it—" Wes starts, but he's inter-rupted by Todd insisting that Taylor has never, ever had a panic attack before, or at least not in front of anyone present. Jaxson seconds this. Wes looks at them like they're all crazy. "What do you mean?" he says, "He had one the other day, when he found Jaxson in the bathroom w-w-with the, um, the razor. He almost had one yesterday w-when w-we w-were sitting in the bathroom together, but I guess you guys were in the other room that time—"

"But he wasn't acting any different?" Todd interrupts again.

Wes wrinkles his expression in confusion. "What do you mean? He gets all quiet and shuts down, his eyes do that thing where he's looking all over the place. And he holds his breath sometimes. Plus, he clearly can't understand anything you say to him—"

"But that's not," Todd tries, "That's just Taylor when he's upset. It's not a panic attack." But the more he thinks about it, the more it definitely is. "Is it?" Guilt bubbles like baking soda and lemon in his gut.

Todd remembers Dalton's mom's funeral. They had it in the summer between fourth and fifth grade. He remembers Dalton's mom's body, bent at funny angles at some of her joints because even the mortician in charge of making her look presentable for the open casket hadn't been able to get her bones to sit right again after a wreck like that. He remembers crying his eyes out, and Taylor standing next to him the whole time, not crying at all, his eyes unable to focus on any one thing.

At the time Todd had taken Taylor's silent presence by their sides the whole day to be a thing of comfort, Taylor protecting them, like always, but now he can't get those unfocused eyes out of his head.

Dalton remembers Taylor showing up at his house one night, it was raining, and Taylor was drenched, and he knocked on his door until Dalton's dad answered it, but when Taylor saw

Dalton's dad he ran off down the street again and Dalton's dad had told Dalton about it and Dalton had chased after him and Taylor had been stone-faced and still but he hadn't responded to anything Dalton said for hours—

and Dalton is so stupid.

He is just now wondering why Taylor ran from his dad.

"Taylor's dad," Dalton whispers.

"Huh?"

"Taylor's dad," Dalton says again. "His dad yells at him."

"He does a whole helluvalot more than yell at him," Jaxson scoffs.

"I'm sorry, what?" Todd says. His toes are rapidly becoming TV static.

"Jax..." Collin cautions, voice high and tight as his hair.

"That's p-probably," Wes stammers, "I mean, that sounds about r-right."

"Alright, Jaxson, Wes, spill." Dalton says, "I don't even care anymore, I just need to know what's going on so I can help."

Wes shrugs, tremors vibrating in his bones, "I don't really know anything, he just flinches when you try to touch him sometimes."

Jaxson says, "Listen, I only know all this shit because our sisters have been friends since forever and Hellen and Juniper-Maisie didn't used to be so tight-lipped. Taylor's dad hits him. Like, beats the shit out of him typa hitting him. He's done it since we were kids."

"Oh, my god." Todd says, and his legs are shaking so he sits down. "And we never—"

"He didn't ever tell you," Collin says, reassuring. "Jax only knows 'cause Juniper-Maisie told him. Seems to me like

Taylor didn't never wanna talk about it."

Dalton chokes out, "Is Hellen—?"

"Hellen's fine," Jaxson says quickly. "They never hit Hellen."

"Then why hit Taylor?"

Jaxson's eyes go to the floor, the first sign Dalton has seen of Jaxson being uncertain about any of this. "Taylor probably isn't... He's probably not biologically his dad's kid."

"Oh." Nobody questions this. Taylor hasn't ever looked like anyone else in his family.

"Yeah, and his parents kinda don't like that."

"So they hit him!?" Dalton cries. "What kinda parent could do that to their own kid!?"

"Taylor's," Jaxson snaps, because he's getting awfully tired of how much coddling Taylor does for his friends. They deserve to know. "And mine. And Collin's."

"Collin?"

Jaxson doesn't give the silence enough time to force an answer out of Collin, whose hands dance between the bowl and the nonstick cookie sheet with a tremor while his eyes dodge every attempt at contact. "Why do you think he can't go home? They'll beat the shit out of him— or make him fast, or fuckin, I don't know, like, lock him in the closet!"

"What!?"

"Jax," Collin says, stilling almost completely, just a thin tremor remaining to differentiate his pale face from a standing corpse. His shoulders have curled in, eyes now rooted firmly in the bowl of dough. "Please, stop. I don't wanna cause a fuss."

Jaxson deflates. He runs a hand through his hair a few times. "Sorry."

Dalton sinks further into the stiff edges of the island barstool. His head is barely buoyed above the flooded tide of new, horrible information. Everything he hadn't known— for thirteen years, he hadn't known— all coming out at once. Across the kitchen, Wes is visibly trying to disappear into the floor. He knew first. *He knew first!* Dalton has been Taylor's best friend for twelve years, and *Wes* knew something was wrong before he did!

Nausea ripples along his organs like a spider, eight legs splayed out and crawling up, up, up his throat. "I'm gonna be sick," he says.

Todd tells him to use the bathroom if he needs to. Todd is trying to remember every time he told Taylor off for picking fights and coming to school covered in bruises, and how many of those times was he chastising Taylor for getting hit. He sets his head on the cool, granite countertop of the island and thinks about how Taylor and Collin had understood each other so clearly yesterday, when Collin panicked at the thought of going home and Taylor had just told him they wouldn't make him. Thinks about how Taylor has always been the last to go home after every sleepover. Thinks about how the only way anyone knew was because Hellen told Juniper-Maisie and Juniper-Maisie told Jaxson.

"God, I feel like a shitty friend," Todd murmurs. Dalton has to agree. They hadn't known. Somehow, they hadn't known.

An oven timer beeps as it is set for twelve minutes. "Now, don't go sayin' that," Collin says softly, shutting the oven door over the cookies. "Y'all have been great friends to Taylor. Yer houses were always open when he needed somewhere to go, and you know he loves you both an' all that."

"But we didn't know," Dalton says, making an incredible

effort not to cry.

"Nobody knew," Wes says. "I didn't know, you two didn't know. None of the teachers or kids at school know. He's pretty fucking secretive."

"I mean, he always said he got in a fight—" Dalton rambles.

"And we fucking believed it," Todd breathes. He's been in gifted and talented programs since diapers, and he's never felt more stupid.

Jaxson shrugs, and he can't keep being pissed when they look so miserable. It's not like they don't care, they just didn't know. "Like Wes said, he's pretty fucking secretive."

Wes goes up at something like nine to check on Taylor. If he's still asleep they might as well just let him sleep until morning, but nobody really wants to leave anyone alone yet. When Wes's panicked yelp echoes downstairs, and his feet pound out time to run back to the kitchen, Todd has already kinda figured out what's up.

"Taylor! H-he's—"

"He's gone, isn't he?" Todd says, feeling his stomach sink and his nerves steel over.

Wes nods, trying to get his breath back.

Todd rubs at his eyes fiercely, feeling preemptively exhausted. "Dalton, can you help Wes calm down?" Todd is bad at calming people down. His bedside manner is the biggest obstacle between him and being a doctor. He's too analytical, his parents say, has no clue how to connect to people. Dalton may not be a whole lot better— not anywhere near as good about it as Taylor is with his smooth distractions and the uncanny ability to force people into calmness— but he's gotta be better than Todd, and Todd isn't sure how well Jaxson and Collin do with stuff like this.

"What am I supposed to do!?"

Todd shrugs, aggravated. They have two priorities right now: calm Wes down and find Taylor. "I dunno, do some of those weird little focus things Taylor used to do with you." Todd knows that Taylor would sometimes spend hours with Dalton when he'd have breakdowns after his mom died. It's something Todd has always been a little jealous of, but he's not complaining now that those interactions could come in handy.

"And where the fuck're you going?" Jaxson asks, eyes looking much more nervous than the rest of him.

Todd slips on his shoes by the door, grabs a coat out of the closet, and calls back, "I know where Taylor went. I'll be right back." On purpose, he doesn't give anyone time to come after him. He's pissed enough as it is, and if anyone comes with them, Todd will spend precious time that could have been spent making sure his best friend doesn't get the shit beat out of him again ranting about how he can't believe he has to chase his best friend down to keep him from getting the shit beat out of him again while his other best friend comforts the first best friend's boyfriend and—

And honestly? Todd would prefer to just get Taylor safe and home and deal with the rest later.

25

Breakdown

Of course, as everyone had guessed, Taylor had snuck out of Todd's spare bedroom looking for a fight. He walked around near the bar, real slow, waiting for some asshole to swagger out drunk enough to oblige him. And, because Taylor is an expert loiterer, he's there when a man built like a freight train with a Semper Fi tattoo on his neck stumbles out mumbling about some enemy with a name he can't even pronounce in his stupor.

Taylor says the right stuff, the usual stuff, and the guy lunges, gets a good whack on Taylor's shoulder where it meets his neck—

And then he stops. And Taylor doesn't immediately see why amidst the adrenaline and the darkness. But he blinks away the bracing and Todd is standing there, in between them, arms up in placation.

And the face of the freight train with the Semper Fi tattoo screws up, confused, and then smooths in understanding, and he spits on the ground, calls Taylor a dirty name, and waddles to his car to get himself a DUI.

Todd turns on his heels and starts walking home before Taylor can get a good look at his face in the awkward glow of the distant street lamp. Taylor hasn't seen Todd upset often enough to be familiar with what it looks like, but from the way Todd is stomping ahead of him, that's what's happening. Because Taylor has been caught. For the first time in his life, he's been caught red-handed looking for a fight. He doesn't know what else he's supposed to do after being caught, so he just starts walking after Todd.

Todd is about the same height as Taylor, but it's mostly in the torso, so he walks pretty slow. Taylor has to waddle with an uncomfortably slow gait so he doesn't accidentally catch up to Todd and have to face whatever he's going to find in Todd's eyes.

If Todd knows, everyone back at the house knows.

Wes is gonna kill him, if Todd and Dalton don't beat him to it.

They walk like this halfway home, and then Todd stops under a street lamp. He stands stiff as a board, and Taylor stops at the edge of the little circle of light, about four feet from Todd. He's never felt more distant from him, and Todd's shoulders hike with the weight of whatever he wants to say. Taylor knows there's not much he can do to prepare himself for it. You can't brace against emotions the same way you can brace against a right hook.

But Todd just sighs out that hike in his shoulders until they're slumped in resignation and Todd scrubs at his face with the sleeve of his Patagonia jacket and it's just then that Taylor recognizes that Todd is crying.

"Todd, dude—"

"You know it hurts, right?" Todd bulldozes past any

placation or apology possible, voice thick enough that Taylor can tell he's been crying the whole walk. "When you hurt yourself? I don't know, dude. It fucks me up." Todd is lost for words. Todd can come up with something to say seemingly whenever he needs to, like water from a faucet. But today he kicks at the slush at the edge of the street around the light pole.

"Like, I have been *right* here the whole time, ya know?" he says. "You could have— I dunno, you could have talked to me, or Dalton— you could have talked to us, ya know? Just told us you need help? I wouldn't have asked if you needed me not to."

Sniffling, facing Taylor now with his eyes swollen from crying, Todd looks miserable, and small, and angry. "You guys are my best fucking friends, and you know I don't have anybody else. My parents are never home, and even when they are they're just filling space. For me, it's just you and Dalton— and now I guess there's Wes and Collin and Jaxson, but it's not the same. You're my fucking family, Taylor. Just—" he laughs, sardonic and piercing and it makes Taylor ache at every joint that isn't already bruised. Bones unsettled. "I don't even know what I'm asking you for, I guess. Just stop hurting yourself."

Of course, Taylor has no clue what to do with that. He knows Todd cares, he knows Dalton cares, he just can't figure out why they care so goddamn much. Why do they bother? Taylor's own mom didn't so much as flinch when his dad broke his nose when they argued about the tater tots that one time. Moms are the metric through which one views love from infancy, and Taylor's mom didn't seem all too bothered when she had to drive Taylor to the hospital a few days after Taylor started complaining about how bad his arm hurt after his dad smacked it when Taylor didn't unload the dishwasher and she certainly didn't seem very upset when the doctor informed them that Taylor had a fractured humerus that was starting to heal wrong. Taylor just got punched once in the shoulder and Todd is crying. Why? He's not dead. The bruise will heal. Taylor is sure that if he were to go home right now and tell his mom that he got into a fight, she would roll her eyes and cross her arms and tell him to stop doing that before they have to take him to the hospital again. He can hear her voice chiding him 'I'm not paying for the ER again, Taylor,' and that is what bubbles tears into his eyes.

He misses his mom. And he knows his mom doesn't miss him back.

Todd doesn't turn around the whole way home. At one point he makes a call, probably Dalton, and all Taylor hears is "Yeah. Yeah. He's fine. Yes, like actually fine. Okay, yeah. Almost home."

Of course, everyone is waiting for them at the spot where the footpath entry to the Richards Estate meets the front walkway of the house. They all look pissed. Dalton falters in his sternness when he meets Taylor's eyes, and Taylor wipes his face with his sleeve to make sure there's no leftover tears on his cheeks. Then Dalton meets Todd's eyes and his resolve returns.

"This is an intervention," Jaxson says. It's half a joke, but this is the most serious Taylor has ever seen him.

Taylor doesn't ask what for. He doesn't ask why. Even if he kinda wants to ask. He's not hurting anybody who isn't looking for a fight just as much as him. He never gets hurt too bad. Nothing that would need a doctor. He's always fine at the end of the day. If anything, Taylor doesn't think Jaxson, of all people, has room to talk after that whole mess in the bathroom last Wednesday, less than a week ago.

What are they chastising him for? For being stupid? For getting hurt? He'd get hurt no matter what he did or didn't do, at least this way he gets to pick the when and the who and the where. Why are they so fucking upset? Why are they angry?

Wes opens his mouth to say something, but a tremor wracks his whole body and his jaw clenches shut and he doesn't open it again. Dalton is trying to look pissed but mostly just glaring between his feet and Todd. Collin is doing a nervous thing where he taps his fingers against themselves. Jaxson is the only one looking Taylor right in the eye.

So Taylor yells at him. "Hit me! You're pissed right? Hit me! I won't even feel it—" and Jaxson does. Punches him right in the jaw and instantly regrets it when Taylor doesn't even falter, just wipes the blood off his lip and says, "See! Doesn't hurt. Do it again."

"Is this what you fucking want, Macready!?" Jaxson screams, "Do you really need someone to rock your shit that badly? Get the fuck over here, I'll do it— I will." And he punches Taylor again, hard enough to send both of them reeling. Taylor's nose starts bleeding and Wes stifles an anxious scream. "You think I like this? You think I wanna do this?" Jaxson cries, "This fucking hurts! It hurts to hurt you! We're fucking friends— aren't we? Aren't we!?"

Taylor doesn't answer. He wipes the blood from his face with his sleeve and tries not to look at his friends' faces. Wes is an angry kind of panicked, with his hands clutching the sleeves of another jacket he's borrowing from Todd; Dalton is rubbing tears from his own eyes; Collin' eyes are blank and unfocused like he's trying to be somewhere else; Todd's expression is hard and tear-stained. Taylor hates this. He doesn't want them to be upset. He just wants to be in control of who hurts him, and when. He wants at least that much!

But this is hurting them. Taylor can't understand why but his tiny locus of control, the point of contact he's desperately trying to balance his rapidly-spinning world on, is hurting his friends.

It's all too much. Jaxson wraps his arms around Taylor's shoulders instead. "Dude, I don't want to hurt you," he says, softly, gently. "I don't like hurting you. What the fuck about that is not getting into your head!?" His grip on Taylor's shoulders tightens and he shouts again, "We are friends, Taylor! Friends don't hurt each other! We're friends, aren't we!?"

Taylor shoves Jaxson off, trying to hide that his eyes are welling with tears. "Then who the fuck is gonna set me right!?" he shouts, eyes blurry and casting wildly from Jaxson to Dalton to Todd to Collin to Wes. He can't look at any of them for long— can't look at the fear in their eyes, water-stained by the tears blotting his vision. "I'm fucked up. If you guys don't let me go get my ass beat once in a while, I might—" he doesn't know how to finish that. He feels like he's choking.

What would he do, if he didn't go get his ass beat once in a while?

He has no fucking clue.

"Fuck. You guys can't— I'm trash!" Taylor screams, "I'm a piece of shit! I'm not good for anything—" Wes opens his mouth to interrupt and Taylor yells over him, "I can't even make a fucking coffee right! And I hurt all of you and I'm an asshole and— and— and I'm—"

"Everything okay, Mr. Richards?" one of Todd's body-guards, drawn by the noise, asks. Taylor's whole body shivers and flinches like an exposed nerve.

"Everything is fine, Austin," Todd says thinly. None of the Richards' bodyguards ever really come near the house, mostly sticking to the perimeter, but there's never usually a whole lot of screaming from the driveway past dark either.

"Are you sure?" Austin presses, eyeing Taylor suspiciously. Looking at him the way everyone looks at him. "He looks dange—"

"Austin, if you say another word I will fire you," Todd snaps. Austin blinks; Todd has never snapped. "Go home for today."

"Yes sir, Mr. Richards." Austin leaves, but the damage is done.

Dalton sees what's coming first, and he reaches out a hand to try and comfort Taylor, but Wes is faster and he manages to wrap Taylor in a hug just before Taylor's legs give out and he's a sobbing mess in Wes's arms and he can't even think clearly enough to care.

"I'm dangerous," Taylor's voice cracks around the words, a hoarse whisper after all the screaming. "I'm bad."

Wes is still shaking too bad to answer clearly, but he holds Taylor close until Todd and Jaxson and Dalton and Collin come sit with them on the pristine, stamped asphalt of the Richards' driveway.

"Taylor," Todd says, "You're not bad."

"And you're no more dangerous than I am," Dalton says.

"And you've been a good big brother to Hellen and Juniper-Maisie," Jaxson says.

"And you keep Jax from doing anythin' too dumb most times," Collin says

308

"You're a good person, Taylor," Wes says.

They go inside when the temperature drops lower. Dalton makes a joke about last Friday night's catastrophe, and how he's not throwing any more of his friends into lukewarm bathtubs, thank you very much.

Taylor is, even tens of minutes later, a sniffling mess, and very embarrassed about it. When not sniffling, he's got a very confusing pissed-off expression that dissolves into tears when Jaxson mentions Hellen and when Wes says things are okay and when Dalton gives him a big bear hug. They sit strewn all over the couches in Todd's basement and try to decide on a movie to watch. They'll be talking about what just happened, but they'll be talking about it when it feels less raw and when their not-yet-eighteen-year-old brains have had time to chew on the incredibly fucked up week-and-a-half they've had.

Dalton, as per usual, advocates for a military movie, but Jaxson says Barbie movies are infinitely better, and Todd mumbles that he would prefer to watch anime. Collin says that an action movie would be fun with this many people (and Dalton shoots that down by informing Collin that no action movie is fun to watch with Mr. Med School Lite (that's Todd) breaking the whole thing into unrealistic pieces and Todd shoots back that Dalton can never leave the imperfections in the theory and symbolism alone). Wes says anything sounds alright as long as they don't watch any of the National Treasure movies, because he just can't stand Nicholas Cage's face. Taylor stays totally silent throughout the discussion, but grumbles in a way that's half complaining and half not when Jaxson wins the rock-paper-scissors tournament and presses play on a pirated online version of Barbie and the Diamond

Castle.

Taylor sings along to some of the songs, even if nobody can hear it because Dalton and Jaxson and Collin are belting out "I feel connected! Protected! It's like you're standing right with me all the time!" in horrible, horrible harmony.

Taylor doesn't tell anyone else that Diamond Castle was Hellen's favorite.

26

God's Least Favorite Fifteen-year-old Girl

"You're doing great, Taylor! Even I didn't pick it up this quick." Which is true, it took Wes a few years to get any kind of proficiency in making coffee.

Taylor scoffs, "You started when you were six, Wes." Which is also true. Wes never did well with sitters, so it was easier for his parents to bring him to the shop with them.

"Taylor?" A voice follows the entry bell and Hellen Macready drops Juniper-Maisie Dixon's hand to run up to the counter and demand, "Since when are you working here!? And can you make hot chocolate!?"

As though he'd expected this (he hadn't), Taylor replies, "Since yesterday, and sure."

"He makes better hot chocolate than I do," Wes cuts in. The part of him that was nervous to talk to Hellen Macready last week has been overridden by Wes' Customer Service Voice™. "He can make you and Juniper-Maisie some, on the house." Wes tells Taylor he'll handle the counter if they get any new orders, and he starts to walk away. Except he hears Hellen ask if Taylor can add cinnamon to hers, and Wes immediately turns on his heel to ask, "Wait, you like cinnamon?"

Juniper-Maisie thinks that's a stupid question, Wes can tell by the way she laughs. Hellen raises one eyebrow and smirks and says, "Yeah? What's it to you?"

Now Wes is kinda nervous again, but he soldiers on. "Taylor hates cinnamon." Hellen glances at Taylor, eyebrow still raised. "I- I uh, just thought it w-was interesting."

Juniper-Maisie leans on Hellen and says, "You know she won't eat you, right?"

Wes actually jumps a little, face flushing, "I didn't mean to—"

"She's teasing you, Wes," Taylor says, nudging him. "Juniper-Maisie, whaddayou want in your hot chocolate— and don't ask for caffeine."

"But I like the jitters!" Juniper-Maisie insists. It's the first time Wes has heard her insist anything. Juniper-Maisie Dixon is about as quiet as it gets.

"Yeah, sure, but who has to go tell your brother that your allergies are acting up?" Taylor says. "That's right, me."

"She's allergic to caffeine?" Wes asks.

"Not a lot, but some. Just makes her stomach hurt, and gives her a migraine."

Hellen smiles the same way Taylor smiles when nobody's looking at him— they both got their teeth from their mom— and says, "Put some toffee syrup in there for her, Taylor."

He nods, wordless, and she makes a very particular face, and he makes it back, and then Taylor does the craziest thing and he *laughs*. Bright and loud enough to make half the coffee shop turn to look at him and a few people even smile with him because when Taylor laughs it's fucking infectious.

Apparently. Not that anybody had the chance to know that before.

Wes actually forgets to breathe for a few seconds, register forgotten. He wants to lift Hellen up and spin her around for making Taylor laugh like that.

Taylor keeps smiling the whole time he's making those two hot chocolates because Hellen keeps talking to him, inside jokes, sibling stuff. Wes puts a cinnamon muffin and a chocolate chip cookie in the food warmer between customers.

Juniper-Maisie says something to Hellen, and Hellen kisses her cheek and Juniper-Maisie skips over to the other side of the counter where Wes is pretending to be busy reorganizing the food display so that Taylor and Hellen can have their time.

"She's been worried about him," Juniper-Maisie says, apropos of absolutely no prior conversation.

Wes almost thinks she's talking to someone else, because her expression doesn't match her tone of voice at all— maybe he's having auditory hallucinations and Juniper-Maisie was talking to someone else she knows in the coffee shop. But she's still looking right at him; she was definitely talking to him.

Wes Post has never spoken to Juniper-Maisie for the reason one doesn't try to stare directly at the sun. She is quiet like the sun, and dangerous like the sun, and will burn you if she doesn't blind you with her dollar-store glue-on acrylic nails. Unless she likes you, a privilege that only seems to extend to her brother, her girlfriend, and her girlfriend's brother.

"Wes Post you listen to me and you listen good," Juniper-Maisie says, and Wes stops pretending to reorganize the food display because he would prefer to keep his corporeal form. Juniper-Maisie's expression is serene, as though they were discussing the weather and Hellen's hair clips, but her voice is made of wrought iron spikes. "My girlfriend loves her brother no matter what she says, and Taylor is just as much my big brother as Jaxson." She gives one succinct up-down glance over Wes, and then hisses, "If you hurt him they'll find your body in a shallow grave near the truck stop."

Wes's whole body seizes in a tic and he starts to stammer out a reply but Juniper-Maisie sighs.

"You're no fun," she groans. "I'm kidding." She probably was not kidding, but the sentiment of pretending to be kidding is nice. "Jeez, how did Taylor end up with a softie like you?" She giggles at Wes's face and adds, "That was a compliment. Taylor's needed a softie for probably about fifteen years."

Wes frowns now, watching Taylor and Hellen bicker across the shop. He's handed her one hot chocolate, and now he must be working on Juniper-Maisie's. "Taylor came in here for the first time in his entire life two years ago. With Hellen," he tells Juniper-Maisie. He has no idea why he's telling Juniper-Maisie any of this. She doesn't need to know. But it seems like she might like to. "He bought her a hot chocolate and they sat at that table right there, in the corner." The corner is currently occupied by Annika Slate and Tia Rodriguez, who are having a conversation in hushed tones (probably about their husbands and potential ways to kill them, their weekly Post Family Coffee Discussion). At the far end of the counter, Taylor says something to Hellen that makes her mock-anger fall flat and dissolve into giggles again. Wes feels his expression, soft and happy, and he feels Juniper-Maisie studying him like a bug on a plate."I'd never seen him smile like that," he tells her. "I made two hot chocolates on purpose instead of just one because it kinda blew my mind that he could smile like that."

In a way that could be accidental, if anything Juniper-Maisie does has ever been accidental, she shatters the calm atmosphere, "Listen, I know he had a breakdown last night—"

"H-h-how could you possibly know that!?"

She rolls her eyes. "Don't yell. I'm trying to give you important advice and Taylor'll try to make me shut up if he knows what I'm trying to tell you— and it's Taylor, so he'll know." She glances off to the side to check that the Macready siblings are still making fun of each other on the other side of the shop. "Wes, I've been watching Taylor for the last ten years. He's quiet, and he's soft, and he's scared all the time."

It's the first time Wes has heard anyone describe Taylor that way, and the quiet, soft, scared look that doesn't extend anywhere outside of Juniper-Maisie's eyes makes him think she knows it just as deep in her bones as the things she knows about herself. The softness evaporates when she continues, "The things I would do to their parents if it were legal are only eclipsed by the things I would do to my own parents," but she shakes that darkness off quickly. "I know what it looks like when he has a breakdown."

All at once she rattles off, "His hands are clenched and his shoulders ride up and his hair's matted under the hat and his jaw is set and his eyes are just a little red and I can see the edges of his bruises when he lifts his arms. I can tell you were there with him because there's nail bites in your arm and Taylor digs his nails into things when he's stressed." She's talking so fast Wes can barely make out the words.

He starts to speak, "Wha—"

"No, you still need to be listening right now, Wes. Are you

understanding my advice?"

Wes's face must answer for him because Juniper-Maisie sighs heavily and scrapes a hand through her hair before answering. "Okay, I'll slow it down: you need to notice these things before it gets bad." She leans over the counter to get in his face. "He doesn't know how to ask for help, Wes," she says. "He acts out because he doesn't know how to tell you he's hurting." Without warning, Juniper-Maisie's eyes well with tears and she sniffles. She holds up a finger to stop Wes from hovering before he can start. "Help him," she says, "please, Wes. Just—" she sniffles again and scrubs at her eyes, "Just keep him away from his parents."

The food warmer goes off behind Wes, and Juniper-Maisie points at it so Wes doesn't continue gawking at her. A customer has come in at some point and Taylor is taking their order. When Wes turns around with the food, Juniper-Maisie has resumed her smile-and-wave exterior. "Ya know, when Hellen and I were, like, ten, we ran away from home. Nobody even knew we were gone except Taylor. He looked for us for something like 6 hours. Didn't tell nobody, just looked all over by himself." That sounds about right. Even with the seismic shock of the discussion he's just speedrun with her, Wes can't stop himself from smiling, a little sweet and a little sad. "He found us hiding in a tree and got us to go home under the condition he'd build us a tree house. Mostly Jaxson and Collin go there now, but it's a nice tree house."

There's no way to discern why Juniper-Maisie is telling him this. She seems to have a very specific point, but Wes is clearly too stupid to get it. He hands her the cinnamon muffin and the cookie from the food warmer, and she takes them. He says, "Thanks," without really understanding what he's been given.

Juniper-Maisie says thanks too, and she takes the food back over to Hellen, who has found them a table by the window with their hot chocolates. Juniper-Maisie gives her a kiss on the cheek and Hellen beams at the free food.

Once the customer has left the register, Taylor comes over and stands next to Wes. "Juniper-Maisie does that sometimes," he says.

"Huh?"

"Just, like, says something absolutely crazy and walks away like she didn't get halfway to solving Fermat's last theorem."

Wes watches the girls for a few minutes. "I gave them a cinnamon muffin."

"Cinnamon is Hellen's favorite."

When the girls are done with their food and drinks, a little over an hour later, they come back up to the counter to say bye. Taylor actually goes around the counter to give Hellen a hug, and then Juniper-Maisie too. "I'm coming back here tomorrow," Hellen says. Before Taylor can say anything, she says, "I fucking miss you, dude."

Taylor looks like he might cry, but he doesn't.

27

Two Feet and Twenty

Collin kinda expected everyone to scatter into their own separate things once Taylor and Wes left for work. Nobody hardly ever sits in the same room for longer than it takes to eat dinner at his house. But it's already lunchtime and Todd, Dalton, Jaxson, and Collin are all still sitting together in Todd's basement. Dalton is messing around with Todd's VR headset, Jaxson is scrolling through social media on his phone on the couch (and occasionally 'joking' about starting a cosplay account), Todd is putting some sort of food together at the definitely-not-a-second-kitchen, and Collin is trying to calm down enough to look like he's scrolling through Instagram. He's not calm though, and no amount of videos of foster kittens playing with cardboard tubes is fixing that.

He pats Jaxson's thigh to let him know he's getting up, and Jaxson grabs the hand without looking up and brings the back of Collin' palm to his lips for a quick kiss. Jaxson doesn't seem to notice that Collin is getting all fidgety, but that quick little hand-kiss settles a little bit of the needless anxiety bubbling in the pit of his stomach and he grins as he tiptoes over to Todd at the bar of the definitely-not-a-second-kitchen.

"Watcha makin' there, Todd?"

"A charcuterie board. It's almost lunch but I'm not great at cooking."

"Shark coochie?" Jaxson says, still not looking up from his phone.

"Charcuterie, darling," Collin corrects.

"How can you two stand being so adorable, like all the time?" Dalton asks, swinging the VR controller in a wide arc (he must still be playing Skyrim).

Collin, anxiously ignoring that comment, rubs his fists together. "Well, I could— I mean, if y'all wanted— er, I uh— I could make lunch. Or somethin'..."

Todd gives Collin a smile that belongs on the face of a 72-year-old. "I would appreciate that, dude. I can help you get the ingredients again, if you want?" Even though it turns his ears a little red, Collin nods. He's not ready to be alone in a small, lockable space yet. Who knows, maybe he won't ever be. He's barely 18, but there are already things that Collin knows he probably won't ever be able to do the way other kids can because of the adults in his life. He tries to shrug those thoughts off his shoulders, but they cling like thick, black oil, drenching his skin and clogging his ears and filling his mouth and nose—

"You coming, Collin?" Todd asks from the top of his basement stairs.

"O-oh, sure! Yeah, I'mma comin'."

"I feel bad making you cook while you're here," Todd says as he hands Collin any ingredients or utensils he requests. "Usually we have a chef, Victoria, but she always gets the holidays off to spend with her family, since it's always just me in the house for Christmas."

"Every year it's just you?"

"Yep. Just me. And whatever bodyguard my parents are hiring that year."

"That's gotta be awful lonely."

"It is." Todd probably means to sound angry when he says it, but Collin just hears sad.

"Well, I sure don't mind cookin'. 'Specially since yer being so nice and lettin' us stay here while we don't got nowhere else."

Todd smiles a little. "You're a sweet little guy, Collin, you know that?"

"I am not little!" Collin says, puffing up. "I'm actually pretty big now!"

Todd laughs. "It's a figure of speech, dude. I don't actually think you're little."

Collin feels his ears go red again, but it feels nice this time. Todd isn't laughing at him. Collin knows this feeling: friends. He has a friend in Todd. Todd is his friend. Todd, the smartest, most level-headed kid in the entire school, has decided Collin is a good person to be friends with. Collin wants to run downstairs and tell Jaxson, *look, look! We have friends! After all that horrible shit when we were kids, now we have friends!*

But Jaxson is downstairs with their other friend. Collin can hear Jaxson yelling something about "High Hrothgar my fucking ass, I wanna go kill Nazeem!" He and Dalton must have switched off on the VR headset.

Collin finishes some garlic-bread grilled cheese sandwiches and Todd cuts up some apple slices ("the extent of my culinary ability" he had joked) and they carry the trays back downstairs to find Jaxson is now upside down on the couch with the VR headset on yelling "For the Empire!"

"Woah, did you speedrun the Civil War questline that fast?" Todd asks.

"Huh?" Jaxson turns toward them, even though he can't see them with the headset on. "Oh, no. I'm fighting a troll."

"Aren't the Stormcloaks the good guys in that game?" Collin asks.

"Not unless you're a fucking fascist," Dalton says. "Thanks for the grilled cheese, by the way— but, no. The Stormcloaks are literally just racist assholes. That's it."

Collin nods and starts nomming on a sandwich. "Oh, man. I've never played Skyrim. My parents— uh, ya know—"

"Yeah, we gotcha," Dalton says, saving him from having to explain the whole seventeen years. "Buuut, if you wanted to play now, it is your turn." Collin thinks that maybe this is why Taylor loves Dalton and Todd so much. You don't gotta explain nothin' to them. They'll feed you and explain video games you don't get and make you feel whole and loved without a word, if you don't wanna talk.

Collin has never played any games with blood or fighting in them. He doesn't hesitate to grab the headset and pull it on and immerse himself in surprisingly good graphics (or, at least, better than the 2012 classic, The Sims 3). The controls are intuitive too, once Dalton and Jaxson and Todd talk him around some of it. It's fun! A little chaotic, but fun too!

He barely hears Dalton tell Todd, "Dude, Toddster, you gotta tell your parents 'thanks' for all of us—"

But he definitely hears when Todd shouts, "Man, fuck my parents!" Collin pulls the helmet off his head and drops the remotes. Todd takes in the faces of three people who don't do well with shouting and lowers his volume. "Sorry, sorry for yelling— it's just—" he sighs heavily. "I dunno, nevermind."

"No, no— out with it," Jaxson insists, "Everyone else has gotten their breakdown. It's your turn, dude."

Dalton and Collin nod to usher Todd on, and he chuckles. "I don't wanna sound like a whiny ass. I've got it all, ya know?"

"Hey, hey, what did my therapist say, Todd?"

"I dunno, Dalton, he tells you a lot of things."

"Martin always tells me, 'don't compare trauma.' Drowning in two feet of water and drowning in twenty both make you dead, so."

"Thanks, buddy."

"So tell us about yer two feet," Collin says. He's smiling like he doesn't know he's the twenty-feet-guy, but the way Dalton nudges him, wraps an arm over his shoulder, and squeezes makes it clear that, at least, nobody else has forgotten.

Todd smiles sideways, then frowns. "It's just— every year since I was twelve, my parents go to this stupid medical science conference in Nashville. Every year! So every year for Christmas and New Years I'm alone, and it fucking sucks! I'm just..." He's looking around at them and he's trying to be angry, but it's coming out sad. He sighs, dropping the facade and just admitting, "This is the nicest winter break I've had in years, because I'm not alone." He starts to sniffle, "I don't know, I just wish my parents would— ya know, be here?" There's the creeping, aching loneliness of having hurts that you hide, Todd knows that just as well as everyone else in the room.

As silly as it feels to acknowledge the heartbreak of parents that don't even know what size shirt you wear, when compared to parents that beat you or lock you in closets, Todd can't run from that hurt forever. He knows that.

Dalton's never been much of a runner away. He wraps him in a bear hug. "How about I'm your new parents?"

"Dude, you're only one person and you're three months younger than me."

"Irrelevant," Dalton says.

"We can be your new parents too," Jaxson says, laughing and also clearly serious. "As long as you're okay with having three dads," that part is a joke.

Todd laughs too, and then he hiccups, and then he starts crying in earnest. Nobody has ever seen Todd cry, and Collin and Jaxson help Dalton give him all the Holiday Hugs he has ever missed from his parents.

* * *

When Wes and Taylor get home from the coffee shop (about an hour later than usual, which is suspicious to Jaxson because the shop wasn't open any later than usual), they find Dalton making cookies for Santa Claus and Jaxson flipping through kids Christmas movies and Collin reading the recipe from a website about how to make mashed potatoes. There's already a turkey in the oven ("where the hell did you get a turkey?" "my parents always leave one in the deep freezer for me over winter break").

Taylor does not fully reveal himself to the people in the kitchen/living room area, instead staying tucked in the alcove next to the garage door, and he grumbles something Jaxson doesn't catch before shuffling back out into the garage.

"Wait, wait, wait," Dalton says, setting down his tray of

cookie-dough balls, "Where are you going, young man?"

"To the garage."

"Why aren't you coming into the kitchen to greet your parents?" Jaxson asks.

"My what now?"

"We decided while you were gone that the three of us are your parents," Collin says. "Todd's too."

Dalton nods, ignoring the part where he's been cracking jokes about being Taylor's parent for at least a year. "So why are you being all sneaky, my son?"

"Stop calling me that, dude, it's weird."

"Answer the question or it's all I'll call you for the foreseeable future."

"I have—" Taylor stumbles over the response that's least likely to get him investigated and comes up with, "I have secrets. Big ones." It doesn't help that he says it totally deadpan, like he's referring to the secrets that got his nose broken in sixth grade, or the ones that make him go out and pick fights with drunk people outside bars late at night.

But Taylor clearly isn't referring to these things because he has a plastic bag hidden poorly behind his back.

Everyone is still too busy holding back laughter at Taylor's horrible, horrible communication skills to stop him from ducking into the garage after telling them, "I'm gonna go hide some shit."

It takes Jaxson (he's not sure about the rest of them) way too fucking long to realize what Taylor is hiding. Tomorrow is Christmas day. Taylor is hiding Christmas presents.

Taylor was so broke he lived under a bridge, and with his first tips and paycheck (if he's even gotten anything like a paycheck yet, after only a few days of working at Post Family

Coffee) he bought fucking Christmas presents.

Not like Jaxson can talk. He's broke with no job and he bought Juniper-Maisie a new sweater and boots, and Hellen some eyeliner and a pair of nice falsies, and Collin some embroidered oven mitts from a creator he likes on Etsy (the embroidery says "No sass" on one mitt and "Eat ass" on the other). You do what you do for the people you love, whenever you can afford it. Jaxson works his ass off every summer to make sure he can afford it.

While Taylor hides his bag in the garage, Jaxson raises his eyebrows suggestively at Wes. "So," he asks, "what's in there that he doesn't want us to know about?"

Wes panics, stammers wordlessly, and shouts, "Drugs!" He calms down once everyone is laughing with him. "It really is a secret though— even I don't know exactly what he bought."

Collin frets, "I hope it wasn't too expensive." He's always worried about people spending too much money on him. Jaxson tries to reassure him with a smile from across the room, and he thinks it works. Collin is getting so much more confident with friends, without his parents. Jaxson is fucking infatuated all over again, and he puts down the TV remote to text Collin as much. Collin won't see it until he checks his texts tonight, but Jaxson is sure that, at some point later tonight, Collin will smile at his phone.

Collin finishes the turkey and the mashed potatoes and Dalton finishes the cookies and Jaxson finds the claymation Rudolph the Red-Nosed Reindeer on PBS Kids.

They eat dinner together, and Dalton makes too many dad jokes, and Collin frets over whether everyone is eating enough, and Taylor insists that he needs to use the kitchen after dinner, and Wes compliments the cooking of the chef, and Todd cries a little bit over having a family to spend Christmas Eve with, and Jaxson soaks it all in with a smile and texts Juniper-Maisie that he'll swing by with her present tomorrow.

They all go to sleep piled next to each other on the basement couch (they watched the animated Frosty the Snowman down there while Taylor used the kitchen for... whatever he needed to use it for, and afterwards Taylor came and joined them and Wes asked Taylor why he smelled like peppermint and Todd said that he definitely smelled some lavender in there too and Taylor denied all of it).

As the last one awake, Collin surveys the scene with a little smile that his body can barely contain, and he runs his fingers through Jaxson's unkempt hair, and he pulls Todd's blanket a little higher over his shoulders, and he looks again at that text Jaxson sent him earlier, and his smile gets a little bigger as he snuggles into his boyfriend and falls happily asleep.

28

Christmas Day

When you're seventeen-or-eighteen-years-old with shitty parents, Christmas morning eventually stops feeling exciting.

Good thing Dalton and Wes don't have that problem.

Wes is up first. He wiggles out from Taylor's iron-clad sleep-grip, takes his meds (retrieved after work yesterday, finally), texts his parents, but skips the daily meditation in favor of sneaking up to the kitchen to find Dalton, who had woken up from Wes's shifting of the cuddle puddle on the basement couch and (while Wes took his meds and texted his parents) crept upstairs with the same idea: Christmas morning breakfast.

In whispering tones, they manage to get through eggs, a fruit tray, a pot of homemade hot chocolate just barely below fragrant enough to bring Jesus himself down, bacon, homemade whipped cream, and Dalton's mom's signature waffles before ninety minutes is through. By then, Collin and Taylor have grumbled themselves awake and managed to drag Todd and Jaxson to consciousness with them, and everyone

327

migrates upstairs, drawn by the smells.

"Holy shit," Jaxson mumbles, still rubbing sleep from his eyes and out of his bedswept hair.

"Holy shit," Taylor echoes, blinking owlishly (adorably) at the nearly-finished and frankly extensive preparations.

Todd grins, wide and childish. He's thinking of six Christmases, a third of his life, spent alone in an empty kitchen, wolfing cereal and frowning at Home Alone reruns in the uncomfortable bar stools. Those same barstools now seem so inviting. He laughs, not even fully feeling his own ebullience yet. "You guys are literally the best. This is the best Christmas on the planet."

Collin, bouncing fast enough to maybe be mistaken for a toddler of immense size, nods and beams. "This is the best Christmas breakfast ever!"

"Well, don't just stare at it," Dalton says. "Food is meant for eating."

Jaxson, who typically wouldn't hesitate to dig in, and isn't even really talking about the food here, says, "But it looks so pretty."

"Don't let it get cold or it'll be a waste of our efforts!" Wes insists, barely avoiding a stammer. He's scooping the fresh whipped cream into a bowl with a rubber spatula, and he has an extra-sappy smile for Taylor, who he has never seen so bright-eyed or purely, unadulteratedly happy.

Call it the magic of Christmas.

Everyone sits at the barstools at the counter and stuffs their faces so full of waffles and fruit and bacon and eggs that, for about an hour after, they don't even have the energy to move. They just sit at the island and talk and talk and talk about the most meaningless things until 12:30 rolls around and Jaxson perks up.

"I gotta give Juniper-Maisie her Christmas present," he remembers.

Taylor nods. "And I've got one for Hellen."

"And there's the one from my parents," Wes says, "They texted this morning, apparently it's hidden in the chimney chute."

"The chimney chute!?" Dalton balks, "Why the fuck would they hide a present wrapped in boxes and flammable wrapping paper in a chimney chute!? What if you guys had started a fire in there!?"

"We never light fires in the chimney." Wes explains, "There's been a family of ravens living there for years, and my parents think it would be bad luck to displace them."

This, of course, gets Dalton and Collin and Todd started in on demanding to know the names of each of the ravens living in the Wes family's chimney, names that Wes had no clue he was supposed to have created. He just knew that the big, fluffy one always dropped colorful bits of trash on the back porch, and the two little ones were learning to do it too, and the sleeker, older one mostly just sat on the of the chimney and scared away other birds.

"So, the sleek one is Screecher, the fluffy one is Sweetie Pie, the little one with the funny wing is Peggy, and the other one is Sir Cornelius Engleton?"

"Perfect— see, even Taylor is getting it!"

"I still don't see why we have to name them."

"Wes, let us have our moment."

"Alright, but it's already one," Wes says, "Don't we wanna go drop off little sister presents?"

"Yes!" Jaxson sings, jumping to his feet and dashing

upstairs to the bathroom where he'd left all his stuff at some point. He scurries back downstairs with a brown paper bag stuffed with magazine pages like tissue paper cradled in his arms. "She's gonna be siked!"

Taylor, with a threat not to follow him, skulks into the garage and emerges with a little white shipping box covered in doodles of cats and rainbows and superheroes and hearts and stars. Wes's heart swells to see that the doodles were done by Taylor. He remembers, a couple weeks ago, that Taylor Macready had been too stone-faced and ice-hearted to do anything like doodle his little sister's favorite stuff onto the box with her Christmas present in it.

Or maybe Taylor Macready has always been this soft, and Wes had been willingly ignoring it— plastering over it with the angry, bruised caricature he had been taught to see by everyone in this tiny little Midwest town— to avoid seeing the vulnerability that made those bruises, still not fully healed, so unbearable to look at.

Maybe Taylor had always been this way, and everyone had been blind to it by some machination of knowing only what they wanted to know for years and years, insulated by the cornfields.

"I like the box," Jaxson says, "Hellen will love it."

"Thanks. Yours has some good color in there."

"Thanks. I stole a Vogue and a Cover girl to make the tissue paper."

"Knowing Juniper-Maisie," Taylor says fondly, "she'll clip the expired coupons and trick the cashier into letting her use them a year late." Jaxson throws his head back in a laugh and agrees.

They set a course of action: Jaxson's house first, then

Taylor's, then Wes's, then back to Todd's. Jaxson's house is farthest, after all, and the rest of the route will be a meandering line back through town.

Halfway into their trek in the snow, half a foot thicker than it was yesterday, to Jaxson's house, it becomes partially about cheering Jaxson up. He hasn't seen his parents in several days, and apparently he didn't leave on friendly terms (Taylor and Collin both point out that, when Jaxson leaves, it's *usually* because he's not on friendly terms with his parents). He becomes visibly worried as they get closer to the house, and even jokes once about turning back and giving the present to Juniper-Maisie at school in a week or so, but he presses on and everyone is right there supporting his back in the face of that harsh, imaginary wind.

At the Dixon trailer, his friends standing a good ways back talking about something else so as not to eavesdrop, Jaxson doesn't even get to the door before it's flung open and Juniper-Maisie bounces out to wrap Jaxson's neck in a hug that's more unguarded than she'll usually allow (it's Christmas, after all, and allowances like this can be made). He shoves his present at her and she shoves her present at him. He beams at the thrift-store-new parka she got him, and she cackles with wild joy at the sweater and boots he got her.

Even Mr. and Mrs. Dixon, peeking from the doorway as timidly as they can allow themselves to be, after everything (it's Christmas, after all, and allowances like this must be made), hand Jaxson an unwrapped present with a single bow on it. It's a Lego set.

Jaxson doesn't like Legos. He takes it with a gracious smile anyway. His parents try to keep him with the promise of dinner. They got a rotisserie chicken from Walmart, and some

331

real vegetables to steam up. He tells them he's got other plans, tells them to tell Jeremy hi for him (if Jeremy ever comes by), and plants a kiss on the top of Juniper–Maisie's head before waving goodbye.

"Well," he says flatly, jokingly, once they're out of earshot, "that was painfully awkward."

"At least they're trying?" says Collin. If anyone else had said it, Jaxson would have had a barbed comment rhyming with 'too little/too late,' but it's Collin saying it. So he just nods. And they start heading for Taylor's house.

Robert Macready doesn't love Christmas especially. Fourth of July is his favorite. He likes the oppressive warmth of an Iowan summer in his hair, even as it thins, and on his skin, even as it wrinkles. He likes the explosive vibrancy of the fireworks, the screams of the little kids. He likes that all he has to do for those days is barbecue and chip into the neighborhood firework money pool.

Christmas, on the other hand, is a pain in Robert's ass. It's impossible to know what presents his wife or daughter will like, and they're expensive, and the tree and decorations always seemed so gaudy to him that he isn't sure why he bothers to tack them up every year, and the gentleness the season is expected to bring out of people is usually more of a burden than a blessing.

But still, watching Hellen gleefully unwrap a new skateboard brings him some warmth. His wife's mirthful eyes meeting his where she's pulled away from him on the couch. She's wearing the new silk robe she had unwrapped from him a few minutes ago. He got his wife that robe ("a higher threadcount than most sheets," the lady at the store had told him proudly, like she'd made it herself or something), some new workout gear, a new monitor for the desktop in her office, some new art supplies (that's what she's been into these past few months), and a nice hat. For Hellen, he got that skateboard, a new laptop, some shoes that she'd pointed out last time the family went to the mall, a subscription to some little online sticker shop or something that she'd talked about, and a stack of new books. Robert is pretty sure he's nailed this year's presents, even if the process of shopping for them was grueling.

Now, he's settled onto the couch, wearing the pajamas Hellen got him and holding the mug from his wife (it reads "Best Husband Ever!" with the exclamation point and every-thing) drinking some of the little coffee pods from the Keurig they had gotten him this year too, and feeling completely content. Yellow light streams in through the windows where the midday sun hits them, breakfast is still a very recent memory, and not one hair is out of place in Robert Macready's life on Christmas day.

And then there's a knock at the door. All three Macready heads crane up to look toward the front door, but it's Robert (not wanting to disturb the domestic little slice of perfection before him) who sets down his Best Husband Ever! mug and says, "I'll get it. Be right back, girls." And he kisses his wife on the cheek and his daughter on the head and he shuffles to the front door.

It's Christmas morning, so they aren't expecting visitors, but Robert suspects it could be the neighbors— Mr. and Mrs. Beaufort— stopping by to wish them the best of the holidays or something. They're sentimental like that. After Thanksgiving, they had dropped by to ask the Macreadys if they wanted any pie, Robert had accepted, but the pie ended up being a little tasteless and he regretted accepting it when he had to force a smile and thank them for their generosity next time he saw them.

Since he expects it to be the Beauforts, Robert does not check the porthole before swinging the door wide open.

It is not the Beauforts.

Robert wishes he had ignored the knock at the door.

It's his bastard son, Taylor. Robert hasn't seen Taylor's face in over a month, and he's annoyed at seeing it now. The black hair that he didn't inherit from Robert or his wife, the crooked nose, the uneven jawline, the patchwork bruises that Taylor has a knack for stitching together on his own skin, the uneven stance even when he's just standing on the front porch. It all pisses Robert off. And even besides the annoyance at having to see him at all, how dare Taylor come on Christmas day? Robert doesn't know what Taylor's been doing with himself these past few weeks, but he must have been doing well enough since he didn't come back, why today? Of all days, why ruin today? Why ruin Christmas?

"Can I see Hellen?" Taylor asks, quietly. There's his standard gaggle of friends, plus a few extra, at the edge of the yard, not stepping onto the edge where the driveway starts. It feels like a judgment to Robert, that they won't step onto his driveway, and it sets his molars grinding a little.

Taylor is holding a little box, covered in shitty little drawings that not even a mother could love. Uneven hearts and lopsided stars and cats drawn with barely any resemblance to the actual animal. Robert feels his lips twitching in a sneer. "No, she's enjoying Christmas," he says. "Besides, I told you I never wanted to see your face, didn't I? What are you doing here?"

"I just have a present for Hellen. Can I please just give Hellen a Christmas present? Then I'll leave."

Behind him, Robert hears the girls stirring in the living room, making their way to the door. His wife is saying "Who is it, dear?" and Hellen's skipping towards him.

Taylor tries to peer over Robert's shoulder, and Robert moves to obstruct his view. "Give me the present," he says, "I'll give it to Hellen." He won't. Anything Taylor got for Hellen is probably corrupting in some way. Hellen has been getting bolder and more disrespectful as she's grown older and closer to Taylor, and Robert would like to nip that bud before it flowers.

Taylor pulls the box infinitesimally closer to himself, protective. He shakes his head minutely and says, "You won't give it to her, you'll throw it away." That's what Robert did for one of Hellen's birthdays, when she was turning thirteen and headstrong and Taylor had declined to inform Robert ahead of time what kind of gift he'd gotten her. He's thrown away any present Taylor has tried to give Hellen since, to protect her from his influence. Taylor's comment is intentionally misconstruing the information, making Robert look like the bad guy, when really he's just protecting his younger daughter from his asshole son, and it fully pisses Robert off.

So by the time his daughter and his wife have reached the door, Robert has punched Taylor in his uneven jaw, left him stumbling back a few feet and spitting blood into the snowbank over the flowerbed. "Get off my property before I call the cops," Robert says. He's said it dozens of times over the years, punched Taylor in the jaw more often than that, but today Hellen comes up behind him, squeezes around him, and stomps on Robert's foot hard in her slippers from last year's Christmas before going to help Taylor up.

"Dad!" she shrieks, a banshee assault to Robert's dumb-struck ears, "I am not sitting by anymore and watching you treat my brother like shit! Leave him alone or I leave with him."

Robert's wife makes imploring eyes at him. She was always softer on Taylor, but she probably can't bear the loss of Hellen. He's half made up his mind to kick Hellen out too, just to make a point, curb her rebellion now, at fifteen, before it's fully grown, but those punks at the edge of the driveway have all come running up the walk now, leaving messy footprints in the clean lines of fresh snow.

"What the fuck is wrong with you?" the Dixon boy shouts. He pulls Taylor up by the shoulder Hellen doesn't already have. "He came to give his sister a fucking Christmas present! It's Christmas, you narcissistic fuck!"

The Richards boy that Taylor brought over a few times stands between Taylor and Robert, and he adds, "Besides, if you want to get the police involved, I wonder whose side they'd take: yours, or your son?" Taylor's other friend, the big one, stands next to the Richards one, arms crossed. Has that kid always been so big?

Robert suddenly realizes that, for a man, he's not that tall. Certainly not that muscular.

There's two other kids— Robert doesn't recognize either of them— but one of them is holding onto Taylor's hand once he's upright and steady, and the other has a look in his eyes that Robert isn't comfortable with meeting or thinking about.

Robert knows he's beat now. He can kick Taylor to shit any day of the week, but his wife will have a fit if he touches Hellen, and Robert can't reasonably fend off six boys who are all his size or bigger. But he won't admit defeat either. "I'm calling the cops," he says, and stalks inside to find his cellphone.

29

That's Not All, Because Of Course It's Not

Hellen's eyes are watery and big and more vulnerable than Taylor has ever seen them. She wraps him in a tight hug. He's too numb to really feel it, but his arms hug her back. Jaxson's got the present he made for her in his hands— Taylor had dropped it in the snow when he stumbled. He hopes nothing in it broke. He hopes he insulated it with enough tissue paper.

"Merry Christmas, Hellen," he says, when he can.

She laughs in that way she does when she can't think of the more appropriate emotion for the situation and nods into his shoulder. "Thanks for the present."

"You haven't even opened it."

Somewhere else, he hears his mom close the door on the two of them, calling Robert, leaving into the recesses of the house.

"You can open it later," he tells her.

"Alright, I will." She still hasn't let him go. She might be crying. Taylor might be crying.

When there's footsteps coming back toward the door, they let go, and Taylor feels his feet directing him to leave. He takes the box from Jaxson and hands it to Hellen. "I'll see you around," he says, and she nods.

The door opens, and it's just mom, looking pinched but not angry. She hands him a plastic-wrapped paper plate with some cake on it. It's the chocolate fudge cake she makes every year for Christmas and New Years. "Here," she says, "I don't have any presents... take this with you." He takes the paper plate with numb hands and a confused face. It doesn't show to her; his mom has never been good at reading him. He knows that all she sees is his same, blank expression. He wishes, just this once, that she could really see him. But he takes the cake and thanks her and he says goodbye again and then he starts down the driveway, following the footprints left by his friends.

They're on the next street over, halfway to Wes's, when he realizes he's not by himself. Wes's hand had, at some point, taken his. And Todd and Dalton and Jaxson and Collin are all right there too, with expressions coloring the whole spectrum of cold to warm to hot.

He feels like he has to say something. It was his problem they had to deal with. It's his blood welling in his mouth where he bit his cheek. It's his cake that he'll eventually have to eat, even if he doesn't want it.

Jaxson beats him to it, and everything feels so much lighter the way he says it: "Well. That was a lot."

Taylor laughs. His eyes are tearing up again, but it's a genuine little laugh.

Dalton adds, "So much. That was so much." His face looks like he just watched someone get shot.

"He wasn't like this every time you guys came over?" Wes asks.

Todd shakes his head, looking about as green in the gills as Dalton. "No, dude. We only went to Taylor's house, like a handful of times."

"It's not like I was excited to show people my sparkling home life," Taylor jokes, and he's relieved when it hits the right cord and everyone else laughs a little too.

"Is your jaw okay, Taylor?" Wes asks.

And suddenly everything feels a little better. A little closer to this new normal Taylor has started, bravely, to feel used to.

Wes's house feels a little like a tomb when they first enter, since they had left so unexpectedly and hadn't cleaned up any messes before they went. It's like a snapshot of five days ago: the nest of blankets Taylor and Wes had warmed up in after nearly freezing to death, the pile of various mealtime dishes in the kitchen sink, Taylor's clothes still in a plastic bag by the TV stand, muddy bootprints all over the laminate flooring.

Wes is the first one inside, and he feels the stagnation in the air run right out the front door to make room for all his friends. The moment everyone is inside, it feels exactly like home again.

He mutters something about how he'll have to mop before mom and dad get home. They've never had to contend with teenager muck, really, since Wes is tidy and had been friendless.

When he texted them this morning, after he took his meds, he had cried a little bit. Happy tears. He'd asked if his parents were doing okay having Christmas so far away (they'd seemed worried in their earlier texts, constantly asking if Wes was okay, if he was lonely, and so Wes had assumed they were lonely), and they had responded that their Christmas was going perfect because their son got to spend the day with his friends, with his boyfriend (as Wes had told them). They had said to make sure everyone was there to open the present they had shoved in the chimney.

Wes shimmied it out and wiped his hands on his pants. "Uh, this one's mine. That one's Taylor's..." There's a third one. "This one is for all of us?"

"But I've never met your parents," Collin says, the first thing he's said since Taylor's house.

Wes shrugs. "I dunno, it just says 'For All of You.'"

"But we've never met your parents," Todd repeats.

"H-hang on. I'll text them."

Taylor, jaw fever-warm where it's starting to swell, hangs over Wes's shoulder, and it removes the feeling of the uncanny from the situation, makes it benign and strange and kind of cute instead of horrifyingly unknown.

The Family Groupchat [1:26]
Wes: hey guys
what's this third present in the chimney?
It says for all of youu
Dad: haha...
That's for you and your new friends, of course!
Mom: Just open it, it'll help you all make some great memories
<3 Love you, kiddo. Merry Christmas! <3
Dad: Merry Christmas, Wes

"They said it's for all of us," Taylor dictates to the group. His 's's sound funny because he's talking around what is rapidly becoming a huge bruise on the lower half of his cheek, and Dalton dips into the kitchen to get an ice pack out of the fridge, wrap it in a clean rag, and hand it to Taylor, who thanks Dalton with a little nod.

"Uh, alright, I guess," Jaxson looks awkwardly at the present, and clutches the new parka Juniper-Maisie got him a little closer.

Wes peels off the wrapping paper of that third, mysterious present, picks open the box, and gingerly dumps the contents onto the pullout couch, while everyone watches.

It's a Polaroid camera. And a notebook— no, not a notebook. It's a blank scrapbook.

There's a note too.

Dear friends,

Thank you for taking care of our son, now and in the future. We can't wait to meet you when we get home. You're all invited over for dinner the first Friday after winter break.

We got you all a scrapbook and camera to share, so that you can put your friendship on page before you've gotten so old that the friendship feels like you've had it forever. Old friendships are wonderful, but new friendships are exciting! Don't forget that!"

Merry Christmas to you all!

Martha and Richard Post

"Why do I feel like crying?" Dalton asks, laughing.

Todd gives a single chuckle, but he's still staring at the note. So is everyone else.

Eventually, just to say something, Jaxson says, "Your parents are literally the nicest, what the fuck?" and then everyone laughs and the paralyzing silence is over.

Everyone badgers Wes into opening his present in front of them (it's a new Switch, with four controllers and some games, plus a note that makes Wes wipe his eyes on his sweater), and they all cheer and insist that they're gonna stay up all night playing Smash and Pokemon. When they try to badger Taylor into opening his present, he resolutely says, "Fuck off, not in front of you fuckers," and they decide to leave that be, since Taylor has had kind of a shitty day.

Wes (with Taylor's help) makes them help him clean up a little (do the dishes, mop the floor, make the bed on the foldout couch), and then they start heading for Todd's. Stomachs grumble along the way, so the first order of business is food. Collin makes everyone grilled cheese and Jaxson sautes carrots.

While they eat, Todd gives the rest of his friends so many long, intense looks, that eventually Taylor snaps, "What, Todd?"

"Huh?"

"Get it off your chest or I'm gonna hit you."

"Why can't you ever express your concern nicely," Dalton sighs.

But Todd shrugs anxiously, pokes at his carrots with a fork, and says, "So, uh, I have Christmas presents for you guys."

Dalton, sitting next to Todd, wraps one arm around his neck. "Aw, Toddster, you didn't have to do that."

"Okay, but I wanted to," Todd says, still looking sweaty, "So Dalton, I got you a new varsity jacket. It's upstairs in a box under my bed if you want to go get it."

"Todd!" Dalton squeals, "Ohmygod, I'll be, like, right back—" and he sprints upstairs.

Turning to face Wes next, Todd says, "I got you a coloring book. And some regular books. There's been a lot of stressful shit lately, and those coloring books are supposed to help people calm down, but I wasn't sure if you would think that was lame, or—"

"Dude, I love those coloring books!" Wes says, sitting straight up, twitching with excited jitters next to Taylor. "I haven't had one in years!"

"Cool," Todd says, breathing out his relief, "yours is behind the TV stand in the basement, if you want to go get it."

Wes hops to his feet, gives Taylor a kiss on the top of the head (which was unexpected, and sends Taylor bright red and flustered), and runs off downstairs.

"You're too nice, Todd," Taylor chokes out between his embarrassed, squeezed expression and swollen jaw.

"Well, don't thank me yet, I haven't given you your present—" Todd says, getting more nervous. "I hope you don't mind sharing with Collin and Jaxson though— I mean, I wasn't even sure if this was the right thing to get you guys, but my parents offered and I told them yea, so I just thought—"

"Whatever it is will be great," Collin cuts in, "I'm sure of it!" Jaxson and Taylor give little, slow nods in agreement.

Todd nods back. "Okay, so you know how my parents own most of the apartment buildings in that subdivision across town?"

"Todd, you did not—" Jaxson whispers.

"Okay, so my parents said they had a bunch of empty units anyway since nobody really comes to Swisher unless they buy a house, so they're just kinda collecting dust, and they're really nice apartments, just nobody in town to move in, so there's empty ones, so I talked to my parents and, uh..." Todd pauses, swallows around the tight collar of his sweater, "Uh, my parents said you can have six months rent-free, and then a reduced rate after that."

"What!?" Collin and Taylor both cry. Jaxson is too fucking

dumbstruck to respond.

"Todd, that's too much, isn't it?" Collin babbles, "You can't let us just move in for free—"

"I don't want to take advantage of you." Taylor adds.

Todd quickly rushes in, "No, no it's not too much because nobody's living there anyway! It's totally fine! This way, at least somebody's using the empty unit."

And then Taylor and Collin are silent too.

Todd rambles, "It's a two-bedroom, one-and-a-half-bath. It has a kitchen. I've seen the units because I go peek at them once every other month for my parents to make sure there's no damage to the property since it's mostly empty— and there's a bathtub in the full bathroom, and it has a balcony—"

Taylor actually stands up, goes over to Todd, and wraps him in a bearhug that pulls Todd's feet several inches off the ground, and then Collin, eyes wet, starts thanking him profusely, blubbering and insisting that he really doesn't have to do this, but thank you, thank you so much, thank you. Jaxson is still sitting on his barstool, fully crying.

"What the fuck," he says. "Dude, you can't be this nice to me. What the fuck."

"I can, actually," Todd says, "so I will."

Dalton returns from upstairs and says, "Woah, what the hell happened!? Why's everyone crying?"

"Todd gave us a fucking apartment," Taylor says, hugging Dalton too. "For six months."

"Ohmygod, he told you? Todd, you told them while I was gone!?"

"I knew you'd get emotional about it," Todd says.

"I wanted to see their faces when you told them!"

"You can see our faces now," Collin says, laughing and

crying at once, which is about what Dalton expected their faces to look like.

"What's going on?" Wes asks, a little breathless at the top of the basement stairs. "Who's crying?"

Todd, laughing, replies, "Everyone, apparently."

But that's not all, because of course it isn't.

Everyone helps make dinner. Even Taylor I-Can't-Cook Macready helps, because Wes is adamant that Taylor can't move into a house with a kitchen and not know how to cook. It helps that they're making little individual, homemade pizzas out of dough and sauce and cheese and whatever toppings that can justifiably (or unjustifiably, if you ask anyone about Jaxson's carrot toppings) be included on a pizza. They shove them in Todd's specially-made, extra-large oven, set a timer, and meander over to the couch to lounge.

Dalton finds a Home Alone rerun to watch, and they enjoy that while the food cooks, and then while they eat their food. Once the movie is over, it's about ten pm, and it's been a helluva Christmas Day, and everyone is kinda tired.

But still, everyone notices Taylor sneak off through the kitchen, into the garage, and return with five boxes and a loose piece of paper. It's all very carefully balanced in his arms, and he sets them all on the table.

"I made you guys presents," is what he says.

And then the room explodes into bright flares of activity as everyone thanks him and grabs their boxes and gingerly undoes the tape and reveals labeled, aesthetically appealing, homemade, and color-coded bath bomb and candle sets.

Wes's are white and green, and they smell like honeysuckle. "You made these?" he asks, bringing the candle to his face to smell.

Taylor nods.

Dalton's are green and blue, they smell like aloe. "Dude..." he whispers. (He's already tearing up).

Jaxson, clutches the purple, coriander-scented candle to his chest. "Macready, you can't do this. I've already cried once today!" he chokes on a wet little laugh.

Todd's hands are dusted with purple and red where he cups a lopsided bath bomb in his hands. "How'd you get mine to smell like thyme?" he asks.

"I put thyme in there," Taylor answers.

Collin is sniffing his pink and blue, chamomile bath bombs, and sneezes when the dust of it gets in his nose. "Does mine have— what is that? Chamomile? Does mine have chamomile in it?"

"Yeah." Taylor says, "They had some oils for sale at the craft store that were supposed to smell like all the stuff, but they only had lavender and chamomile, and I couldn't smell them to see if they even smell close, so I just went to a garden shop and took some bits of the plants that made me think of you guys."

"Aw, babe," Wes coos, wrapping Taylor in a hug (which is the only thing earning him forgiveness for the shoulder-to-chest blush igniting on Taylor's skin. He's still not used to pet names. It will take him multiple years to be used to pet names).

"You picked up plants because they made you think of us?" Dalton asks, heart in his throat and his eyes. "When did you become such a little sweetheart, dude?"

Everyone fawns over Taylor's character development for a minute or two, and then he tells them, "Shut up, shut up. I got something to say." And he finds that loose piece of paper under the boxes, and he clutches it in both hands. They can see him shaking a little, where he has that too-tight grip on that loose piece of paper.

"Dear Dalton, Todd, Jaxson, Wes, and Collin,

First of all, sorry for being such a huge pain in the ass lately— don't interrupt. I'm only gonna be able to get through this once— Sorry for being such a huge pain in the ass lately. I promise I'm gonna do my best to be less of a pain in the ass going forward. You guys— uh, you guys are my closest friends. I know you're my only friends, but you're also the only friends I'd ever want. You all have—" Taylor is crying, again. Wes leans into his side for comfort. "Have helped me more than you can know. I can't thank you enough for that. I hope the candles and bath bombs are a start. If you ever need anything at all, I'm here.

Merry Christmas,

Taylor."

30

Epilogue

By the time Wes's parents have unpacked their suitcases, the pullout couch is folded away and Taylor's clothes are no longer piled on the living room floor. Wes had assured them so many times that Taylor was fine, he has an apartment with Jaxson and Collin now, stop worrying, oh my god. Still, the loss spurred Richard and Martha to plan a dinner for all Wes's new friends sooner rather than later, and so on the Wednesday before school was set to resume, five teenage boys arrived at the door one by one.

Todd, of course, arrives early with a nice bottle of wine. When Richard, who answered the door, raises a playful eyebrow, Todd flushes to match the color of the Merlot and splutters, "It's not for us! It's a gift! For you and Mrs. Post!"

Richard cackles and waves Todd in and Todd deposits the bottle on the kitchen counter while Martha bites back a cackle of her own and reprimands Richard for teasing people he's never met. She's cooking up some ground meat in a pan, and completely ignoring the boiling pot of noodles on the back burner.

"Oh, he can handle it," Richard tells them both. "He's got a head built for witty banter."

Todd has no idea what this means. Nobody has ever described his head in any particular way, but Martha appraises him slowly and nods, understanding, as if this is some obvious truth about him.

It is an utter relief when Wes thunders down the stairs and meets Todd in the kitchen.

"Todd! You made it!" His grin is blinding.

Todd reaches out for a hug, and Wes reciprocates. "I said I'd be here, didn't I?"

Wes shrugs. "You did."

The doorbell rings again, and Richard chases the sound, and the sound of more embarrassed spluttering precedes Dalton's entrance to the kitchen. He sets a bottle of Merlot on the counter next to Todd's and squeezes up next to him at the island. "I thought *I* was bringing the wine!" he hisses.

"No, I said—" Todd starts to say, and then just pulls out his phone and scrolls through the texts, with Wes and Dalton peeking over his shoulder.

Dalton: We gotta bring a gift toddster
  Theyre respectable parents and they got our boy for us
  Gotta show them WERE respectable parents too u feel me
  Todd: A gift is a good idea
  could get some wine
  Merlot maybe?
  Dalton: Yessss i like merlot that seems like a respectable parent thing to drink
  Todd: We are not drinking it
  Dalton: I knowwww but it gives us a certain je ne sais quoi

Todd: so you can spell that but not government

"In my defense," Todd whispers, "My parents have a wine cellar that I snagged something good from. *You*," he whirls to give Dalton a scathing up and down glare, "shouldn't have legally been able to *get* wine. I know your dad doesn't drink Merlot."

"Well, I thought my boy was depending on me!" Dalton hisses back. "I got my big sister to help me."

"You have a sister?" Wes chirps.

"Kinda," Dalton shrugs. "She's way older. Moved out a year or so after mom died. But," his tone is buoyant, his smile mischievous and proud, "she comes in clutch when I need it."

"We didn't 'need' it," Todd mutters, "now we've given the Posts two near-identical wines."

Wes giggles. "Nah, they'll like them both," he lies smoothly, "they like to have a sip with any new baked goods they're thinking about adding to the menu." His parents haven't drank casually in years, but he knows they appreciate a gift given with good intention more than they care what gift it is. The Merlots will reach the bottom of their bottles, eventually.

The doorbell rings again, and Richard chases it again.

"Perfect timing," Martha says, "the sauce is just about done." While the boys had been bickering about text mis-communications, she had turned a pan of ground meat into a rich red sauce, and now she's pulling a tray of roasted veggies out of the oven.

Jaxson and Richard visibly get along like a house on fire, because of course they do, and they are already combining their penchants for tomfoolery to the end of turning Taylor bright red, while Collin pats his back and tries to pretend he

351

doesn't find this just as funny as his boyfriend does.

"Are we making Taylor the butt of a joke?" Todd asks, grinning.

And Dalton throws an arm over Taylor's shoulders. "Count me in! Taylor, buddy, what are we making fun of you for?"

When Wes approaches, searching expression leaning into Taylor's personal space, Taylor shakes off Collin's patting hand on his back and Dalton's arm around his shoulders to fly a few steps back. "Nothing," he says, voice sharp and low and only the uneven grumble of it, and the pinkness in his cheeks, marks that he is so different now than he was when he was first set onto the Post's living room couch.

Jaxson's grin is still as Cheshire as ever though when he says, "Just warning him about the dangers of native flora." Then he slides past them, following Richard into the kitchen and calling, "Mrs. Post that smells *delicious.*"

"Is that flirting?" Wes asks, to nobody. "Is he flirting with my *mom!?*" he asks, now to Collin specifically, who shrugs, finding this hilarious.

"If he doesn't, I will," Dalton tells him. "Wes, why is your mom *that* fine?"

"I will kick you out," Wes bites.

"Your dad's attractive too!" Collin promises, as if the issue here is the inequality of the compliments.

"They are both married!" Wes cries, and before Dalton can say something bisexual about that, he adds, "*Happily.*"

Taylor rolls his eyes and starts walking to the kitchen. Wes had been between the two, so Taylor uses himself as a bulldozer to shove him, and by extension drag the rest of the group from the entryway into the kitchen.

"There you all are," Richard says, "I was beginning to

wonder if you got stuck in our flytape." This joke is funny only to him and Martha, but they don't let that stop them from laughing as if the whole room is in on it. Everyone is invited to grab plates and serve themselves from the big pot of noodles and the pan of meaty spaghetti sauce and the baking tray of mixed veggies, and everyone fills their plates about as they would be expected to: Dalton is all protein, Todd stocks veggies, Jaxson overloads noodles, Collin takes a tasteful amount of each, Taylor gets mostly noodles and veggies with just a dollop of sauce, and Wes pretends the way he mixes all of them together in an unholy mash is anywhere close to normal.

They eat, and the biggest surprise comes to the Post parents in how *loud* six teenage boys are, compared to one. They shout over each other and bicker and laugh in ways that rattle the 9x5 picture frames on the walls. This is them on their best behavior, and it is louder than the coffee shop is most days.

It's kind of nice.

"Jaxson, the HVAC guy came yesterday, right?" Todd asks. "My parents said he was supposed to but *someone* didn't text me."

Taylor, who had been telling Dalton about the old, somewhat busted, but still usable telescope he'd found for free on Craigslist, goes for an instinctual middle finger before freezing, making awkward eye contact with Richard and Martha, and then switching to a thumbs down. "I did text you, dipshi– Todd. Check the groupchat. Anyway, the tripod is full broken, but if you're okay holding it yourself–"

"And it's fucking *heavy*," Jaxson groans, before replying to Todd, "Yeah. His name's Mike. Great guy, actually, offered me an apprenticeship if I wanted, just because he's starting to get up there in years and—"

"Jax, you could get a bird to offer you an apprenticeship in flying," Collin says, and in his laugh it's hard to tell if this is a compliment or if he's teasing. Either way, the joke is missing the crucial component of pointing out that Jaxson doesn't have wings, so it's good that only Wes, the only person present who might be able to match Collin in politeness, heard it.

He gives him a fake laugh before turning back to Todd and saying, "Anyway, that's so sweet your parents are doing that."

"Doing what?" Dalton asks, leaning over to hear past Martha and Richard discussing the upcoming hour distribution for their new employee load and Jaxson and Collin bickering about the correct way to eat spaghetti.

"It's smaller than they normally do for presents," Todd says, "but after I told them how much it bothers me that they spend *every* Christmas away, they did some research, and decided they're gonna do at least the big Christmas traditions with me this year, late or not."

Taylor grins, really smiles from ear to ear. "That's awesome, man."

"Oh my god, *Todd*," Dalton coos, and he stands from his chair to stand behind his buddy and squeeze his head in a one-sided hug.

Todd, embarrassed at being the center of attention, bats him away. "Get those beefy football arms off my head before I catch sportball disease."

"Oh speaking of!" Jaxson interjects, "Dalton, you still gonna do the football pickup league in the spring?"

"Hell yeah, I am," Dalton replies. "You thinking of joining?" This is not said with much enthusiasm, because Jaxson is built more for cheerleading than football, but he could maybe make a good runningback or kicker. Maybe.

"Absolutely not," Jaxson says immediately, "Collin, on the other hand," Collin is visibly attempting not to shrink into his seat, "has only not joined before because his parents didn't let him and because he didn't know anyone there."

"Oh, *fuck yes*– sorry, Mr. and Mrs. Post, I meant *frick* yes."

"Of course you did, dear," Martha replies.

"We're gonna be football buddies!" Dalton whoops, and Collin cheers, quieter but just as excited, with him.

Martha and Richard have been clued into almost none of what transpired over winter break, but Wes did tell them about the reason Jaxson and Collin are moving out of their houses with Taylor, so they know which of these kids they might need to check on a bit more.

"Collin," Richard asks slowly, "Where do your parents think you are? Now that you're not living with them, I mean."

"I texted them once from my old phone," Collin says, and perhaps the fact that he is a visitor here, not a child, buoys him. Perhaps it's the fact he has somewhere to go back to now that is fully his own. Perhaps it's the fact that he's already faced his worst fears and lived to explain them to others. "I said that I'm an adult now, I turned eighteen in October, and that if I see them approach me for anything I'm filing for a protective order."

"Good," Richard says, unsure if and how he means it, "That's good."

"And if I see them, I'll break their noses," Taylor adds. Under the weight of multiple unimpressed glares, he amends, "Or I'll just firmly, verbally tell them to go away." The words are very clearly practiced under Jaxson's tutelage, but what nobody but those two know is that they have a secret agreement that, should the Donahue parents ever show up, Taylor will in fact break their noses, and Jaxson will have a rock solid alibi for him if the police ever get involved.

Everyone insists on doing the dishes, which turns into a rock-paper-scissors tournament to decide who does them, and so it is decided that Wes and Jaxson will rinse the dishes and load them into the dishwasher, respectively, Dalton will wipe down the counters, Todd will clean the stove (which the Posts all insist is overboard, but Todd insists is perfectly reasonable), Collin will package up leftovers, and Taylor will collect the dishes from the table.

He's just finished that when Martha beckons him into the living room.

"Yeah?" he asks, and the way his eyes don't crackle like the lightning trapped in dark clouds is so much different than just ten days ago when she saw him last. He doesn't chafe at her and Richard's presence. Good.

Martha smiles, "I just wanted to say that, even with the new apartment, we expect to see you around here frequently. It wouldn't do to be on bad terms with our son's boyfriend." Taylor goes pink around the ears at that, and Martha giggles. It's a mother's joy to embarrass her children with affection, and eventually-potentially-in-law is close enough.

"I'll come by sometimes," Taylor promises. "You'll see me at the shop too."

"Good! Wes needed more help and I couldn't ask for a sweeter employee."

Then she lets him go. She'll wear him down until he accepts her compliments as easily as breathing.

Everyone walked to dinner, so there's no cars involved to offer rides home, but still everyone leaves at the same time so they can walk in the same direction a little longer than is strictly necessary. For the same sappy reason, Wes walks them to the porch and, sensing something, most of the group says a quick goodbye and bolts ahead to the end of the driveway, walking slowly but surely out of earshot.

It's just Wes and Taylor on the porch. Taylor looks that half-angry brand of nervous, and his eyes keep darting between the Post's front door, the retreating backs of his friends, and the overhand of the porch. Wes follows his gaze to each, and when he looks up, he sees mistletoe.

There's no avoiding it now. Taylor says, resolute and maybe a little terrified, "I'm gonna kiss you now. If that's okay. If it's not okay—"

Too late, Wes already has one hand on the back of Taylor's neck and the other on his jaw and is pulling him in for a kiss that would probably be more perfect if both of them weren't so nervous that it's setting their nerves on fire.

They both forget to breathe for long enough that when Wes pulls back, they're a little winded.

"D-d-don't build it up like that," Wes says. "It makes me nervous."

Taylor giggles, a wobbly, airy, brand new sound straight from his lungs. He leans back in, and he kisses Wes again.

About the Author

A writer whose genre is the Venn diagram of "happy endings" and "things where people get punched in the face," Brittney Hart goes about life trying to defy traditional categories. As early as 20, she started publishing her own books where queer characters got to be protagonists who get their own happily-ever-afters, in every conceivable genre. If you can see bits of her lived-everywhere, cat-obsessed, messy-family, anti-establishment lore between the lines, that is a personal problem you can take up with your therapist.

Also by Brittney Hart

Assassin x Demon King

After seven years working as the renowned mercenary, The Inevitable Blade, Salvador has had enough. To seal his resignation, he tosses his sword in a river and vows to save 1,441 people, one for each life he took, in hopes that the smell of blood will stop chasing him to sleep. But the ex-king, Kain, who has a smile that could blot out the sun and who was supposed to be Sal's final job, starts to follow him around, and then Sal gets infected with a slow-acting poison for not killing him. Can he save the people he wants to save with only a year left? Can he keep it all a secret from Kain, who insists on worming his way into Sal's heart and life?

Are You Still Awake?

When some conspiracy nutjob blows up every government building in America, leaving the country in ruins, Lucy takes shelter in the hospital room of a co-matose stranger, who she names Charlotte. Months later, Charlotte wakes up with no memory, and Lucy must maintain the lie as they set off on a trek across the corpse of America.